The Fugitive

The Fugitive

Menno Simons

Spiritual Leader in the Free Church Movement

Myron S. Augsburger

Foreword by
Timothy George

Herald Press
Scottdale, Pennsylvania
Waterloo, Ontario

Library of Congress Cataloging-in-Publication Data

Augsburger, Myron S.
  The fugitive : Menno Simons, spiritual leader in the Free Church
movement / Myron S. Augsburger.
      p. cm.
  Includes bibliographical references.
  ISBN 978-0-8361-9409-8 (pbk. : alk. paper)
  1. Menno Simons, 1496-1561—Fiction. 2. Anabaptists—Fiction.
3. Mennonites—Fiction. I. Title.
    PS3551.U387F84 2008
    813'.54—dc22

                                        2007050896

THE FUGITIVE: MENNO SIMONS
Copyright © 2008 by Herald Press, Scottdale, Pa. 15683
  Published simultaneously in Canada by Herald Press,
  Waterloo, Ont. N2L 6H7. All rights reserved
Library of Congress Catalog Card Number: 2007050896
International Standard Book Number: 978-0-8361-9409-8
Printed in the United States of America
Book design by Joshua Byler
Cover by Sans Serif
Cover sculpture of Menno Simons by Esther Augsburger
Photo by Wayne Gehman

13 12 11 10 09   10 9 8 7 6 5 4 3 2

To order or request information please call 1-800-245-7894 or visit
www.heraldpress.com.

To my siblings,
Fredrick, Donald, Anna Mary, Daniel, and David,
committed Christians who have lived
as disciples of Jesus Christ our Lord
in faithfulness to the Mennonite church

Acknowledgments

Thanks to Gerald R. Brunk, as consultant in historical scholarship, and to my granddaughter, Caitie White, for her remarkable and helpful work in editing with the young reader in mind.

Contents

Foreword

In the summer of 1985 my family and I moved to Switzerland, and we lived for a year on the shores of beautiful Lake Zurich. As a student of the Reformation, I wanted to be close to the epicenter of the events that did so much to reshape the course of Christianity in the West. Each day I would take the bus into the city, where I studied at the University of Zurich. At lunchtime, I would often climb the steep stairs leading to the famous Lindenhof, an open space from Roman times overlooking the Limmat River.

As I sat there looking down on the swirling waters, I often thought of an event that took place just a few feet below. In January 1527, Felix Manz became the first Anabaptist to be drowned in Zurich. As Ulrich Zwingli and other leaders of the city looked on, Manz was placed in a cage and forcibly lowered beneath the icy waters of the river until he was dead. The last words he was heard to utter were "Into thy hands, oh Lord, I commend my spirit."

Later that same year, Michael Sattler, the former prior of a Benedictine monastery who had become an Anabaptist pastor, was burned alive at the stake in Rottenburg on the Neckar River in southern Germany. His wife, Margaretha, was executed by drowning in the river two days later. Like her husband, she had refused to save her life by recanting her beliefs.

In the following year, a similar fate befell Balthazar Hubmaier, another Anabaptist leader who held a doctorate in theology from the University of Ingolstadt. He was burned at the stake in Vienna on March 10, 1528, and his wife was drowned in the Danube River three days later. In 1529, the imperial Diet at Speyer revived

9

the ancient Code of Justinian, which specified the death penalty for the practice of rebaptism.

Today it is difficult for us to conceive that baptism was once deemed so important that some Christians were willing to die for it and others to kill over it. In contemporary American culture, baptism seldom involves personal sacrifice or hardship of any kind. Today where (or whether) one goes to church and what one thinks about the practice of baptism or the meaning of the Lord's Supper are usually matters of supreme indifference, issues of personal preference, like choosing vanilla or chocolate at the local ice cream shop. However, it is important to recognize that the Anabaptist tradition was forged in the context of persecution and martyrdom. Something was decisively at stake for those who are willing to accept the loss of livelihood, the forfeiture of home, land, and family, and even torture and death "for the testimony of God and their conscience" as Menno Simons put it.

When Manz and Sattler were suffering for their faith in Zurich and Rottenburg, Menno, the son of Simon of Witmarsum, was busy with his parish duties as a Catholic priest in the Dutch village of Pingjum. In 1531 he was transferred to the Catholic Church in his home village of Witmarsum. Already he had begun to entertain doubts about the dogma of transubstantiation and the meaning of infant baptism as taught in the tradition of the church. He was most reluctant to break with this tradition in which he had been baptized as an infant himself. His ordination vows also weighed heavily on his soul.

For several years he continued to "toy with Babylon," as he later described this phase of his life, pulled between his conscience on the one hand and the tradition he had always known on the other. In the midst of this spiritual turmoil, he experienced an evangelical awakening: "My heart trembled within me. I prayed to God with sighs and tears that he would give to me, a sorrowing sinner, the gift of his grace, create within me a clean heart, and graciously through the merits of the crimson blood of Christ forgive my unclean walk and frivolous easy life." Menno himself was then baptized as a believer in Christ and soon thereafter was ordained an elder by Obbe Philips, an Anabaptist preacher from Leeuwarden.

From his ordination in 1537 until he died in 1561, Menno exerted a remarkable influence on the Anabaptists of the Netherlands and northern Germany. During most of those years he lived the life of a hunted heretic, preaching by night to secret conventicles of brothers and sisters, baptizing new believers in country streams and out-of-the-way lakes, establishing churches and ordaining pastors from Amsterdam to Cologne to Danzig.

When we consider the dangers Menno faced, we are amazed that he died a natural death at the age of sixty-six. For instance, in 1542 Emperor Charles V published an edict against Menno, offering one hundred guilders for his arrest. Menno referred to himself as a "homeless man," but he did not have only himself to think about. His wife, Gertrude, and their three children suffered the same fate. In 1544 he lamented that he could not "find in all the countries a cabin or hut in which my poor wife and our little children could be put up in safety for a year or even half a year."

Gertrude and two of their children preceded Menno in death. The earliest portraits of Menno show him with crutches, and it is certain that he lived his last years as a cripple. From the beginning of his career, Menno knew that there was no way for the true Christian to avoid the cross. "If the Head had to suffer such torture, anguish, misery, and pain," he said, "how shall his servants, children, and members expect peace and freedom as to their flesh?" On the twenty-fifth anniversary of his renunciation of the Roman Church, Menno died and was buried in his own garden at Wüstenfeld in Holstein. Today a modest memorial stands near the site of what is believed to be Menno's grave.

Some sixty-five years ago, Harold S. Bender of Goshen College presented his inaugural address on "The Anabaptist Vision" as president of the American Society of Church History. Since that time, scholars from many perspectives have mined this long-neglected tradition to give us a fuller and more textured understanding of the "radical reformers" who stood on the margins of the established churches and who forged their own distinctive pattern of ecclesial renewal in the sixteenth century. The three major emphases Bender identified as core commitments of the Anabaptist movement are still relevant today: (1) a new conception of the essence of Christianity as discipleship; (2) a new conception of the church as a brotherhood; (3) a new ethic of love and nonresistance.

No one in the sixteenth century better embodied this Anabaptist vision than Menno Simons. Following Jesus—discipleship—was at the heart of true Christianity for Menno. The church, he believed, could not be defined ultimately in terms of budgets, programs, ceremonies, or clerical leaders. The true church was a covenanted community of brothers and sisters in Christ, separated from the world for the sake of service in the world. Finally, Menno, in keeping with the example of Jesus himself, advocated a pattern of life marked by self-giving love and nonresistance. "Christ is our fortress," he wrote, "patience our weapon of defense; the Word of God our sword; and our victory a courageous, firm, unfeigned faith in Jesus Christ."

Throughout his distinguished career as a pastor, educator, and Christian statesman, Myron Augsburger has also been an effective and winsome advocate for the Anabaptist vision. Now, in this engaging book, he has woven together the disparate threads of Menno's harried life into a coherent and fascinating narrative. Menno emerges as a real, life-and-blood character, not the mythic founder of a denomination, but a faithful disciple for whom the path of obedience was not a straight line but a zigzag pattern through the shadows and byways of his fugitive life. The Marxist philosopher Ernst Bloch had more sympathy for Thomas Müntzer than for Menno Simons, but he has written a fitting epitaph for Menno and all the radical reformers, who struggled against the stream for the sake of conscience. Their legacy is a vital part of our common Christian heritage:

> Despite their suffering,
> their fear and trembling,
> in all these souls
> there glows the spark from beyond,
> and it ignites the tarrying kingdom.*

Timothy George
Beeson Divinity School
Senior editor of Christianity Today

---

* See my *Theology of the Reformers* (Nashville: Broadman Press, 1988), p. 306. I follow the translation in Hans Jürgen Goertz, ed., *Profiles of Radical Reformers*, trans. Walter Klaassen (Kitchener, Ontario: Herald Press, 1982), p. 9.

Preface

Accounts of the life of Menno Simons have been told in various ways, but to my knowledge there is no serious English-language attempt to present the story in narrative form in a way that is true to Menno's life and work. This book is an attempt to interface his life with his writings and events of his time. Although this is a fictionalized account, it is also a historical study. I have used English spellings of some of the Dutch names.

Readers of my previous historical novels have asked me to write a similar piece on Menno Simons because there is no easy reader on his life. I am well aware that there are many others who could do it better, and I wish that I had more literary creativity. But even so, here it is. I have carefully researched and consulted with others on the story, put together associations, and created conversations, but it is still limited. I share this knowing that if some of what happened to me in the process of writing happens to others in reading, it will have been well worth it.

There are limited insights into Menno's family, but there is evidence of three brothers, one of whom died young. There is nothing definite about his sisters except in a German novel that gives no source. For this story, I have included one sister to make the family more complete. There were three children from Menno's marriage to Gertrude, including a son who died young and a second daughter who died as a young woman. Gertrude died in August 1559. I have read with appreciation Louis A. Vernon's *Night Preacher*, a brief and selective story of Menno through the eyes of his children, and I borrowed the names of those three children.

The story is as accurate as possible from the sources I have studied. It is an attempt to present consistently the pilgrimage and service Menno rendered to the church during his twenty-five-year ministry. I have used numerous excerpts from his writings to keep the story informed. There are also many references to Anabaptist martyrs, taken from actual historical accounts. I've presented these primarily to emphasize the threat to Menno's life and the gauntlet he was continually running.

As an Anabaptist leader, Menno escaped martyrdom and was able to die in his own bed. This stands in sharp contrast to many of his contemporaries who were the early founders of the Anabaptist movement in Switzerland and south Germany. Conrad Grebel (who died probably of the plague in August 1526, though other sources suggest it was syphilis), Felix Manz (executed by drowning in Zurich on January 7, 1527), Michael Sattler (burned at the stake on May 20, 1527, at Rottenburg on the Neckar), and Georg Blaurock (burned at the stake on September 6, 1529, at Clausen). They lived for only a few years of the free church movement before their death.

I have benefited from my seminary professor Dr. Irvin B. Horst, with his expertise as a very careful historian. He is without doubt the greatest living scholar of Menno Simons' life and work, and one to whom I am deeply indebted. I also pay tribute to Dr. J. C. Wenger and his remarkable writings, and significantly in this writing by the counsel of Dr. Gerald R. Brunk, a historian who has given much attention to the unique ministry of Menno Simons. As a special favor, Dr. Brunk has read this manuscript several times and made editorial comments and given counsel on various historical matters to provide authenticity to the presentation of this work. I have sought to be as accurate as possible with the use of available works. I give my compliments as well as recognition to the important contribution that he has given me as a consultant and in reviewing this novel.

Various trips to Europe guiding tour groups to review

Anabaptist history on site have taken me first to the Netherlands. There I have been exposed to the setting from which this historical novel emerges. The changes to the landscape by dikes and contained lakes are great advances over the condition of the land in the sixteenth century. However, much of the beauty and the customs of the people remain. The story of Anne Frank from World War II gives lasting witness to the integrity and character of the Dutch peoples.

The Mennonite church in the Netherlands continues to be one of the expressions of the faith of Menno Simons, a faith that has thousands of adherents around the globe.

"For other foundation can no man lay than that is laid, which is Jesus Christ" (1 Corinthians 3:11). Soli Deo gloria!

Myron S. Augsburger

Prologue

1544

Menno Simons ran around the corner of the last cottage at the end of the street. His heart beat rapidly and his breath came in great gasps. His meeting had been interrupted when a messenger called out that the beadles were coming to arrest him.

"Farewell, my friends," Menno had cried out. "By God's grace, I'll be back." He leapt from a little platform in the barn and was out the back door, scurrying between the cottages and down a narrow street, carrying his crutch.

As he passed the last cottage, he paused to decide what to do. To return to the village would be suicide; the police would take him without a doubt. Some months earlier, it had been announced and spread widely that Emperor Charles V had put a price on his head—one hundred guilders. This had made Menno a fugitive. But recently the regional magistrate, Regent Maria, had given orders that he be arrested. She offered to pardon any prisoner whose family turned Menno over.

Menno trembled from the chill, or perhaps from a surge of fear. He knew this threat was serious, for his friend, Jared Renik of Kimswerd, a little village near Leeuwarden, had been executed for nothing more than showing him hospitality.

He thought of his family in Oldersum to the east, in the comfort of their home on the Von Dornum estate, and he wished he were there with them. But he jerked his thoughts back to the present. To take the road to Leeuwarden, a city he knew well and where he could find a place to hide, was not feasible; the horsemen would soon overtake him.

"Lord, what do I do now? I am your servant, and you have promised to walk with me." With those thoughts in prayer, he gazed at a dike across the lowlands on his left. Looking back at the village, he recognized that the cottages would hide him from the view of his pursuers for a short time. Turning away from the little street down which he had just come, he quickly made his way across the dike. On the other side he turned to his right and hid himself in the brush along the edge of a marsh that farmers had been draining. Menno could hear voices in the village as his pursuers called to one another. He was quite certain that they would not plunge their horses into the marshy land in pursuit, and they probably wouldn't use the dike.

Several hours later, having made his way across the country as rapidly as his feet would carry him, Menno came to a sheepcote. Carefully he opened the door and stepped inside, gently speaking to the sheep and easing himself down just inside the door. They stirred but made no commotion. With the warmth of the interior of the little cote, Menno began to relax, but sleep eluded him as he reflected on what all had brought him to this time of his life. Just as he was dozing off, he heard footsteps.

1
Early Years in Witmarsum

1496-1521

The streams of milk made muffled sounds as they danced across the foam in the wooden pail. Menno sat on his one-legged stool, his head in the flank of the cow. His hands skillfully drew the milk from the animal's teats. The milk's warmth felt good to his knees as they gripped the sides of the bucket. He glanced over at a cat by the stable door and shot a stream of milk at it, getting some on its face. The cat licked the milk from its fur.

Menno's brother Peter stuck his head in the door and spoke brusquely. "Are you about finished? Breakfast will soon be ready."

"Almost done," Menno replied. "And you? It must be cold out there."

Peter drew his jacket around himself, his breath visible in the cold air. "Yes, it's cold, and those porkers ate like everything. It took me a while to feed them." After observing Menno for a few moments, he added more congenially, "It is good to have you back from Pingjum. We have missed you around here." He paused, and then added, "I'll go on ahead and not wait."

Peter walked across the lot. Menno could hear the swish of his pants as they rubbed with the movement of his legs. While it was cold outside the lean-to stable, inside it was comfortable, warmed by the body heat from several cows of the family's small dairy farm. The milking stall near the house at the edge of the village was on a large mound to keep it above the water. The creative work of the people of the region had rescued this lowland from being swallowed by the sea. The dikes that the people had carefully built protected the village and the farms, with their fields surrounded by draining ditches. Each polder was a small cow-pasture or vegetable field; Menno's family made its living from selling milk and vegetables.

Menno poured some milk into a pan for the cat. He turned to carry the pails of warm milk to the house. As he stepped out through the doorway, the strutting cock threw up its head and crowed, welcoming the sunlight that was breaking above the polders and would warm the day.

Menno looked down the narrow street leading into Witmarsum and noted the neat rows of houses lining each side. The tiles on the roofs were covered with frost.

In the early morning light he could see his friend, Leenaert, who worked for the baker and was delivering fresh bread in the early morning. As Leenaert came near, Menno called out a cheery greeting, unable to wave as his hands gripped the bucket handles. Leenaert called back and hurried on his way.

Menno thought of Peter's words welcoming him back from the several months he had been with their cousins at Pingjum, just a short distance to the northwest Witmarsum, where he had worked during the summer season. He had missed being with the family, but for the past several years this had been his job for the summer. Now he was back at Witmarsum, and the fall weather was already quite cool. He breathed deeply and stepped briskly toward the house. Yes, it was good to be home.

As Menno entered the house, his mother met him at the door of the kitchen. Her blonde hair framed a smiling face under a white muslin headdress. She had been waiting for the milk and took the pail from his hand, saying, "You're just in time, Menno. I have breakfast on the table." She quickly strained the milk and placed a large pitcher on the table. "You may call the family," she said. Menno's sister, Altjie, assisting their mother, nodded toward the adjoining room.

He stepped to the door to the next room to find that his father and two brothers had heard and were already moving to the door. As they all sat at the table, they bowed their heads, and his father led in the prayer of blessing.

Menno looked at his mother and said, "It is a fine table, as usual." Then he added, "You are a wonderful mother."

The youngest boy, Theo, added, "That goes for all of us."

She smiled with pleasure as she glanced at Menno.

Altjie said, "He's just hinting for another piece of your fresh bread."

"That's what makes him more stocky than the rest of us," Peter quipped.

Menno reached over and jabbed him in the side. "It wouldn't hurt you to add a bit on those ribs," he said.

They all laughed, and their father added, "Just be thankful that we are not hungry as many are."

⁓

The family was close and had deep respect for each other. They also were quite reserved, as befit their Frisian culture. From early childhood, Menno had been consecrated for the service of the church. Born in 1496, he was thirteen years younger than Martin Luther of Germany, about the same age as Ulrich Zwingli to the south, and thirteen years older than John Calvin of France. These were men he'd soon come to know. Like them, Menno had no idea of the role they would fill in the future of the church and the coming Reformation. Even so, Menno did a lot of thinking about the church and the nature of its service in the community.

Menno's parents were devoted members of the Roman Catholic Church in Witmarsum and believed that loyalty to the church was one of the greatest things they could do for God. As a young man, Menno well knew that his parents wanted him to become a priest and that they wanted to place him in the care of the monastery at Bolsward.

Yet while it was his parents' wish that he study to be a priest, he had to decide for himself. He recognized if he chose the priesthood his life work, his life would change radically. True, he would find security in this role, but it would limit him. But Menno knew that he needed to make this decision, for he was now in his early twenties and his parents let him know they were concerned about his uncertainty.

~

Menno found family life meaningful and enriching, but it was not without pain. He and his brothers, Peter and Theo, with their sister, Altjie, had survived their younger brother, Jan, who died of the plague in his early teens. Peter, the eldest, now worked in the town of Witmarsum while Menno worked with his father on their little farm. They had opportunities to talk together because Peter lived at home and walked to work. But deep conversation was limited by their different roles and schedules. Both of them were serious thinkers and engaged in heated conversation at times. The youngest boy, Theo, had gone with Menno to Pingjum and found a job. This was an adjustment for the family. Theo was now working for a distant relative and continued on there, but Menno had returned to Witmarsum to process the matter of his future with his parents.

In addition to his family, Menno enjoyed his neighborhood friends very much. Several knew he might become a priest and encouraged him as he contemplated going to the monastery. When Menno thought of his neighbors, he also thought of Gertrude, a girl he had known from childhood. She was a close friend of a neighbor, Marty, whose parents had earlier moved to Groningen. But while there, her mother had died and Marty had come back to Witmarsum to become the foster-daughter of the carpenter Nonno Zylman. Marty was a close friend of Altjie, and through their times together Menno had come to know her like a sister.

Gertrude's time with Menno had been brief. When she was a young girl, her home burned and the family moved north to Groningen, where her father was able to get work. Menno remembered her well, and Marty frequently read him notes she received from Gertrude.

Marty told Menno that Gertrude was considering becoming a Beguine and living in the service of the church. He admired her commitment to the church, even while it raised questions in his mind of the implications for her future. His heart warmed as he recalled her beauty, the sparkle in her shining eyes, and her cheerful expressions. It would be easy to love her and even to share his life with her. But Menno knew that if he became a priest, there would be no such relationship with her or anyone else. And if she became a Beguine, that would also prohibit marriage.

Menno dared to think that perhaps Gertrude had turned toward becoming a Beguine after she heard that he was going to be a priest. But he shook his head and put the thought aside as presumptuous, though it continued to resonate inside him. His mind was set more and more on entering the monastery and pleasing his parents. But he was still hesitating, knowing the sacrifice it would involve.

∼

After breakfast, his father said, "Come, Menno. Little Altjie can help mother. We need to work on the polders today. We have to clean the draining ditches in case of another flood."

Menno got up from his chair and simply said, "Yes, we never know when we might be inundated again."

He well remembered the last flood, in 1516, when he was nearly twenty years old. It had been very destructive. The waters of the sea had breached the dikes and flooded the lowlands. Like many of their neighbors, Menno's family had their house on a raised area with dikes around it and the garden, so they had been able to secure their personal things. But the polders had been badly damaged. For weeks they had kept the cows inside their little barn and fed them hay. The saltwater so destroyed the field that, without this feed, the cattle could not have survived. In fact, across the region, the deaths of cattle created serious losses. Menno worked hard with his father and Peter to recover from the devastation.

Menno's father told stories of other floods, which had been more frequent before the government built dikes and windmills, which pumped water from ditches at one level into ditches at the next level, until it eventually flowed into the sea. Menno's father said there had been seven such floods from 1502 to 1516, and these were the stimulus for the lowlands government to raise money and hire people to construct and maintain the network of dikes.

"This changed our country," his father said. "It is much safer now and has made our land a wonderful area for agriculture. The people in the cities could hardly have survived without the markets being regularly supplied by the farmers. Among other things, it improved relations between the aristocrats and the peasants." He chuckled as he said this, and Menno smiled.

On many days, Menno and his father worked together in the polders. Menno was a strong young man, and he enjoyed feeling his muscles flex as he bent to the task. As the two worked, they talked of incidental things in the neighborhood, of their associates, and of the demands of their business. Frequently they talked of Peter in his work and of Theo in his new job at Pingjum. But recently, with the issues before Menno and the decision he needed to make, the conversation readily turned to the monastery.

"Father," Menno said, "I have been giving a lot of thought to my future. I know that you and mother want me to be a priest.

But this choice means no marriage, no family, no life like you have known. That is giving up a lot, even though it would open a whole other life for me. But I can't keep putting off this decision. I must decide whether that is really what I want to do."

"Yes, son," his father replied, "I understand, and I've pondered this much more than you may know. While you were away in Pingjum, I often asked myself whether we have been fair to you by encouraging you to enter the priesthood."

He paused. "But your service assisting the priests during mass has given you an opportunity to test your feelings. Your mother and I do believe that the church is primary, and we dedicated you to this from your birth. We've lost one of your brothers and we believe this service will represent the family as an expression of our submission to the Lord. This calling will also be a wonderful service for you."

He hesitated, then continued. "Your mother and I, with Peter, Theo, and Altjie, will support you. I'm quite sure it will be worth the sacrifices you have to make."

"I realize that," Menno said. "I've known of your deep interest in this from my childhood, in fact. And I have tried to push the matter away."

He paused, and picked up his shovel. "But it hangs there in my mind. It must still be my decision and it isn't an easy one. Such a decision shapes the whole of one's life."

Menno began to work, his thoughts now to himself. He was aware of his father's studied reflection and knew that he would have said more, but Menno didn't look up. He continued his work, attempting to think honestly of what this role would mean.

Like everyone else in Witmarsum, Menno was a faithful Roman Catholic. He had been involved in the church at the center of the village since he was a child. It was really his life. He had been carried to church by his parents and baptized as an infant. His early education had been in the parish school. As a lad he had started serving as an altar boy, taking turns with several of his friends. He continued serving at mass when he became a teenager, and it had been very meaningful to him. From this background he thought he had some understanding of the priest's work.

Among the numerous programs the church had developed to prepare young men for their future work, the nearest was at the monastic school in Bolsward. While Menno had continued living and working on the farm with his parents in Witmarsum into his early twenties, his parents had taken the initiative and made preliminary arrangements for him to attend monastic school.

Bolsward was not far away, less than thirty kilometers to the south. In the other direction was Pingjum. Pingjum was where his father had grown up, so it was something of a second home for Menno and his siblings. But Bolsward was unknown to him and offered new interests in addition to the monastery. Menno actually thought he wouldn't mind being away from home at this stage in his life.

~

One day Menno's father said simply, "Son, pack your bag, and this afternoon I will walk with you partway to Bolsward. We have frequently walked together to Pingjum to visit my relatives, but today we go the other direction. I'll walk with you for a while, and then you can make your way on to the monastery."

Caught off guard, Menno did not respond, so his father continued. "I know that you have been giving this much thought, and we don't mean to control your life, but this decision shouldn't wait longer. It is time for the school term to begin, and you should be enrolled to test this out for yourself. Your mother and I think that you might try this for a term and then you can decide more definitely for your future. At least a year of experience at the monastery will give you a better understanding on which to base your decision."

That latter point had its appeal to Menno. It relieved the concerns over the finality of the decision he was making.

In a matter-of-fact way, Menno packed to leave. His mother helped him. It didn't take long to select the clothing: leather leggings and his leather jacket, typical Dutch garb. As his mother selected other things he would need, he watched her work. He was sure he could detect tears in her eyes as she placed things before him. Once he saw her wipe her eyes with her apron. "Son," she said, "things will never be the same again, but don't forget how much you are loved and how proud we are of you." He nodded, his own eyes moist as he heard her words of love.

Peter, to whom he had become increasingly attached, bid him farewell and wished him the best in his venture.

As Menno walked down the road with his father, the sun was high in the morning sky; its rays felt warm on his face. He looked back to see his mother standing in the door. He waved and in turn she raised her hand in farewell. Menno thought of the change he was facing. He was leaving the comfort of home—not just the house and community, but the comfort of family.

After they had walked about ten kilometers, his father said, "This is as far as I go today. You will have to go on alone. So it will be for you now." They stood at the fork of the road and he bid his father *adieu*. They embraced briefly, an unusual gesture for them, and Menno turned to walk on alone. His father choked back tears as he called, "*Tot ziens*," ("Farewell until we see each other again"). Menno knew that although he could come home to visit, the rigorous disciplines and the monastic schedule would seldom permit it.

As he made his way along the broad path, he observed the waterfowl by the edge of the canal. He had often watched them when at work; they were awkward yet beautiful, and free and graceful in flight.

～

It was very late in the afternoon when he arrived at Bolsward. He found his way to the monastery by early evening and introduced himself as Menno, son of Simon of Witmarsum. The proctor, who knew of the earlier contact by Menno's father, showed him to his room. Not long afterward, a bell summoned him to the evening meal. There he joined with new acquaintances as they sat at table and partook of warm cabbage soup. He was relieved when he could return to his room and rest from the long walk.

Once he was admitted to the school, Menno plunged into his work with diligence. He had always enjoyed reading, although he had never had a regular discipline of study and prayer. But he knew that the studies would go well for him.

For the other young men who were entering, the monastery was a new experience, just as it was for Menno. As his friendships developed, the discipline and the rigor of his studies seemed to decrease, and he enjoyed a lively social life.

In his classes he studied many subjects, but the languages were the most demanding. While he soon learned to read and write Latin, he mastered only the reading of Greek. He even questioned why he had to learn Greek, for he had never read the Scriptures and had no special interest in doing so. But Greek study was required, and he was told that the discipline would be a good aspect of his development.

There was social unrest in the area and an amazing amount of religious conversation all around them. This was especially so among the students, even though they were in a monastic school. They were hearing much about the radical thought of Martin Luther, whose views the instructors considered heretical. For several years now, the story had been told of Luther's stance at the Diet at Worms in April of 1521. There was something thrilling in his words "Here I stand, I can do no other; I cannot go against the dictates of my conscience. So help me God!"

This story, and that of Luther's escape, impressed Menno. He pondered the news that Luther's translation of Scriptures into common language was introducing the Bible to the common people across the country, which the Catholic Church regarded as anathema. It held that such freedom of interpretation could only lead laypeople to confusion. But say what they would, the common people were very much involved in learning to read and in gaining some understanding of the Bible.

Luther worked in Germany, but his broader influence reached into Friesland, and as a consequence, many people were raising questions about various doctrines of the Catholic Church. These questions included such matters as indulgences, infant baptism, the meaning of the sacraments, and the authority of the church. Menno heard them but simply shoved such questions aside, assuming they were heresy. His goal was to become a priest and to live in the comforts of a role of service in a parish.

⌒

Menno's life at home had been quite disciplined. In many ways, his parents guided his lifestyle as well as the schedule of his work. But here at Bolsward, he had fewer constraints and soon became known as a rather carefree young man. He found the freedom of being on his own exhilarating. As he and his fellow freshmen played cards together, he was often the life of the party. They found considerable time to socialize, visiting the little pub nearby, playing cards, and drinking. The older students would taunt them, often asking favors, saying the new students had yet to mature and fully share the meaning of monastic life. Menno's little group continued their parties, but they did so with caution, lest overindulgence should lead to their being called before the officials and disciplined.

Hands that once were skilled at milking cows now became deft at cutting the deck and thumbing through the cards. Sometimes in Menno's bouts of drinking, the thought would cross his mind that this was hardly what his parents visualized when they sent him to this monastic school. Although he and Peter had frequently visited the pub, it had not been in excess. His conscience bothered him, especially when he thought of his parents.

As Menno retired to his own room, an inner conversation was happening in his thoughts. Day after day he became increasingly conscious of his own emptiness. "This is not the role for a priest who is to be a representative of God to the people," he thought. Something was missing in his life, and it wasn't being answered either by his socializing or by his religious observances.

He rolled over on his cot, pulled the thin blanket up to his chin, and waited for sleep to come.

2
Life in the Monastery at Bolsward

1522–1524

There was a loud knock on his door, and a voice called, "Time to gather for prayers, Menno." It seemed to Menno that he had just crawled into bed. The headmaster of his quarters had indeed done him the favor of a call, or he would have missed morning prayers altogether.

Menno swung his feet to the floor and stood up beside his cot. It was time to begin his morning routine. He bathed himself, stepped into his trousers, pulled the knitted shirt over his head, and tied the string at his waist. Then he joined his colleagues as together they made their way down the hall to the chapel. There they shared the cycle of prayer and confession, then everyone hurried to the dining room to eat and to chat as friends.

"You almost missed prayers, Menno," Justin quipped. "You would have been down in spirit all of the day."

"Speak for yourself," Menno growled. "You came in last in the group, I noticed."

Hans said, "Justin should be tired. He works all night sawing timber. You can hear him all over the dormitory."

"That must be what I heard," Menno replied. "We'll have to do something about that so the rest of us can sleep."

When they all laughed heartily, several of the older monks looked at them with frowns of disapproval. Normally the atmosphere at mealtime was quieter than the spirited interchange that Menno and his colleagues were expressing. As they met in the dining area, they greeted one another with a freedom not allowed in chapel. Their jovial spirit and even ribald comments showed that they needed the chapel experience to condition their lifestyle and personalities to solemnity.

Their meals were meager because a serious famine had spread across the land. The weather had been difficult, which limited the production of food in the region. Because of his own background on the farm, Menno understood these problems well. The monastery kept some cows for milk and calves for meat, and Menno was quite accomplished at caring for them. He soon made it his mission to visit farmers around the monastery and assist them in some of their labors. In doing this he made new friends and created good relationships for the monastic community. In turn, he usually brought cabbages, turnips, and eggs back to the monastery, all of which helped with their diet. This won him the respect of other monks, who benefited from his kindness.

Latin had at first been quite difficult for Menno, but soon he was finding it a more ready study. His instructor encouraged him and said that by his second year, language study would become almost routine.

∼

Near the end of his first term, his superior gave him a special privilege: leave to make a trip home. He walked toward Witmarsum with much joy. As he entered the street and made his way to his home, all the familiar surroundings gave him a sense of belonging. He was well aware that he was now a part of a different world, but it was pleasant to be with his family, to see his parents and Peter and Altjie.

His time with the family was short, and he told them that he was now sure of his calling and expected to continue at the monastery.

Altjie was full of questions: "What is your room like? Are your meals good?"

"Not mother's cooking, or yours, you can be sure of that," he said. She smiled with his compliment, continuing to keep him engaged in conversation.

Peter interrupted and asked about more serious issues. "What have you heard of Martin Luther, Menno? Are they talking about him at Bolsward?"

"Yes," Menno replied. "And of course it is seen as a real issue for the church of Rome and for us."

"But he is calling people to a more personal faith rather than to simply trust in the sacraments and the rituals of church practice."

Menno was surprised. "You're more aware of his influence than I realized."

"Well," Peter said, "one doesn't have to be in a monastery to think about the church and about the meaning of faith."

Menno smiled and nodded. He thought of his association with new friends at the monastery. His life there had opened up new dimensions of reflection and the conversations were stimulating, but so was this discussion with Peter.

"We'll need to keep up this conversation, Peter." Menno noted his mother's expression of satisfaction with his statement.

Time went quickly, and after fond farewells, Menno was soon on his way back to Bolsward. He was grateful that his superior had allowed him to visit home at least once each term. Later, as Menno thought back on this visit, much of the conversation, even about the monastery, was merely social. But his discussion with Peter had opened new challenges.

~

Menno pursued his work with renewed enthusiasm. His studies introduced him to new insights into the faith, the church, and many practices that, as a layman, he had little understood.

One of his first new insights had to do with the spiritual benefits that came, the church taught, from the practice of indulgences. Indulgences were considered to be the leftover benefits or superfluous merits of Christ, Mary, and the saints. The priests claimed to draw on these merits to reduce the needed cleansing in purgatory for sins. Menno would jest with his friends about this benefit whenever they engaged in their bouts of drinking and playing cards.

This practice of indulgences had called forth Luther's wrath in his Ninety-Five Theses, posted on the cathedral door at Wittenberg in 1517.

As Menno studied the church of his day, he came to further understand the sacraments as visible signs of invisible grace. The sacraments, Menno was sure, were more important than the so-called indulgences; they were active functions of religious practice. The church emphasized seven sacraments: baptism (which had been administered to him as an infant), the Eucharist (of which he partook regularly), confirmation, penance (which he did to find peace in his conscience), ordination (which he anticipated eventually), marriage (for those not in the priesthood), and extreme unction (for those near death). Someone properly ordained in the line of apostolic succession administered these sacraments, and Menno regarded them as his basis for salvation. In fact, he was taught and believed that there was no salvation outside the church.

More and more, Menno gained a reputation of being insightful and studious. Early on, he was known to be a good student and a dedicated man. It was clear to him that his superior held him in high esteem, and he sought to live up to his mentor's expectations. He was determined that if he was to be a priest, he would be a very effective one.

Menno's instructor told him and the rest of the class preparing for the priesthood that one of the most important things a priest does is administer the sacrament of the Eucharist. In this sacrament, the spiritual powers of the church were made visible, and Menno identified deeply with this meaning.

The instructor took time to carefully explain that in the Eucharist, the words of institution were expressing the greatest of all mysteries. Menno was gripped by his explanation: "In the words 'This is my body' the elements of bread and wine are transformed into the body and the blood of Christ. This is a change called transubstantiation. But only the substance of the elements are changed, not their appearance or taste. While they remain the same, the body of Christ is actually present in the consecrated host."

He paused, then continued. "As a priest, you should always look at the host with devotion and with prayer, and hold it so before the people. As to the wine, once dedicated, it becomes the blood of Christ and is to be handled with extreme care. As a priest, you are responsible to drink the wine to the last drop, then to wipe the chalice so that no drop of the blood of the Lord shall be spilled."

Their instructor warned them to take a strong stand against an aggressive movement known as the Sacramentarians, which was spreading across Friesland. This group took exception to church teaching on the sacraments. They held that the elements were only symbols that represented the body and blood of the Lord; they were not changed into the actual body and blood of Christ. With this interpretation, the instructor said, this group was apostate from the true meaning of the sacrament.

"It is an attack," he said, "on the very central aspect of our faith in the Savior."

Menno shrugged his shoulders, concluding that the group had little ground for its position. He thought of his years as a young boy at Witmarsum and the times he had served as an altar boy. Throughout his life, he had been taught that, in receiving the sacrament, he was receiving the actual body and blood of Christ. It was without question for him.

~

As the months went by in his second year, Menno was reading broadly and freely. He became intrigued with the Latin
fathers and found special joy in new insights from his studies.
Day after day he read Tertullian, Cyprian, and Eusebius. He relished the *Confessions* of St. Augustine, which opened new win-
dows of self-understanding for him. He was especially absorbed
by the spirit of Tertullian and his convictions about piety's personal dimensions of spirit.

Menno was also captivated by the work of Erasmus and his
very clear humanism. The very human presentation of Jesus
that Erasmus expressed was different from Menno's sacramental orientation, and it stimulated his thinking. He became so
engrossed in this new field of reflection that he spent hours
poring over the few writings he was able to find.

He recognized that this disciplined kind of study was what
his parents had in mind for him at the monastery. In his more
serious thoughts, he knew that they would be impressed by his
study, but they would also be disappointed by the times of
idleness and frivolity he shared with his friends. This, he knew,
would need to change.

He remembered his father's words to him: "You should not
milk cows all of your life; there is much more in the world calling for your involvement." But, in fact, the change from farming to study was something of a luxury. He was free from the
demands of the farm and even now his parents were helping to
support him financially. He needed to make good for their sake
as well as his own.

Menno loved the Netherlands. Many of the people lived in
large cities such as Amsterdam, Haarlem, Leiden, Gouda, and
Delft, but nearly half were spread across the rural countryside.
The country was under the control of the Holy Roman Empire,
which was ruled by Charles V, grandson of Maximilian. Charles

had grown up in the Netherlands. He also had studied at Utrecht under the famous professor Adriaen, who had become pope in 1522, a transition that happened so far away that it had made little impression on the young Menno.

Charles V had acquired a strictly religious but gloomy view of the world. When crowned at Aachen, Germany, on October 22, 1520, he was a devoted and faithful servant of the Roman Catholic Church. As emperor, he had opened the Diet at Worms on January 28, 1521. The Diet placed Luther under the ban of the empire, an act heralded by an edict posted on May 26 of that year. Charles meant to crush Luther's challenge to the church. But despite the emperor's efforts, what Luther's followers called a reformation continued to take its course.

⌒

Menno's studies engaged his days fully. The work, he thought, continued to progress well. He had a keen mind and an aptitude for systematizing the concepts he was learning. His instructor went beyond the content of the lectures and challenged Menno to discipline his own life as a monk by studying monastic piety. Menno thought of his own father as he heard the instructor comments. "Even lay piety is modeled upon the ideals of monastic piety," he said. "This has been emphasized especially by the lay religious communities of Beghards and Beguines, who are current expressions of this piety. Their spirituality is marked by an emphasis on poverty, chastity, and separation from the world."

As Menno thought on this, he remembered Gertrude. He had heard that she was now a member of such a Beguine order. He was pleased when he thought of how her pursuits of spiritual disciplines must be quite similar to his.

Menno was now finding more stimulus from the works of Erasmus than from the older sources. One challenge was the development of a growing desire to broaden his knowledge. The humanism of Erasmus quickened his interest to engage in fields of study besides theology. He was impressed that Erasmus, with all of his creative thinking and challenge to the church, actually chose to stay with the church rather than to withdraw as had Luther.

Menno became known for his interest in Erasmus. When challenged by his fellow students, he simply said, "Erasmus is my man."

Soon after the start of his third year, Menno's superior called him to his office.

"Menno," he said, "I have sent a recommendation to the bishop at Utrecht that he examine you, and assuming you do well, as I expect, you will be ordained to the priesthood and given an assignment."

Menno exclaimed in surprise, "Already? I'm only in my third year at the monastery."

"Yes," his superior said, "but you are of a mature age, a bit older than your fellow students. You have served at the altar for several years, and you are ready to move to a more responsible assignment. I have told the bishop that I would arrange for you to make a trip to Utrecht and spend a bit of time there. Perhaps you might even take in a few classes at the university. That would give the bishop time to form his own impressions and make his decision about your ordination."

Menno was silent for a moment, then looking up at his superior, he said, "Your Holiness, this is a compliment. I am deeply grateful to you for your confidence and recommendation. This will be a privilege for me."

Menno knew that the trip to Utrecht could be a wonderful experience for him. He became more enthusiastic as the time approached. His appointment for an audience with the bishop was a special honor, but he looked forward to the meeting with some measure of fear. An association with the bishop would benefit him after ordination; in any later assignment it would be a privilege to be under the bishop's call.

His heart beat more rapidly when he thought of the possibility that while in Utrecht he might pursue studies during a term at the university. At least he would get acquainted with this center of religious and cultural activity. Perhaps it would be there that he'd find some answer to his inner unrest. His studies at Bolsward were a satisfaction, but beyond his intellectual achievements, he had a haunting feeling that something was missing in his own soul. His religious exercises seemed increasingly routine, if not perfunctory.

~

Utrecht was quite a distance south and not an easy trip because of the inland sea. Menno considered going east and south, but the population was sparse in that direction. His advisers recommended that he go from Bolsward to Workum, and from there cross the lake by canal boat to Twisk, then journey south through north Holland. He would make his way from Twisk to Hoorn, then through other towns on the way to Zaandam and on to Amsterdam, which he wanted to visit as well on this trip. His destination, Utrecht, was south of Amsterdam.

Menno finally set out on his long journey. As he passed between small lakes and crossed the dikes, he was impressed with the human ingenuity that made the land usable for farming. Near Amsterdam, he made his way along the Zaan River, admiring the new windmills providing power for grinding grain and pumping water. He never tired of watching their arms turn lazily in the breeze.

Most nights, he would stop at the home of a farmer and offer to milk cows or do other menial tasks for a night's lodging. Usually the farmers were hospitable, and when they learned that he was in a monastery, they frequently didn't ask much of him in work.

He made a long rest stop in Amsterdam, and for several days enjoyed the city's sights, its bustling streets, its network of canals, its art galleries, and its social centers. But his destination was Utrecht, and he was soon on his way again. After several days, he finally arrived at that very impressive city and made his way to the monastic quarters adjoining the bishop's residence. There he found that lodging had been arranged for him.

After spending several days with the priests in the cloister, he made his presence known to the bishop's assistant and was summoned early on the third morning to the audience.

To visit the bishop was a great honor, and Menno entered the bishop's office with trepidation. He trembled as he knelt and took the bishop's hand to kiss his ring. But the bishop soon put Menno at ease, and their conversation encouraged him.

"It is a pleasure to meet a young man so committed to study and preparation for the priesthood," the bishop remarked. "Your superior has written me, highly recommending you for an early assignment."

"He is most kind," Menno responded, "a remarkable man and a gracious mentor. I am grateful to be able to study under his direction." Menno knew that he owed special thanks to his superior for having written the letter of introduction and for the recommendation that he be given special attention by the bishop.

As the visit continued, Menno learned that the bishop was well acquainted with Pingjum and with Menno's home community. This mutual interest seemed to Menno the beginning of a respectful friendship.

With the bishop's encouragement, Menno arranged to extend his visit in Utrecht for a few months. This would enable him to enroll in several classes at the university, even though it was a bit late for the current term. He soon found himself deeply involved in classes. He especially enjoyed the library and the variety of books and writings available to him. And he was thankful when he was able to extend his visit for the whole term.

The university setting was quite different from the community at the monastery, and Menno appreciated the broader exposure he now enjoyed, as well as the stimulus of his classes. The university was a much larger community, but he soon developed meaningful friendships and enjoyed socializing with these new friends.

Menno liked the gaiety of the people on the streets of Utrecht and the social life of the pubs. He was a few years older than many of his peers and, as he moved with his new circle of friends, they looked to him as leader in their parties. He enjoyed the freedom, and often they tried to drink each other under the table. Card games died by the players' inability to continue.

With all this activity, Menno found his life taking on new aspects of social and cultural refinement. His education was not only what he learned in the classroom, but even more in what he learned from his peers. His experiences in the city taught him the social graces he never learned in his small, provincial village.

Menno had two very close colleagues with whom he enjoyed playing cards, drinking, and talking. George was a robust fellow but quick with his hands. Wolfgang was smaller but sharp and witty—the life of the group. Menno was the more exacting of the group in discipline and integrity, and he was a good student. His disciplined patterns came from the quality of his upbringing. But he had very little knowledge of the Bible, while his colleagues were much better instructed in Scripture. Menno's interest was sparked as he listened to them discuss various passages, but though he listened, he actually didn't read the Scriptures for himself.

His friends had been exposed in a small way to some of Luther's teachings, and they enjoyed seeking to refute them from their own perspectives. As he pondered over their interpretations, Menno actually gained new understandings of Luther and the Scriptures. He had generally perceived God's grace as the source of all good things, but he knew little of the personal meanings of grace. From his readings back at Bolsward, Menno knew something of St. Augustine and his emphasis on grace, but he did not know Augustine's own experience of grace. But having grasped a few concepts from *Confessions*, these became a part of his thinking. All this served to quicken his spirit's inner drive toward the meaning to which his religious rites were always pointing.

～

Because Menno stayed in Utrecht for several months, the bishop got to know him well. He was further impressed with Menno's character and with his academic record. He was especially amenable to Menno serving back in his home community. In another audience with the bishop, they discussed the implications of an appointment in that region. It was possible, the bishop suggested, that Menno might even be assigned to Pingjum. This had a special appeal to Menno, although at the time he reacted with neither pleasure nor caution.

The bishop urged him to go back to the monastery to finish the last term of his work there. "It will be better, Menno, if you do not leave anything incomplete in your role there. We want your reputation to be without fault."

"I understand," Menno said, "although a trip back there and then a return for ordination will not be easy. However, I respect your counsel and understand this to be important."

The short term passed too rapidly for Menno, and he soon found himself journeying back to Bolsward and the monastery. When he passed through Amsterdam, he didn't spend much time in the city, for he had a long trip ahead of him. In the next days he passed through the small towns, crossed the sea, and then headed north toward Bolsward. As he traveled, he remained troubled that he had not found an answer to the inner disturbance of his soul.

As he faced the prospect of ordination, Menno was haunted by questions. How could he serve as a priest when he lacked so many answers in his own mind? Even so, the lot was cast for his life and future. He would not go back to the farm, of that he was certain. He was sure that the priesthood was his calling, and he knew his parents were proud of his prospects for the future.

Despite his questions, Menno was pleased about the prospects of becoming a parish priest. At least one of his associates would be no stranger, for his friend George of Utrecht had gained the respect of the bishop and was able to negotiate a promise of appointment to serve with Menno. Together they would assume their joint assignment at Pingjum.

The possibility of serving as priest so close to his home held a special satisfaction for Menno. He could easily visit Witmarsum and his family and friends on occasion, and Theo was living near Pingjum. He thought of his friends there, people he had come to know quite well during his summer months of work in the community. He knew that everything was now to change in his relationship with them, for they would view him quite differently as a priest. Yet as he thought about the service he would render, he was aware of his own personal need for fulfillment. Perhaps that would come as he moved ahead into the priestly order.

⁓

As he neared the Bolsward monastery, Menno hurried his steps. It had been another long journey. As he stepped onto the grounds, Justin and Hans welcomed him back with enthusiasm. He had long earned the respect of his colleagues, and they wanted to hear all the details of his trip.

But first he had to report to his superior, so Menno made his way to the priest's office. As he stood before the open door, waiting for a summons to enter, the priest looked up. "Menno, come in, come in," he said, standing to greet him. "Welcome back."

As Menno entered, the two men bowed to one another.

"Have a chair," his superior said. "We must talk. Tell me about your time in Utrecht, and your interchange with our esteemed bishop."

Menno smiled with pleasure and began. "It is a long but

beautiful trip, and I included special time in Amsterdam, but Utrecht itself is a very remarkable city. I enjoyed the culture, the university, and the many new associations."

"And your time with the bishop?" his superior asked eagerly, leaning forward in his chair.

"He is a very remarkable man," Menno said. "He is very encouraging, very understanding, and I would say very insightful."

"Yes, and what was his response to my proposal?"

"He took your letter very seriously. But that is one reason he urged me to stay for several months, to take some classes at the university but also so that he could get to know me better."

"And his decision?"

"He has affirmed my ordination. I'm to return when I've finished my studies here, and he will administer the ordination vows." Looking at his superior, Menno added, "It would be a great honor if you would accompany me."

"This is wonderful news, Menno. I'm so pleased and so proud of you. It would be an honor to be present, but I think not. It is too difficult a trip for me." He paused a bit and then added, "And as for you, we can share some funds and you can take the barge on the canals that will carry you at least quite near to Amsterdam. That will make it easier."

Menno nodded. "That would be nice."

He rose from his chair, bowed to his superior, and excused himself. When he joined his friends at the table for the evening meal, their conversation continued. Justin and Hans were full of questions. They had never been to Amsterdam, much less down to Utrecht. He answered many of their questions and shared the details of his trip, especially insights from his classes. But he didn't comment about his talks with the bishop or his coming ordination. Word of that would come from his superior in due time.

3
Ordination and Early Priesthood

1524–1526

While he was still a student at Bolsward, Menno made one final trip to visit his family in Witmarsum. He was due to be ordained in Utrecht in March 1524. On that final visit home before becoming a priest, Menno enjoyed being with his family and walking in the familiar countryside. He helped his father in the polders for several days and savored his mother's fine meals. He had made the trip to invite them to be present at his ordination.

"It would mean a lot to me to have you there," he told his father. "This has long been your dream for me."

"And we would like to be there so very much," his father replied, looking over at Menno's mother. "But it is a difficult trip and too much for Mother." He paused for a moment. "I will not come alone. We will plan to be present for your installation at Pingjum. That will be a special occasion as well."

Menno was disappointed with his father's decision, but he understood the reasons. And as he returned to the monastery, his step was quickened by awareness of their strong support.

In March, the bishop summoned Menno to Utrecht for his ordination. Before leaving Bolsward for the final time, Menno bade farewell to his superior and Justin and Hans. The day he set off on the long journey, they walked with him the first few kilometers, knowing they might never work together again.

Spring was breaking across the country, but the cool wind chilled Menno. Yet his journey this time would be easier. He was able to afford secure passage on a boat across the lake to north Holland.

After staying overnight in the small town of Twisk, he traveled south to Hoorn, in the Zuiderzee region, finally reaching Zaandam. After a brief rest, he resumed the trip along the Zaan River to Amsterdam. As on earlier trips, he was impressed by the canals and the windmills that made the country inhabitable. This was his land, his country, and he enjoyed each day.

Menno made only a brief stop in Amsterdam and visited a few now-familiar places. Then he made his way south and was finally back in Utrecht. Though he enjoyed some of the familiar cultural privileges, his mind was on his coming ordination.

Early on the morning of the ordination day, Menno attended prayers and sought to prepare his soul for the coming commitments. A few hours later, several young acolytes accompanied Menno as he made his way to the cathedral of Utrecht. There he would be immersed in all the symbolism and ritual of the Roman Catholic Church.

Upon his arrival in the bishop's sanctum, Menno was briefed by the associate to the bishop, who told him to be relaxed in spirit and to focus on entering into the sacredness of the service. The bishop soon joined them, and Menno bowed before him and kissed the ring on the hand held out to him, expressing the customary respect for the bishop and his office.

As they entered the large and vaulted hall, the entourage of priests moved slowly to the front and stood in reverence before the altar as the singing of the chancel choir echoed through the cathedral. Menno was overwhelmed by it all—the religious exercises, the beauty of the cathedral, the symbols, and the sacramental meaning of ordination.

As the bishop led him through the ordination exercise, Menno expressed his vows and submitted himself humbly to the church. At the proper time and place in the service, he knelt and prostrated himself before the bishop. The words intoned would long ring in his ears, commitments that would shape his life in all his future and service. He arose from the floor in the identity of his new calling and heard the words of dedication.

Menno knelt again, this time for the bishop's sacramental anointing and the prayer of blessing. It seemed to him that he arose a very different person. The weight of the finality of this calling rested on him. He had entered a covenant of holy orders, and now he would live in service to the Lord and the church.

$\sim$

Several days later it was time to travel again. Menno bid farewell to the city of Utrecht and began the long trek north to his new assignment as a parish priest in Pingjum. The senior priest there was soon to retire, and Menno would take his place. Menno welcomed being installed there as a priest.

He came this time not as a workman but as a priest, as evidenced by the robes and other symbols he wore. His appearance made it easier to find lodging, as people welcomed him and gave special respect to the new priest. Several of the overnight stops were in homes where he had previously stopped on his way to Utrecht. Now his hosts were almost in awe, very interested in his new role and his reports from the big city.

While his destination was Pingjum, he passed through Bolsward, and this enabled him to spend several days visiting at the monastery again. His superior was elated about Menno's ordination and assignment. He apologized for not coming to Utrecht for the ceremony but said his age made it too difficult. He would, of course, be at Pingjum to serve in Menno's installation.

After a few days with the superior and with his friends, Menno bid them farewell and traveled on to the northwest, to stop at his home in Witmarsum to see his parents. He wanted to explain that, while the journey had been too far for them to come to Utrecht, he did want them to be present at Pingjum for his installation.

⌁

Menno's parents were delighted to see him, and his mother embraced him warmly. Later he and his father took a walk out across the polder for a father-son conversation. Menno's father became teary as he told Menno of the great joy the family felt about his ordination. For him, to have a son as a priest was the fulfillment of his dreams. The talk between father and son was brief, but it meant a lot to Menno that his calling brought such joy to his father and to the family.

On their return to the house, the bantering with his siblings took on the old form of teasing.

"Altjie, we needn't worry about our sins," Peter said. "We have a special priest to cover for us."

"Right, Peter," she replied. "And maybe we won't need to pay tithes now. He knows us well enough that we don't need to purchase his attention."

Then mother spoke up. "You had better not bother Menno. This is a new role, and he needs your support."

"Ach, mother, we understand," Peter said. "We just want him to know that we are the same people he's always known."

Menno broke in. "I am the same man, and if you should forget it, I'm sure that I won't."

"Theo will be eager to see you," his mother said. "He may have a surprise for you!"

"Mother, I will go to call on Theo just as soon as I am settled in," Menno said. While the farm where Theo worked was some distance from the church, it would not be difficult to visit.

⌁

As he walked, Menno reflected on his visit at Witmarsum.

It had been great to see his mother and to feel her arms around him, and to greet his father in the old familiar way they had known while working together. Menno and Peter had embraced warmly and slapped each other on the back, like they did when they were boys. Menno was pleased that the family would be in Pingjum for the installation. They all wanted to witness his appointment as parish priest.

A few days after Menno settled into his quarters at Pingjum, he set out early one afternoon and made his way to the farm where Theo was working. As he approached, he recognized his brother at work in a polder near the barn and called to him. Theo dropped his fork and ran to meet him.

"I heard about your ordination," Theo said. "This is wonderful. We are so proud of you. And now you are assigned here in Pingjum!"

"I'm so pleased to be back in this community," Menno said, "with so many friends here. And I'll be so close to home too. I hope you can come to my installation. Everyone else is coming."

"Of course," he said. "And I want to introduce you to my wife, Annakin. Come."

Menno exclaimed, "This is good news, Theo. Mother and Father didn't tell me, only hinted that you might have some news for me."

As they walked toward the cottage where Theo and Annakin lived, Menno asked, "And this will be another person with the family at the installation?"

Theo nodded. "Menno, we are all proud of your ordination to the priesthood, and we look forward to your ministering among us." He paused, and then added, "But, as you know, there are many currents of thought just now, and Peter and I have been talking about these new movements, and we're eager to know your thinking."

"Well, brother, I'm a servant of Christ and his church, and that gives you a sense of where I am as I enter this role."

"Yes," Theo replied, "but the servant of Christ has a commitment to follow wherever our Lord may lead. We are not sure that the church of Rome is the full expression of the work of Christ."

Menno cut the conversation short by expressing his desire to meet Annakin. But as they approached the house, they learned that she had gone to a neighbor's home to help a young mother with a new baby. Menno left with Theo's assurance that he and his wife would be present the next week for the installation.

Menno made his way back to Pingjum, but as he walked his thoughts were on Theo's statement about the church and the current talk in the region. There was something in Theo's tone that gave him concern for his brothers, a concern that remained on his mind for some time.

∼

On the day before his installation, Menno arose early, went to morning prayers, and assisted in the early mass for the community. Then he set out for Witmarsum. It was early morning, and the sun had broken through the light clouds as the mist was lifting off the polders. Menno wanted to walk with his family as they traveled the few kilometers to be present for this special occasion. They had left quite early, and he met them less than halfway to the village. He embraced his mother and greeted his father warmly. Then he turned to greet Peter and Altjie, and they presented Altjie's old friend Marty from the priest's manse at Witmarsum.

They walked along the narrow road together, chatting freely as they passed through the green fields of Friesland.

"I've called on Theo," Menno said. "He and Annakin will be there. I'm eager to meet her."

"Did you and Theo have time to chat during your visit last week?" Peter asked.

"It was all too brief," Menno said. "He did tell me that the two of you talked about the radical movements against the church."

"Whether the movements are radical and against the church depends on one's stance," Peter said. "We've talked with father about this as well, and we all have our concerns for clarity on the meaning of faith and the church."

Menno looked over at his father with some surprise, but his father continued walking silently beside them.

Soon the thatched roofs of his new parish home at Pingjum came into view, and Menno showed the family where he was living. Lodging for them for the night was not a problem. They would stay with his father's relatives and be at the church for the early morning mass that preceded the installation. Menno was certain that his father was quite pleased, if not downright proud, that his son had been appointed to serve as a priest in Pingjum.

Menno pointed in the direction of the farm where Theo worked and suggested that they walk that direction, and perhaps Theo would join them. Theo saw them coming and, after calling his wife, the two of them were soon greeting his parents. Then he turned to Menno and presented his wife, saying with a twinkle in his eye, "This is Annakin. I trust that she meets your approval."

Menno's gaze met hers as she peered out from under her bonnet. He looked into her sparkling blue eyes. He put his arm around her, smiling as he embraced her. "She has more than my approval; she has my admiration. How did you succeed in winning the hand of such a beauty?"

Theo turned to his sister and brother with warm greetings to both. Then he paused as he turned to Marty. Theo knew the young woman, but as Peter introduced her he explained that the primary reason for her presence was her involvement in the work of the local parish, acting as housekeeper and hostess at the manse.

As the small group surrounded Menno and walked on together to the village church, a spirit of joy moved among them, a celebrative spirit.

~

The installation service was rich in symbolism, similar to his ordination but without the special rituals administered by the bishop. Menno's superior from Bolsward had been asked to represent the bishop and did so in good style. He had brought Justin and Hans too. Menno made the required commitments of faith and consecration to the church and its order. He promised that he would administer the parish to the honor of the church, the mother of the Lord, and Christ himself. And he promised to administer the sacraments with the full endowments of the church as the presence of Christ.

Menno's installation meant that he would be second in responsibility, associate to his superior, but a leader among the several other priests in the Pingjum parish. During his ordination service in Utrecht, he had been moved by an inner sense of fulfillment as he listened to the bishop recite the liturgy of his consecration. With elation over the momentous calling and with a deep feeling of responsibility, he had expressed his vows before the bishop. But now, in a different way, sharing the confirming sacrament and then hearing the words in the related vows of his installation as priest in this parish, Menno felt a new sense of responsibility.

After the service, the family shared a meal together and then took a walk along the main street that led through Pingjum. As they returned to the court adjoining the church, the group took a brief look into Menno's rooms. Marty teased Menno that he loved his books as much as she loved her flowers in the manse garden.

Even in the brief conversations they were able to share, Menno was impressed again with Peter's keen mind and his interest in matters of faith. His brother was a few years older than he and had been a good influence in his life. Menno himself was now twenty-eight; to have achieved his goal of becoming a priest by that age was quite commendable.

Yet he felt slightly unsettled, even disturbed, about a question his father had asked as they walked together: "Son, how is it with you? Are you at peace with yourself about this role?"

Menno had answered, "Yes, Father, I have owned it for myself and I look forward to serving. I don't want you and Mother to feel that you have pushed me into this."

His father reached out, and as they gripped each other's hands, he simply smiled and nodded. Yes, he owned it as his personal calling, but he knew that he still needed answers in the work he was now assuming.

During their meal, Menno introduced the family to his colleagues. After they had eaten and taken a brief walk through the parish, the family wanted to get on their journey back to Witmarsum. Menno offered to walk partway to thank them for coming. They had all been very supportive, and it was evident that they were pleased by his appointment.

Menno walked beside his mother, but it was not easy for him to put his gratitude into words. "Thank you, Mother, for all that you have done for me in life," he said. "It has not been easy to look out for myself in the many details that you covered so graciously. But I've learned, and much of that comes from you. I have always known that I am loved. Family is not something that I have run away from. From here on, it seems I must rely on the people around me." He paused, then added, "And of course I rely on the Lord."

His mother smiled with understanding, squeezed his hand, and said, "Son, I gave you away to the Lord and the church years ago. We've lived with that understanding." Then she lifted her apron to wipe her eyes and quickly walked on along the roadway.

Altjie and Marty gave him their goodbyes. "Menno, when you visit the church in Witmarsum," Marty said, "I'll be there to attend your needs."

"I envy the care you are giving the manse," Menno said. "I'm sure I will not get the same at Pingjum."

~

The priests of Menno's new parish worked out a careful order of responsibilities for one another as colleagues. Menno's ministry, although second to his superior, for the most part seemed routine. Actually, he didn't need to do much study, for he could draw on his knowledge of the church fathers and make his own adaptations in his work. He knew the liturgy well, and the administration of the sacraments was a regular role for him as priest.

After a few weeks, the newness of his assignment faded, and he and his colleagues sought things to do in their extra time. Many of those hours they spent in idle conversation, and they filled some of their free time by playing cards and drinking. Menno had never gotten into the Bible, and he was scarcely interested now. He really didn't think that he needed to pursue more than the orders of sacred rites as he knew them.

He did enjoy the regular services of the parish, the daily rites of group devotion, and the saying of mass. He found it meaningful to think of how well he performed, and he enjoyed the compliments of his associates. In this calling, he had taken his place as one of a thousand priests who served the 100,000 inhabitants of Friesland. Since he was new to the role, he felt himself to be something of an apprentice to his superior, who continued on for a short time.

It was only a few weeks until his friend George arrived from Utrecht. He had been sent by the bishop to work with Menno because the older priest was retiring. Having served as vicar, or *jongerpriester*, Menno was now the lead priest, with George as an associate and Hans, the third member of their group, as canon. Each of them enjoyed a limited education, although the two associates had pursued some academic training. They had come to this assignment by recommendation from the bishop and the approval he had asked of some of the local patrons, the landowners in the parish. Menno, thinking of his appointment, was not certain how much the fact that his father was born in

Pingjum influenced the bishop's decision to place him in this assignment.

In this small parish church, the high mass and the benediction were not sung daily. High mass was celebrated primarily at the ordinary Sunday services and on the four great feast days: Christmas, Easter, Pentecost, and the Assumption. Menno, as priest in charge, was responsible for administering the sacraments, but he was assisted by George and Hans. George was especially qualified to serve the parish in religious education. It fell to Menno to regularly deliver the homily at mass, and this he enjoyed.

Menno's contact with the parishioners was especially pleasant. Some knew him from his time working in the community and accepted him warmly. He enjoyed baptizing infants and the complementary gifts from the families. He knew this tradition well, and before he baptized a child, he explained to those present that the baby, while under the wrath of God, would be reborn through the sacrament of baptism.

After this explanation he began the rite, interpreting each part of the ceremony. First, he blew over the child just as Christ had conferred the Holy Spirit on the apostles. Then he exorcised the devil by an invocation of prayer. This he followed with a blessing for the child, stroking its eyes with saliva and placing salt on its tongue. He then made the sign of the cross over the infant and baptized it as its godparents held it above the baptismal font. After some expressions of pleasure from the parents and friends, he would conclude the ceremony by anointing the infant with oil, then ceremonially laying his hands on the baby and saying a prayer of blessing.

As the parents and godparents went back to their homes, they spread the word of their great esteem for Menno and the beauty of the service in which their infant had been baptized. Menno soon became a highly honored priest, somewhat independent of church authority, and was respected by the laypeople as one of them. There were few, if any, problems of anticlerical feelings on the part of the parishioners.

In Menno's own mind there was no serious question as to the efficacy of infant baptism. He had been baptized as an infant at Witmarsum and always answered the questions in his mind about his salvation by reminding himself, "I have been baptized into the Holy Roman Catholic Church of Jesus Christ."

Menno was well aware of the continuing religious turmoil in the region. Emperor Charles V was committed to eradicating all movements that challenged the authority of the Roman Church. But everyone was surprised when news came that the 1524 Diet of Nuremberg had sided with the Lutheran cause. Charles's efforts to win the Protestant princes to his side had failed. This seemed to bode a new phenomenon: the empire would now have two streams of life and faith, Roman Catholic and Protestant.

～

But the outer turmoil was not the only thing that impacted Menno. As time passed, he was made increasingly miserable by a struggle within his soul. Questions and even doubts plagued him. His father's inquiry about his personal peace stuck with him, even taking on dimensions that his father may not have meant. One Sunday morning in 1525, as he lifted the bread and the cup in consecration during mass, he was startled by his doubts about the reality of the rite of religion he administered. Did these items of bread and wine actually become the very body and blood of Christ? If Christ was, as the Apostles' Creed said, sitting at the right hand of God, how was he shared all over the empire in these sacraments?

At first Menno attributed his thoughts to the devil, but this gnawing doubt led him to reflect deeply on this question. He discovered the works of another scholar, a Hollander by the name of Cornelius Hoen. In 1521, Hoen had taught that the elements used in the Lord's Supper were not actually transformed into

Christ's body but were to be seen as symbols of the suffering and death of Christ. Now unbidden questions began to rise in Menno's own thinking. But he did not talk of this with his colleagues.

He had to find an answer to this. Quite frequently, as he served the host at the celebration of the sacrament, he would again question how the bread becomes the very body of Christ. And when he blessed the wine, pouring water into the chalice with the wine to signify Christ's suffering on the cross, and when as priest he lifted the chalice and drank the wine, was it actually the blood of Christ? And further, if Christ had died once for all, why this reenactment of the death of the Savior?

In the middle of one of their games of cards, George suddenly asked, "Menno, have you heard of the Sacramentarians and of their flamboyant spokesman Melchior Hoffman whom many of them quote?"

"Of the Sacramentarians, yes, but not of Hoffman," Menno replied. "What is this rebel teaching?"

"From what I hear, he has a very apocalyptic message and talks a lot about the imminent coming of Christ. In preparation to meet the Lord, he calls for a deep spiritual experience of meditation and sensitivity to the Spirit of God. His influence has reached to the north and he has many disciples in this region. Among them is an aggressive young person, David Joris from Ghent. He left the Catholic Church several years ago and is very fluent in his preaching."

"This emphasis on the Holy Spirit—how do they know whether it is the Spirit of God or their own spirit?" Menno asked.

"Well, they are so sure of this and of his direction that they have the audacity to question whether the bread and wine are actually being changed into the flesh and blood of Christ!" he replied.

"George, that is heresy," Menno muttered, even while in his own mind he was curious about it as well. But then he added, "We know better than that. The church fathers were very clear about transubstantiation. When the wafer is blessed and the words *hoc est corpus meum* [This is my body] are spoken, it becomes the very flesh of our Lord."

"And the wine, when it is blessed," the younger Hans chimed in, "it becomes a part of us!" The others looked at him somewhat surprised, then their laughter pealed out, and they went on with their game.

But suddenly George said, "Are you sure, Menno, about that claim you just made? There is a great mystery in this, in spite of our easy answers."

Menno lifted his brow in surprise. True, he was not at peace. It seemed that George sensed this and that he himself might be wrestling with doubts. Menno's quick answer had been something of a cover for his own doubts, but he didn't offer any further comment to George.

$\sim$

As the weeks passed, Menno continued his reflection, even while he efficiently carried out his service as priest. He became aware that up the Rhine River, in Zurich, the reformer Ulrich Zwingli had, like Martin Luther in Germany, rejected the very doctrine that Menno was questioning. Menno learned from George that all was not peaceful in Zurich. Many of Zwingli's Bible teachers were pushing his reforms further than Zwingli himself wanted to go.

"At Utrecht there was discussion of this before I left," George said. "It was thought by Professor Vogt that anything more radical might cause Zwingli to lose the support of the city council."

"He is scarcely another Luther," Menno said. "Rome is not finished with him yet."

George chuckled. "You sound like Professor Vogt. You really believe in the faith, and Rome's power, don't you, Menno?"

"I have little reason to believe these newcomers have found anything more satisfying."

Menno had little interest in what was happening in Zurich.

But he wondered whether these questions could be settled by political considerations or only by careful study of the Scriptures. And so he continued to wrestle with the questions. He tossed on his bed many nights, unable to sleep, but he kept it to himself, searching to find answers. More frequently now he asked himself what it meant when he administered the sacraments and quoted the words of institution.

Menno read various works to find answers for himself. The writing of Cornelius Hoen, the Hollander, focused the questions for him. But Menno's reflection on the issue was made even more difficult through this reading. One thing Hoen pointed out that Menno could not ignore was that at the Last Supper, when Jesus instituted the sacrament, it was before his death, and he was actually sitting at table in his body when he broke the bread. What Jesus said may have been a promise in those words, "This is my body given for you." And Jesus' blood was still in his veins when he said, "This is the new covenant in my blood shed for many." This was his promise to give himself to the death on behalf of his own.

As Menno pondered, he recalled numerous conversations and readings that had challenged his thinking while at Utrecht. In addition to the works of Hoen, there was another writing that he wanted to pursue further—that of one Jan de Bakker, known as Pistorius. He had been arrested in May of that year and was executed in the Hague in September of 1525, ostensibly for his having married as a priest and refusing to renounce the relationship. But from the little Menno had read, there must have been other accusations. Like Luther, Pistorius called for true believers who could know a new life in the Spirit. He placed a strong emphasis on the supreme authority of Scripture, rejecting papal authority and the teaching that the sacraments were valid only when administered by a priest. Though Menno pondered these ideas in his mind, their deeper meaning was as yet lost to him.

George brought news of unrest in Ghent, Brussels, and

across Flanders. "There are many prominent persons in Flanders who are speaking of the spiritual life in a much more personal way than the generally accepted patterns of participating in the orders of the church."

"Tell me," Menno responded, "what is the character of this spiritual life they espouse?"

"Well, for them the church and its dogma have lost their authoritative character. The focus is on *imitatio Christi*. This they affirm to be the meaning of genuine faith."

Menno looked at George silently for a moment, and then said simply, "The imitation of Christ is not a new concept in the church. I've read much of this from the twelfth-century fathers. It doesn't seem to me that there should be harm in it."

Now as Menno administered the sacraments he could not escape questions of what Jesus was actually saying about the bread and wine. How did they represent Jesus and convey his body and blood to the adherents of the faith?

4
Introduction to Scripture

1527–1530

Menno lifted the chalice and recited the prayer of consecration. His mind was numbed by the recurring questions that troubled him: Is this now actually the blood of Christ? Is Jesus here present in these sacraments? How so if he is at God's right hand?

Very deliberately he pushed the thoughts aside and went on with the mass. It was clear to Menno that his role as priest was to provide people with the promise that the church extended to them certainty of their salvation. Behind the altar at which he ministered was a large painting of the final judgment, a constant reminder that ultimately each of us answers to God. In light of this, he sought to give to the sacraments all the meaning that he could share. As he addressed the congregants, he was especially emphatic about the call to penitence. As he made his presentation of the *contritio*, he called for heartfelt repentance on the part of each person.

Being their father confessor, Menno sought to help his parishioners prepare perfectly for confession. To do this, he selected various penitential books to enrich his own thinking on this subject to add meaning to his presentations. The insights of these books spoke to his soul, and he began asking himself how genuine and perfect his own confession was.

Menno practiced and taught his parishioners the necessary fast that was to prepare them to receive the sacrament of the body and blood of Christ. He taught them to avoid combining the host with excessive use of food and drink. He gathered a catalogue of sins from various Bible references in his reading, noting especially that all expressions of immorality, sodomy, incest, adultery, and fornication had a corresponding specified penalty. Menno assured his parishioners that exercising penance would shorten their time in purgatory. He became known for his piety, and he expected the same from his parishioners.

His colleagues, though they had studied the piety of penance common at the time, didn't take it as seriously as Menno did. While they respected him for it, they did not imitate it.

Menno was amazed that he continued to be haunted with questions that he couldn't answer. The most immediate continued to be about the mass, probably because he administered it so regularly. Then one day in early 1527, at a bookstore in Pingjum, he found some of Martin Luther's writings and purchased them, telling the proprietor that the books needed to be examined. In the privacy of his room he read the tract "The Babylonian Captivity of the Church," in which Luther emphasized that "human injunctions cannot bind unto eternal death." There were references from Scripture that were unfamiliar to Menno. This reading, however, opened a window for him to think more freely about what Luther called "human injunctions."

Menno found it increasingly difficult to be free in his ministry of the sacraments. He went to confession himself to share his doubts, but he was unable to find release from the turmoil in his mind. As vicar, he needed to settle this, but the nature of the issue was such that he could not be secure in the dignity of his office while at the same time discussing his personal questions with his associates.

Occasionally Menno would open conversation with his associates about aspects of Luther's emphasis. At times the discussion shifted to the emotional movements among the peasant society, which helped him evade his own questions.

"George," Menno asked one evening, "what do you know of the preaching of these radicals who are all about us? Have you heard any of them? We spoke earlier of the movements in Flanders, the tensions in Ghent, but what have you heard here in our region?"

"I actually heard one of Hoffman's disciples preaching in the marketplace the other day. He was bold and articulate, emphasizing what I would call a spiritualism that we have studied in Utrecht that was known in the medieval period."

"It may be harmless unless it challenges the church," Menno suggested.

Hans broke in with an observation. "It seems that many of the peasant workers give their attention to these spokesmen. I've seen them listening attentively and giving their affirmation."

"Perhaps this is our challenge," Menno said. "We must make the meetings at the church attractive to the public so they find good reason to attend our services." And with this, he broke off the conversation.

Menno now had at least a limited understanding of the thinking of his associates. But he kept his mind at some peace by engaging fully in the tasks of his office, which he carried out with finesse.

~

One day Menno was brought word of a parishioner living a few miles from Pingjum who was on his deathbed. One of the man's farm laborers came to the parsonage and asked Menno to hear the dying man's confession and administer the last rites to him. Menno sent for an acolyte to assist him and invited a few villagers to accompany them. The acolyte was one of Menno's pupils, and Menno was confident that this would be an important learning experience for him.

The acolyte walked ahead in his surplice, ringing a bell to draw the attention of passersby to the procession. All reverently knelt in the mud of the road leading from the village to the farm, observing the procession. A second assistant carried a burning lamp before Menno, even in broad daylight, as a symbol of Christ, the everlasting light. This light was carried to precede Christ himself, who was physically present in the host carried by Menno in a pyx, a decorated box. Several other representatives of the parish followed Menno, symbolizing the priests' full awareness of their responsibility for the salvation of fellow villagers.

This short but impressive procession made its way through the flat and bare countryside to the parishioner's home. There was a salty tang borne on the west wind, a reminder of their proximity to the sea. Menno reviewed the teaching of the church as to how a dying man, in his last will and testament, could secure a shorter stay in purgatory by providing for the daily bread of the parish priests. And suddenly he was shocked that his thoughts turned to an estimate of the dying man's prosperity.

As the weeks went by, Menno thought back over this experience. It disturbed him that he had thought so superficially about the death of his parishioner. The routine administration of the sacramental rites continued to give Menno uneasiness. He finally had to admit that he had some doubts about the efficacy of what he was administering. Yet Menno kept himself busy with his services.

After nearly two years of these tenacious doubts, he decided that he could not hide behind the church fathers; he would have to examine the Scriptures for himself. If Luther was right and the Bible is the sole authority, then Scriptures should confirm the teaching of the church. Though he was a priest, Menno knew very little of what was between the covers of the Bible. He now thought that he needed to read it for himself.

Menno was able to find a copy of the New Testament translated by Erasmus and began his study. References to the Psalms and the prophetic materials led him to turn also to the Vulgate translation of the Old Testament. But he continued reading the New Testament, with special interest in the Gospels and in the epistle to the Romans.

As he read the four Gospels, the matter of the Lord's Supper was ever on his mind. In searching the concluding chapters of each of the four, as they recounted Jesus' last meal with his disciples, only three of the texts spoke of the sacrament; the fourth recounted how Jesus washed his disciples' feet.

To Menno's amazement, these readings did not support the views he had been taught. He could find no evidence that the wine was transformed into the blood of Christ nor the bread into his flesh. In this context, it was clear to Menno that Jesus did say to his disciples, "This is my body," and "This is my blood." But at the Last Supper, he was actually at a table in his body and his blood was in his veins. Jesus must have been giving the disciples a special symbol.

Menno also noticed Jesus' words, "Do this in remembrance of me, for as often as you eat this bread and drink this cup, you do show the Lord's death until he comes." This made the emblems at the table something of a pre-symbol of his coming death, an event that Jesus was predicting. In other words, Menno concluded, Jesus was saying that the bread and wine were special symbols around which his disciples would gather as the sign of their faith and as a memorial of his coming death. Jesus was preparing them for his death by giving them an interpretation of what was to happen on the cross.

Out of curiosity, Menno compared these new insights with some of Luther's writings, especially Luther's rejection of transubstantiation. The Wittenberg reformer convinced Menno that he needed to turn from human doctrine to the way of the Scriptures. Luther had taken the liberty of interpreting Scripture for himself, but in doing so he continued to hold a high view of the sacrament. He emphasized that taking these symbols by faith meant that they became to the believer the body and blood of the Lord. Luther was calling this interpretation by a term new to Menno—consubstantiation. Luther emphasized the ubiquity of the body and blood of Christ, meaning that Christ could be present everywhere in these emblems. Now Menno's reading of the Bible took on a new immediacy for him, and he began to engage in careful interpretation of the Scriptures himself.

~

Stories continued to circulate about evangelical movements spreading among the people. The religious unrest was not only Luther's challenge to the Roman Church, for it was evident that among the general public there was a broad quest for meaning and freedom. This interest was spreading like wildfire. Menno had heard much of this activity in Flanders, especially reports from Ghent and Brussels. Now he learned that to the south, in Nordlingen, Germany, the city's parish had been baptizing both infants and adults for two years, since 1525.

Another story was that further south, in the Breisgau of south Germany, a peasant uprising was disturbing the country, and there were disputations and violence between opposing groups. One leader among the spreading movement of the Anabaptists was a dashing figure named Hans Hut, formerly from the Low Countries. He was proclaiming an apocalyptic message, and it was catching on with the people. This, Menno was sure, would increase the mysticism that seemed to have such an appeal to the populace.

Another shocking story came down the Rhine of an execution for difference in faith. The authorities had put to death a former monk named Michael Sattler, prior of St. Peters in the Black Forest. He had given up his position as a "lord among men," a designation Menno understood, and had become a leader in the Anabaptist movement. After some months as a leader of the movement, Sattler was imprisoned at Horb in Bavaria. Fearing a riot in which the prison would be broken into and Sattler released, the authorities brought two hundred troops on horseback and took the prisoners to Binsdorf.

In the spring of 1527, a trial was held at Rottenburg on the

Neckar River, and Sattler was convicted and sentenced to death. He had been gruesomely tortured with red-hot tongs and his tongue had been cut off. He was finally burned at the stake beside the river. His widow, Margaretha, refused to recant her position, and several days later she was placed in a large bag and drowned in the same river. Menno was stirred by the story, but concluded that the couple must have been religious fanatics.

Charles V continued his authoritarian efforts to quench the spread of these movements, but he was unable to silence the divergent voices within the empire, nor could he prevent the divisions they fostered. In fact, the spread of this Anabaptist movement was seen now to be a threat to both the Protestant and Catholic churches. Some concessions had been made between Protestants and Catholics, but their mutual oppression of the Anabaptists actually solidified their agenda.

∼

Menno could no longer live with his uncertainties. He continued what for him was a new experience: opening the Bible to read it for himself and searching Scripture for answers to his questions. He needed to find answers, no matter what. The light that at first was a small torch penetrating the darkness now began to shine more brightly. At first he refused to admit to the facts that impressed themselves on him, but now he was gripped by new insights. He saw the life and death of Christ differently from the perspectives of his sacramental teaching; he derived more mystical interpretations.

Jesus, Menno now recognized, was a living person. He called believers to be disciples who would walk with him in life. So it seemed that if one acknowledged Jesus to be Lord, it should mean following his teaching as a way of life. This view of salvation was transforming Menno. It meant that he had a covenant with the Lord. And with this idea of covenant, he now found Paul's teachings on the Lord's Supper as a call to something beyond the mass, beyond reenacting the suffering and death of Christ. Paul seemed to interpret the Lord's table as a call to covenant, a new covenant in the blood of Christ, a covenant that meant a new relation among those who identify with Jesus.

As Menno began to wrestle with this, he was now confronted by a dilemma: which of the two authorities was he going to follow, the Catholic Church or the Holy Bible? Others had faced the same questions because of new insights on justification by faith. Menno was especially indebted to Luther for the reassurance that it was not a mortal sin to consider these questions, and they did not lead to the loss of eternal salvation.

With this new freedom, Menno sought out Luther's other writings. He read the pamphlet "Instruction on Several Articles." It spoke directly to Menno and some of his needs. The booklet "On the Freedom of a Christian Man" convinced him that violation of man's commandments, many of which dominated the church, would not lead to eternal death.

The writings of Luther and Erasmus convinced Menno that Jesus' call to repentance in Mark 1:15 was not, as the church taught, a reference to the sacrament of penitence; rather it was an emphasis on a lifelong attitude of repentance. In Luther, Menno discovered that true evangelical penitence was not a precondition of faith but instead was a consequence of it. It was faith, not penitence, that was the key to receiving forgiveness of sins.

The dawning of light in Menno's mind came like the rising of the sun across the polders, shimmering on the waters, steadily bringing more and more visibility. Christ is not in the bread; the bread is only a symbol. We do not eat our Lord but, as Luther believed, we celebrate Jesus by identifying with him. We who believe are the body of Christ, and we celebrate our covenant with him by sharing symbols of it: the bread and the wine.

Even though things were not yet fully clear, this change of view was a radical one. It came into focus for Menno in late 1528. He continued to wrestle with his doubts, but not in despair.

Instead, he sought more insight from Scripture. But even with his doubts, Menno continued to administer the mass, leaving his congregation with the belief that the church was right in its teaching.

A new challenge confronted him when a booklet about the age of baptism came into his hands. Its emphasis was on freedom of choice. Rather than insisting that infants be baptized, the pamphlet said that believers should have an understanding of their faith and choose to make a commitment to Christ before they are baptized. The booklet came from south Germany and was written by a preacher named Theobald Billicanus. With this new insight that baptism should be a testimony of one's covenant with Christ, Menno began to question the rite of infant baptism. This had serious implications; infant baptism was a requirement needed for the registry of each person's citizenship. No infant was to be missed.

Menno shared this question cautiously with George, who in turn mentioned a work of several years earlier by J. J. van Toorenbergen. The emphasis of this writing was on the baptismal vow as the beginning point for a new life, as a sign of dying to the old life and being resurrected to a new life in relation with Christ. According to Van Toorenbergen, the real difference between people was not, as the Roman Church described it, between laity and clergy. The difference was between believers and unbelievers. It is the believers who will live by love, and this will change society.

Menno listened. "You amaze me," he told George. "You have read this and you understand this man."

"Understand? In a sense," George replied. "But from what he says of the meaning of baptism, it is more than can be understood by an infant. He seems to be calling for an adult baptism. But he has remained faithful to the Catholic Church. So this matter of believing must be a developing awareness for the child who is baptized."

Menno was a bit frightened by the questions his thoughts

were raising for him. Was he going to defy the Roman Church, as Luther was doing? Was it not his calling to be a priest and serve the church? This had been the reason for his studies. His parents were counting on him to fulfill the ministry of a priest. To be a priest, he had given up a deeper relationship with Gertrude. He thought of her now and of how he admired her grace and beauty as a young woman. But he pushed aside those thoughts, which could have no meaning for him now. He brought his mind back to the present and recalled that he was in a role in which his friends respected him and in which he should be happy.

But as a priest, he was called to serve Christ, not an institution. He continued to push the doubt from conscious reflection and to give himself to his work as a priest. He admitted to himself that he was avoiding the issues and that someday they would need to be resolved.

～

Menno was kept busy ministering to the many parishioners who were suffering from a disease known as the English "sweating fever." While there were some deaths in the Pingjum area, the more general problem was the inability of people to work for the several weeks they spent recovering from the illness. Most homes had at least one person who was ill, and the family needed to tend them.

Menno and his colleagues were busy making calls and encouraging parishioners with rites of healing oil and exorcisms. He would hold the cross over the person and together they would pray the Our Father and the Hail Mary. He was never sure that anything more happened in this ministry than the encouragement of the family in their vigil.

Time went by slowly. Over the next weeks, Menno continued to hear reports of unrest and of new religious voices. He learned of the death of numerous Anabaptists in the city of Alzey, county seat of a Hessian province, and the region of the Palatinate. The burgrave of Alzey, Dietrich von Schonberg, was responding violently to the Anabaptists, and this created a major stir. Those operating by his authority were so very severe that Pastor Johann Odenbach, at Moscheln in the territory of Zweibrucken, made a powerful appeal to the judge at Alzey for a more merciful approach. Nevertheless, during the summer of 1528, more than 350 people were executed in the region. As many as twenty at one time were taken forcibly from their homes and executed without trial. Odenbach's protest—a very forceful call for more tolerance—was published by the end of the year, and the document fell into Menno's hands.

Months went by, and in 1529 something remarkable brought a new hope of freedom for Protestants—although not for Anabaptists. The Diet at Speyer had granted religious freedom to those who had separated from the church of Rome, who were now being called Protestants. At the Diet, it was agreed that each imperial estate could conduct its ecclesiastical affairs according to the religion of the ruling prince, who "could answer for it before God and the emperor."

However both Catholics and Protestants now agreed to work to crush the Anabaptists. While this reality would not have spared Michael Sattler or any of the other radicals, it opened a new window of tolerance. As Menno heard of these distant events, the firm convictions of these groups challenged him to continue asking why tolerance was extended to some dissidents but not to other?

As the weeks passed, the impact of the movement now called Anabaptist became closer to home for Menno. By 1530, more voices were preaching the emphases of these radical people.

The radical proponents were not all alike. Some seemed to be quite different from reports Menno heard of Thomas Müntzer, the former follower of Luther. Some were markedly different from another people known as Münsterites in northwest Germany, where the heretics had a central base. And now

Melchior Hoffman, the charismatic preacher whom George had mentioned earlier, was preaching in the Lowlands around Pingjum. He had fled Strasbourg to avoid arrest and was now in the north. Whether Menno liked it or not, Hoffman had suddenly become a major influence in the religious conversation among Menno and his colleagues.

One day George came in from his trek across country and said, "Menno, I heard that man I mentioned earlier today, Melchior Hoffman. There was a gathering of people by the canal, and I stood at the edge and listened. He is a leader in this movement of the Sacramentarians and was there with one of his followers who also spoke, a Jan Volkerts Trypmaker from Hoorn in the north."

"And what are your impressions?" Menno asked. "You are a learned man yourself." Menno respected his colleagues, for they had more extensive education than his own. They had each attended the University of Rostock and knew the languages well. Menno looked up to them and had continued his study of Greek and Latin under their tutelage. This he did to carry himself beyond the limited learning in the languages that he had achieved at Bolsward.

"Well, you have heard of Hans Hut, that zealous apocalyptic orator who stirred up the crowds to the south," George said. "This man is different. True, he has something of the same apocalyptic tradition as Hut, but Hoffman counsels his followers to absorb violence, not to inflict it. Today he spoke of wielding only the 'sheathed sword.'"

"To me that sounds like the words of Jesus in the Sermon on the Mount," Menno said. "As you know, I've finally gotten into the Scriptures for myself, and I am especially interested in the teachings of Jesus."

"Well," George replied, "I'm not sure about his following the teachings of Jesus as much as that he emphasizes inner spirituality and the yielded spirit."

"He is not so revolutionary, then, as what I have heard of Hut."

"Perhaps not," George said. "Even so, his invective against the emperor, the pope, and what he called 'bloodsucking anti-Christian Lutheran and Zwinglian preachers' was scathing. And he is predicting the arrival soon of the kingdom of Christ on earth. And would you believe it? Today he even presented himself as the Elijah who was to precede the 'coming again' of the Lord. It seems that there are many people who are taken with his message." He paused, then added, "I could be taken with this myself, except it is going to carry a terrible price, and I am not ready for that."

"Tell me more about the influences at Strasbourg that led Hoffman to flee the city," Menno said, changing the focus.

"I don't know a lot, but I've learned a little about the scholar Hans Denck, who was discharged from a teaching position at Nuremberg for his views on adult baptism. He puts a strong emphasis on our need to be lovers of the truth and lovers of what he calls the 'inner word.' He says that the Lord is accepting of all those who truly seek him. He came to Strasbourg in the summer of 1526."

"Inner word," Menno mused. "That's an interesting concept. I'm quite involved in the outer word just now. That will hold me for a while. But what about this Hoffman, and the influence of Hut—tell me more of him."

"Hut is an interesting one," George said with a smile. "He's a bookseller, and he's traveled all across the land. That former follower of Luther, Thomas Müntzer, spent some time with him, and Hut even signed Müntzer's "Eternal Covenant." Hut then spent time with Denck in Nuremberg while he tried to get Müntzer's "Vindication and Refutation" printed. But Hut seems to have retained more of Müntzer than of Denck, although he did emphasize the need of the living Spirit of God in all believers."

"That I like," Menno said simply. "But that in itself is not enough to make one a revolutionary."

"No, but speaking against infant baptism and the sacraments is," George replied. "He spoke of a three-fold baptism—Spirit, water, and blood—and he tied baptism to a willingness to suffer. It's in suffering, he says, that we are brought into the fullness of God. He was something of a mystic on this matter. Like Müntzer, he too called for a *Gelassenheit*, an inner spirit that gives primary place to God's will."

"George, you are quite well informed and very insightful. I am impressed with how much you have learned of these voices, and I am grateful to you for this information," Menno said with a smile.

As he was breaking off the conversation, George said, "One more thing. I have just learned of a mandate from the emperor, issued on January 4, and we should have known of it. It states as 'protector of the most holy Christian faith,' he had ruled 'that each and every Anabaptist and rebaptized person, man or woman of accountable age, should be brought from natural life to death with fire and sword and the like,' and that this is elevated to imperial law."

Menno said, "That was reaffirmed at the Diet of Speyer. Both our Roman Catholic Church and the Protestants agreed to work together on this."

"It was from one of the warrants for Hut's arrest that I learned something about him," George said. "It describes him as a very learned, clever fellow, a fair length of a man, a rustic person with cropped brown hair, a pale yellow mustache, dressed in gray woolen pants, a broad gray hat, and at times a black riding coat. It shouldn't be difficult to spot him." George chuckled.

"Well, I'm glad I'm not on a poster," Menno replied.

In a short time Menno and his colleagues learned that Hut had died in prison. As an apocalyptic preacher, he had become identified as an effective spokesman for the Anabaptists. He was arrested several months after an Anabaptist synod in which he had participated at Augsburg in August 1527. Hut had been convinced that Christ would return to earth on Pentecost Sunday 1528. So he had set out to gather the 144,000 elect, the number spoken of in the book of the Revelation, and to "seal" them by baptizing them with the sign of the cross on their foreheads. But because of his strong influence as an Anabaptist he was imprisoned and died in his cell on December 6, 1527, during a fire. It wasn't known whether he knocked over a burning candle while he slept or whether he set the straw afire to induce a prison escape, something the jail keeper suggested to perhaps cover for his own failure.

Menno was struck with what this intensity of arrests and suffering might mean in Friesland. There were many groups now being called Anabaptist. This hit him with special force a few days later when he learned that his brother Peter had become a follower of radicals under the influence of Hoffman. He felt so deeply concerned that he set out for Witmarsum to talk to Peter.

As they conversed, Menno said, "Peter, tell me, what is it that you seek? What appeals to you in this man's message?"

"I'm not so well read as you have become," he replied, "but I do think for myself. I am yearning for a cause that can give me purpose and peace, can change our society, can liberate the peasants, and can give us a future. This is more than simply being tied to the church and going through the religious rites Sunday after Sunday."

"Yes," Menno assented, "I have come to know that faith in Christ is a very personal thing. It is not simply exercising religious rituals. But you must be careful, Peter, as movements for such freedom can get you in trouble with the authorities."

Peter responded defensively. "We believe that even they need to be confronted. They need to hear the voices of the people. The leaders are not a class by themselves, but they must recognize the voice of the people they rule."

"That sounds good," Menno said, "but it is also a dangerous course of action. Walking with God is to be our privilege and passion, but it is not to create division within the church."

"But Menno," Peter asked, "is it the church that we worship or the Lord of the church?"

Menno smiled and nodded to Peter, acknowledging a point well taken. Then he added, "We've been taught that Christ is known only in the church."

At the conclusion of their conversation, they embraced as brothers, and Menno made his way back to his church in Pingjum. Now he would wrestle with his own thoughts. As he walked along the road, he fixed his eyes on the steeple of the church with its cross high above the land. His mind kept asking questions: What was the meaning of Christ's death as a sacrifice? How did the sacraments extend that meaning into the life of the penitent? If he came to reconcile us with the Father, in what manner was this to be experienced, and what of this in my own life?

Menno began to reflect on the Old Testament meanings of sacrifices in the orders of worship that God gave to Moses. God slew the firstborn of the Egyptians and spared the firstborn of the Israelites. But later God claimed the firstborn of the Israelites as redeemed and therefore as belonging to him. "Is that the meaning of redemption?" Menno wondered. Does this mean that the redeemed belong to the Redeemer, that because of the cross we now belong to the Lord? This Menno pondered as a very immediate and personal insight.

And when Israel was instructed to keep the Passover with the Paschal Lamb, the lamb was a sign of the cost of their Passover. The actual exodus was signified as promise that was yet to be fulfilled. Similarly, Menno thought, in the Lord's Supper the bread is called the body and the wine the blood of the Lord. In this expression as signs they signify the reality. He reasoned that the symbol is not actually the flesh and blood of Christ, but the reality is the resurrected flesh and bones with which he ascended into heaven and sits at the right hand of his Father, immortal and unchangeable, in eternal majesty and glory. It is a sacrament, for it is the sacred symbol Jesus expressed when seated with his disciples, a sacrament communicating grace.

"Communicating grace, yes," Menno thought, "but the administration of the sacrament in the church was designed to mediate grace." He pondered at length how this was so.

With these thoughts Menno made his way back to the church at Pingjum and was immediately surrounded by his priestly duties. He well knew that he needed to arrive at his own position of faith, just as he had needed to make his own decision about the priesthood. He thought carefully over his conversation with Peter. Then he thought of his father, recalling that he wanted him to have inner satisfaction in his calling and ministry.

5

The Dawning of Personal Faith

1531–1532

Menno had been a priest at Pingjum for about two years when he was summoned one morning to meet a visitor at the monastery door. To his surprise, it was his brother Theo, who stood there waiting to see him. Theo had tears in his eyes.

"What is it, Theo? Is something wrong?"

"It's father, Menno. He died this morning, and we need to go to Witmarsum to be with the family. Peter sent word that they are preparing for his burial and that Mother wants you to be there with us."

Menno opened his arms to Theo, and the brothers stood in an embrace of grief.

"Father is gone. Of course I will come at once," Menno said. With a quick preparation and explanation to his associates, he was soon on the way with his brother. They talked as they walked. Theo reviewed what he had been told of their father's illness, a problem they had each hoped he could overcome. But the illness became more severe and finally caused his death. The local priest, Bonifaz, had come to their home and given him the last rites to confirm his faith. Now his body was being prepared for burial.

When they arrived in Witmarsum, Menno went at once to his mother and held her tenderly, expressing his sorrow. He looked into her blue eyes with compassion and said simply, "How much we will miss him. His influence was so strong in each of our lives."

Altjie wept and threw herself into Menno's embrace. Peter came into the room and reached for Menno's hand. They looked at each other through damp eyes, each knowing how deeply the other cared.

"Let's walk out to the cemetery, and I'll show you where we are going to bury him," Peter said. Theo joined them, and they walked to the open grave that several neighbor men had prepared. They stood there looking into the grave, knowing that tomorrow they would be placing their father's body there. "Death is so final," Menno thought, "and we are left with little on which to rest but the claims of the church." Deep within him was the awareness that he could no longer talk with his father, and this was a great loss.

As they were walking back to the house, Peter said, "We must make a call at the manse. You will want to see Marty."

"Marty?" Menno asked, a bit dazed by his grief.

"Marty Noneka. You remember, the foster daughter of Nonno Zylman the carpenter. She was with us at your installation."

∼

As they came to the household of the priest, the young Marty met them at the door. She was attractive with her long blonde hair. Her tears and the expression in her greeting conveyed her sympathy.

"God alone understands this," Menno said. "He knows what is necessary and what is not. Our father is in his care."

Marty said, "He was so good, so good. It seems that he couldn't do anything which was contrary to God."

"That is a beautiful word, Marty, a wonderful tribute from you," Menno said.

The brothers turned and walked on to their home, each with his own thoughts about their departed father and the affirmation they had just heard from the young housemaid.

Their mother requested that Menno sprinkle the holy water on his father's body and that he assist the local priest in the funeral rites. Menno complied to please his mother, functioning almost in a perfunctory way, as his mind was on his father and their many conversations. As the family stood around the grave and watched the men shovel dirt on the coffin, it seemed to Menno that a large part of his own life was closing.

After spending some time with his mother, Altjie, and Peter, Menno gave the family a blessing and said goodbye. Then he and Theo began their trek back to Pingjum. He became a priest in fulfillment of his father's dreams, and now his father was gone. Menno felt quite alone.

The two brothers walked by the cemetery as they left for Pingjum. Menno asked Theo to wait a moment; he wanted a brief time by his father's grave. In something of a prayer he said, "Father, I will be true to your expectations. I don't know yet what all of this means, but I will remember our conversations and your expectations for me in the role of priest. Your family will be represented in the work of his church."

Menno and Theo made their way back to Pingjum with limited conversation. As they came to the town, they bid each other their best wishes, and Theo went home to his wife. Annakin had not come to the funeral because she was heavy with their expected child. As Menno walked on to his parish residence, he met a number of his neighbors, who expressed their sympathy. He was loved and respected by the community and had developed a very wholesome relationship with his parishioners.

In the next days, Menno thought repeatedly of his father. He remembered looking into those gray eyes, which seemed to see right through him. Menno could hear his father's admonitions. "To invest one's self for God in his church is one of the highest callings in life," he'd said. "I could ask no more for you, Menno." And now it was a reality. But even in this role Menno had to ask himself whether he was really doing this for the Lord or for his own benefit.

~

Some weeks after his father's funeral, Menno learned of a tragic event at Leeuwarden. The graphic news of March 20, 1531, was a real shock to him. A well-known tailor by the name of Sicke Snyder, had been beheaded for his faith, and then his body had been burned.

Snyder had come to believe that a personal conversion by faith in Christ was a prerequisite for baptism. Two weeks before Christmas, he had confessed his faith and been baptized while on a trip to Emden. Because he had persisted in his new understanding of faith, he had been sentenced to death by the court of Friesland. "What an embarrassment for Friesland," Menno thought. "Snyder was publicly executed simply for being baptized as an adult."

Executions were being carried out in the Netherlands against this free church Anabaptist movement. But those who put Snyder to death claimed they were simply carrying out the edict of Charles V to rid the country of heretics. The Diet convened at Augsburg in 1530 had issued a mandate to destroy Anabaptists and made it an imperial law. Now, nearly a year later, Snyder had been killed.

As a Catholic priest, Menno was expected to support the edict and the intense opposition to these Anabaptists. But his inner reaction to Snyder's death and the general expectation that he support the church resulted in a deep inner conflict. Menno could not shake the conflict he felt between his role in the Roman Church and this inhumane act.

As he thought about Snyder and his execution for having been rebaptized, Menno was confronted with a new issue to ponder and study. He had worked with his doubts about the sacrament of the Lord's body and blood, but now the questions involved infant baptism.

~

Several months later, Menno received word that another Diet

had been convened in Frankfurt. This one, held later in 1531, may have been convened in response to the execution of Snyder. The mandate of death to Anabaptists was reaffirmed. Further, it added that people who were negligent in carrying out the decrees of the Diet were to be punished. Charles V was the dominant voice at this meeting, signifying that he claimed absolute power to determine the fate of dissenters.

Snyder's execution so impacted Menno that he began his own inquiry into it. He wanted to understand how a man's faith could lead him to die rather than to recant it. Why would a man die for his beliefs? And what beliefs were worth dying for? Menno himself had lived quite an easy—even sheltered—life, and this cut to the quick in his soul.

First he wanted to learn something about the preacher Jan Volkerts Trypmaker, who had baptized Snyder in Emden in East Friesland. What was the nature of this man's message? What, if anything, had Trypmaker learned from Hoffman? And how had Hoffman's teaching shaped the teachings of the little band in Leeuwarden with which Snyder had been associated?

As he pursued his inquiries into this, Menno developed a renewed interest in understanding more of Hoffman's teaching. Was it Scripture or Hoffman's own form of spiritual piety that formed his thought? While in Utrecht, Menno had read the report of the council at Nuremberg, which dismissed Hans Denck from his teaching position because of his "free church" emphasis. But Menno wanted to know what, if anything, Hoffman had learned from Denck, an advocate of adult baptism. It could be that Hoffman had gotten to know Denck while in Strasbourg and was teaching the same things Denck emphasized. From what Menno had discovered, Denck was a spiritualist, much like some of the people around Luther, and very individualistic in his views.

But the more Menno learned of Hoffman from talking to people who had heard him speak, the more he was impressed that this counter-movement had something he needed to understand. Some of Hoffman's teaching matched Menno's own quest for meaning beyond the religious rites in which he ministered, and Hoffman's influence was inescapable as the Sacramentarian movement spread widely across the Lowlands.

Though many other Anabaptists had been executed, the proximity of Snyder's death engaged Menno's thinking in a more personal way. Parishioners continued to ask his opinion on it, so in conversation with George and Hans, he carefully inquired about what kind of person this Sicke Snyder of Leeuwarden was to have deserved to die in such a cruel way. From what he was told, it was evident to Menno that Snyder was a moral and pious man, highly esteemed in the community.

"Why then," Menno asked carefully, "was he executed?"

The answer Hans gave was scornful: Snyder was an Anabaptist and a heretic who didn't think his baptism in the church was good enough.

George was more cautious, replying, "The church will need to review its way of dealing with those from whom we differ. There must be some room for diversity in our society."

Menno responded, "I agree with that, George. It seems to me the more rigid the church becomes in its approach, the more we give cause for such movements."

While this matter of adult baptism instead of infant baptism had only recently come up in Menno's mind, it was a question he could not shake off. He wrestled with the concept that baptism is preceded by faith, and this meant an adult perception and understanding of faith. After weeks of pondering Snyder's execution and searching in all his church literature, Menno could find no answer as to why a man should die for a "second baptism."

Finally Menno opened his questions to his senior associate, who had long served as pastor at Pingjum. The priest listened to him and finally admitted that there was no evidence in Scripture for infant baptism. "But," he insisted, "reason says that the teaching of the church is right, and we are to follow the church order."

"But do we follow reason," Menno thought, "or Scripture?"

～

In the little library of the monastery, Menno located the writings of Theobald Billicanus. As he perused them, he found quotations from Cyprian showing that he had, long years before, been an advocate of adult baptism. This presentation by Billicanus had a special appeal to Menno. He knew and respected Cyprian as one of the greater church fathers. Menno felt that Cyprian's writings merited further attention.

Menno next turned to writings of the Protestant leaders in reform, Luther especially, but found that all of them taught that infants should be baptized. Some argued that infant baptism was similar to circumcision, which God had instituted in the Old Testament as a sign of covenant. But was not covenant something one had to engage in by deliberate choice? Yet while Luther wrote that baptism requires faith, he argued that the faith of the parents bringing the infant for baptism could in grace be transferred to the child. These views only seemed like rational explanations to Menno, lacking clarity from Scripture.

Reading Scripture, Menno found that Jesus had said, "He that believeth and is baptized shall be saved." Baptism, it appeared, was for converts to faith in Christ. But what of children who were born into a Christian home? He read Peter's words in Acts. 2: "Repent and be baptized for the remission of sins and you will receive the gift of the Holy Ghost." Then, as he read of the baptism of persons in Samaria, of Cornelius and his household, of the Philippian jailer and his household, Menno began to see baptism as related directly to one's expression of faith.

Now that he had finally begun to read the Bible, he more regularly closed the door to his room and turned to the big book he placed on his desk. Almost fearfully, Menno opened the heavy cover and began to page through it, seeking answers. He enjoyed browsing the Psalms, but usually he made his way directly to the

New Testament, reading again the story of Jesus in Matthew's Gospel.

In the crucible of prayer and study, Menno came to recognize in a new way that faith was a response to grace, and faith was more than trust in the sacraments to mediate that grace. As he contemplated the sacrament of baptism, he soon admitted to himself that there was no basis for infant baptism in Scripture. Baptism was not so much a sacrament as a confession. It did not in itself wash away original sin, but like the elements of the Lord's Supper, it was a symbol of the inner cleansing of the heart and of a baptism with the Holy Spirit.

Menno heard Hoffman's comments that Jesus himself had not been baptized until the age of thirty. It was evident that John the Baptist, and later Christ and his disciples, called adult people to repentance and then to baptism. Jesus' instruction had been to baptize those who believed. The focus was on calling people to come to Christ and follow him as disciples. The way of salvation, as taught by Hoffman, was first a conversion to Christ. Baptism should then follow this conversion as a public confession of one's covenant with God.

"That, I may be able to accept," Menno thought, "but all of Hoffman's apocalyptic emphasis confuses the issue for me."

Menno also read of how Jesus referred to little children who came to him. When his followers restricted them, Jesus said, "Suffer the little children to come unto me, and forbid them not, for such is the kingdom of heaven." Menno noted that Jesus further said to his followers, "Unless you become as little children, you cannot enter the kingdom of heaven."

"So," Menno wondered, "is it true that children are under the wrath of God, as I declare at each baptismal rite, and do innocent children need to be baptized as children if the kingdom of heaven is of such?"

Despite all the searching, reading, and reflecting, Menno still had too little time for study. He needed to push his reflections aside at times, as he was being pressed to exhaustion by his priestly duties. His work was very demanding just then; it was 1531, and a serious plague was raging across the region. Many had already died. All the medical ministries seemed to be of no avail, and Menno found himself performing last rites and practicing exorcisms in one home after another. The most effective approach to the plague was to use quarantine as a means of trying to check its spread. This made it difficult for the priests to minister to people and be in direct contact with families.

The country was so ravaged by this plague that the population was noticeably diminished. Menno and his colleagues viewed this apocalyptically, and many believed that the Lord was preparing society for his return. This stimulated in most of them a more intense reading of the Scriptures, as they tried to find a fuller understanding of God's work.

$\sim$

As Menno read the Sermon on the Mount, he became deeply convicted. Baptism, he now recognized, should not be made the first consideration; rather the issue is conversion, a definite response in faith to the Word and will of God. This call of Christ to a life of discipleship opened a new awareness for Menno. The Gospel of Matthew pictured a different Christ than the mystical Christ of the crucifix and of the sacrament. As he concluded his reading of the Gospel, Menno was confronted with the wonder of the resurrection of the Lord, the living Christ at God's right hand, our Lord and our contemporary. Menno was gripped by the words "All authority is given unto me in heaven and on earth." He recalled the words from the Apostles' Creed that he repeated so often: "From thence he shall come to judge the living and the dead."

His heart raced as his mind pursued again the meaning of the words "All authority is given unto me." In his experience, authority was in the hands of the church. How was Jesus the authority? Exalted at God's right hand, how was he reigning as King of kings and Lord of lords? True, he had died for the salvation of humanity, but was the focus on his death or on his resurrection as certifying the gift of life? Menno sat quietly thinking about the implications of these questions in light of his observance of religious exercises. Why do we focus on the crucifix rather than on the glory of the resurrection? And why is the pope the authority rather than the word of Scripture?

Menno suddenly felt that this risen Christ had now laid a claim on his life. This conviction drove him in further study of the New Testament but with more painstaking care. He began to preach on the very questions he was raising. He preached from the biblical passages rather than the lectionary, and he soon gained a reputation for being an evangelical preacher. Many received his ministry within the parish enthusiastically, but for others it raised questions. He felt driven to share these new insights with his parishioners and to call them to search for a personal and satisfying faith.

Menno found some peace from his study and inner convictions, and he found some limited answers to his doubts. As he made his search known to his colleagues, they cautioned him strongly. "You are following the path of Luther," they warned, "and, you know, that is a dead-end street."

Menno responded, "I am simply searching the Scriptures. It is my conviction that the truth of the Word of God is to be our guide in faith and life."

As his perceptions of New Testament authority for faith and life grew, Menno began preaching a series of sermons based on the Gospels. He was taken aback by how many people, in his parish and beyond, began to come to him for counsel. He was being regarded as a Catholic priest who preached the Word of God. As a consequence, he pursued his studies with even more diligence to be certain that he had a biblical base for his teaching.

George, whom he regarded as a close friend, came back from

one of his times out in the village and reported that a group of rebaptizers in the Hague had been judged by the sword, which means that after they were condemned by the council they were immediately beheaded, before a crowd gathered. The leader was Trypmaker, a Hoffman follower who had earlier baptized Sicke Snyder. Now Trypmaker, with seven others, had been executed for their stance on rebaptism. This news stirred Menno to pursue a better understanding of why these reformers were gripped so deeply by this issue. "Was it baptism or their understanding of conversion to Christ?" he wondered.

"George," Menno said, "I need to continue studying the Scriptures on that issue for myself. I don't want to identify with such persons, but I can't afford to be uninformed on the issue."

George responded abruptly. "Menno, do you realize how prominent you have become in the church? You are very popular and are now a much sought after preacher. You are known especially for your evangelical emphasis, your biblical homilies, and this is attracting people to our audience. You can't jeopardize this. Stay by the church, Menno."

He pondered George's comments for a moment and then replied, "But it is not a reputation I am seeking. It is simply following my own inner yearning after the truth."

The two men looked at each other with mutual understanding. George nodded and turned to walk away. Menno turned to go back to his room. There he could be alone and reflect on the insights that were calling for changes in his life.

Even with this new evangelical focus in his ministry, Menno continued his usual priestly functions. He conducted the high mass, led the prayer rituals, and baptized the infants who were brought to him. What he knew in his head to be true from the Scriptures he had yet to put into practice in his ministry. Others were seeing him as a good moral man, but conflict raged within him about his newfound convictions and the struggle to be honest about them. The challenges to conventional thinking disturbed him. "What if," he thought, "this inner struggle leads me to open conflict with the church?"

6
Influences of the Anabaptists

1532–1533

The countryside around Pingjum was peaceful, with the farmers busy at their work. Menno enjoyed occasionally visiting the farm and talking with Theo. He still found pleasure in his ministry and was flattered by the very affirming responses from the people. As he continued his evangelical preaching, he knew that his role would be under question. He considered carefully the implications of his developing faith and knew he had to decide about his future in the ministry. Was he to be shaped by the traditions of the church or the teachings of Scripture?

Menno increasingly found a lack of support in Scripture for much of what he had been practicing as a priest, especially with respect to the sacraments, but also on the matter of authority. In his readings from Luther, he had come to realize the authority of Scripture as the Word of God; this was the apostolic authority. But as Menno's preaching reflected his new insights, the warnings of his associates only sharpened the inner conflict.

As Menno read Paul's letters, he was convicted by the apostle's experience in Ephesians 3:17-19, where Paul knelt to pray for the Ephesian believers and their understanding of the mystery of Christ. Now Menno was led to pray that God would also reveal to him the full meaning of this mystery. Menno now knew that he needed the same spiritual insight that Paul had requested for the Ephesian believers.

Menno continued studying Luther. He read Luther's treatises on justification by faith and Paul's letter to the Romans. All that Menno had heard against Luther now suddenly took on a new and positive meaning, and it appeared to him that Luther was more right than Rome.

Menno still struggled to understand the nature of faith, but Luther's call for repentance as a lifestyle meant that faith was more than acknowledging Christ. Faith was the opening of a new order of life, a life directed by Christ.

~

A few years earlier, far to the south in the city of Augsburg, Germany, the Anabaptists of south Germany and Switzerland had convened another synod. For several years Menno had known a bit about a February 1527 meeting, the Schleitheim Synod, led by Michael Sattler. The news of that synod reached the Netherlands; it would hardly have come north except that it accompanied the story of Sattler's execution. The stories of the Sattlers' martyrdom had been carried to the Low Countries by itinerant Anabaptist evangelists, who carried copies of the Schleitheim articles with them to share with others.

When Menno first read the articles, he had not been impressed by their emphasis on separation—the identification of the church as a separate people in the world. But their emphasis that the Christian should not use the sword had challenged him, and its implications stuck with him. He pondered the idea that "the sword exists in the hands of the state outside of the perfection of Christ."

Now he learned of a second synod convened by this same group on August 20, 1527. At this gathering, Anabaptist leaders reaffirmed their faith and commissioned all who attended as evangelistic proponents of the faith that motivated them. Reports were that they had not limited their travels to Austria and the Bavarian or south German territories, but had continued north down the Rhine. The people in Menno's region, especially in Amsterdam, were now hearing them. Their work in the city, where there was great diversity of thought, was resulting in increasing tension.

Menno was impressed that the message of these evangelists was different from that of the radicals from Münster, a city of Westphalia in northwest Germany. The Anabaptists from the south were a people of peace. They were calling believers to be disciples of Jesus, not of some earthly leader. They urged Christians to follow Jesus' teachings on peace and to have no involvement in violence. Menno learned that these Anabaptists called themselves Swiss Brethren. Many of them had come to a personal faith under Zwingli's preaching, but now that they had broken from Zwingli, they were being severely persecuted.

It was the political authorities who referred to these preachers as Anabaptists because of their insistence on the baptism of adult believers. Rebaptism was seen not only as discounting the baptism they had received as infants, but also, perhaps more importantly, as negating a pledge of loyalty to the state.

Many were dying for their belief in believers baptism. Menno learned that the Anabaptist leader Conrad Grebel had died of the plague in August of 1526. But his close associate, Felix Manz, had been brought to trial after a number of imprisonments and was condemned in January 1527. He was sentenced and then drowned by Zwingli and the Zurich city council in the Limmat River. The impact of Manz's witness remained a unifying power in the movement.

It was partly in response to the martyrdom of Manz that the Anabaptist synod at Schleitheim had been called. The Anabaptists had met to unite a very diverse movement that was spreading across Switzerland and Austria and was now following the Rhine into Germany and on to the Lowlands. When he read the copy of the Schleitheim articles that George had shared with him,

Menno was impressed with the references to the Holy Spirit working among them to unite them as one body in Christ. This was refreshing language.

However, the questions Menno's parishioners brought to him now were not only about Luther and the Swiss Brethren, but also about another voice, the radical Lutheran spokesperson Bernhard Rothmann, who had been in Münster with the radicals there who had tried to set up the kingdom of God. The emphasis on establishing a kingdom, Menno learned, was primarily the message of Rothmann's associate, Jan Matthys, a very militant man.

Earlier, when Hoffman preached in the region, he spoke as a man of peace, albeit one with an apocalyptic emphasis. He had prophesied that Christ was soon coming, but he would first send Elijah and Enoch. Hoffman had even suggested that he himself was Elijah. But now Matthys as a millenarian was claiming that he was Enoch, and the kingdom of God was soon to be set up in Münster.

~

Menno was concerned for Peter, who had become quite involved in another counter-movement. Menno knew that Peter was a man with a deep faith commitment but who held his own opinions. Since their earlier conversation, Peter had become very actively involved with a group following a man known as Jan van Geelen, a fluent spokesperson. On one brief occasion when Menno and Peter were together, they discussed this revolutionary group and its views.

Menno cautioned him, "Beware of getting involved with them, Peter. They are fanatical about the apocalyptic emphasis of Jan of Leiden and of Jan Matthys, both of whom are making ridiculous claims."

"Yes, Menno, I understand your concern, but we can take seriously the scriptural teachings about end-time conditions and expectations without following the pattern of the Münsterites."

"That may be true," Menno responded, "but there is so much in the New Testament about the meaning of faith and of covenant with Christ in life that I don't see the necessity of so much emphasis on the apocalyptic predictions. And as to those developments, I believe the Lord himself will take care of his plan. The claims of men like Hoffman, Matthys, and Leiden are heretical."

"You may be right, Menno, but I am finding something in the emphasis of this group that has made me think more of the work of the Lord than I ever found in the church in Witmarsum."

In the several weeks since that conversation, Menno learned that Peter associated himself fully with the leader, Van Geelen, and had become a prominent worker with him. Although having come from Münster, they were not directly related to Jan of Leiden, even though they were also apocalyptic in their emphasis. In response to what they had learned from Hoffman, they were seeking to help establish the New Jerusalem.

The spread of this movement resulted in a large number of arrests under the edict of Charles V. Opposition to the Anabaptists was now being carried out across the region with a vengeance. There were continuous reports of executions. Menno did not regard this with the same seriousness as the death of Snyder at Leeuwarden, because most of the recent executions were of people connected with the violence of the Münsterites. Snyder was merely a simple tailor who had come to a meaningful faith, not a violent revolutionary. Even so, Menno was not convinced that violent oppression by the church was the answer to this false faith. He believed there was a place for direct conversation to expose error and emphasize the truth.

Since the populace was lacking in an understanding of the Scriptures, Menno was sure that his ministry was to inform his parishioners and enter into conversation with those who were being enticed by the Münsterites. But confronted by the various reports of persecution of these heretics, Menno could not shake the deep conviction that a true church must emerge in society. His conversations with Peter had sharpened his thinking, and he believed that such a church was needed to guide the many misled people in the social context that both he and Peter knew well.

∾

Menno continued to ask his colleagues about Hoffman. Since last talking with Peter, he had been motivated to better understand Hoffman's message. While there were some things that he found refreshing, there were others that he rejected, especially the man's more apocalyptic views. He liked what Hoffman had to say about the work of the Holy Spirit. Hoffman emphasized the transformation of believers through a spiritual yieldedness, which he called *Gelassenheit*. Menno also understood him to say that the quest for holiness, which Menno also taught, was a lifelong enactment of one's faith. This was a change from Hoffman's earlier stance, conditioned by Luther's view of being "justified and a sinner." Now Hoffman was emphasizing the Spirit's work as something of a progressive "divinization" of human beings.

Menno was fascinated by this emphasis. Since Hoffman had broken with Luther to follow this form of spirituality, Luther now regarded Hoffman as a *Schwärmer*, one of those heretical rabble-rousers who were spreading across the land like a swarm of bees.

George was quite informed about Hoffman's break with Luther as well as his present teaching. He related how Hoffman had fled north from Strasbourg in the early summer of 1530 to escape arrest and had come to the city of Emden, where there were many members of the Reformed faith. Hoffman had at first found acceptance and was even permitted to rebaptize three hundred people in the city church. This created no small stir, and many of those he had baptized became very active evangelists, especially Jan Trypmaker who carried their message into the Lowlands.

Menno was sure that Hoffman's influence could not be ignored. Indeed, it was spreading across the Lowlands, south to Amsterdam, and to Leeuwarden and the Groningen district to the north. George reported that there was a group of rebaptizers in Leeuwarden. Menno learned of Hoffman's view on the nature of Christ from George, who had heard Hoffman preach.

George said, "It sounds like some of the heresies we studied in our classes.

"Please tell me about it," Menno said. "We can't be too careful about the mixtures of doctrines being taught the people."

"Well, to begin with, Hoffman holds that as the Son of God, Jesus was born of the virgin Mary and lived among humanity. But he did not receive his human nature from her. He was sinless because as God's son he was given human form in Mary but not of Mary. His was a 'celestial flesh.'"

"This has some appeal," Menno said. "I have always had some difficulty in my mind as I sought to understand the virgin birth and the degree to which the man Jesus, as the Christ, was shaped by this human birth."

They broke off their conversation, but Menno could not break off his reflection. For him, the virgin birth expressed a great truth of incarnation, but it remained a mystery. He pondered at length the confessions of Nicea and Chalcedon and the issues of Christology.

~

Menno could not ignore the turmoil in the Lowlands—the itinerant preachers impressing the peasants. But of more importance to him was the continued search for his own answers to conflicting questions of faith. As a man of the church, he had no interest in joining any of these movements. But as he read the Scriptures, he was especially gripped by Paul's words to the Corinthian church, "For other foundation can no man lay than that is laid, which is Jesus Christ." These words rang in his mind.

Taking them as a true word meant that his faith need not rest on traditions, religious orders, the sacraments, Rome—on nothing but Christ himself.

A deep conviction gripped Menno as he recognized how important it was for him to correctly understand Christ from the Holy Scriptures. This drove him repeatedly to the study of the four Gospels, as he sought to understand Jesus as fully as he could. But with this, he was soon called to think carefully beyond the Gospel story to Paul's interpretation of the gospel, of what it means for the believer to be, as Paul wrote, "in Christ." Since Christ is risen and is at God's right hand, discipleship must involve a covenant of relationship with him. This must mean that saving faith is to live by a faith identity described by Paul as being "in Christ."

While reading in the second letter of Paul to the Corinthians, a particular verse caught his attention: "If any one is in Christ Jesus he is a new creature." "A new creature," Menno contemplated, "must be the meaning of the new birth of which Jesus talked with Nicodemus. This must be what Paul meant by a spiritual resurrection." Menno knew that he had not experienced this new birth. But he had a dawning awareness that it must become true in his life, and he could not be at peace with himself unless he pursued it in his study and in prayer.

Menno recognized that his identity had not been with Christ but with the Roman Church and all of its religious rites. His life was not ordered by Christ as Lord but was directed by his own interests, achievements, and popular success. His faith was not that of a trusting relationship but was simply an endorsement of concepts that he had mastered in his study. Reviewing his own life, it wasn't clear to him what Paul meant by being "in Christ." But he discerned that when one becomes a new person in Christ, one's life must be marked by discipleship.

He had previously read about this concept of discipleship in the fourteenth-century writing *The Imitation of Christ* by Thomas à Kempis. The book had appealed to him, and now he began to study it more thoroughly. Its insights offered him a new concept of the Christian life, and he now began to think of the life of faith as a matter of covenant, of relationship with the Lord. This meant something more than observing rites and ceremonies in an effort to please, even appease, the Lord. If this new perspective was right, Menno knew it would be a radical new direction for him.

Menno pondered whether he could really embark on a life of faith with these new principles and motives beyond ritualistic religious observance. He wrestled day after day with the implication of his insights. Night after night he tossed on his cot and found that sleep did not come readily. In the morning, when he served mass, so many questions would arise in his mind that he doubted the words he spoke over the bread and wine and the validity of the claim that these elements actually became the body and blood of Christ.

He knelt at the altar and then looked up at the crucifix before him. "Lord, I want to be true to my vows," he prayed, "but I need to know the truth. I need to know you and not just things about you."

7
Promotion to Witmarsum and the Revolt at Oldeklooster

1533–1535

In early 1533 Menno received notice from the bishop that he was being given a new assignment—to a parish in his hometown, Witmarsum. Menno's heart beat rapidly as he heard this surprising news.

Such an appointment was a unique privilege. Just the thought of it gave Menno a thrill but also a little tingle of fear. What would it mean to be among his people as their priest?

He was given a few weeks to make preparations and move to the manse at Witmarsum. He felt strange as he said farewell to Pingjum and his colleagues he had liked so much. But he resolutely and with excitement made the short journey between the villages to the familiar streets of Witmarsum and his new dwelling at the manse.

Upon his arrival, he stopped at the edge of Witmarsum and made his way to the cemetery where his father was buried. Kneeling by the grave, he said, "Father, I'm back home, priest in the very church in which you and mother were so faithful. I will try to be just as faithful. While I will do so in your memory, it will be primarily in faithfulness to the vows of ordination which I have taken in the church."

His next stop was the parish residence. First he visited with Marty, the matron of the manse. She filled him in on some of the happenings in the house and the patterns of his predecessor at the church. After a brief orientation, he walked to the little cottage where his mother lived. She had aged, he saw readily, but she was her same loving self and expressed her delight that he was now priest in Witmarsum. Together they recalled wonderful times they had shared with his father and the family.

Altjie had married and lived some distance to the north, so their mother was now alone in the cottage. She assured Menno that she was well and was able to look out for herself, but she also said, "It is a special gift to have you so near and while you are my son I will look to you as priest in your ministry here."

Humbled by her comments, Menno said, "Mother, you have in many ways been a priest to me as a lad in my growing up."

"A priest!" she exclaimed. "Far from it. But I have sought to guide you in reverence for God."

"That you have, Mother, and that is a priestly function, whether recognized as such by the church or not."

~

Menno felt alone in his new setting. He missed Pingjum and the people with whom he had developed an extensive program for the parish. While serving there, Menno had been able to give guidance to the other priests in the care of cattle and farmland the monastery owned at the edge of town. Now, just as the farming season was beginning, he had left that behind.

This assignment was a bit unusual, and Menno regarded it as a calculated risk. It may well have been an expression of the bishop's confidence in him, but Menno wondered if the bishop had heard of some of his recent questions and felt that Menno's hometown people might help keep him in balance. Perhaps the bishop believed that the expectations of the home community would help settle him and keep him from taking some of the new directions on which he was reflecting.

But it appeared that for the people of this small village, Menno's appointment was a special satisfaction. They welcomed him with great warmth. Their own son had come home and was now minister among them. Many friends of his youth graciously received him. The community knew him, and they trusted him.

Menno walked the familiar streets, often stopping by his old homestead and meeting members of families he knew. He was a good preacher and his popularity was evident by the attendance at his services. He was especially complimented for his homilies.

By now, Menno was a well-matured man. He had found new spiritual meaning in turning to Scripture as the basis for his faith while remaining faithful to the Roman Church. He conducted his ministry effectively while continuing to search in his thinking and prayers for direction to engage the future of his work. As he reflected on his new assignment in Witmarsum, he admitted with a little chuckle to himself that being the sole priest would give him personal prestige and a good income. To his pleasure he was paid a much better salary, in fact one of the highest in Friesland— around eighty guilders.

When he looked back on the period, he interpreted his decision to accept this assignment as a "lust for gain." "Relying upon grace I did evil," he wrote many years later. "I was as a carefully whitened sepulcher. Outwardly before men I was moral, chaste, generous, there was none that reproved my conduct; but inwardly I was full of dead men's bones. I sought my own ease and men's praise more zealously than God's righteousness, honor, truth, and Word."

∽

Menno enjoyed being back in the community of his boyhood, though he was so busy that he rarely had time for leisure.

Several times, however, he walked to the edge of the village, to the polders where he had worked with his father. He stood there gazing over the land, recalling not only the labor but also the conversations with his father, whose direction had brought him to his present place.

But Menno could not rest, despite his success and satisfaction. Once the newness of the appointment wore off, the same troubled thoughts that had dogged his spirit at Pingjum emerged in the new parish at Witmarsum. The experience of reaching out to God on his knees brought a new focus to his life. He was driven to pursue a deeper understanding of his next steps of faith and found himself praying over the Scripture in a quest for spiritual satisfaction.

It was not long after his move to Witmarsum that Menno heard of several Anabaptists who had come to the community and met with some of his parishioners. He had not encountered them personally, but talk spread of an "association of believers," as they called themselves. They were urging people to seek more than what the Catholic Church was offering and to join in covenant with one another as disciples of Christ. Their pattern of thought was conditioned by the south Germans and Swiss Brethren of whom Menno had earlier received reports. Most of these people, he learned, were peaceful and in no way connected with the Münsterites.

Menno learned that numerous Anabaptists had earlier made their way across the channel to the east coast of England. Some had managed to infiltrate London by hiding themselves among the people in the churches of England. But in 1534, King Henry VIII issued a royal proclamation that ordered them out of his kingdom on pain of death. Consequently, many of them were now making their way back across the channel to the Low Countries in Flanders, Delft, and Antwerp, and north to Amsterdam. These people were mixing into the society of Friesland and seeking employment as artisans and textile workers. Menno knew about them, but from his previous location at Pingjum he'd had no contact with the group. His colleagues were quite concerned about additional heretics coming to the region in which they served. Now several of them had appeared in Witmarsum, and Menno hoped to meet them.

During 1534 he had encounters with a very different group. Several people who had been followers of Bernhard Rothmann of Münster came to Witmarsum and were also talking to members of the parish. This small group had broken from Rothmann and had come into association with Melchior Hoffman's followers. They were ardent in seeking to gain participants for their movement. In fact, these men were very aggressive and even militant, and Menno engaged them in public debate. The people of the community were greatly impressed by his debating skills on behalf of the church, and many commented that "he silenced them beautifully."

Menno was pleased with the compliments he received, but he was also concerned for the people who were being influenced by these visitors. He followed his public debates with private ones in which he asked the men to leave Witmarsum. When Menno met privately with them, he learned much about their conditioning by Rothmann before they had become proponents of the teaching of Hoffman. They were very effective in their public discussions and were known around Witmarsum as "Melchiorites."

These men spoke of Hoffman as their leader, although he had gone back to Strasbourg and then been imprisoned in May of 1533. Even so, his followers believed that he would be released and that he would set up the true messianic kingdom. On this matter, Menno sought to dissuade them privately. He saw the Melchiorites as a special challenge, and through his conversations with them it became clear in his mind that they needed help. Without Hoffman's leadership, they were prey to other revolutionary voices. Menno was sure that unless they were guided to a better position, they would be more of a disturbance than a blessing in his community.

As Menno talked with the Melchiorites, he inquired about

what they knew of Rothmann. They were glad to share from their experience and reported that Rothmann had for some years been preaching an evangelical message in the region of Münster. Several groups now controlled the city of Münster: the council, the guilds, and the Catholic bishop. The city had sought to silence Rothmann, but he had gained a considerable following, which gave him at least some power.

More recently a spokesman named Heinrich Rol, an ex-Carmelite monk, had come to Münster and brought with him a Zwinglian emphasis. The resulting conversations had impressed Rothmann and led him and his group to begin questioning infant baptism, much as the Swiss Brethren had done, and they soon recommended a move to adult baptism. Hundreds were baptized as adults. But another man had arrived, Jan of Leiden, having been sent there by his mentor Jan Matthys. Leiden at first allied himself with the Anabaptist group, for the movement was now so strong that even the bishop gave it some support, apparently because it was the bishop's best political option.

As Menno listened to their detailed review, he began to see more clearly the difference between Hoffman and those who were leading the radically militant movement in Münster. Within a few days, Menno had gained rapport with the Melchiorites, even though he disagreed with them. As he became better informed, he grew concerned that not all of Hoffman's followers accepted his call for disciples to be peaceful.

Some of the Melchiorites were preaching Rothmann's radical views, including justification for using the sword in these last days, a position based on the Old Testament and the expectation of the kingdom of the Messiah. In turn, some of these itinerant evangelists also continued to be followers of the new revolutionary leaders in Münster, Matthys and Jan of Leiden. These men claimed to be called of God to establish the "new kingdom." They had now begun a program of setting up their new kingdom in Münster, which was already a center of so much turbulence.

As Menno learned from various conversations, Matthys, an egotistical, uneducated baker from Haarlem, Holland, had become powerful. Hating the upper classes and equipped with a fanatical imagination, he had come to Münster in early 1534, while Menno was still at Pingjum and hadn't paid much attention to what was happening at Münster. Matthys became the leader of the city when his Anabaptist group managed to win an election on February 23. He soon ruled a radical regime and ordered all inhabitants to either accept baptism or leave the city immediately. Under pressure, several thousand persons were baptized. The "perverted sect of Münster," as Menno described them, now ruled the city.

Matthys and his associates announced that Christ was to come on Easter 1534, and with this expectation the countryside was abuzz. Menno told his parishioners that "no one knows the day or the hour" according to the words of Jesus. Easter Day came and passed, and there was no cataclysmic event.

$\sim$

The errors of the Münsterites, with their blatant heresy, now became a focus of Menno's preaching. It also engaged him in almost daily confrontation. Though he had come to speak more openly against patterns of life in the Catholic Church of which he disapproved, his antagonism to the Münsterites was more evident and kept him in better grace with church authorities. Menno recognized that the need for change in the church must be grounded carefully in the Scriptures and not be built on individualistic egoism, which is what he saw in the Münsterites.

Another thing that troubled Menno was the way the movement in Münster had taken on a political tone that did not emphasize the freedom of faith. Matthys, having developed a strong following, had become the city's dictator. He first overthrew the upper classes, then expelled the Catholic bishop. Now he was promising to set up the kingdom of God on earth and to establish the New Jerusalem. He had marshaled his forces and was engaged in battle against his Catholic opponents in the surrounding areas.

Menno was especially disturbed by the fact that Matthys and Jan of Leiden had sent out "apostles" across the country to announce their new kingdom and to call people to the "New Jerusalem." Several of these apostles came to Witmarsum to propagate their doctrines. As he had done with the Melchiorites, Menno engaged these men in a public debate in direct refutation of their positions.

After a few days, news came that the Catholic bishop had begun a military siege of Münster, planning to bring this regime to an end. Reports followed that Matthys' forces had been defeated, and he himself killed in battle. But the movement did not stop with his death. Jan of Leiden installed himself as Matthys' successor and, in September 1534, he proclaimed himself king of the new Israel and of the whole world, seeing himself as the reincarnation of King David.

"The reign of God has come," Leiden announced presumptuously, and he believed he was leading its inauguration. The new coins for use in the city carried an inscription of John 1:14, "The Word was made flesh and dwelled among us." Others had Jesus' words from John 3:5, that one must be born of the Spirit if they are to enter the kingdom of God. But Menno did not see the claims of Leiden as related directly to these texts, and he denounced Leiden's claims in his next homily.

"Münster the New Jerusalem, bah" Menno muttered in derision to his congregation. "This Jan of Leiden is no 'second David,' no matter what he claims for himself. As for his leadership, it is one thing to be called by the church, or the people of God, and another to elevate oneself to a position of power." Menno's message was an impassioned call for his congregation to stand firm in allegiance to the Catholic Church and not become swayed by the message of such a man.

Within a short time came an amazing report of nearly three thousand people from north Holland who had come south by boat to Münster. They had disembarked at Hasselt and were there met by the authorities and arrested. This large group now filled all the prisons across the region. The influence of the Münsterite heretics had spread far beyond Münster. Menno felt that, as priest, he needed to speak of this to his congregation, and he made plans to do so on the coming Sunday.

But in his preaching from one week to the next, Menno's preference was to focus more on the person of Jesus, the One who is Lord of all. He tried to avoid spending a lot of time dealing with the problems of these sects and instead systematically developed the themes of his messages from the Sermon on the Mount, as a call to discipleship. His study had convinced him that the use of the sword was not the way to promote or secure the church of Christ. His emphasis carried a new directive for his parishioners: peace can enrich society in a way that violence can never do. His preaching of this more effective way of peace was given as a very clear challenge to the messengers from Münster.

Menno's brother Peter had been in the congregation at Witmarsum several times. When he heard Menno's comments about Münster, he met Menno at the door.

"Menno, we need to talk," he said. "While they may be far off in their emphasis, there are some other groups with a 'free church' emphasis that I respect, and I think you should know about them."

"I'm eager to talk," Menno replied. "I respect you and your sincerity, and I really care about your involvements with this radical movement. I do need to understand why you are so committed to this cause. Let's get together soon."

Within a few days they were able to meet. At Menno's invitation, Peter came by the manse, and they began a conversation as the same free and jovial brothers. Menno was impressed with his brother's insights; with limited formal education, he gave clear evidence of an intelligent faith. It was also evident to Menno that Peter was seeking to walk in the way of Christ as best he understood the Christian faith. Peter's associations of the last few years had stimulated his growth in perception and his ability to share ideas, and Menno sought to help him rethink his relationship with the church.

~

Menno's influence in the region was phenomenal for a young priest. Because of the fanatics about the country, and their confusing teaching, many parishioners sought his advice. He was embarrassed to be received as a "lord and prince" among the people wherever he went. The support of his bishop enhanced his prestige, and he enjoyed the elation this ego boost brought.

For Menno, his popularity confirmed the importance of his role as a priest, which he fulfilled effectively and diligently. But his many questions still confronted him. The issues continued to hang over him as he went about his work, like a shadow following every step. He could not but search for his own peace.

Once again, Menno turned to the ideas of Thomas à Kempis in *The Imitation of Christ*. There he found some direction for personal piety and a measure of satisfaction in his spirit. He resonated with the emphasis on seeing Christ as the model for life. Yet he was unclear about Kempis's idea that following Christ was not simply a human effort but needed to be done by the special work of the Spirit. If one confessed Christ as Lord, it followed that one should follow his lifestyle, including his teachings.

Menno's interest in the integrity of the church meant that he needed to keep abreast of what was happening with the groups spun from the movement started by Martin Luther. He continued to gather news of this so-called Anabaptist movement, which was spreading across Friesland in a variety of expressions. The movement was also spreading in Germany to the east and to the south between the Lutheran and Catholic communities. Menno was sure that there was a way to achieve respect among those with various perspectives on faith.

On March 16, 1535, word came from Leeuwarden to the north of another martyrdom. A rebaptizer, Andrew Claessen of Drourijp, had been arrested and taken before the open court at Leeuwarden. After making his confession of faith, he was condemned and then publicly beheaded. His body was placed on the wheel in ignominy and left there for three days, until finally some associates in faith came at night and took it away for burial.

Like the execution of Sicke Snyder several years earlier, Claessen's death challenged Menno's faith in the church and in the political system that dominated West Friesland. Because these executions had been carried out simply for differences in belief, Menno came to believed that tolerance of differing views was the better way for the authorities to proceed.

Menno had asked himself first what motivated these men. What was the essence of their faith? He was impressed that they held to their belief so deeply that they would die for it. Conversely, he was asking himself about the validity of the church using capital punishment for matters of difference in faith.

⁓

Peter came by again to chat. He informed Menno that he had become a leader in a group that he had joined. Their position was different from the Münsterites', but they identified with the numerous and varied Anabaptist movements. As the movement spread across Friesland, Peter had been called to a role of leadership in this freewheeling association.

This gave Menno no small concern for him. This group espoused an emphasis on revolution and the use of violence to achieve their goals. "There must be more peaceful ways of bringing about change in our society," he said. "The kingdom you seek is the rule of God, and we can know that reality in other ways than expressions of power."

But Peter did not respond as Menno had hoped. On March 30, 1535, his group took a bold and unique action. It's main leader, Jan van Geelen, along with Peter and about three hundred others, occupied the Oldeklooster, an old monastery at Warffum, in the northeast province of Groningen. Menno knew of this place and of the knights of St. John, who had once occupied the monastic quarters. Van Geelen set up a community there and used the monastery as a base from which they intended to establish "the kingdom of God."

But tragedy struck. In early April, government troops moved in and decimated Van Geelen's group. Menno soon learned that Peter had been killed early in the battle. Overwhelmed with sorrow, he knew he must go as soon as possible to their mother to provide whatever comfort he could offer. To Menno, his brother had perished for a cause that could not survive.

The battle had lasted several days and many had perished. After the dissidents were defeated, thirty-seven of them were beheaded at one time, and 132 more were taken west to Leeuwarden, where another fifty-five were executed. With the death and capture of so many of their group, the remainder surrendered. By April 7, when Menno learned all this, the remainder of the original three hundred had been imprisoned or executed.

As he walked to his mother's cottage, Menno pondered the futility of violence as a course of action. He considered what he'd been reading in the Gospels about Jesus' arrest in the garden of Gethsemane. He recalled how Peter the disciple came to the defense of his Lord by drawing a sword and slicing off the ear of the high priest's servant. Jesus rebuked Peter and ordered him to put his sword back into its sheath. "He who wields the sword will perish by the sword," Jesus admonished.

Peter's death brought Jesus' very words to life for Menno. Suddenly, the blood of his brother and the others impacted him like a hot knife searing his own soul. They had died for what they believed to be the truth, but as a priest of the church,

Menno was unwilling to act on what he believed to be truth. If only he could have spoken more clearly to Peter and warned him with Jesus' words of taking up the sword. If only he could have pointed the members of this group to the Sermon on the Mount, where Jesus said, "Love your enemies, and do good to those who hate you and despitefully use you."

These thoughts troubled Menno as he made his way slowly across Witmarsum to his old home to call on his mother. He walked slowly through the village and pondered how to minister to her in their mutual grief over Peter's death. He had little to offer, other than that Peter had given himself to what he believed to be right.

Menno found his mother sitting quietly in the house, tears on her face, yet quite composed. Altjie was there, comforting her. Menno had the impression that his mother respected Peter's deep dedication and had been impressed with his new insights and convictions.

She said softly, "He did what he believed to be right, Menno. I can say no more." He nodded in affirmation but could only share the comfort of his presence. He had no answer to give her to the unspoken question, Why?

A few days later, Theo arrived from Pingjum, explaining that he had come as quickly as he could upon hearing of the tragedy. Their mother expressed her gratitude to Theo, saying with deep emotion, "Our family circle is smaller now, only the three of you, but you are each important to me."

~

Day by day, Menno saw his duty with an increased clarity. If he was truly a servant of God he could not evade his responsibility to preach the truth and guide erring sheep into the way of God. In deep anguish of soul, he turned to the Lord, pleading for grace and forgiveness, and for a pure heart and the courage to walk in the truth as he knew it. He wrote in his journal, "The blood of these people became such a burden to me that I could not endure it nor find rest in my soul."

~

They had just come through the Easter season, and Menno had given several homilies concerning the resurrection of Christ, a theme well received by his parishioners. In his own soul, however, he was wrestling with the implication of a new perspective. "Since Jesus is risen and lives at God's right hand," Menno thought to himself, "he is my contemporary. This means that I engage in a relationship with him, talk with him, and walk with him. This adds a special reality to spiritual fellowship. This is something far greater than all that I have been expressing in the sacraments and the rites of religious observances."

Suddenly, Menno dropped to his knees and began to pray. He was searching for light, torn in his spirit with the heaviness of uncertainty. He was a long way from inner peace, but search for it he must. His studies of the Scriptures and his preaching had pointed him along a new path, and he was increasingly aware of the call of the Spirit. In his prayer this day he sought to honestly reach toward God and to sincerely open his mind to think with God in the Scriptures. After some time on his knees, Menno felt a measure of inner peace. He sat at his desk and wrote in his journal.

> My heart trembled within me. I prayed to God with sighs and tears that He would give to me, a sorrowing sinner, the gift of His grace, create within me a clean heart, and graciously through the merits of the crimson blood of Christ forgive my unclean walk and frivolous easy life and bestow upon me wisdom, Spirit, courage, and a manly spirit so that I might preach His exalted and adorable name and holy Word in purity and make known His truth to His glory.

A new peace and assurance came into Menno's life. He expressed a new joy, and his preaching took on a new evangelical emphasis. He became quite specific in calling people to take seriously the matter of their own faith confession. In many ways, Menno recognized, he was preaching out of his own search and of the yearnings of his own heart. For the rest of 1535, he sought to carry out an evangelical reform in the church, hoping to do this from his position as priest of Witmarsum.

But a day soon came when he knew he had to make a more radical commitment. It had become clear to him that just as Luther and others had done, he needed to renounce his fidelity to a church with which he no longer was in agreement. The call of God for a full surrender to the lordship of Christ was increasingly clear in his ministry. This surrender, he felt sure, would lead him in a new direction. Kneeling on the floor of his room in April of 1535, his heart trembled as he prayed with great wrenching sobs:

> Lord, I am a troubled sinner, grant me the gift of grace, through the merits of the crimson blood of Christ, cleanse my heart and forgive my unclean walk and my ease-seeking life. Bestow upon me wisdom, candor, and courage, that I may preach your exalted and adorable name, your Holy Word unadulterated and make manifest your truth, to your praise.

Menno was called by Christ to a new course of action: a life of daily discipleship. Reflecting on Jesus' teachings in the Sermon on the Mount, he wrote in his journal:

> The regenerated do not go to war, neither do they engage in strife. They are the children of peace who have beaten their swords into plowshares and their spears into pruning hooks, and they know no war. Since we are to be conformed to the image of Christ, how then can we kill our enemies with the sword? Spears and swords

of iron we leave to those, alas, who consider human blood and swine's blood as having well-nigh equal value!

Such a stance made him a radical, he knew, but one of a different sort than others in the Lowland. On the one hand, he rejected the sacramentalism of the Roman Church, as had Martin Luther. On the other hand, he was rejecting totally the heresy and the militaristic spirit of the Münsterites in their revolutionary ways.

This, Menno reflected, must be what Luther meant by *sola gratia*, for it was by God's grace alone that he was called into this new life of faith, one of love and peace, a life of equity and justice, a life of freedom and mutual respect. This would be the focus for his ministry in the new community of the regenerate. Of this he was certain.

8

Further Confrontations with the Münsterite Sect

1535–1536

Menno was wrung out emotionally. He had been wrestling with serious questions about whether to leave the Catholic Church. He was increasingly aware of the difficulties of working for change and spiritual renewal within church structures. He began to think about when he might renounce his role as parish priest and how to make it known. A secondary question was whether he should join another group as a base from which he could share his faith.

These issues were now the primary concern of his prayers. He would not act until his course of action was clear, though he was aware of what God was asking. His long identity with Rome and his participation in this tradition was not easily broken.

Menno was impressed by what he knew of the group of Anabaptists called Swiss Brethren. They were a dedicated and peaceful people, and he encountered them frequently. They were a peaceful expression of the separatist movement, with roots in what was being called a believers church movement that had emerged in Zurich, far to the south. While the group was reviled in Menno's Roman Catholic circles, the new Protestant movements of both Lutheran and Reformed churches also rejected it. In turn the Swiss Brethren group set itself off from the violent revolutionaries of Münster, which in Menno's mind was absolutely necessary.

The Swiss Brethren's strong emphasis on religious freedom was an affront to both Catholics and Protestants. The latter had moved to solidify their authority through the power of the prince of each territory, which had been a decision at the Diet of Speyer in 1529. This interchange between Charles V and the Protestants resulted in an imperial mandate that carried two articles condemning the Anabaptists without distinction between the peaceful Anabaptists and the Münsterites, different as they were.

The Swiss Brethren emphasized a separation from the state and its power; they sought to live only by the priorities of the Christ's kingdom in love and peace. Menno admired this high ideal, though he questioned whether such a movement could survive in the controlled political environs.

Menno had frequently heard criticisms of this Anabaptist group; some of his associates at Pingjum, though Roman Catholic, frequently quoted Luther in calling them *Schwärmer*—comparing their activity across the country to an uncontrollable swarm of bees seeking their hive. They felt this was a very good description and was appropriate language. In Reformed circles, the language about Anabaptists was even harsher, calling them fanatics, scatterbrains, scoundrels, and mad dogs. Despite all the attention and denunciation, the Brethrens' impact could not be ignored.

∼

Months had passed since Menno had come to Witmarsum, but for him, it seemed an eternity. He had become a different man since stepping into the pulpit at Witmarsum a year and a half earlier. In late April 1535, Menno was not planning to resign, but he was very deliberately preaching his personal convictions. On that day, though still Catholic, his flock began to hear the evangelical gospel. Just as he had read about Luther and Zwingli, Menno was attempting to proclaim from the pulpit the truth as he now saw it in Jesus. This course of action, he thought, might help to answer his questions about when he would need to resign the priesthood.

Through the end of 1535, Menno's ministry remained popular, and people continuously sought him out for counsel and direction. His preaching repeatedly called the congregation to discipleship in Christ and authentic participation in faith. He spoke forcefully against the Münsterites, their so-called kingdom, their self-proclaimed king, their polygamy, and their use of violence. Countering their emphasis, he very carefully presented a message of biblical faith and behavior for life. But after about nine months, he became more explicit in his expectations.

Much later, Menno wrote in his journal of this time:

> I began in the name of the Lord to preach publicly from the pulpit the word of true repentance, to direct the people unto the narrow path and with the power of the scriptures to reprove all sin and ungodliness, all idolatry and false worship, and to testify to the true worship, also baptism and the Lord's Supper according to the teaching of Christ, to the extent that I had received grace from God.
>
> I also faithfully warned every one of the Münsterite abominations, viz., king, polygamy, earthly kingdom, the sword, etc., until after about nine months when the gracious Lord granted me His fatherly Spirit, aid, power and help, that I voluntarily forsook my good name, honor and reputation which I had among men and renounced all the abominations of Antichrist, mass, infant baptism and my unprofitable life, and willingly submitted to homelessness and poverty under the cross of my Lord Jesus Christ; in my weakness I feared God, sought out the pious and, although they were few in number, I found some who had a commendable zeal and maintained the truth.

Behold thus, my reader, the God of mercy, through His abounding grace which He bestowed upon me, a miserable sinner, has first touched my heart, given me a new mind, humbled me in His fear, taught me in part to know myself, turned me from the way of death and graciously called me into the narrow path of life, into the communion of His saints. To Him be praise forevermore. Amen.

~

The Münsterite heresy, which had by its influence led to the death of Peter, was a constant cause of disturbance for Menno. Somehow it had to be answered. Jan of Leiden had to be exposed and his insidious views refuted. For the government to overthrow the city by the sword, as would surely happen, was not in itself an adequate answer, for often violent confrontations only spread the ideas they were meant to stifle. The use of violence was like trying to stamp out a fire with wind.

Beyond this issue, Menno had been seeking to carry out an evangelical reform at Witmarsum. He was concerned that in promoting reform his emphasis had to be distinguished clearly from these fanatics or his congregation and the community would misunderstand him. But, on the other hand, he didn't want his attack on the Münsterite heresy to be understood simply as his defense of the forms of Catholicism he was now challenging but rather as a call to personal conversion by identifying with Christ as Lord.

Under the decrees of Charles V, opposition to the various dissenting groups was forceful and quite effective in meeting the purposes of the state church. The enactment of the decrees cost the lives of scores of people. On March 6, 1535, five were put to death in the city of Amsterdam. One of those Anabaptist leaders was Hendrick Biesman, who had been in prison with two other brothers and two women. The men were each beheaded and the women were drowned. The injustice of this act hit Menno force-fully. He was certain that such violence was self-defeating for the country and that it should not continue.

In late 1535 and early 1536, Menno took pen and paper in hand and wrote pointedly a pamphlet he called "The Blasphemy of Jan of Leiden." (The full title of the tract was "A Plain and Clear Proof from Scripture, Proving that Jesus Christ is the Real, Spiritual David of the Promise, the King of kings, the Lord of lords, and the Real, Spiritual King of Spiritual Israel, that is, of His Church, which He has bought with His own Blood. Written to all the true Brethren of the Covenant scattered abroad, against the great and fearful Blasphemy of Jan of Leiden, who poses as the joyous King of all, the Joy of the Disconsolate, so Usurping the Place of God.") He wrote to expose the man's claim to be king and the present David of God's promise. In his tract, Menno emphasized that it was Christ who fulfilled God's promise of a "David" to come. He con-trasted the kingship of Christ and his style to the claims of this so-called King Jan and his use of violence.

Menno wanted to make a distinction between two kinds of revolution: the kind promoted by this heresy coming from Münster and brought on by the sword, and the kind brought on by the transforming power of Christ through the way of love and nonre-sistance. "It is forbidden," he wrote, "for us to fight with physical weapons." He figuratively asked Leiden whether he had been bap-tized with a sword or with the cross.

> If Christ fights his enemies with the sword of His mouth, if He smites the earth with the rod of His mouth and slays the wicked with the breath of His lips; and if we are to be conformed unto His image, how can we, then, oppose our enemies with any other sword? Does not the Apostle Peter say: "For even hereunto were ye called, because Christ also suffered for us, leaving us an example

that we should follow his steps, who did not sin, neither
was guile found in his mouth: who, when he was reviled,
reviled not again: when he suffered he threatened not;
but committed himself to him that judges righteously?"
This agrees with the words of John who says: "He that
abides in Christ walks as Christ walked."

With the realities of his new commitment to the Lord, Menno
was amazed at how the Scriptures had become so important to
him. This he saw as evidence of his new birth, a special benefit of
the regenerating work of the Holy Spirit. He regularly spent more
time in prayer and study. He knew that he could not be at peace
without calling people to move beyond the expectations of the
Catholic Church to a new obedience to the Word of Christ. In his
prayer and waiting before God, he asked the Lord for a special
blessing of the presence of the Holy Spirit. This he enjoyed with
an inner freedom and assurance that he well knew was for his aid.

Menno began boldly calling his people to join him in rejecting the abominations of the antichrist, mass, infant baptism, and
unprofitable living. "As God touches us," he said, "he will give us
new minds, humble us in his fear, teach us to know ourselves,
turn us from the way of death into the path of life, into the communion of his saints." This preaching would at least give people
an understanding of what was happening should he need to
resign his position.

As "The Blasphemy of Jan of Leiden" was copied and passed
around, Menno became known for his clear and bold attack on
heresy. Consequently he was subjected to increased criticism, and
both Leiden's sect and his colleagues in Catholic Church began
to oppose him.

In his writing, Menno carefully expressed his own scriptural
insights. As he exposed Leiden, he was also developing his own
unique theology and articulating his differences with Rome as well.

His mind and heart exalted as he expressed his conviction.
Having given his key verse on the title page—1 Corinthians

3:11: "For other foundation can no man lay than that is laid, which is Jesus Christ"—he appealed to his readers to be faithful to Christ and to the word of Scripture:

> There is but one true King and Lord, namely Jesus Christ. He is the one who possesses all authority in heaven and on earth. He is exalted at the right hand of God, the place of all power. It is the church which is his spiritual kingdom, a kingdom of love and peace, whose weapons are spiritual and not the armaments of the world.
>
> The eternal, merciful God who has called us from darkness into His marvelous light, yes, has led us into the kingdom of his beloved Son, Jesus Christ, must keep us upon the right way, that Satan by his wiles may not deceive us and no root of bitterness spring up among us to make confusion and many be defiled, as alas happens to some these days. It must be that sects arise among us that those who are approved may be made manifest.
>
> Let none stumble at this but let all give heed to the Word of God and abide by it, that they may be delivered from the strange woman, as Solomon says (by which woman we should understand all false teachers), even from the stranger which flatters with her words; which forsakes the guide of her youth, and forgets the covenant of God.
>
> This is the true nature of all false teachers. They desert the pure doctrine of Christ and begin to traffic in strange doctrine. They get others under their spell so that they cannot believe the truth and they use smooth talk as Paul says: By good works and fair speeches, they deceive the hearts of the simple. They leave their master Christ, whom alone they should hear as the Father testifies saying: "This is my beloved Son in whom I am well pleased; hear ye him." But this voice from the

Father all false teachers forget and they leave their only master, Christ Jesus, for since they are not of His sheep, they do not hear His voice. The false teachers forget the covenant of their God and that to which we should give most heed they ignore. . . .

Let everyone behave himself in accordance with the example of the divine Word which he has received from the apostles by faith and love; let everyone remember that he has not learned Christ except by suffering. Abide in it. For in Christ is an upright spirit; He is the Light of the world; he who follows him shall not walk in darkness, but have the light of life. The Lord reigns; let the people tremble; he sits between the cherubim; let the earth be moved.

All believers are the sheep of Christ and there is but one fold, of which Christ is the Shepherd. From this it must follow that Christ is the only Shepherd, and that no one else can be that. For this reason Peter calls Christ the chief Shepherd, and Paul says: "Now the God of peace, that brought again from the dead our Lord Jesus, that great shepherd of the sheep, through the blood of the everlasting covenant, make you perfect in every good work to do his will."

Christ is the only Shepherd; for all believers must hear His voice and the voice of none other. From this it follows at once that He is also the promised David, according to the words of the Lord; David my servant shall be King over them; and they shall all have one Shepherd. Besides this God says, my servant David shall be their Prince forever. I trust that no one is so foolish (unless a root of bitterness be in him and he be given up of God to a perverse mind) as to understand these words of some man—that a man shall be our eternal prince—for it is written that God alone is eternal, He only has immortality and dwells in a light to which none can come. No man can be our eternal Prince.

But Christ is our eternal Prince, and His kingdom is an everlasting kingdom as it is written, "Thy throne, O God, is forever." Paul and Peter say that Christ's kingdom is eternal; and the angel said to Mary: "The Lord God shall give him the throne of his father David, and he shall reign over the house of Jacob forever, and of his kingdom there shall be no end." Again the prophet says, "His seed shall endure forever, and his throne as the sun before me. It shall be established forever as the moon, and as a faithful witness in heaven." From this everybody realizes that our eternal prince is none other than Christ; therefore our Promised David is none other than Christ.

Menno's writing were copied and passed from hand to hand. His parishioners were proud of their priest and quoted him in their conversations. Clearly he was no Münsterite, but a fresh voice within the church.

With Menno's more evangelical preaching, the pattern of church life steadily changed in his parish. He adjusted his approach from administering the mass to sharing a simple Lord's Supper. He only occasionally performed infant baptisms, suggesting to parents that they delay the baptism until the child became mature enough to make its own commitment. But the matter of believers baptism continued to trouble him.

Not everyone accepted his changes with good grace. Some of his parishioners spoke to his fellow priests in the region. His colleagues from Pingjum became increasingly confrontational about the changes he was making. They were committed to the church of Rome, and they warned Menno that he should not become a second Luther. They reminded him that Luther had been protected by the German princes, and Zwingli by the city council, but there was no one in Friesland who would do that for Menno, in spite of his popularity.

There was considerable tension, and the confrontation meant that he needed to think carefully about a break from the church. He would have to make a decision: should he continue his attempts at reform in the church or change his religious identity. This had its dangers, he knew, for reports continued of executions of Anabaptists in various parts of the Netherlands. If he broke from the Catholic Church, he was placing himself in grave danger.

Menno had been deeply shaken a year earlier, in April 1534, when at Aalsmer, to the west of Amsterdam, two inhabitants named Jan and Johannes Dirks had been put to death for their beliefs. The report that Menno received declared that they were steadfast in their faith, "going to their death like sheep, so that it was amazing to see." They had been arrested in the countryside where they had sought hiding places in the swamps and marshes and were then brought to the city for execution.

Another report that came earlier in May of 1535 concerned ten Anabaptists, including Adriaen Cornelisse, who were executed near Amsterdam. Adriaen had been baptized by Gerrit Boeckbinder and stated boldly that he did not regret this baptism. These reports of martyrdoms were a warning to Menno, since he had questions about the sacrament similar to those that several martyrs had expressed. Even so, he continued to rethink carefully the meaning of his own baptism.

During the summer and fall, Menno was almost obsessed with study. He was driven to find further confirmation in the Scriptures of convictions that were growing in him and that continued to disturb his peace. He found no teaching in Scripture that mandated infant baptism. Rather Scripture taught that the administration of this ordinance was best following one's confession of believing in Jesus.

The Protestant and Catholic troops continued the siege of Münster and by early 1535 the city was expected to collapse. Leiden's gathering of his subordinates and having himself crowned the "king of righteousness over all" on Easter Sunday 1534 had, in Menno's thinking, marked the doom of the city. Leiden also had summarily inaugurated polygamy in a literal imitation of Old Testament practices. Three times a week he would appear in the marketplace in royal robes as king and receive homage from his subjects.

On June, 25, 1535, Leiden's "theocracy" came to a bloody end. Defeated by the besieging troops, he and two of his associates were captured. They were first tortured with red-hot tongs and then put to death. Their bodies were put on display in iron cages that hung on the tower of St. Lambert's Church in the heart of Münster. The corpses remained there indefinitely as a witness to the victory of the bishop over such heretics. Menno's thought was directed toward the many people who had been misled by this fanatic, and he wondered who would be a shepherd to them.

Having written against Leiden, he was quite sure that the man had met judgment for his errors. In his teaching Menno sought to make clear his new sense of the authority of the written Word and what he believed to be a correct interpretation. He was not calling people to follow him but rather to commit themselves to Christ and his Word. Menno felt very deeply that the error of the people in Münster had come from a man; people had blindly taken up his claims and an inner mystical spirituality without any base in the Scriptures.

～

Soon his colleague priest in Pingjum urged him, "You must decide whether to be one of us who are working with Rome, or whether you are one of the dissenters working against Rome."

"I have no other commitment than to be true to our Lord Jesus Christ," Menno replied, "for he is head of the church. I don't want to be thought of as a dissenter."

"But in a particular way you are, gracious as you may be about your evangelical preaching. You say a lot about the meaning of the symbols, but you minimize the symbol itself. At least it appears that way in the options you have given about baptism."

"Yes, it may look that way. But you know me personally, and I want to assure you that I have no other goal than to interpret the meaning of the Word of God to my congregants and call them to the true meaning of penance before the Lord." His former partner nodded with understanding and turned to walk slowly away.

Menno knew that should he leave the Catholic Church, he would have to live with threats against his life. This was a price he needed to consider. He didn't take this lightly, and over the next weeks, he weighed the implications of the decision toward which he knew he was moving.

Altjie came to Witmarsum to visit their mother and stopped by to see Menno. She and her husband, Jan, lived near Leeuwarden, far to the north, and she didn't make the trip often. As they visited, Menno shared some of his inner struggle with her, and in turn she told him of the spread of the Anabaptist groups in her area. In fact, she and her husband had attended one of their meetings. A small gathering had met in a home near theirs, and they knew the people as good neighbors with integrity and peaceful intent.

"They are wonderful people, Menno. They are committed to walk with Christ and to live by his teachings. They really are not revolutionaries in any way like the Münsterites."

"I understand," Menno replied. "I think they are shaped more by influences from the south, from the Swiss Brethren, with an emphasis on the freedom of the church and a lifestyle that includes a rejection of the sword."

"That is my impression," she said. "Although, I haven't attended enough of their meetings to be an authority on it. Jan tells me to stay away from their gatherings, that we don't need trouble with the authorities." She paused and looked intently at him. "And you, Menno, from what I hear you have quite an effective ministry and are preaching a very evangelical message."

"I preach what I am finding in the Scriptures and what has become a reality in my own life. Faith is much more than rites of religion, Altjie. It is a covenant relationship with the risen Christ. This is a joyful reality of peace but also a demanding covenant in a call to faithfulness."

To Menno, her words were further evidence of a work of God's Spirit among the people, a work not limited to the trained clergy. The Spirit was calling laypeople to the reality of faith in Christ, and this was touching his sister. In the words that he had read just that morning from the book of the Acts, he had to say with Peter, "Who am I to withstand God?"

9
Menno Resigns from the Priesthood

1536

January 30, 1536, was a cold Sunday morning, but Menno had a warm heart. He had met God on his knees, made a decision, and surrendered his life and his future to the Lord. He went into the pulpit that morning with mixed emotions—but clear resolve. He was giving up his position, his security, his income, and life as he had known it.

Menno went first to his mother and informed her of his decision. He shared his steps of faith and asked for her understanding. He told her that he was sure his father would respect his reasons for the decision. After speaking to her, he made his way to the church for the morning service. As he looked out at the congregation from the raised pulpit, he spoke with choked voice. "My beloved brothers and sisters," he began. "This morning I am resigning my position as parish priest."

The congregation gasped. But then a hush settled over them, and Menno continued.

"I do this to be true to my convictions, which you have heard me declare from the Word of God. I seek only to be faithful to the Word of the Lord and faithful in my walk with Christ. I must be free to follow him in obedience and not be bound by traditions that have no meaningful life in faith. I invite those who can join me in this step to walk with me as disciples of Christ, to share with me the fellowship of his resurrection."

Menno carefully stepped from the pulpit and walked slowly down the aisle, nodding to individuals in the assembly. There were a few who looked at him with disapproval, even hostility, but there were many others whose eyes were wet with tears. As he stepped out the door, he looked up toward heaven and said simply, "Lord Jesus, I've done what I felt you have asked. Now the future is in your hands."

Later he would write in his journal:

> With God's Spirit, help, force and hand, I left my good
> fame, honor and name, which I had with people, and left
> all the anti-Christian errors, masses, child baptisms, easy
> life, and everything else. Voluntarily I went in misery and
> poverty under the burden of the cross of my Lord Jesus
> Christ, in all my weakness, fearing God, searching for
> real and true believers in God.

⌇

Menno knew that he needed to leave Witmarsum for his own safety. The church and state authorities would not take his resignation lightly. From here on he would be a fugitive priest.

Some friends stopped by the manse in the afternoon to express their regrets that he would no longer be their priest. Several expressed concern that he might be facing danger or discipline for this decision, which he knew. He would leave quietly the next morning without telling anyone.

It seemed to Menno that he was now on a long and lonely journey. Even so, he was amazed at the inner peace he felt about his action. He had pondered it for so many months that he felt there were few surprises; he had thought over every aspect of the decision.

As he walked along the narrow paths between the various

waterways, the peace of the water reflected the calmness in his own spirit. He would face threats and persecution, he knew, for he was well known. A priest didn't just renounce his parish and allegiance to Rome without it becoming an issue for the church.

Having known of the believers church group at Leeuwarden, he set out on a journey to the north. The trek took him through familiar countryside. As a fugitive, he would need to be careful finding this believers church. For her safety he would not call on Altjie, but he would find some of the people of whom she had spoken.

Once he arrived in the Leeuwarden, he rented a room. Then he cautiously inquired of the landlord about independent movements that had broken from the church of Rome. He assured the landlord that he was not a member of any such group but had reasons to seek them out. The landlord steered Menno to some neighbors who could help him find the group.

These neighbors were cautious, however; it took some time before they believed that this priest was sincere. After a few days they introduced him to their leader, Dirk Philips, and several of his associates. A number of them had heard of Menno Simons and his evangelical message at Witmarsum. But upon meeting him, they needed to test what they had heard with his own answers to their questions of faith. It was soon apparent that Menno and Dirk shared a special affinity in their way of thinking and of expressing faith. A new friendship was begun.

A few days earlier, several leaders of the local group had gone to a neighboring region to meet with Obbe, Dirk's older brother, where he was speaking to a gathering in a barn. They had told him of this man, Menno Simons, a priest of prominence who had left the church of Rome and was now asking about joining them. Obbe had been urged to visit Leeuwarden secretly and meet with this priest from Witmarsum.

The meeting was held in late afternoon in a barn near the village. It began with a time of getting acquainted with Menno.

Then the group prayed, asking for God's guidance as they pursued their interchange. The group turned to Obbe, the senior elder in the fellowship, and asked him to lead the conversation. Many of the questions focused on teachings of Jesus and on Menno's commitment to a full rejection of violence and the sword. As the interchange proceeded, they were satisfied with Menno's expression of faith and his commitment to discipleship of Christ.

Following the meeting, it was agreed that Menno should have some continued meetings with the Philips brothers. These meetings followed in the next several days, and on those occasions Menno simply gave his testimony of personal faith. "Brothers," he said, "I have wrestled with the issue of my relationship to Christ and his sacraments for a number of years. Ever since the execution of Sicke Snyder here in Leeuwarden, the question of the meaning of the sacraments and the nature of faith in Christ has plagued my mind. In the last year I have come to know in Jesus Christ the reality of becoming a new creature. In his grace he has granted me a new birth and in this new life I am committed to be his disciple."

They continued to ask him a variety of questions about his faith struggles, almost in the style of an interrogation. Obbe wanted to discuss in more detail Menno's approach to Scripture. Menno responded freely out of his readings in the epistles and his particular focus on the Sermon on the Mount. He sought to be clear on his understanding of salvation in Jesus and his call to the way of nonviolence.

After the lengthy interchange, Obbe responded, "Menno, this is a wonderful word of faith, and it marks you as our brother. We are not asking that you identify with us as such, even though many of my followers are called Obbenites, but we are interested primarily in calling people to know and walk with Christ. We will be glad to sit with you as opportunity makes possible in study of the Scriptures together. This will help us to see even more fully the evidence of his work in your life, which so impresses us. It is great to have a person with your experience and insight to become a part of our fellowship. We will search with you to find the further leading and will of God for your future."

Obbe and Dirk met with Menno on various occasions. They usually met in the morning and talked until noon. Each of them appeared to enjoy spending these hours with him, discussing their faith as well as his. In turn, the Philips shared their thoughts on the movement's central emphasis—the call to follow Christ in life. They talked of the commitment to walk with Christ as disciples and of their concern for faithfulness to Scripture. They asked Menno to be clear with them about his insights into Scripture. Again Obbe asked, "What were the essential aspects of faith that led you to make this break with the Roman Church?"

Menno carefully related the transitions in his own life, emphasizing his study of Scripture, his approach to interpretation, and his understanding of the centrality of Christ in what Menno called his lay theology.

"First," he said, "I came to an awareness of God's grace and the call of the Spirit to a new life. In my response of faith, the Spirit's work of regeneration gave me this new life. He has continued to witness in my spirit the assurance of my salvation and has brought a transforming change into my life. Old things passed away and my life has been made new.

"Second, I have found that discipleship is not simply a profession but is walking daily with Christ. This discipleship, I believe, means that we are to live like Jesus. The Lord has made clear to me his expectation of the way of love and a complete rejection of the sword and violence. Our mission in society is one of witness, of calling people to join in covenant with Christ. It is the building of free communities of love and holiness, communities that will practice justice in relation to every person and will live in the mutuality of peace."

While speaking deliberately and carefully, Menno watched their faces to discern any reactions. He was especially clear that his quest was now to find fellowship with those who would take the words of Jesus seriously as a lifestyle. This, he said, meant to take up the cross daily and follow him, to love even one's enemies, and to give up the sword.

Obbe and Dirk spoke of their understanding of the New Testament concept of the church and, listening to Menno's response, the two brothers affirmed his perceptions. They also stressed the importance of the redeemed community as a voluntary fellowship of the regenerate. They emphasized this as being in sharp contrast to the state church, which was neither voluntary nor encouraged an act of believing on the part of a mature person.

They further emphasized that the members of the community are responsible to hold one another accountable to the covenant of faith. This fit with Menno's thinking, for he was convinced that the new creation meant a new covenant with the Lord, and such a covenant carried accountability.

Obbe and Dirk responded to Menno's expressions with warmth and affirmation. Dirk, who was the better-trained theologian, commended Menno for his quest to understand Scripture in its disclosure of God's full revelation in Christ. He affirmed Menno in his recognition of the importance of the new community as the body of Christ.

~

At a gathering a few evenings later, Menno shared his faith with the small group led by Obbe and Dirk. He was quite impressed with the spirit of fellowship among them. Truly this fellowship was in the spirit of Christ.

Menno took his time getting acquainted with the group and giving consideration to joining them. As the next week passed, he felt at rest in his spirit about identifying with these people. While this group was labeled Anabaptist, they were quite different from the Münsterite Anabaptists. Their faith centered on

Christ, not on a man, and their emphasis was on nonviolence. They were committed to being a community of disciples that followed Christ, sharing the faith with others and living in peace and love.

Menno contemplated the next steps in his faith. He had not experienced an adult believers baptism for himself, and he now wanted this covenant experience. But it would make him a marked man, and once he took that step, there would be no turning back. But he was convinced from the Scriptures that regeneration did not come from baptism; rather regeneration preceded baptism, and this regeneration he had experienced. The ceremony of baptism would actually be the testimony to his new life in Christ.

Menno had resigned his priestly office, given up salary, status, and the security the position offered. To Dirk and the elders, he declared, "Without restraint I renounced all of my worldly reputation, name and fame, my unchristian ambitions, my masses, my infant baptism, my easy life, and I willingly submitted to distress and poverty under the heavy cross of Christ."

A short time later he asked for believers baptism and membership in the group. In a simple service Menno shared the witness of his faith in Christ and his desire for baptism. As he stood before the congregation, Obbe asked him once again to express the vows of his commitment to Christ. Then Obbe asked him to enter into covenant with the church as a visible fellowship of believers. Menno responded with a clear affirmation that he was doing this willingly and in the freedom of Christ.

Upon his affirmations, Menno knelt before the men. Obbe took a pitcher of water and poured it on his bowed head, repeating the age-old formula: "I baptize you with water in the name of the Father and of the Son and of the Holy Spirit." Obbe reached down and took Menno's hand. "Arise," he said, "and like as Christ was raised up from the dead by the glory of the Father, even so you also shall walk in newness of life."

Menno rose to his feet, the thrill of these words bringing

warmth to his heart. "Like as Christ was raised, so too he would walk in newness of life." Yes, this he had found as a transformation of his inner being and now, in this baptism, he had publicly embarked on this new life as a disciple of Christ. Most important, he felt the inner witness of the Spirit in confirmation of his covenant, a baptism not by water in an external way but as an inner reality given him by his Lord. Menno was exhilarated with joy and deeply at peace in his soul.

The people gathered around and offered words of encouragement, most of them giving him their promise of prayer for his walk with the Master. His baptism marked him as one of them, one who would share the dangers of discipleship with his fellow Anabaptists. Having made this break with the Roman Church, Menno now began to think about his future in a different light.

⁓

A few days later he made a very secret trip back to Witmarsum to check in on his mother. He wanted to see how she was getting along but also to share with her what was happening in his own life.

She greeted the news warmly but with some restraint. "What a major step, Menno. Are you sure this is the right thing?"

"I've never been more sure of anything, Mother. I am at peace. I am confident that this is the will of God for me." He paused. "It will not be easy, even dangerous, but I am his disciple."

Her eyes filled with tears, and she reached out to take his hand and squeeze it. For one who was not inclined to overt expressions of her feelings, this was very meaningful to Menno.

He soon returned to Leeuwarden, where he now celebrated his new family of faith. After several weeks there, he relocated to a rural community to the east. He felt that he needed to find such a place where he could live for the next period of his life. His new home was nearer to the city of Groningen in northeast Holland. There he could read, study, and carefully think through the implications of his steps of faith. He was able to remain hidden and to live without threat, but he could also meet and converse with his friends Obbe and Dirk.

∽

It was after some weeks in the Groningen community that Menno's mind turned to Gertrude. Altjie had told him that Gertrude now lived in the Groningen region. He had clear memories of her, and he was sure they needed to meet again. But he felt that he needed more time to find direction in his life before any conversation with her.

In his study of Scripture, one of the issues Menno wrestled with was interpreting the incarnation. He talked with Dirk about this at some length.

"It is my understanding" Menno said, "that Melchior Hoffman held that Jesus, as God's Son, received his full nature from God."

"That is Melchior's interpretation," Dirk replied. "He has taught what he calls 'celestial flesh' and uses this concept as his way of interpreting the phrase 'born of the virgin Mary.' Hoffman held that Jesus received his nature only from his Father and not from Mary. But this is not designated in the creeds, and we need to be careful that we don't wrest the Scripture to some theory that appeals to our minds."

"If Hoffman was right, this would mean that Jesus received essentially nothing from Mary, would it not?" Menno asked.

"If you accept Hoffman's interpretation, yes, that would be true. However, Paul speaks of Jesus as having been 'in very nature man' in Philippians 2. In other passages, Paul speaks of Jesus as the last Adam, one who is true humanity. As the creed expresses it, he was very God of very God and very man of very man."

Menno left the discussion still wrestling with the deep aspects of the issue. The incarnation was a mystery, true, but how was one to interpret the incarnation as true humanity, a humanity expressed in the sinless nature of Christ? Believing from Scripture that the Holy Spirit conceived Jesus as the Son of God, he readily attributed the full nature of Jesus to this divine identity. But as he contemplated the mystery of the physical conception and birth of Jesus by the virgin Mary, Menno was troubled by the question of how the divine nature of Christ could be incarnate through sinful flesh. He regarded Jesus as a new creation of human flesh in Mary, yes, but Christ being formed in Mary still had the nature of his Father and did not fully take on Mary's flesh. Menno's understanding of the biological factors of procreation were focused primarily on the simple biblical references that a man begat a son. This biblical statement led him to regard a child as receiving its nature from its father.

Menno was sure from the Scriptures that Jesus was the Son of God, and therefore it followed that Jesus' human nature came from his Father. But he was not settled in this. He knew that this issue needed further resolution to make clear to him how the Christ "became in very nature man." He was deeply gripped by Paul's statement in Philippians 2. There was mystery here, just as Paul had written to Timothy.

He fasted and prayed over the incarnation, asking God to reveal the mystery of the conception of his blessed Son. After some weeks of reflection and prayer, Menno felt that he had now come to a satisfactory conclusion: In the incarnation, Christ was given human flesh in Mary as the last Adam, but Menno did not see this as being born of Mary's flesh. He would need to study it further for his own satisfaction, rather than for teaching others.

~

Menno thought of Gertrude more frequently. He soon learned that she was no longer with the Beguines but had become a member of another Anabaptist fellowship that was meeting in a Groningen neighborhood. She also lived not many kilometers from his new residence. In his mind, this was the providence of God. His heart beat faster as he thought of her, a sensation he hadn't experienced since he was a young man. It made him somewhat self-conscious, yet he was eager to meet her again.

After finding out where Gertrude lived, Menno called at her home. The family was surprised by his visit but welcomed him. Gertrude responded warmly to him as an old friend yet somewhat shyly. It was wonderful to see her, and Menno knew the emotion was mutually shared, for her eyes sparkled as they talked.

Menno's resignation from the priesthood meant that he could pursue friendship with Gertrude. To his amazement, his mind even considered the prospect of a future with her. She too had renounced her vows, so there was no barrier to their relationship. A meaningful friendship would develop, renewed readily by the memories of their childhood in Witmarsum. After an enjoyable visit, Menno excused himself, agreeing that they should meet again in a few days.

During their second meeting, Gertrude's faced flushed as she admitted to Menno that she had kept informed about him. Marty had told her that he had left his parish at Witmarsum. It was now a rather simple matter for them to renew their acquaintance.

Menno found himself making excuses to call at her home. Usually Gertrude's sister Griet was with them as something of a family presence during their times of sharing. The conversation among the three of them was meaningful, as Griet had also developed a deep interest in the believers church with which Gertrude was now associated.

Menno was hesitant to become very intimate in his conversation. Courtship was a totally new experience for him, so he was somewhat reserved. But as he became more relaxed during their times together, his emotions became more evident. He hoped that Gertrude felt the same way he did, and he thought that she couldn't help but see his special interest in her.

Gertrude sensed Menno struggling with the newness of this relationship and his new freedom to love. For her, it was not as difficult; she admitted to herself that she had never forgotten him through the years of their religious life. It soon became apparent to Griet that Gertrude and Menno had a growing affection, and she would take her leave from the room where they were meeting.

Menno began to open his heart more intimately. "Gertrude, you are more than an acquaintance; you are a special grace in my life. I really can't tell you all that it means to me to come here and spend time with you. It's an inner refreshing of my spirit. You are very, very important to me."

She looked at him with a smile and said simply, "I know, Menno. And you are a wonderful friend to me. I'm so thankful that we have renewed our acquaintance and that we find so many common interests."

"I need some time to find my way in this new freedom," Menno said. "Perhaps our friendship can become something more. But for the next steps I must be sure of my future and how it might include you."

"You are speaking of marriage," she said. "I don't think we're ready to think of that."

But Menno was talking about continuing to live in the region so that they could pursue their friendship with more time together. The lodging that he had acquired in the countryside near Groningen, while a good place for study and writing, was isolated from family and friends. With his family scattered in Witmarsum, Pingjum, and Leeuwarden, and not having the association of the parish church, he felt very much alone. Reflecting on this he became increasingly caught up in the prospect of a loving companion. He could not think of living alone for much longer.

As a priest, Menno had not been totally alone socially; he spent time with his associates. In his earlier years, he had shared with his fellows in the revelry of their drinking together and card playing. But now he was a new man, a disciple of Christ, and such empty practices had no appeal. He needed someone with whom he could share his walk of faith, one who would provide him with support and with the love that would make his life more complete. As the weeks passed, Menno became increasingly certain that Gertrude was that person.

Menno also had a new freedom to relate to others through his faith in Christ, and he enjoyed the satisfaction of this fellowship. He had begun to interpret his growing understanding of discipleship to Christ as having a unique social dimension. This social emphasis also made place for partnership, not holding an individualistic faith but working out its implications with others. He began to share this feeling with Gertrude as honestly and openly as he could.

They were mature adults, and their times together became a testing of both their mutual understanding and their love. Almost without conscious effort they found themselves beginning to think and talk of a future together. They talked of the satisfactions it would bring but also of the dangers that would confront them as they contemplated the implications of marriage.

Menno began meeting in various small groups of disciples, and sometimes Gertrude was there. After one of their meetings, as Menno walked Gertrude home, she told him simply, "I have come to the same faith, Menno, and I'm sure it is the work of the Spirit in me."

On Menno's next visit to Gertrude, he learned that Griet planned to marry Rein Edes, and the couple would live at Pingjum, only a few kilometers from their old home in Witmarsum. After Griet's announcement, Gertrude and Menno sat together and shared the different aspects of their faith walk. Menno reviewed the effect of his faith on his life calling, and Gertrude discussed her decision to leave the Beguinage.

As Menno spoke more of his thoughts for the future, Gertrude suddenly asked shyly, "Is it a partner that you need?"

"Yes, I need a partner, Gertrude, and I came today to ask you to share my life. I don't know all that it means to love and to be loved, but I can learn. I'm sure that what I feel for you is more than just simple friendship." He took a big breath and than said, "I am in love with you."

Her heart filled with joy, and she responded to his affirmation of love. "Menno, I was sure of that, and I love you. We will learn to love more deeply, for we both know God's love, and ours will be wonderful! I've been expecting this moment."

They embraced each other for the first time, and it was the opening of a new experience of intimacy. They looked into each other's eyes with the warmth and excitement of love. Their long kiss sealed a bond that they knew would never be broken.

"Wherever life takes us, it will be together," Gertrude said. After a brief pause she added, "And whatever the call is that comes to you in this new movement of the believers church, it will be of God, and we'll share it."

They began to plan for their wedding. It could not happen at the church in Witmarsum. That was out, for Menno was *persona non grata*. But with many friends at Leeuwarden, Menno was certain that he could arrange to be married by Obbe or Dirk in the new fellowship. And Obbe knew Gertrude; he had baptized her in a service in Groningen. It seemed best to both of them that they should be married in the larger congregation at Leeuwarden, especially because they did not want to call attention to their marriage and bring criticism to her parents. It was not possible for them to be registered and married by the officials of the state church because they were Anabaptists, so they would be married with Leeuwarden congregation as witnesses of their covenant. Gertrude would prepare her belongings and wait for Menno to come for her. Then, with the blessing of her parents, they would travel together to Leeuwarden and be married there.

Menno embraced Gertrude, and they held each other for a long time. Then with a tender and lengthy kiss, he took his leave.

Menno's step was much lighter as he made his way back to his quarters, softly singing as he walked along the path. There was a warm glow in his chest, and he knew that his heart was singing as well as his voice. Now he must get back to his lodging and prepare for the trip to Leeuwarden to make the wedding arrangements. He wanted to be on his way by early morning.

When Menno arrived in Leeuwarden, an enthusiastic group of friends greeted him. As he shared plans for the marriage, they were impressed that he had met someone of similar faith with whom he had been acquainted years before. All promised to do everything they could to make the wedding a wonderful— although quiet—celebration.

Within a week, Menno made the trip back to Groningen to get Gertrude. Her family had given their blessing to the marriage, even though her parents had deep hesitancy over being present. Menno and Gertrude both understood this and excused them from attending the wedding, and the two were soon on the way to Leeuwarden. They made the trek west from Groningen with light steps, enjoying the trip together and often walking off the main roads in the difficult areas along the polders. They crossed the fields on paths that Menno had been using and knew quite well. Occasionally they were fortunate in securing a ride from a farmer part of the way in his wagon. It was the beginning of a new chapter in their lives.

Upon their arrival at Leeuwarden, they went to the home of the Jantz family, friends of Menno's. Obbe and his wife were already there. Obbe's wife made arrangements for Gertrude to stay with her while plans for the wedding were completed. Two evenings later, the group met in response to word passed from one to another that there was to be a wedding of the former priest and a former member of the Beguinage.

The wedding was a simple but beautiful service. Menno and Gertrude stepped into the center of the little group and stood before Obbe. He gave a brief message about marriage and the sanctity of this covenant. He explained to them and to the gathered group that their believers church movement, being separate from the state and unrecognized by it, meant that the congregation was the only witness to this marriage.

He then led Menno and Gertrude in the exchange of their vows before the congregation and before the Lord. Menno was struck by the words in his vow, "With my body I thee worship," an expression that they were joined as one flesh. Upon their affirmations of commitment, Obbe pronounced them husband and wife in the grace of God, stating that he did so by the authority of the Word of God and with the witness of the gathered group.

After the wedding, Menno and Gertrude took the late summer of 1536 as their special time together. Sharing their love, they found great joy in each other. They also found opportunity to get better acquainted with the circle of friends gathered by the ministry of Obbe and Dirk Philips. Menno was strongly affirmed by the community in his abilities to interpret and to teach Scripture.

~

By the end of a month Menno and Gertrude were living in the region of Groningen, near her family. Now Menno could share regularly with Obbe and Dirk in a ministry of teaching and preaching. The group had great respect for his experience as a priest and sought to include him in various services and ministries.

Menno and Gertrude visited with numerous people in the community of faith and were impressed with the quality of those who had joined the believers church. For the most part they were strong people with dedication and good spirit. They had come to the believers church because, like many others about them, they were seeking a new sense of intimacy with God. They wanted something beyond the rites of religion, beyond trusting sacramental participation to mediate with God for them.

Menno was able to speak very personally on this matter. He could share the struggles, questions, and doubts that had haunted him when he served the sacraments. He described how he doubted that the bread and wine he consecrated at mass actually became Christ's body and blood. He now taught that they should be regarded only as symbols that communicate the rich meaning of participation in grace through faith. They do not in themselves mediate grace to people who may often lack the immediacy of faith. It was one thing, he held, to say that the sacraments communicated grace but quite another to claim that the sacraments in and of themselves mediated grace.

Menno spoke frequently of life in fellowship with the risen Christ, which he interpreted as participating in the power of the resurrection for victorious living. Gertrude urged him to put some of his thoughts in writing. He often remembered from his own baptism those special words Obbe had quoted from the sixth chapter of Romans: "Like as Christ was raised from the dead by the glory of the Father, even so also shall we walk in newness of life." With this in mind, and with Gertrude's encouragement, he wrote a meditation called "The Spiritual Resurrection."

He opened the little pamphlet with his favorite text from 1 Corinthians 3:11: "For other foundation can no man lay than that is laid, which is Jesus Christ."

> Awake you who sleep, and arise from the dead, and Christ shall give thee light. The Scriptures teach two resurrections, namely, a bodily resurrection from the dead at the last day, and a spiritual resurrection from sin and death to a new life and a change of heart.
>
> That a man should mortify and bury the body of sin and rise again to a life of righteousness in God is plainly taught in all of the scriptures. Paul admonishes saying, "Put off concerning the former conversation the old man which is corrupt according to the deceitful lusts, and be renewed in the spirit of your mind, that ye put on the new man, which after God is created in righteousness and true holiness. Put off the old man with his deeds, and put on the new man which is renewed in knowledge after the image of him that created him. Mortify your members that are on the earth."

This was his first writing that shared his understanding of Christian experience. He wrote at length on this spiritual reality, seeking to make this new dynamic understood.

> Behold, so we must die with Christ unto sin, if we would be made alive with Him, for none can rejoice with Christ unless he first suffers with him. "For this is a sure word," says Paul, "If we be dead with him, we shall also live with him; if we suffer, we shall also reign with him."
>
> This resurrection includes the new creature, the spiritual birth and sanctification, without which no one shall see the Lord. This Paul testifies in his words saying, "In Christ Jesus neither circumcision avails anything, nor uncircumcision, but a new creature." Again, "If any man be in Christ, he is a new creature; old things are passed away; behold, all things are become new."
>
> A spiritual resurrection introduces us to the freedom and the character of the new creation, for we are persons born of the Spirit. We now share the privilege of being filled with the Spirit and walking in the Spirit.

Menno worked carefully at expressing his thoughts; he had not done any serious writing since his lengthy article addressing Jan of Leiden. He completed the pamphlet, and soon it was being passed from hand to hand.

Many readers appreciated Menno's insights. One reader who responded to the "Resurrection Living" pamphlet was a young man who had recently joined the local group, Nikolaas van Blesdijk, from the province of Overijssel. He was quite well educated and had been deeply influenced by Hoffman. He was now attracted to the believers church movement, which held a position totally opposed to the Münsterites, whose emphasis he also rejected.

Nikolaas was deeply impressed by Menno's focus on spiritual resurrection and a faith relationship with the risen Christ. He liked

Menno's insights and his emphasis on life in the Spirit, which fit with his own convictions on a piety that meant personal relationship with the Spirit of Christ. He was soon able to help Menno negotiate the publication and distribution of the pamphlet.

Menno and Nikolaas spent a considerable amount of time together discussing Scripture. "I think that Nikolaas is a gift from God," Menno remarked to Obbe. "He will become a strong leader for us in the fellowship."

Obbe responded enthusiastically. "I feel the same way about him. In fact, Dirk and I have talked, and we want to see him included in our fellowship. We need to encourage him in his growing understanding of Scripture. He may be of service in the future in a call to ministry."

Menno responded emphatically, "We need every voice that we can find who will speak clearly from the Scriptures for the enrichment of our fellowship. Furthermore, we need people who will speak out against the heresies of the Münsterites so that our own break from the Roman Church is not confused with their actions and beliefs. We need to seek the Spirit's help to unite our people as faithful disciples of Christ."

Obbe chuckled. "It is good to hear you say 'our fellowship' and to see how deeply you have identified with us."

"I feel that I belong, that I have come home. This is the work of the Spirit of God, something I've longed to find. It is not a perfect group, but one honest in a faith that reaches beyond forms of religion to relationship with the living Christ."

Obbe nodded in assent. "This is the heart of our faith, the centrality of Jesus Christ and his rule in our lives. How I regret all that I went through before understanding his calling and before coming to know the transforming power of his grace."

"You are not alone in that. We all have regrets for attempts to secure our own relationship with God. It is not by rituals of religion but rather by simply opening ourselves to the Spirit of God by faith."

The two men sat in silence for a few moments, deep in their own thoughts. Then Menno said, "Obbe, let's pray together and place this before the Lord."

They knelt by their chairs and Menno began to pray, thanking God for his grace and asking him to give them a fresh anointing of the Holy Spirit that they might walk in humility, in confidence in his grace, and in the joy of his love, sharing his mission. After Menno closed his somewhat lengthy prayer, Obbe led in a similar one. As he closed they stood up and wiped tears from their eyes.

10
Menno's Second Ordination

1536–1538

Scarcely a year had passed since Menno's baptism when he answered a knock on the door to be greeted by eight leaders of a nearby fellowship. Most of them had traveled from Leeuwarden to Groningen. They had tracked down Obbe and Dirk and came with the pair to Menno and Gertrude's tiny cottage, where the group now crowded in.

Gertrude listened carefully to the conversation. She prepared tea and, opening her cookie jar, graciously served the men as they talked with Menno, who was surprised by the visit and sensed a major concern among them. Finally, a spokesman for the group confronted him with their intent: they had come with a commission from the larger "Obbenite community" of faith, which prompted Obbe to raise his hand.

"No, I wish we wouldn't use that designation," he implored. "We as a fellowship are disciples of Christ, and I wish that we would stay with the name of Christ."

"That is fine," the spokesman responded, "but people use that designation. When there are so many in dissent from the church of Rome, it is important that we identify which group we are with."

Obbe nodded, and the conversation went on. Their intent in coming was to extend a call for Menno to accept ordination as an elder in the movement, which they said was the wish of the congregation they represented, a wish expressed at their recent gathering.

"We are here to present this to you as a calling from the Lord, and we believe that it is from him as head of the church."

After a period of further discussion, Obbe spoke for the group. "Menno, you have been ordained a priest and have had a remarkable experience in church leadership. Now that you have received believers baptism, you've become a brother and a colleague with us. We feel that since you have heard the call to openly join this Anabaptist movement, it is our responsibility before the Lord to call you to a leadership role among us."

Menno listened intently but remained silent as he pondered this affirmation. He looked over at Gertrude. Her head was bowed, he was sure, in prayer. Menno was impressed that they were inviting him to a leadership role in the fellowship. The group believed he was God's chosen instrument for leadership in the development of a believers church.

Obbe and Dirk both knew something of Menno's evangelical faith and preaching at the Catholic Church at Witmarsum. Further, as Dirk commented, Menno's emphasis on a biblical faith and the way of peace—an outspoken difference from the Münsterites—was especially significant to each of them. The men had discussed this together and had prayerfully reflected on it. They were sure Menno was needed to help clarify the new aspects of faith being discussed by the emerging believers church.

Obbe picked up the conversation again. "We are in agreement that you should accept ordination by the elders as a call of God. We are asking you to become an elder in the movement you have joined. We will not press you, but we would like you and Gertrude to give this careful thought and prayer."

The group stood in a circle around the couple, the men smiling, knowing they had fulfilled their mission. At Obbe's request, one of the brothers led the group in a simple prayer for the Lord's confirmation of the next steps in his calling. Each man shook hands with Menno and Gertrude and said they would pray as they awaited a decision. He could only promise to seek in prayer to know God's will.

Shaken by the visit, Menno stood in the door and watched the men make their way down the lane. When they came to the main road they separated, one group heading for Groningen and the other toward a neighboring village to the west.

"They were of one heart and soul with me in their belief and life (as much a person can judge) blameless," Menno wrote in his journal, "separated from the world according to the witness of the Scriptures, subjected to the cross, who had turned away not only from the Münsterites, but also from all the world's sects, curses and abominations."

Menno had come to know and trust some of the men who had called him, especially the Philips brothers, Obbe and Dirk. They hailed from the region of Leeuwarden, and both had been illegitimate sons of a Dutch priest. This was a story that was not uncommon in the religious orders, as Menno well knew. They had been introduced to believers baptism from two members of the Melchiorite movement who previously had some connection to the Münsterites. But upon their baptism and further study of Scripture, both rejected any identification with the Münsterite group. In fact, they carried deep regret that it was followers from this group who had called them to their personal faith.

Once they had heard Menno's sharp attack of the events in Münster, they wanted to make their own very similar position clear to him. One special distinction was that each of the Philips brothers took seriously Jesus' teaching to live by love and reject violence. But it was evident from the conversation in Menno's cottage that they sorely needed his help, and their associates had come to stand with them in encouraging him.

Menno and Gertrude spent considerable time talking about the implications of him becoming an elder. Then with deep sincerity, Menno and Gertrude fell to their knees. Together they prayed for direction and the Spirit's confirmation of his leading. As they rose, they quietly pursued their own thoughts. Menno wondered whether he was ready to accept the role of shepherd and overseer of the brotherhood.

Eventually it became clear to Menno that he could not avoid the leadership role. He had previously decided to declare himself a member of the free church movement by being baptized. This was his "training," a gift from God. He was one with the believers in their commitment to discipleship of Christ, to a life of peace and self-sacrificing love, and to rejection of the sword.

Yet as he wrestled with the call to be an elder, he looked to Gertrude for confirmation. While they were still newlyweds, he and Gertrude were both mature and could speak freely and realistically to each other about what such a leadership role could cost them.

After several days of reflection, Gertrude shared her thoughts. "Menno, with your gifts and perspective, I think you have little choice but to give yourself in a service of leadership to our church."

"That is not an easy decision," Menno replied, "because it involves you as well, and both of us will be under the watchful eyes of those who oppose this movement."

"I'm well aware of that, but that is a price we must pay in our discipleship. Perhaps this is part of what Jesus meant when he said we must take up our cross and follow him."

Menno became aware that he was really seeking her support for a direction that had, in fact, become quite clear to him. But he knew that each step he took from here on would shape their future together. Menno took her hand, bowed his head, and began to pray:

> Lord Jesus, I am blind, do thou enlighten me,
> naked I am, do thou cloth me;

wounded, do thou heal me;
dead, do thou quicken me.
I know of no light, no physician,
no life, except thee. Amen.

A few days later, Gertrude told Menno that she was at peace over this question. "I also recognize a new freedom in your life," she added. "It seems to be something very personal and inward for you, evident in your spirit but also socially in the freedom with which you meet others."

Menno smiled and put his arms around her in a close embrace. "You are a special gift of God, and I love you."

Menno also came to peace with the decision. As he told others about it, he spoke of the Spirit's presence to guide and create a new life in Christ. His emphasized the cross—but also the resurrection of Christ and the freedom Christ grants disciples to walk with him in life.

~

It was 1537, and Menno was entering a new chapter of his life. He was now deeply involved with this free church of disciples, and he had an enlarging circle of friends with whom he shared in faith.

Menno sent an answer to Dirk and Obbe, saying he would become an elder. About two weeks later, his ordination was set. The Philips brothers, other elders, and the congregation assembled in the barn of a farmer who belonged to the group. Other leaders from elsewhere in the free church also came for the ordination.

The little meeting space in the barn was packed. The people gathered in a spirit of great joy, and Menno sensed a high level of support for his calling. Several men kept watch, in case the meeting was interrupted. Obbe and Dirk led the congregation in worship. First they sang softly, so as not to be heard at any distance. Then Obbe led a meditation from Scripture. He explained more fully the occasion for the meeting, then presented Menno and

Gertrude, asking the congregation for affirmation of the call and a commitment to prayerful support.

Dirk then brought a short message from chapter 3 of Paul's first letter to Timothy, which describes the qualifications of deacons and bishops. After a prayer by another elder, Obbe invited Menno and Gertrude to stand before the congregation.

Turning to Menno, he asked him, "Do you accept this call willingly as a part of your commitment to Jesus as Lord and Master?"

Menno responded simply, "I do."

"Are you committed to preach the Word, to lift up Jesus as the one Lord of the church, to give yourself in the work of shepherding the flock and to do the work of an evangelist?"

"I will endeavor to do so."

Turning to Gertrude, Obbe asked her, "Will you accept this calling for your husband to serve as a bishop in the church of believers, and will you support him with your love, your prayer, and your partnership?"

She answered resolutely, "I will, by the grace of God."

Obbe continued. "This commitment is made with the awareness that you are a part of a community of believers and that we serve one another, holding each other accountable to be consistent in the discipleship we profess. We expect you, Menno and Gertrude, to share in this work together as examples to others of the sanctity of marriage and partnership in service."

He asked Menno to kneel, and the elders gathered around him and put their hands on his head. In the solemn hush, Obbe referred to Acts 13:2: "Just as the Holy Ghost said to the early church, separate me Barnabas and Saul to the work to which I have called them, so today the Holy Spirit is saying, separate to me Menno Simons for the work to which I have called him."

With the laying on of hands, they ordained him to be a bishop, or elder, in the church. Dirk announced the commission "to preach the word, to administer the signs of covenant, to hold the fellowship accountable in faithfulness to Christ, and to do the work of evangelism." As Menno heard these words, he responded with a strong amen.

The commission had special meaning for him. He had been ordained as a priest at Utrecht to serve at Pingjum; this was his second ordination, now to serve in the development of a free church and as a minister of the gospel of Christ in the freedom of the young Anabaptist church. Menno pondered the difference, the former with all its pomp, regalia, and sacramental symbolism, and this one with the simple calling by brothers in Christ and the voice of the local congregation. Without pomp or regalia, in a simple service, the elders spoke for the congregation and commissioned Menno to serve as a pastor, for sure, but also to be a pastor of other pastors, a shepherd of the flock.

Obbe stressed to Menno that in serving as a bishop he was to preach the Word, shepherd the congregations he served, proclaim the gospel of new life in Christ, and be an extension of God's grace for all to whom he ministered. Then Obbe led a prayer emphasizing commitment and inviting God's blessing. Dirk and several other elders also prayed for him.

As Menno arose from his knees, the elders embraced him and wished him God's grace and wisdom. The congregation began singing softly a hymn of gratitude for God's grace and love. Dirk then pronounced a benediction, quoting from the book of Jude: "Now unto him that is able to keep you from falling, and to present you faultless before the presence of his glory with exceeding joy, to the only wise God our Savior, be glory and majesty, dominion and power, both now and ever. Amen."

The service ended, and Menno took Gertrude's hand as they faced the congregation. Many greeted the couple and assured them of their support. For safety, the congregation dispersed slowly, several people leaving at a time to make their way down the road or across a dike.

～

Life now had a new excitement for Menno. He and "Gert," as he called her, were a team. They were partners in love but also in the new ventures of faith and leadership in the free church. But Menno was well aware that this meant for both a new life of caution, as they would now be constantly under threat of arrest.

Menno later thought back over the significance of this calling for their future and wrote in his journal:

> When I heard this call my heart was greatly troubled. Apprehension and fear was on every side. For on the one hand, I saw my limited talents, my great lack of knowledge, the weakness of my nature, the timidity of my flesh, the very great wickedness, wantonness, perversity and tyranny of the world, the mighty great sects, the persecuting state churches, the subtlety of many men and the indescribably heavy cross which, if I began to preach, would be the more felt; and on the other hand, I recognized the pitifully great hunger, want and need of the God-fearing, pious souls, for I saw plainly that they erred as innocent sheep which have no shepherd.
>
> When the persons before mentioned did not desist from their entreaties, and my own conscience made me uneasy in view of the great hunger and need already spoken of, I consecrated myself to His gracious leading, and I began in due time, after having been ordained to the ministry of the Word, according to His holy Word to teach and to baptize, to labor with my limited talents in the harvest field of the Lord, to assist in building up His holy city and temple and to repair the dilapidated walls.

Menno undertook his work with diligence. He admitted to Gertrude some sense of fear, partly because reports of various executions continued. One told of the beheading of Adriaen Cornelisse at Zierikzee, on June 2, 1537, for buying and reading a book on the holy sacrament by the reformer Johannes Pomeranus.

Menno knew the book and in fact had raised the very same questions that were in it. He now faced the same danger as Adriaen.

Menno's labors in the church immediately plunged him into travel, preaching, and writing. His first field of work was nearby, in the Groningen area, where he ministered to various groups gathered for worship. In the summer months he worked westward into West Friesland, around Leeuwarden. He enjoyed this region, with all its beauty. These Waterlanders had made remarkable achievements in developing polders for farming, and they excelled in their dairy products, especially in producing cheese.

Gertrude was able to travel with Menno in these areas, and they enjoyed the hospitality of the Anabaptist fellowships they visited. She often helped the women in their work with cheese production. Menno had little time to share in this way, though he did when time allowed, for it reminded him of his earlier years. He was remarkably successful as an evangelist, and his reputation brought many people to the gatherings and to faith in Christ.

⌒

In 1537, a new governor was appointed in Groningen—Schenck van Toutenburg, who had served as governor of Friesland. He took a strong position against the rebaptizers. Obbe was arrested and imprisoned, and Dirk and Menno fled with others into East Friesland. Here the two were able to serve with more freedom, often doing so together, moving from city to city in the proclamation of the gospel. They especially united in prayer for Obbe to be released soon.

"This is some of what it means to bear the heavy cross of our Lord," Menno said to Dirk.

To avoid arrest, they often traveled in the early morning, just as dawn lifted the darkness, finding their way across the fields before others were out and about. Gertrude frequently went with Menno, and more than once, in the semi-darkness, one or both of them slipped from a dike and landed in the water or mud. But they wanted to travel when officials were not yet to be found on the roadways.

They blended in well with other workmen, although Menno did not wear the traditional short sword on his left side that almost every man had for protection. He did have a short sheath with a good knife, but it was not for protection or use against any person. Rather, it was needed to meet their domestic needs. He often used the knife to cut up vegetables given to them by farmers as they traveled through rural communities.

Menno and Gertrude shared special intimacy in their work. With the insights the Spirit gave him into the sixth and eighth chapters of Romans, Menno developed sermons that interpreted dying with Christ and being resurrected with him into a new life. He drew from the little pamphlet he had written, "The Spiritual Resurrection." His sermons frequently used the quotation on the title page, "For other foundation can no man lay than that is laid, which is Jesus Christ."

~

In late fall of 1537, Menno found lodging for Gertrude with some friends. He said goodbye with a warm embrace, then traveled west alone. He slipped secretly back to Witmarsum to visit his mother and to call on a few special friends. Opposition to the free church movement was quite intense by then, and he faced arrest if found by the authorities.

Menno spent an afternoon and evening with his mother. For her safety he did not stay the night but stayed with a free church brother who had also come to share the Anabaptist faith. After he left, the *stadtholder* of Friesland learned of Menno's visit and arrested his host. This saddened him, but made him all the more careful lest his presence in the service of Christ should endanger others.

He thought of Pingjum and wanted to visit there when it was feasible, but he knew that the priests at the church held him under judgment. He thought of Theo, whose move to Pingjum some years before had led to his marriage to Annakin, daughter of the farmer for whom he worked. Menno remembered that her pregnancy had prevented Annakin from attending their father's funeral.

Theo and Annakin continued to live at Pingjum, and Menno learned from his host at Witmarsum that they had attended meetings of the Anabaptist fellowship there. It was especially good news to Menno that they had become believers and were baptized. They now shared the same faith—and the same dangers—that Menno and Gertrude knew.

Menno made his way back to the east, avoiding Groningen and staying off the main roads. Earlier, in June of 1536, Groningen had become a part of the Hapsburg Netherlands. Maria of Hungary, sister to Emperor Charles V and governor of Brussels, had been given the government of Groningen. The former governor, Karl von Gelre, had "departed with silent drum," a formality paying respect to his office but not to his person. Now the word was that the new governor, Regent Maria, sister of Charles V, would follow the wishes of the emperor and would not tolerate the spread of the rebaptizer group.

It was widely known that Menno, the prominent preacher of Witmarsum, had defected from the Catholic Church and was now a leader in the Anabaptist circles. He was a wanted man, and the authorities made it known. They ordered anyone who knew his whereabouts to report to them, and they offered a tidy award for such information.

With this awareness, Menno and Gertrude secretly traveled further east, to the village of Oldersum, on the Ems River, south of Emden by the sea. Earlier, Ulrich von Dornum had been tolerant and actually welcomed Anabaptist refugees to his estate. Various Anabaptists had reported to Menno of their good relationship with him. But he had died on March 12, 1536, and a nobleman named Hero was now lord of Oldersum. But Hero was reportedly continuing the practices of his predecessor. So Menno and Gertrude, along with Dirk and his wife, chose to go to Oldersum and see if Hero would accept them.

Dirk and his family decided to seek a dwelling place in Norden in East Friesland. Menno soon learned that with Dirk's remarkable success in evangelism he had extended his ministry into Emden. Because they could no longer minister in the Netherlands, it seemed an answer to prayer to find a new base in East Friesland. They hoped that Oldersum could be the center of their operation at least for the next several years. Through mutual friends, Menno was introduced to people at the Von Dornum estate. Hero was gracious to the couple and welcomed them to stay.

Menno and Gertrude helped the family with work around the castle. The family told Menno that as Ulrich's health had declined, an elder in the Anabaptist group had prayed with him and encouraged him in reaching out in faith to Christ. They were so grateful for this experience of faith. It had of course been a deep sadness to the family when Ulrich died. Menno and Gertrude offered the family their comfort and support.

Ulrich's death left the family at a disadvantage, but with Hero as administrator they were enabled by the resources of the estate to continue their lives in relative ease. Several members of the family, especially Ulrich's daughter Essa, had become ardent disciples of Christ, responding to the new understanding of faith that Menno and Gertrude shared. Hero was less supportive; he was caught between his deep interest in free-church developments and his political responsibilities.

It was good news when, a few weeks later, Menno learned that Obbe had escaped from prison in Groningen and was now with Dirk in Emden. The brothers were once again engaged in sharing the gospel, leading to a good number of converts.

During the first few weeks at Oldersum, Menno concentrated primarily on writing and publishing. He worked dili-

gently on his booklet about regeneration, "The New Creature."
Part of it read:

> The regenerate, therefore, lead a penitent and a new life,
> for they are renewed in Christ and have received a new
> heart and spirit. Once they were earthly-minded, now
> heavenly; once they were carnal, now spiritual; once they
> were unrighteous, now righteous; once they were evil, now
> good, and they live no longer after the old corrupted
> nature of the first earthly Adam, but after the new upright
> nature of the new and heavenly Adam, Christ Jesus. Their
> poor, weak life they daily renew more and more, and that
> after the image of Him who created them. Their minds are
> like the mind of Christ, they gladly walk as He walked;
> they crucify and tame their flesh with all its evil lusts.

Menno's pamphlets were being passed quickly and widely
by hand. This he found to be almost as effective in spreading
the gospel as his preaching. His writing increased his influence.
Menno himself had been blessed by written materials, and he
recalled how meaningfully the accounts of the Swiss Brethren,
including the story of Michael Sattler and the description of
the Schleitheim Synod, had stimulated his earlier thinking.

The articles from the synod, known as the Schleitheim
Confession, had been carried down the Rhine to the Low
Countries and passed to many people in the region. It was said
that the writings of both Zwingli, in *Elenchus*, and the young
reformer John Calvin criticized this confession. Zwingli claimed
that wherever one found an Anabaptist, one also found a hand-
written copy of the Schleitheim Confession.

Menno regarded this passing of written materials as a great
strength of the movement that was difficult for opponents to overcome. With this in mind he hoped to see his own pamphlets
spread across the country. It was a great risk to carry these printed
materials, and Menno admired believers who took that risk.

~

At Oldersum, Menno met a new friend, Peter Jans. At first, the thoughtful man had serious questions about Menno's beliefs. But it was evident that he had even more questions about the Catholic Church. Menno recognized that Peter was a man of deep thought who made steps of faith only after he had sufficient evidence to which he would then commit himself in full honesty. It was an especially joyous day when Menno heard Peter's confession and prayed with him. With a few other believers present, Menno baptized him in a canal running through a field just outside Oldersum.

Peter wanted to spend time with Menno and occasionally accompanied him on preaching and evangelizing missions, which left Gertrude to spend more time at Oldersum. Though she was happy that Menno was not traveling alone, she missed him dearly.

On one of their trips into Friesland, the two men stayed with Jared Reynertszoon, who was called Renick. From his farm in Kimswerd, a short distance from Leeuwarden, Menno could make short trips to meet with various groups. Renick was a sincere man with an inquiring mind. Menno and Peter enjoyed lengthy and intense discussions with him. They helped Renick place his faith in Christ and see Christ, rather than creeds and ceremonies, as the true focus of faith. It was a special joy to Peter to help Renick make this commitment to Christ.

Upon Renick's confession, Menno and Peter baptized him in a canal late in the evening. It was a simple service with his family and a few friends. Renick was well known in the Leeuwarden community, and his aggressive testimony encouraged others in a similar decision. His example became a witness to the dynamic of a new life in Christ and encouraged others to lives of diligent discipleship.

As they returned to Oldersum, Menno and Peter met up with Dirk and Obbe in the region of Emden. The brothers were on the move, so their time together was brief. But Menno found such times of reflection and prayer with the Philips brothers to be encouraging. Dirk was a very competent thinker, quite interested in doctrine and theology, and Menno enjoyed the interchange with him. Obbe was more practical and pastoral in his approach, and he offered Menno good counsel.

Though Menno was in a hurry to get to his Gert, he sensed that Obbe needed to talk with him. And indeed, Obbe opened his heart. "It really grieves me," he said, "that I ever had association with those messengers from Münster. Their movement has proven to be a real heresy. I'm especially embarrassed that those sword carriers ordained me. I am troubled that it was their call that led me into the ministry."

"But ordination is a call of God," Menno responded, "even though the instruments he has to use at times are very imperfect. You were called by the voice of a group of believers; you are a free man in Christ. You are not responsible for the developments of thought within that group. We have all come to reject them. You are called to your leadership role by this new church, by the group of believers who were present in prayer and affirmation at your ordination."

"True, Menno, and I felt the same way about the calling extended through the faith community when we ordained you some months ago. But I still feel that I am tainted by that earlier association. You will need to pray for me."

Dirk joined Menno, and they all knelt with Obbe in prayer. Each laid his hand on Obbe's head and asked God to renew in him a sense of calling to the ministry of the gospel.

When they left and were well on their way, Peter said, "Menno, I have felt a special encouragement in discovering how many brothers and sisters we have who are clear in their commitment to Christ and who reject the beliefs of the Münsterites."

"Yes," Menno said. "The teachings of Jesus are focused on reconciliation with God, and the life he calls us to is far more peaceful than the claims of those radicals. They seek to justify violence to achieve their goal of bringing their kingdom to dominance."

Following the trip into Friesland, Menno spent the next weeks with Gertrude on the estate, enjoying their time together and working in the fields. Frequently he met with small groups in the region and shared with them in the teaching of Scripture.

⌒

It was some months later when Menno felt that he must make another brief journey, this time to the south and then west. These were territories he knew well, and he was able to find hospitality with other believers.

Before leaving, he folded Gertrude in his arms in a warm embrace and whispered softly, "It will be difficult to be away from you these weeks, my darling."

She sighed and said, "But you must go—they need you—and I know that you are driven by an inner sense of direction."

"There are so many who do not know the Savior; they only have their forms of religion and the emptiness of routine practices. They do not know the truth of the gospel, nor do they know the joy of assurance of salvation."

He paused. "And even when they come to know Christ, they are in need of fellowship, of a community of believers. True faith is not an individualistic matter; it is participation with a community of disciples. This I must bring to them. And in addition there are many Flemish refugees who are believers yet need ministry in the region where I am going."

Gertrude nodded, tears in her eyes. "That is our calling, to share what it means to be members of the kingdom of Christ, a kingdom that is 'righteousness and peace and joy in the Holy Spirit.'"

Menno remembered those words each day as he made his way across the lowlands to the west. Eventually he traveled north to the region around Pingjum, having a longing to visit with Theo and Annakin. While Menno had heard this good news of their confession and baptism from others, he wanted to hear from Theo himself and to encourage him and Annakin in their walk as disciples of Christ.

When Menno arrived, Theo said, "I will get word to others, and we will have a gathering at our house this evening. You must share with them the word of faith that you preach. They are our neighbors, and we've been sharing in our limited way, and I want them to hear you."

Menno responded warmly, "I accept your hospitality, but if I could lodge elsewhere it would be better for you. Please let me find a place where my lodging will be less known to others. A night of rest will do me good, and I will be delighted to share the faith of Christ with your neighbors. I also made many friends in the neighborhood when I served them as a priest, and I want them to hear what God has called me to."

"Stay with us," Theo said. "One of my neighbors, Quirin Pieters, has become a believer. It would be wonderful if you would be the Lord's servant and baptize him."

"If his faith is clear, that would be a pleasant ministry," Menno replied.

Later that evening, a group of about fifteen met for a time of singing and prayer, and Menno preached on Peter's words from chapter two of Acts, "Repent and be baptized each one of you in the name of the Lord Jesus and you will receive the gift of the Holy Spirit." Menno emphasized that there are two baptisms, the outer baptism with water, which in itself doesn't save but is a witness of the saving covenant one enters with the Lord. The other baptism, which does save and transform a person, is with the Holy Spirit, a baptism that the living Lord gives as an inner experience of the Spirit.

After the message, Menno gave opportunity for response from the group. Quirin, Theo's neighbor, stepped over to Menno. With a smile he knelt before him and said, "I would like to be baptized as an expression of my faith in Jesus Christ."

With Quirin's voluntary request, Menno said, "I am here as the servant of Christ to minister to you." He asked Quirin to affirm his repentance from the old life and his commitment to

Jesus Christ as his saving Lord. Quirin expressed his faith clearly to Menno and the group.

"And do you commit yourself to walk with Jesus as a disciple, to receive the Holy Spirit, and to walk in the Spirit? Will you share in the community of the reborn the responsibilities of nurturing one another and in giving and receiving rebuke?" To this Quirin gave his further affirmation of commitment.

Theo brought a bowl of water. Menno cupped his hands and filled them with water. He slowly released the water to flow on the bowed head of this new brother in Christ, and said simply, "Brother Quirin, upon the confession of your faith I baptize you in the name of the Father, the Son, and the Holy Spirit."

An audible breath of joy rushed through the little group. Menno took Quirin by the hand and said, "Arise, like as Christ was raised from the dead by the glory of God, even so you also now rise to walk in newness of life."

The group was in awe, and one after another they spoke words of encouragement to Quirin. Some spoke a bit hesitantly but said they admired him in taking the step of faith. The fellowship lasted late into the night, which allowed the group to slip off to their homes undetected.

Menno had a restful night of sleep and a good breakfast with Theo and Annakin in the morning. Without saying where he was going, he was on his way back to Gertrude and their dwelling in Oldersum. Being home with Gertrude was the most satisfying thing in his life.

"My dearest," he said as he held her close, "I thought of you most every hour I was away. And I remembered your words in sending me off, especially the quotation from Romans 14, of Paul's words about the kingdom of God."

"And I was thinking of you, and praying for you most every hour. I'm so thankful that the Lord gave you a good trip and brought you back safely."

As they sat together, Menno found satisfaction in telling her news of Griet and her husband, of Theo's and Annakin's faith and of Quirin's confession and baptism in Theo's home.

~

A few days after Menno's return to Oldersum, in early February 1539, Dirk came to visit them with sad news from Leeuwarden. A few days prior, on the eighth, Renick had been arrested and executed for hosting Menno.

Menno was stunned. His friend Renick—executed! The authorities, of course, were really after Menno. Renick had died in his place. "Had I known this would happen," Menno said to Gertrude, "I would have slept in a sheepcote rather than accept his hospitality. But he was a wonderful brother and so gracious."

"Menno, you must not punish yourself. You could not anticipate this. We must rest this with God."

In mid-February, Gertrude came to Menno with something special to share. He could see by the little smile across her face that it was important and he pulled her into his lap. "What is it, my Gert? You have a secret?"

"Yes, Menno," she answered, "but it won't be secret for long." She very joyfully broke the news to him that she was expecting a child.

He was excited but at the same time very concerned. He wondered how they would manage if they needed to be on the run. "It will be wonderful to have a child, my dearest Gert," he said, "but it will not be easy. We are increasingly threatened and sought by the authorities. We may need to keep on the move. But I'll help you, and we will find places of lodging."

"I know," she said. "I thought much about that before sharing this with you. I don't want to be a burden, nor do I want our children to suffer, but this is part of our walk with God."

Menno sat down and wrote to Griet, Gertrude's sister, and told her the good news. He also shared his concern that they did not have freedom to set up a permanent home but needed to avoid detection by those who sought them. He was sure that Griet would not give them away. He sensed she was impressed by the faith he and Gertrude shared. Even so, he didn't tell of their actual location. Perhaps in the future, they could have a permanent home and could try to host Griet and her husband. As he wrote of their joy in expecting their first child, he wished Griet the same good fortune. He smiled to himself, thinking that he had to brag just a bit.

He did let them know that he and Gertrude were not in Friesland but in Germany, quite some distance from where Griet was living. This might at least assure them that the search for Menno would not be a threat to them.

11
Travels Between Groningen and Oldersum

1539–1541

Hearing of the death of Renick, Menno and Gertrude decided that they should dare another very secret trip to Leeuwarden. They both felt they needed to join their many friends and share their sorrow. Gertrude insisted that she go along, confident that she would have no problems traveling for a month, even though she was midway in her pregnancy.

Menno and Gertrude slipped out of Oldersum without informing anyone of their destination, traveling slowly because of Gertrude's pregnancy. They planned to slip quietly into the town and go immediately to their friends and be secreted with them. It was well known in Groningen and Leeuwarden that Menno was now a leader among the Anabaptists.

For their meals along the way they ate little. Gertrude had fixed food for the first day, which Menno carried in a bag. On the second day they were able to buy some turnips from a farmer and some bread from a country bakery they passed. They could smell the fresh bread long before they got to the house, and Gertrude went to the door to make the purchase. Stopping in the country some time later, they sat under a tree by a canal. Menno took out his large knife, which he carried for such purposes, and peeled and cut the turnips. He then added a slice of bread for each, and they enjoyed their luncheon together.

The travel was not easy for Gertrude. On several occasions, they were able to negotiate a ride with farmers, who very carefully arranged for them to ride on their cart. On the first ride, they climbed into the load of fresh, dried hay and covered themselves from view.

As the wagon rolled along, Gertrude asked, "Menno, can you trust this man? He might take us to the *burgomeister*."

Menno replied, "I looked into his eyes and they weren't shifty. I'm quite sure he can be trusted."

When they arrived at the barn where the farmer was to sell the hay, he took them to another man he knew and said, "This neighbor is going further in the direction you are traveling. He can give you a ride, but it won't be very comfortable, as he has unloaded his hay." This he said with a chuckle as he looked at the empty wagon.

The neighbor said simply, "Climb on. I'll give you a lift for part of your journey." As they rode along the bumpy road, it was evident what the farmer had meant. It was not very comfortable, but it was better than walking. Menno took off his coat and formed a pillow for Gertrude to sit on, relieving some of the bumps. When they arrived at the man's home, Menno expressed his gratitude and the two started walking on. The man said, "Just a minute. You are tired and it is late afternoon. You should stay for the night."

"That would be great," Menno said, "but we have already been bother enough."

The man smiled and said, "No bother. We have an extra room, and my wife will add two more bowls for the evening soup. But please don't give me your name. I'm sure I know who you are, and if I am asked later, I'd like to say that you never gave me your name."

Menno nodded. "I understand. We will accept your kindness."

After a night of rest and a good breakfast, Menno prayed for the family of new friends, and he and Gertrude were on their way. They were in familiar territory now and were able to follow paths that kept them from the main road. They arrived in the Leeuwarden region in late afternoon and made their way carefully into the town just before dark.

They had often been welcomed into the home of the Jansz family, so they went there now and knocked softly on the door. The Jansz's were members of the local Anabaptist fellowship and accepted the dangers associated with it. When the door opened, there was a cry of recognition, and they pulled the couple quickly inside. Menno and Gertrude responded with deep gratitude.

Frau Jansz was a gracious hostess, and the family offered them many kindnesses, especially in view of Gertrude's pregnancy. "You should stay here until some time after the baby is born," she said, "and let Menno do his travels from here."

"Yes, Menno," Jon Jansz said, "you can go and come carefully in your ministry in the area, but your wife should stay here until the child is born and it is strong enough to travel."

"You are most gracious," Menno said, "but this would mean several months at least. That would be too great a risk for you. Just think of what happened to our friend Renick simply for giving me hospitality."

"Ah yes, I know. But we run no greater risk than what you are running. And after Renick's execution, who would suspect that you'd be back in the area? Keep inside during the day, Menno, and we will ask the congregation to keep your presence secret. We all know that you live as a fugitive."

This was a special encouragement to Menno and Gertrude, though they would need to be doubly careful to avoid detection. They had felt that coming there was God's will. Now Gertrude needed rest after the strenuous trip.

Menno was grateful to the Jansz family but deeply concerned

for the risk his presence meant for them. He and Gertrude were sure they should not stay very long. Once they had ministered to Renick's family, they would move on from Leeuwarden. That evening Menno spoke to the gathered group, telling them that in the face of the violence confronting them, they needed God's grace for a spirit of love and forgiveness.

"We cannot be shaped by what happens to us," he said. "We are formed by the work of the Spirit within us. The children of peace do not retaliate, do not go to war, do not use violence, but live by the Spirit and teachings of our Lord. He taught us to act in freedom, to turn the other cheek as evidence that we are free to behave by our own inner convictions. This is the freedom of Christ and it is worth dying for. We must help our society and our leaders to understand the true meaning of the gospel, to respect differences of convictions and grant tolerance for those different views. It is in this freedom that we can then participate with others in a conversation about our faith. Above all, we must maintain the integrity of our life in faith."

~

By the middle of the week Menno and Gertrude bid the Janszes farewell and slipped away late one evening without saying where they might be going. Menno planned to spend some time in another home in the region, where he was quite sure they would find Dirk and his family. He wanted to discuss theology and experiences in the Lord's mission.

Menno and Gertrude made their way in the darkness, benefiting from the bright moon. After several hours they came to the house where Menno was confident Dirk would be. He was correct. The man of the house welcomed them, as did Dirk and his wife, Marika. She and Gertrude, along with their hostess, talked together. Upon learning of the expected child, Marika said with alarm, "Menno, you know, is a fugitive priest. You must be careful."

"Yes," Gertrude nodded, "That we try to be. We have been keeping on the run, not staying at the same place very long."

Menno and Gertrude felt it was important for them to leave this home soon too. They decided that the Oldersum estate was the best place to live during the final months of Gertrude's pregnancy.

Before they left, Menno and Gertrude wanted to meet again with their very special acquaintance, Elizabeth Dirks, a vivacious young convert who was a very effective Bible teacher and had accepted baptism in an Anabaptist home to the south.

Her story was unique. As a young girl living in the convent of Tienge, she had come to faith at the age of twelve by finding and reading a Bible. When a visiting priest caught her with the Scriptures, she was arrested and given a year of confinement for her daring to read the Bible for herself. The nuns at the convent negotiated to have her released into their custody, which led merely to another form of punishment.

Elizabeth worked around the convent but then came up with a plan of escape. She had developed a friendship with the neighborhood milkmaid, who delivered milk almost every day. One day they exchanged clothes and traded places, and it was Elizabeth who walked across the grounds carrying the buckets as though she were the milkmaid.

She went first to Leer and stayed with the Lambert family, and within a few weeks she was baptized in the canal near their house. Now she was staying near Leeuwarden with a widow named Hedgie. Hedgie was a woman of special interest to Menno because her husband had been ordered to play the drum at the execution of his close friend, Sicke Snyder, whose martyrdom had so gripped him. Now in meeting her, the story came together for Menno.

Hedgie's husband, Fritz, not wanting to cover for the execution in this way, drank heavily the night before to become more insensitive to what he was to witness. But the next day, in the freedom of his semi-drunkenness, he spoke boldly to the people gathered, giving witness to the integrity of Snyder and declaring emphatically that the real reason for this execution was Snyder's faith. Fritz had to flee to save his own life. He was never heard of again, and Hedgie knew nothing of his whereabouts.

Now Hedgie and Elizabeth were living together and leading Bible studies in the area. They had been working primarily in the immediate region but also worked south of Leeuwarden into Warga and east, around Groningen.

Menno and Gertrude wanted to encourage Elizabeth and Hedgie in their work. A meaningful partnership had developed among them while they were guests of the Jansz family. They were impressed with Elizabeth's winsome spirit, her keen mind, and her ability to teach the Bible. During their few days together, Elizabeth and Hedgie traveled with Menno to several small villages in the region and shared in a ministry of teaching. It was evident to Menno that the reputation of these two as effective teachers had grown in the region, and Menno gave them all the support and encouragement that he could.

As the time came for Menno and Gertrude to leave, they admonished the women to use care lest they be arrested. They assured them of their continuing friendship and support, even though they had to travel back to Oldersum. They said they would attempt to meet frequently and share ministry in the region, though all of them needed to keep on the move to avoid detection. But the positive side was that their travels enabled them to serve in many areas of the free church.

∼

Before leaving Leeuwarden, Menno met with both Obbe and Dirk to talk about leadership in the church. The brothers had brought along David Joris, whom they had introduced to Menno earlier. David had been converted to Christ as a follower of Hoffman. Since their earlier meeting, David had been ordained by Obbe in a trip to Delft, just one year earlier. He was a very effective spokesman for the gospel, and the Philips brothers wanted Menno to help them lead David to better understand the way of discipleship as emphasized by their community of peaceful Anabaptists.

Menno had thought long about his previous conversation with David. He had carried with him a few reservations about David's thinking. But meeting again they now shared in a meaningful and refreshing conversation. Early in their talk, David commented that he had reread Menno's "A Spiritual Resurrection" and found it stimulating and meaningful. With this common ground, David spoke of the inner transformation that Menno emphasized as an expression of his own spirituality.

"But," Menno said, "your mentor, Melchior Hoffman, as a spiritualist seems to not give enough place to the authority of the Scriptures and its authority as God's word written. Tell me, where do you place the ultimate authority for your message, on the Scriptures or on Melchior's position?"

"Well, it is the Scriptures, of course," David responded. "But with the inner word of the Spirit."

"The inner word of the Spirit, yes," Menno said, "but this must be tested by the outer word of Scripture."

"Indeed," David replied, "I believe that. But the outward must not be turned into a law. It is the Spirit that quickens life, as you have said in your pamphlet. I seek to share that spiritual resurrection more than anything else."

"As do I," said Menno. "This is the special work of the Spirit, and he guides us in the interpretation of the Word so that we catch its meaning and thereby know the Word of the Spirit."

They discussed at some length their understanding of Jesus' expectations for a life of discipleship within the freedom of grace to which he calls disciples. Menno was especially interested in knowing that David took a stance for peace and nonresistance, rejecting the sword as a disciple of Christ.

"As ministers of the truth of Christ," Menno said as they parted, "we need, as we have said, to follow the example of Christ and balance the inner and outer aspects of his call to discipleship. This should be expressed in the love of God, which never violates another person but treats them in the peace of Christ."

From a brief earlier meeting with Obbe and Dirk Philips, Menno learned from them more of David's background, which provided Menno with an increased affinity and respect for him. He learned that David had been a well-known glass painter in Delft and had already become known in the city as an eloquent spokesperson for the gospel. In needing to flee, and coming to this region, he was preaching primarily from a Melchiorite orientation. His convictions and spirit had impressed Obbe and Dirk, and they engaged him in extended conversation to broaden his perspectives. He had responded so favorably that his ministry among them soon led to the call of the congregation for his ordination.

Menno saw how effective David was in interpreting his new faith to the people and sought to encourage him. With the political and state-church denunciations of dissenters, persecution of the new church was on the rise. Menno recognized the increased ill treatment they were experiencing in Friesland as "the heavy burden of the cross." He spoke freely of the fellowship of believers as being a free church in society.

While David affirmed his agreement with Menno on this, Menno thought that he tended to overemphasize the inner spiritualistic aspects of faith experience and minimize what the apostle Paul called the "obedience of faith." It was Menno's conviction that David needed to balance his spiritualism with the authority of the Scriptures. When they parted, Menno had the feeling that David had heard him and had taken his counsel seriously.

Menno told his colleagues that he hoped to continue a free and candid interchange with David, for he recognized his strengths. David had helped many people come to a new and personal faith.

He was six years younger than Menno and had actually broken from the Catholic Church ten years before Menno did. During that decade he traveled freely across the country, preaching the gospel. These factors served to recommend David to Menno, despite his reservations, and he wanted to support what the Spirit might be doing through this man.

Menno bade his colleagues farewell and slipped off to the home were he and Gertrude were staying. Talking later with her, he shared some things he had learned of David's significant activity in Delft several years earlier. David had led the socialite Anneken Jans and her husband Arent to faith. He had baptized them in Delft. Anneken was of a high social class, and their conversion to the new movement was an affront to the authorities. The couple had fled to England when they were threatened with arrest.

They were there for some time, during which Arent died. Anneken had then come back to Delft to settle some financial accounts and had met with David to talk about her continuing a leadership role in the movement. But the authorities soon learned that she was in Delft, and she was arrested. After a time in prison, during which she wrote several letters, she was sentenced to death by drowning in Rotterdam.

While being prepared for execution, she pled with the crowd for someone to take her fifteen-month-old son and care for him, offering a purse from her wealth for their kindness. Even with this offer, the intense fear in the crowd hindered response, but after some time a baker stepped forward and said he would add this little lad to his six children. Anneken was very expressive in her gratitude and asked a business associate to fulfill her promise of gratuity. She was twenty-eight years old when she was executed, leaving behind the boy, who would now carry the name Elias de Lind.

"I wish we could have known her," Gertrude responded to Menno's intense account of the story. "How difficult to leave a little child behind, when facing death itself is hard enough."

Menno nodded, knowing that she was thinking of the threats

to them and what it would mean if they were arrested and had to
leave the little one she was expecting.

Sitting quietly for a moment, Gertrude said, "It would have
been a privilege to have accepted her little son into our family."

"Yes, that would have been a remarkable privilege, but not
easy for us to achieve."

They soon learned that the account of Anneken's return to
Delft was only the beginning of the story. Many other independents were traveling to the Netherlands from England, where a
decree against Anabaptists was published in 1538. Their association with the brothers and sisters in Friesland gave an increased,
yet unwanted, visibility to the Anabaptist movement. In his
preaching, Menno encouraged his people to be hospitable wherever possible. But the coming of this group of independents to
Friesland was not to be an escape. The report was that thirty-one
of them were arrested at Delft, and then the shocking news: on
January 7, 1539, sixteen men were beheaded and fifteen women
were drowned.

~

Menno and Gertrude stayed in the north far longer than
anticipated. Their work had been important and fruitful, especially the new association with Elizabeth. Menno recognized her special abilities in leadership and teaching and encouraged the congregations of the region to support her. But Menno and Gertrude
agreed with Dirk that it would be wise to return to Oldersum and
to leave as secretly as possible.

Menno and Gertrude sat together at the table that evening
and discussed their moving on. They both had a sense that it was
time to leave the area, and together they sought the Lord's direction. Menno picked up the Scriptures and read from Psalm 25:

> Unto thee, O Lord, do I lift up my soul. O my God, I
> trust in thee: let me not be ashamed, let not mine ene-

mies triumph over me. Yea, let none that wait on thee be ashamed; let them be ashamed which transgress without cause. Show me thy ways, O Lord; teach me thy paths. Lead me in thy truth, and teach me; for thou are the God of my salvation; on thee do I wait all the day. Remember, O Lord, thy tender mercies and thy loving kindnesses; for they have been ever of old. Remember not the sins of my youth, nor my transgressions: according to thy mercy remember thou me for thy goodness' sake, O Lord. Good and upright is the Lord: therefore will he teach sinners in the way. The meek will he guide in judgment: and the meek will he teach his way. All the paths of the Lord are mercy and truth unto such as keep his covenant and his testimonies. For thy name's sake, O Lord, pardon mine iniquity; for it is great. What man is he that fears the Lord: him shall he teach in the way that he shall choose. His soul shall dwell at ease; and his seed shall inherit the earth. The secret of the Lord is with them that fear him; and he will show them his covenant. Mine eyes are ever toward the Lord, for he shall pluck my feet out of the net.

As he concluded, Gertrude said a soft amen. After a brief pause she added, "Menno, you should write a sermon on that psalm and have it printed. It would encourage many to whom it can be passed, many who may not get to hear you preach but would be blessed by reading your thoughts."

"Thank you for that suggestion," Menno said. "I shall try to do that." And delaying their departure for the next two days, he worked at writing this message, which he entitled "A Meditation on the Twenty-Fifth Psalm." He asked Dirk to have it printed and distributed among the congregation and beyond. Although it was a meditation from the Old Testament, Menno again placed on the title page the words of 1 Corinthians, "For other foundation can no man lay than that is laid, which is Jesus Christ."

In the sermon he wrote of how he frequently felt like "a derelict in mid-ocean without mast, sail or rudder, driven by fierce winds and boisterous waves," expressing his frustration at the constant threat of persecution.

He gave the pamphlet to Dirk, and with the help of several others they copied and passed the message to others. The response to the meditation was so positive that Dirk assured him that he would seek diligently to get it published. Strongly encouraged to work at expressing his understanding of faith in Christ by use of the pen, Menno agreed to give more time to writing.

~

They stayed with the community of believers for several days. One evening Menno said, "Gert, since hearing of Anneken's leadership and of her execution, I have been pondering the need for more women to be commissioned as leaders in our circle. What is your thinking on this?"

She looked at him with a surprised expression. "I think that it is time for you men to recognize this. The women of our fellowship will be better served if there are some women in leadership." She paused a moment and then asked, "Are you thinking of Elizabeth Dirks?"

"Yes," Menno replied. "It seems to me that with her ability and reputation as a Bible teacher, she should have the added authorization of being commissioned by the church just as we commission elders. I think that I should bring to the elders the possibility of commissioning Elizabeth as a deacon."

When Menno was later with the elders, he raised the question. "She has proven herself as a teacher and this would give her a strong base of authority to serve," he said. In the discussion he reminded them that for some time now in their fellowship many men referred to their wives as "sister" to emphasize that they were equal in partnership.

One of the men quipped, "Men of quality are not threatened

by recognizing the gifts of women and giving them equality." Menno smiled and nodded his head. Now, with little hesitancy, the group came to agreement, and Menno asked Dirk to arrange for Elizabeth to meet with the elders before the next service. Two days later, the congregation were to gather in a local barn, so the elders met early with Elizabeth.

At first she was very hesitant, saying that this was such a new step for her. But Menno reminded her of the nuns who served widely from their convents. He asked why the free church should not have women serving in the freedom of their fellowship.

Elizabeth said simply, "I will submit myself to the voice of the congregation."

As they met with the community of believers, Menno and his colleagues shared their conviction. Upon his interpretation of Paul's words in Romans 16 about Priscilla as a deacon of distinction, and of other women serving in the church, the congregation gave a strong affirmation for the commissioning of one they called "our own Elizabeth."

Menno turned to Paul's letter to Timothy, where he set conditions for a woman to be set apart for such deacon service. And he noted Paul's words, "I want women to learn, in modesty and not usurp authority," emphasizing that the women of the movement were becoming quite learned. After a short homily, Menno, with the elders, invited Elizabeth to come to the front and to stand before the group.

Menno led the ceremony, asking Elizabeth questions about her commitment to Christ and his church, as he usually did when ordaining ministers. Upon her positive response he invited her to kneel and asked Dirk and the elders to join him in laying hands on Elizabeth's bowed head while he spoke words of commissioning to the role of deacon.

She rose, her face wet with tears, and the women of the congregation gathered around to assure her of their support. Menno watched, his own eyes wet as he witnessed this wonderful expression of love and spiritual community. He looked at Gertrude, and her eyes were shining, filled with tears of joy.

The following evening, before departing, Menno gave a final sermon then led the group in a time of free discussion. Someone asked him, "Tell us, how are we to answer those who say that we are heretical because we've left the Catholic Church with its 'apostolic succession'? As you know, the Roman Church claims that the pope is the true successor of St. Peter."

"Ah, we too believe in an apostolic succession," Menno replied, "but the succession is in the apostolic word, not in a hierarchy of persons. We have one Lord and he is the head of the body, and we are mutually together as his servants."

The conversation continued late into the evening. Menno emphasized that their commitment as Anabaptists was to be a genuine church, not a sect. "We are clearly church," he said, "for we elevate Jesus above all else as Lord of the church, and in placing him above everything else, we seek to follow him daily in life. This is to truly be his church, his body."

There was a general affirmation of respect for Menno's teaching. He enjoyed the interchange with the local groups, and he was hesitant to leave the community. In extending their stay, he and Gertrude found lodging with different families in the congregation, seeking to keep from being identified at any one location.

As their stay lengthened, Menno continued to work diligently during the day to revise and complete a major treatise he was writing, "The New Birth," a work he had begun much earlier and carried with him. Now, after a few more days of work, he finished it. Turning back to the title page, he again wrote his favorite Scripture, from 1 Corinthians.

Menno believed this was his most important work so far, and he trusted Dirk to make arrangements for printing. Dirk told him of a printer whom he was certain would undertake it.

"Now," Menno told Gertrude, "I am at peace about our leaving." With Dirk's advice about places they could stop and rest with other believers, the two made their departure. They slipped away quietly and began the long trek to Oldersum.

Gertrude's pregnancy was now in the seventh month. Menno was very sensitive to Gertrude's condition and sought a place to hide and rest during the day. They were tired but at peace as they covered the miles, quite certain they would be welcomed back by the Von Oldum family. The quarters they were given there were quite satisfactory, and to the weary travelers the prospect of being back seemed especially inviting.

The congregations where Menno had just ministered gave him substantial offerings, and he would be able to again pay rent to the Oldum family. Menno was also satisfied about having left several of his writings with Dirk to be published.

~

The first day of their trip home, Menno and Gertrude made a brief stop east of the Groningen region to visit a group of Anabaptist believers. The assembly gathered in a weaver's shop for worship and discussion in late afternoon, a time when many people took a short rest. Later in the evening they gathered in one of the member's homes with a small circle of people eager to hear Menno.

Early the next morning, before the sun rose, the two continued toward Oldersum. They walked along with people on their way to work in the fields. Menno was sure that the Anabaptist hunters would look for him in more socially significant places, in view of his reputation as a leader; they would not expect him to be found in early hours walking with working peasants.

It was almost two weeks later when Menno and Gertrude arrived at Oldersum. Both were very tired, but Gertrude was especially exhausted from the long trip. Their fatigue was not only from the rigors of travel but also because of the strain of taking extreme caution to go undetected by Anabaptist hunters.

There were days when they continued in hiding rather than be seen on the road.

They attended an evening meeting held a few days after their return. Both were enriched by the spirit of fellowship and were encouraged by the growth of the community of faith. There were a number of seekers whom Menno was now privileged to help in their next steps of faith. Within a few days he was able to lead a service of baptism. This was a joy for Menno and Gertrude and an exciting time of celebration in the group. In Menno's message he emphasized the new covenant in Christ, a relational righteousness that came from the grace of God and not by their power alone.

The weeks moved by as Menno helped around the estate grounds, working with Hero and building a wholesome relationship with him. From the gratuities he had received, Menno was able to give Hero a good bonus for his family. He explained that it was only fair since he and Gertrude benefited so much from Hero's work. His host thanked him for his gracious gift and the help that he offered on the estate.

As the next several weeks passed, Menno reflected on the many questions that had been brought to him in the various meetings. Studying and thinking on these as systematically as he could, he became eager to begin writing again. But Gertrude urged him not to get too involved in another writing project until after their child was born. Menno made use of those days for study and careful thought as they waited on the child's coming. He felt he needed this time to enrich his mind with fresh biblical treatment for his presentations.

But there were nearly two months until their baby would be born, and after a few days Gertrude urged Menno to go ahead with the writing project. She was aware that he needed something to occupy him. Menno knew it was important for the strength of conviction within the free church community, so he wrote a treatise called "Christian Baptism."

As Menno began writing, he stressed the necessity of first being converted to Christ in response to Christ's call into a covenant of discipleship. This was a believers covenant and as such could be made only by those old enough to understand its meaning.

In several weeks he completed the work, and the title page again carried his favorite Scripture, 1 Corinthians 3:11. The verse was especially appropriate, for he had argued that there is no other foundation for baptism than a believer's covenant with Jesus Christ.

This pamphlet was a strong statement from the New Testament on the nature of believers baptism, the outward sign of a new covenant with Christ. It stressed the significance of baptism as a witness to one's experience of the new birth and one's commitment to discipleship. The commission of Christ, the teaching of the apostles, and the Scriptures all made clear that baptism was to be administered to believers, not to infants.

While he drew at length from Scripture, he also quoted Tertullian and Rufinus from the third and fourth centuries. Their writings recognized that salvation was not in mere rites of religion but in a pious faith relationship with Christ. Menno also distinguished that the outer baptism with water is a sign of a new covenant with Christ, but the true transformation comes from a baptism with the Spirit, which the Lord himself gives.

Menno also argued that the idea of godparents is a human institution, tracing this practice to Pope Hyginus, bishop of Rome in the second century. It was not a biblical teaching or practice, he wrote, but could only be a privilege of extended community. Baptism itself is for believers who in their maturity and in faith enter a responsible covenant with the Lord.

In this treatment of believers baptism, Menno wanted to answer critics of second baptism, so he pointed out the significance of Acts 19:3-7. There Paul rebaptized twelve men when they came to faith in the full work of Christ. These men had previously been baptized with a baptism of repentance. But Paul called them to a response to Christ and a baptism as their covenant with him.

> Now listen, dear readers, for I would here present to you and to all the world three points, which you should impartially consider and judge according to the Word of God. First, was the baptism of John of God? I know you will give an affirmative reply. If now the baptism of John is of God, as indeed it is, and if Paul still considered this baptism from above as insufficient and imperfect in these disciples because they did not know the Holy Ghost, and if he after preaching Christ to them, baptized them again with the baptism of Christ Jesus, as is mentioned by Luke, then what must we think of the baptism of children who are naturally unable to understand the divine Word? Can you think that they are able to acknowledge Father, Son, or Holy Ghost, and can they distinguish between truth and lies, righteousness and sinfulness, good and evil, right and wrong? Does not this prove infant baptism to be useless, vain, and futile as administered and received without the ordinance of God?
>
> And if we acknowledge this by the Word of God through faith, then does it not become incumbent upon us to be baptized with the baptism of Jesus Christ, as Christ has commanded it, and as Paul has administered it to these disciples? I say verily that if we do not receive such baptism, there is according to the Word of God neither faith, regeneration, obedience, nor Spirit in us, and therefore no eternal life, as we have frequently shown above.
>
> In the second place, judge for yourselves, kind readers, since Christ Jesus himself and also the holy apostles, Peter, Paul, and Philip, have commanded and taught no other baptism in all the scriptures of the New Testament

than baptism on confession of faith and in witness of it, and since the whole world nevertheless teaches and practices a different baptism; one which is neither based on the commandment of Christ nor on the teachings and practices of the holy apostles, namely, infant baptism; and since the world supports it, not by the Word of God but solely by the opinion of the learned ones and by long usage and by the bloody and cruel sword; therefore judge, I ask, which of the two we should follow. Shall we follow the divine truth of Christ Jesus or the lies of the ungodly world?

Third and finally, judge whether the ordinance of Jesus Christ which He commanded in His church and which the holy apostles learned and administered as from His blessed mouth, can ever be changed and broken by human wisdom or dignity. If you answer in the affirmative, you must prove it by the divine and evangelical scriptures or else we should not believe you. But if you answer in the negative, as you should, then you must acknowledge that they (no matter who they are, whether they lived at the time of the apostles and were even their disciples), who say that the apostles baptized infants err shamefully and ascribe falsehood to the apostles, yes, speak their own opinions and not the Word of God.

Menno folded his arms and leaned back in the chair, reflecting on what he had written. He had a satisfying peace and found it especially satisfying to get this long treatise ready for print. He prayed that it would strengthen the faith of the believers and help them to understand the biblical base for the Anabaptist teaching about baptism.

Menno had written this treatise to challenge the thinking of people in the larger circle of his influence. He was well aware that the spread of his writings would make the authorities more aware of his leadership role, which would add to the threat of his being apprehended. With this in mind he traveled as secretively as possible, and he and Gertrude prayed constantly for the Lord's protection.

~

For some time Oldersum had been their home, and it was good to be back and settled in. Menno hoped and prayed that they would be able to stay for a while, especially for Gertrude's sake. She was now heavier with the child, and he didn't want her to make even short journeys. They were accustomed to living as fugitives, but they enjoyed their time together in the secure setting of Oldersum and were eager for the birth of their first child.

Menno occasionally left Gertrude to make short trips, meeting with groups of disciples and teaching them the Word of God. Often the meetings were at night, in a home, a barn, or even outdoors. Occasionally other leaders accompanied him, but on many occasions it was with Dirk, who had moved back to Emden and frequently joined him in meetings. Menno and Dirk together taught and baptized new converts.

As the movement continued to grow, Menno would often help the small congregations to select an elder to serve them as "shepherd." Sometimes Dirk was present to witness this calling by the congregation and join Menno in ordaining the person to the ministry of the gospel. Using Paul's words, Menno admonished them to preach the Word, to care for the flock, and to be steadfast in the face of increasing opposition.

Late one evening, after returning from a trip he had made west into Friesland, Menno told Gertrude softly, "Today they almost got me. I had taken a seat on a boat because I was tired. As we passed along through the canal, several soldiers rode up to the edge on horseback and called out, 'Is Menno Simons on board?' We were near the opposite bank, and I gathered up my things quickly and leaped ashore. I called back to the startled pilot and said, 'Tell them that you are sure Menno is not on board.' I hurried down a narrow street long before the soldiers could ride to a crossing and come to find me. I hid in a gardener's shed and rested for an hour until I was quite certain that it was safe to travel on."

Gertrude's hand was at her throat as she tried to catch her breath. She looked at Menno with tear-filled eyes. "Thank God you are safe. Had they taken you, I don't know how I could live!"

She hurried to place their evening meal on the table, and they sat down together to sup. As they bowed their heads for the blessing, Menno prayed, "We thank Thee, Lord God and Father, Creator of heaven and earth, for all Thy good gifts which we, O Father of lights, have received of Thee and receive daily out of Thy liberal hand through Jesus Christ, Thy dearly beloved Son, our Lord. Thou hast clothed our bodies with the needed covering and have satisfied them with the natural bread."

Menno spent more time at home for the next several weeks. He wanted to be near Gertrude as they anticipated the birth of their child. The nine-month period seemed much longer to Menno than it actually was, because the months had been filled with so much activity. It would be better for Gertrude as well that he be there when the child was born.

Menno told Gertrude that he would now stay at home so he could write. Many new believers were requesting material from him. He explained to her that this was not a project calling for immediate completion, but one that would continue to challenge him and that might become his most influential work, *The Foundation of Christian Doctrine.*

He began writing, and as was his custom, he placed the 1 Corinthians Scripture on the title page: "For other foundation can no man lay than that is laid, which is Jesus Christ." Menno wrote of the centrality of Christ, the authority of the written Word, and Christ's call to walk with him as disciples in love, holiness, and peace. He urged his readers to look beyond religious rites to a faith identification with Jesus as Lord in life. In turn he also argued eloquently for religious freedom.

Do not excuse yourselves, dear sirs, and judges. You are the servants of the Emperor. This will not clear you in the day of vengeance. It did not help Pilate that he crucified Christ in the name of the Emperor. Serve the Emperor in imperial matters, so far as scripture permits, and serve God in divine matters. Then you may boast of His grace and have yourselves called after the Lord's name.

Do not usurp the judgment and kingdom of Christ, for He alone is the ruler of the conscience, and besides Him there is no other. Let Him be your emperor in this matter and His holy Word your edict, and you will soon have enough of storming and slaying. You must hearken to God above the emperor, and obey God's Word more than that of the emperor.

Early one evening, Gertrude was sure it was time for the baby's arrival. She told Menno to send for the midwife, and he hurried off to get her. Menno tried to be of help but as the midwife tended to Gertrude, she told Menno that he was in the way. She said firmly, against his protests, that he should wait outside the room. For half an hour he paced the floor in the adjoining room, waiting for the baby's birth and for relief for Gertrude, whom he could hear crying out in pain.

Suddenly he heard the baby's cry, and he almost shouted as he exclaimed, "Praise the Lord." The midwife called him into the room, and there on the bed beside his Gert was a little round face that already tugged at his heart with love.

"It is a girl," she said softly, and looked down at the little face with a warm smile. "Let's name her Bettjie, alright?"

"If that is your choice, it is mine as well," Menno said. "So it shall be. Bettjie." He again softly to himself, "Bettjie Simons."

The birth of their daughter brought a new sense of love between Menno and Gertrude. While the evening Bettjie was born was a special time of blessing, each day increased their joy as they watched the remarkable signs of growth. Every smile on her little face touched Menno with an inner joy. This was his daughter!

He was especially careful now to keep their dwelling secret from any adversarial authorities. It was much too early for Gertrude and their little one to be on the move with him. And traveling from place to place was in itself no security, for they could be detected in their movements as readily as in a local lodging place.

～

News came that Charles V had returned from Spain declaring that he needed to discipline rebellious Ghent. He issued a mandate from Brussels calling for eradication of the Anabaptist heretics. But the more the persecution intensified, the more the free church spread. Many Flemish fled north into the Lowlands because of this persecution.

Menno was sure this community of believers would not only survive but also would be heralds of a new age. He predicted that society would need to move to a new level of freedom and eventually people would come to recognize that the state and the church were two separate aspects of the social order.

A special disappointment to Menno came that year, 1540, in his role as bishop. Obbe decided to renounce his ministry and leadership in the movement. He remained troubled about having been ordained by "those sword bearers," as he called them. Obbe's defection from their fellowship was a serious loss. He was an effective leader but had been increasingly disillusioned and dissatisfied. He told Menno that he needed to withdraw from the ministry and the Anabaptist cause.

"And why such a radical step?" Menno asked rather sharply when they finally got to discuss it.

"Menno, it is my integrity," Obbe said simply. "It has haunted me that I had direct contact with those who were involved in the heresy of Münster. I cannot forget that I was baptized and commissioned by those sword bearers! Now that I have found in Christ the way of nonviolent peacemaking, I can hardly accept the fact that my very baptism was at the ministry of such preachers."

"I understand, Obbe, and I agree fully with your rejection of their position. But your identity is with the communities of peace. Your calling is from God, and you must rest in that. You are not accountable for the human imperfections that marked the men he used to call you."

"Of course, I know, and imperfect though it was, those messengers brought me to see the need to break from mere faith in the sacraments to experience a new faith in Jesus Christ. This has been rewarding. But those who know my past association find it difficult to hear me in the community of peaceful disciples. I think it best that I resign from leadership. I've talked with Dirk about this and he has agreed to carry on and continue to work with you. Perhaps, if it becomes known that I have resigned, the authorities may give me a bit of respite."

From that statement Menno wasn't sure to what extent the persecutions had contributed to Obbe's decision. But he held to it, though Menno tried to persuade him that there was sufficient validation for Obbe's ministry and that Christ is present more significantly in the midst of the gathered community of believers than in any figure of authority. A call to ministry was much more significant when viewed in that context, and this should far outweigh the limited association Obbe had with the disciples of Jan Matthys and the Münsterites.

Obbe still insisted on withdrawing. Menno spoke to others of Obbe as a "Demas," one like the apostle Paul's partner who forsook him and was described as "having loved the present world." But Menno recognized the depth of the inner turmoil his friend had been experiencing, and he knew that he needed to accept Obbe's decision.

Out of this reflection Menno wrote "Hymn of Discipleship," hoping that as the hymn was used it could help in healing and

refocusing faithfulness for the church. As he composed the lines
he prayed that it convey the spirit of the servant who loves the
Lord and has chosen to suffer affliction with Christ. It was his
prayer that the hymn would serve as a call to faithfulness in the
service of the Lord.

> My God, where shall I wend my flight?
> Ah, help me on upon the way;
> The foe surrounds both day and night
> And fain my soul would rend and slay.
> Lord God, Thy Spirit give to me,
> Then on Thy ways I'll constant be,
> And in Life's Book, eternally !

> When I in Egypt still stuck fast,
> And traveled calm broad paths of ease,
> Then was I famed, a much-sought guest,
> The world with me was quite at peace;
> Enmeshed was I in Satan's gauze,
> My life abomination was,
> Right well I served the devil's cause.

> But when I turned me to the Lord,
> And gave the world a farewell look,
> Accepted help against the evil horde,
> The lore of Antichrist forsook;
> Then was I mocked and sore defamed,
> Since Babel's councils I now disdain;
> That righteous man is e'er disclaimed !

> I'd rather choose the sorrow sore,
> And suffer as of God the child,
> Than have from Pharaoh all his store,
> To revel in for one brief while;

The realm of Pharaoh cannot last,
Christ keeps His kingdom sure and fast;
Around his child His arm He casts.

In the world, ye saints, you'll be defamed,
Let this be cause for pious glee;
Christ Jesus too was much disdained;
Whereby He wrought to set us free;
He took away of sin the bill
Held by the foe. Now if you will
You too my enter heaven still!

The community of believers, while recognizing that the leadership role of Obbe was now vacant, expressed to Menno their strong affirmation of his leadership. People spoke of his role as bishop as in the wonderful providence of God, that in God's plan he had been called to be a leader in the church. His influence was wide, and many people supported him and prayed for his safety. Many of his fellow disciples, at risk to themselves, sought to provide hiding places for Menno and his family.

It was of special importance for Menno's leadership that Dirk stood by him. The two of them continued to share a rich ministry. Menno emphasized that his call to leadership in the church was from God and was extended through the voice and calling of the congregations of believers. The community of believers was the unique channel by which the Lord of the church carried out his work.

With Obbe transitioning out of leadership, the focus was on Menno more than ever. He had become increasingly known as the primary leader of the Anabaptists, which he did not take lightly. He told Gertrude that he wanted people to know that their leader is the Lord Jesus Christ. Anything that he might do must witness to his Lord.

With this in mind Menno wrote a tract called "Why I Do Not Cease Teaching and Writing," in which he sought to clarify

Anabaptist doctrines and elucidate his dedication to spreading the gospel. His boldness in doing this encouraged many other leaders.

The pamphlets he had written in 1539 were so well received that Menno continued to put more of his teaching into print. It was more difficult for him to meet with congregations in person, but his writings could be passed from hand to hand. He saw this as a teaching strategy, and he began writing, expressing his faith:

> Behold, beloved reader, in this way true faith or true knowledge begets love, and love begets obedience to the commandments of God. Therefore Christ Jesus says, "He that believeth on him is not condemned." Again at another place, "Verily, verily, I say unto you, He that hears my word, and believeth on him that sent me, hath everlasting life and shall not come into condemnation: but is passed from death unto life." John 5:24

Menno paused to reflect and pray before he continued. He wanted to express the core of an evangelical faith.

> For true evangelical faith is of such a nature that it cannot lie dormant, but manifests itself in all righteousness and works of love; it dies unto the flesh and blood; it destroys all forbidden lusts and desires; it seeks and serves and fears God; it clothes the naked; it feeds the hungry; it comforts the sorrowful; it shelters the destitute; it aids and consoles the sad; it returns good for evil; it serves those that harm it; it prays for those that persecute it; teaches, admonishes and reproves with the Word of the Lord; it seeks that which is lost; it binds up that which is wounded; it heals that which is diseased and it saves that which is sound; it has become all things to all men. The persecution, suffering and anguish which befalls it for the sake of the truth of the Lord is to it a glorious joy and consolation.

All those who have such a faith, a faith that yearns to walk in the commandments of the Lord, to do the will of the Lord; these press on to all righteousness, love and obedience. These prove that the Word and will of our beloved Lord Jesus Christ is true wisdom, truth and love, is unchangeable and immutable until Christ Jesus shall come again in the clouds of heaven at the judgment day.

Menno now gave seven signs of the true church as he perused this writing: (1) No leader should be appointed unless he knew Christ and followed his doctrines as an evangelical preacher; (2) no message should be proclaimed but the true gospel of Jesus Christ; (3) true faith and life in Jesus Christ will prove itself in deeds of love; (4) only true Christian baptism, first with Spirit and fire and after with water, should be practiced; (5) no other supper should be celebrated than the Supper of Jesus Christ; (6) all strange ceremonies contrary to the Word of God should be abolished from worship; and (7) all magistrates should be converted so that they rightly administer and execute their office in the fear of the Lord for the protection of the good and the punishment of the evil.

His seventh point on government raised questions from many elders. They asked him whether he was encouraging an Anabaptist government, as there were Protestant and Catholic governments. Menno said his vision was not of a church governing society; it was a free society in which those who governed did so with integrity in their faith and respect for all others.

$\sim$

During the remainder of 1540 Menno gave a lot of his time to supporting Gertrude and didn't take as much time for writing as he wished. But he found a special joy in being a parent and especially with the freedom the family shared in the small castle at Oldersum. Looking into Bettjie's little face, he believed that he was seeing the *imago Dei*. Menno knew that each life is created in the image of God, and he saw her in this light. Soon she was crawling between the two of them, from one lap to the other, and as the year passed she began to totter around the room.

It was a special thrill to Menno to help Bettjie as she learned to walk. "It is much like helping people in the steps of faith," he said to Gertrude. "They are slow at first, need to find their balance, and then they begin to walk with confidence."

There were numerous small congregations with which Menno shared in fellowship. The demands of preaching, instructing converts, and conducting baptisms kept him very busy. But a new challenge soon emerged for him. As congregations gained some cohesion, they needed to be led in the exercises of church discipline to safeguard integrity. Menno regarded this as a primary need if the scattered and diverse church was to have the unity it needed to be true to its Lord.

As he wrestled with promoting his vision for a true, authentic church, he sought to engage the local leaders of each congregation in holding members accountable to one another and to the Word. Whenever there was need for disciplinary action, it should be the voice of the group and not the word of an authoritarian elder. As their bishop, Menno sought to help them in the process of discipline but not to displace them.

In his ministry, Menno emphasized that for a group of believers to be a true church there must be biblical accountability. But this accountability was primarily positive rather than negative. Holding one another accountable meant challenging each one to be the best possible disciple in faithfulness to Christ. Church discipline began with brotherly assistance.

A number of the elders requested that he write a pamphlet on this matter, which he did. It was called "A Kind Admonition on Church Discipline" and was completed early in 1541. When he finished the writing, he turned back to the title page and there placed his favorite verse of recognition of Christ as the one sure foundation.

Discipline, Menno urged, should be tempered with kindness and love, never be harsh and severe:

> If you see your brother sin, then do not pass him by if his fall be curable, from that moment endeavor to raise him up by gentle admonition and brotherly instruction before you eat, drink, sleep, or do anything else. . . .
>
> Brethren, understand correctly. No one is excommunicated or expelled by us from the communion of the brethren but those who have already separated and expelled themselves from Christ's communion either by false doctrine or by improper conduct.

After he completed the pamphlet, Menno wanted to write more about the calling of faith in Christ. In late 1541, he took up his pen and began a draft of what he called "Fundamentals." With all the threats on his life, he was driven to express himself as clearly as possible. As always, the title page carried the words, "For other foundation can no man lay than that is laid, which is Jesus Christ." He worked carefully on this manuscript, searching the Scriptures to develop a clear presentation of the essential aspects of faith for all who are disciples of Christ. Menno saw it as a major work and took his time in study, reflection, and writing. He couldn't help but wonder when he would complete it. However, he wanted to be at home with Gertrude and Bettjie, and he took the respite from travel as his opportunity for writing.

The substance of the pamphlet was the nature of a believers church. He focused on the need for a personal relationship with Jesus as the one in whom we are reconciled to God, on each believer's sincere commitment to the community of faith, and on a clear emphasis on the way of love and peace as a nonviolent answer to oppression.

Since then for reasons stated I cannot teach publicly, I will serve you nevertheless in writing as long as the Lord will permit me and I live, with my small talent, which the gracious Father has granted me through Christ out of the abundant treasury of His heavenly riches. I say with Paul, to serve is my desire, not with exalted words of human wisdom, for I posses and know them not. I let those seek them who desire them.

My boasting, however, is with Paul to know Christ and Him crucified, for to us the knowledge of Him is eternal life. Therefore God cannot endow us with better wisdom than with this even if it be such rank folly to the world, for she is more precious than gold and silver, pearls and precious stones; there is nothing under heaven to be compared with her. Her ways are ways of pleasantness and her paths are peace; she is a tree of life to them that lay hold upon her, and happy is everyone that retains her. . . .

With this wisdom—so much as the gracious Father, the Giver of every perfect gift, has given me through His Son Jesus Christ—I desire with all my heart to serve not only our brethren and sisters but the whole world. I desire this in order that the hungry and thirsty souls who would gladly live according to the Lord's will . . . may be clothed from above with this heavenly wisdom and may learn to know God through His Son and Word in the Spirit: the God who says: Let not the wise man glory in his riches: but let him who would glory, glory in this, that he understands and knows me, that I am the Lord which exercises loving kindness, judgment, and righteousness in the earth: for in these things I delight, says the Lord (Jeremiah 9:23, 24).

Menno drew voluminously from his wealth of memory of Scriptures, exalting the Lord and emphasizing the wonder of his grace. Paragraph after paragraph and page after page, he addressed the claims of the papists, of the Lutherans, of the English, and of the Zwinglians. He gave his own clear interpretation of faith centered in Christ, which he expressed as a call "to accept the thrust of the whole Scriptures, that of the whole Christ from head to foot, both inside and outside, visible and invisible, God's firstborn and only begotten Son. All who can believe this as certain and true are sealed through the word of God in their spirit, are inwardly changed, and receive the fear and love of God."

Addressing of the movement's persecutors, Menno wrote,

The common proverb is, "The wolf will manage to get his hide through the forest, but the sheep will be forced to give up his pelt."

When will you turn your backs to their deceiving lies and face up to Christ? When will your deadly and cruel sword finally be wiped clean of innocent blood and put back in the sheath? When will you hear and fear God more than you do lords and princes? When will the abominations of the Antichrist be grubbed out of your heart and the doctrine of Christ be planted in its place? When will you let yourselves be put to silence by unblamable lies and have enough of the blood of innocent saints?

When will Christ Jesus with His Word, Spirit, and life be conceived in you through faith in very deed be born in you? Never, I fear; for your heart is so earthly and carnally minded, the eyes of your understanding so darkened, that you desire the world far above heaven, lies above the truth, sin above righteousness, the honor and praise of man above the honor and praise of God.

Since then these selfsame sheep are born of the truth and have Christ together with His truth, and therefore

His Spirit dwelling in their hearts, nothing but the honest, plain truth of Christ, by which they were born into
righteousness and converted, will be found in them. Yet
it is manifest that no matter how piously and unblam-
ably they live, our lying, adulterous, lewd, idolatrous,
drunken priests and monks openly rob God of His
glory and arrogantly murder those whom Christ purchased with His precious blood. They defame them
before the whole world, betray them, and bring them to
the stake. . . . Dear Sirs, when will these foul traitors,
this murderous bloody seed with their Judas-like betray-
als, be motioned aside and turned down by you?

Menno laid down his pen and leaned back with a sigh. What
he had just written was not easily said. He really meant to encourage the new disciples and unite the Anabaptist movement in discipleship and peace. But it seemed necessary that he set his views
against what people were hearing from other groups, which, he
recognized, might tend to be overly defensive.

Menno discussed with Gertrude his desire to be more positive.
She reminded him, "It isn't by putting others down that you have
found your greater strength; it is simply in lifting Jesus higher."

12
Itinerant Preaching in Amsterdam and the Zaan

1541–1545

Menno fell to his knees in prayer and a soul-searching renewal of his commitment to the Lord. He had just learned that Maria, regent of the Netherlands, had authorized the courts of Friesland to pardon any penitent Anabaptist who would betray Menno Simons. The authorities were committed to crush the Anabaptist movement, of which they regarded Menno a leader. He tried to discern whether his concern was over the threat to his life or whether it was because of what his death would mean to his family and to the church. Some of both, he decided.

"I am not in a hurry to die," he said to himself.

"A church free of state control is a threat to the establishment," Menno told Gertrude. "But this freedom is needed for the church to be true to its Lord. I need to continue my ministry. God has called me to it, and in faithfulness I've been preaching and teaching across Friesland, right in the regent's backyard. In these several years I have helped many converts to form congregations. I wish the Regent Maria understood that we are not a threat to government. We are simply exercising the freedom that each person should know in God's grace. I am sure it is God's work, and I must continue."

207

"I understand, Menno," she said. "But you must be careful. Remember, it is the Lord's work, and you don't need to do it all. It might be good to lay low for a while in view of this threat."

A few weeks later Dirk came to talk with Menno and to make certain that he knew of Regent Maria's edict. Dirk gave a word of warning: "I want you to be aware, Menno, that the focus of the authorities is on you as our more prominent leader. You are better known than others of us, and they are aggressively searching for you. The margrave of our home region has written a letter of response to Maria, and I came to share this with you. He sent this on May 19. Clearly his intent is to make the search for you well known, and a copy was posted in Leeuwarden, calling for your arrest."

He pulled a folded paper from his pocket, unfolded it carefully, and said, "Let me read it to you."

> Most gracious Lady, the error of the cursed sect of the Anabaptists which in the last five or six years has very strongly prevailed in this land of Friesland . . . would doubtless be and remain extirpated, were it not that a former priest, Menno Simons who is one of the principal leaders of the aforesaid sect and about three or four years ago became fugitive, has roved about since that time once or twice a year in these parts and has misled many simple and innocent people. To seize and apprehend this man we have offered a large sum of money, but until now with no success. Therefore, we have entertained the thought of offering and promising pardon and mercy to a few who have been misled if they would bring about the imprisonment of the said Menno Simons.

Menno was silent for a few moments, sitting with his head bowed. Then, looking up at Dirk, he said simply, "Our Lord calls us to take up the cross and follow him, even to the death. I won't deny that this gives me some fear, but it is not his will that I surrender to fear. This is our calling as his disciples, as being aliens in an unfriendly world, of bearing the heavy cross of Christ."

After Dirk left, Menno told Gertrude about the report. He could see the fear in Gertrude's face, and he spoke gently to her. "I am not indifferent to this. It does stir fear within me. But this work is God's calling, and we will keep on sharing his gospel. This message of the grace of Christ must be shared with the whole world and even if it is a risk to us. This is a prophetic word, and I do believe that God will bring about a change in society for more tolerance and freedom."

"Menno, I do understand," Gertrude responded softly. "But when you are gone I wonder whether you are safe and if you'll return. When you are here we live in fear that we'll be apprehended. It is difficult. Without the grace of the Spirit giving us courage, it would not be possible to be true to our calling, but we will be."

Menno looked into her eyes with a smile, "My Gert, you are the greatest! What a wonderful partner. I am so blessed to have a wife who is always there with me in the service of our Lord."

∼

Menno continued his work despite the dangers. He was encouraged by the growth of the free church, which had spread across Friesland and into north Germany. In spite of the opposition, many people supported the Anabaptist idea of freedom in faith. Many were making confession, repenting, joining covenant with Christ, and being baptized.

Menno continued to travel secretly, yet he was very forthright in his preaching. His messages called believers to personal conversion and regeneration through the Holy Spirit, and to walk in the way of the Spirit in love and peace. But the secret nature of these gatherings made it difficult for Menno to nurture the new believers. He delegated much of this responsibility by appointing leaders and ordaining pastors, deacons, and bishops who would shepherd new members in a pattern of life that expressed their discipleship of Christ.

As the work of the free church progressed, government opposition to it grew. Within a year, the earlier edict was followed by a new announcement placing a price of one hundred guilders on Menno's head, equal to the annual salary of a priest at Witmarsum. Such an offer would be a temptation to most anyone. In 1542, an imperial edict, which carried the authority of Emperor Charles V, was drawn up at Leeuwarden. It read, "No one is to receive Menno Simons in his house or on his property, give him shelter, food or drink, or even speak with him, or read any of his books under penalty of loss of property and life as a heretic."

Menno continued his secret visits to West Friesland, his fatherland. He usually left Gertrude at Oldersum with the Von Dornum family on these trips. While this was a necessary caution to avoid arrest, it was especially important because Gertrude was carrying their second child.

From gifts that came from various congregations, Menno was able to pay rent to the Von Dornum family. This helped them to justify their lodging to Hero, the caretaker, who often expressed to Menno his concerns and fears for the property.

Even with the danger to himself, Menno made another secret trip to an area near Leeuwarden with the intent of strengthening the community and elders after the loss of Obbe's leadership. He made the long trip very carefully, traveling in the early morning and hiding during the day. When he arrived, the leaders sent the word around, and the congregation gathered in a barn for a late-afternoon meeting.

In spite of the dangers, the group shared a very joyful time of fellowship. The spirit of the meeting was positive, and the response to Menno was especially encouraging. But one of the guards they had posted suddenly burst into the meeting, calling out that the beadles were coming.

"Farewell, my friends," Menno quickly said. "By God's grace, I'll be back." He leapt from a little platform in the barn and was out the back door, scurrying between the cottages and down a narrow street, carrying his crutch. He ran around the corner of the last cottage at the end of the street, his heart beating rapidly and his breath coming in short gasps.

He paused to decide what he should do. To return to the village would be suicide; with the reward being offered for his capture, the police would soon have him, without a doubt.

Menno trembled from the chill and from a surge of fear. He thought of his family back in Oldersum, in the comfort of their home on the Von Dornum estate, and he wished he were there with them. But he jerked his thoughts back to the present. To take the road to Leeuwarden, a city he knew well and where he might be able to hide, was not feasible, for the horsemen would soon overtake him. "Lord, what do I do now?" he prayed. "I am your servant, and you have promised to walk with me."

His gaze turned to a dike across the lowlands to his left. Looking back at the village, he thought the cottages would hide him from the view of his pursuers for a short time. He wheeled around, turning from the little street he had come down, and quickly made his way across the dike. Once on the other side he turned again and soon hid in the brush along the edge of a marshland being drained by the farmers. He could hear voices in the village as his pursuers called to one another. He was quite certain they would not plunge their horses into the marshy land in pursuit and perhaps would not use the dike.

Several hours later, having made his way across the country as fast as he could, Menno came to a sheepcote. Carefully he opened the door and stepped inside, gently speaking to the sheep and easing himself down just inside the door. They stirred, but made no commotion. With the warmth of the interior he began to relax, but sleep eluded him as he began reflecting on what all had brought him to this time of his life. Just as he was dozing off, he heard footsteps. He held his breath as the door slowly opened. The sheep tender called for the sheep to follow him, and Menno sat quietly, watching the little flock make its way out of the sheepcote.

Menno bowed his head and thanked God for his providential care. He prayed for protection on his journey back to Oldersum and his family. He rested for some time, but he slipped out late in the afternoon, before the shepherd returned with his flock. Menno made his way east. Some days later he was in north Germany and headed to their house by the castle, to Gertrude and Bettjie.

⁓

A few weeks after his return from West Friesland, Dirk joined Menno on a short trip north to the coast where Dirk and his family were living. He wanted Menno to visit the believers there and had arranged for him to preach in a warehouse on the fishing wharf.

Menno preached from one of his favorite passages, the last half of the second chapter of Paul's letter to the Ephesians. He spoke of the work of Christ in reconciliation, of removing the barriers between estranged peoples, and of the new community of the Spirit. Menno emphasized the covenant of grace and the enabling of people to live in unity and peace and to transcend their differences by a new sense of mutuality.

"He is our peace," he said, quoting the Scriptures, "who has made of both one and has broken down the wall of partition between them, having abolished in his flesh the enmity, to make in himself of two one new humanity, so making peace. . . . He came and preached peace to you that were afar off and to those who were near."

Menno prayed that the hostility, violence, and persecution they were seeing would be brought to an end in the sovereign work of Christ.

"But," he continued, "that text says that this new peace has been made possible in that he has reconciled both unto God in one body through the cross. The continuing work of God is not without the meaning of his cross nor the experience of the cross for each believer. At the cross of Calvary a sacrifice was made on behalf of God's covenant with humanity, a sacrifice expressed in his self-giving love. This sacrifice is at the heart of reconciliation and, as seen in the text, it is not a private transaction but has a social aspect in that it includes the reconciliation between peoples of diversity. We too must bear the heavy cross of participation in his suffering."

At the close of the service, Dirk said, "Menno, your message gives us hope. It is not easy for us to bear our cross in following Christ, but when we see what he did and the power of his cross in redemption, it inspires us in our walk."

Menno nodded. "Yes, and I have come to believe more and more that the cross is the central expression of grace that transforms those of us who follow him."

It had been quite a long day with Dirk, and it was late when Menno bid the Philips family adieu. He stopped to sleep a few hours in a stable and arrived in Oldersum in the early hours of the morning. He was eager to be with Gertrude, and was especially concerned that the birth of their second child be without any problem for her.

Menno made his way carefully to the edge of the village. He avoided the heavily traveled heart of the village by turning to follow several small streets that were less public and led to the Von Dornum estate. When he arrived at the house, he paused to knock softly on the door, a signal that he knew Gertrude would recognize. Soon the door was opened, and they were in each other's arms.

〜

For the next several months Menno spent considerably more

time at home. He helped to care for Bettjie while Gertrude, heavy with child, looked after her knitting and other aspects of preparation for the expected birth. Menno tried to help in the cooking, and they joked about the borscht he made and the bread he helped her to bake.

But the day came when Gertrude called to Menno with some anxiety. Her pains were beginning. Menno again hurried across the village to a neighbor who would serve as midwife. She was one they could trust not to insist on registering the child for baptism or reporting the birth. This time, Menno assured the midwife that he would stay out of her way and trust Gertrude to her care.

But that was not easy. He paced the floor, going repeatedly to the closed door to listen to the sounds from within. Suddenly he heard the cry of a new baby and threw the door open with joy. Gertrude looked at him with a smile, her face sweaty and her hair damp across her forehead. But it was over, and the child was born.

"It is a boy," she said softly.

Menno was quite elated with the birth of their son, their second child, who they named Jan. This child might grow to be the man who could carry on Menno's work. He knelt by the bedside and held Gertrude in his arms as they looked lovingly at their little baby.

"Gert, this is our greater privilege, to be the parents of two wonderful children. It is a difficult world into which they have been born, but we will trust in God for their future."

She smiled with full understanding of what he meant.

Little Bettjie was so excited to have a baby brother that she tried to assist Gertrude. She could rock the little cradle, whisper her few words to little Jan.

Yet with the birth of this second child, Gertrude continually struggled with her health. She could not regain her strength. Menno watched her with tender care and sought to be helpful around the house. He limited his time away and made fewer trips for the next several months. The emotional effect of the dangers of persecution and the strain of their repeated moves had taken a toll on Gertrude. Menno prayed for her health and rejoiced as she slowly regained her strength.

Menno had recently suffered a few health problems of his own. His difficulties were not so stressful while he was home, but some affected him in his occasional travels. Earlier he had severely strained his left leg and hip slipping from a dike as he hurried to cross a polder. More recently he was suffering from pain in his lungs that made his breathing difficult. But the greater difficulty for Menno was to watch Gertrude suffer.

As the months passed and Jan grew, they were confronted with the risks of staying in Oldersum. The price offered for someone to betray Menno was well known. While their hosts continued to guard their secrecy, Menno knew they'd welcome freedom from the constant unease. Gertrude agreed that it would be wise to relieve their hosts and find lodging elsewhere for a while. This was not easy, because lodging was always dependent on friends and travel was rarely easy or comfortable. While traveling, they often stayed in a barn or a cellar where a family was willing to conceal them. This was very difficult for Gertrude and for the children, who could scarcely understand all the moves and the secrecy. At times it was almost more than Menno could bear.

They decided to move about more frequently in various areas of north Germany. Many believers, some of them friends of the couple, were being martyred in Friesland, including a number in the city of Amsterdam. The fear that it could happen to Menno weighed heavily on Gertrude. Every time he was out on a mission, she prayed continually for his safety.

Several times it was reported that Menno had escaped the Anabaptist hunters hoping to gain their reward. He would travel through the fields to avoid the well-used roads and often traveled at night or in the very early hours of the morning, especially when traveling to areas where he had ministered earlier, for there he knew some familiar paths.

Months after he had been in Leeuwarden, Menno heard that Souck Hayes, his friend from there, had been fined quite severely for being in a crowd listening to Menno preach. Hayes was living under orders not to leave the city for the next six years. Menno thought to himself, "It will take more than that to stop the wind of the Spirit, for this is God at work among us."

~

Menno came home early one evening from a secret mission, and sitting down in his chair, he gathered the children in his arms. He bowed his head over theirs and whispered his words of love. He told them why he was so often away in his service for the Lord, and he wanted them to understand that they were in this together as a family in the service of Christ. Bettjie nodded with her childlike understanding, but Jan was too young to get even a simple understanding of what he meant.

Menno snuggled the children deeper in his arms and told them stories from the Bible. He smiled at Gertrude as they observed how Bettjie seemed to understand, her large eyes wide as he told of Joseph being sold into Egypt by his brothers. Later, Menno promised, he would tell them the rest of the story, of how God used Joseph to bring blessing to his brothers and to his father.

Menno and Gertrude talked about how they should educate their children. He had once served at Bolsward as a teacher of boys from the community, but he couldn't do that here, as it would give away his presence. Gertrude could teach the children to read, and they decided to try to seek out the small school gatherings that parents arranged in many of the communities. It would be good for Bettjie and Jan if they could sit with other students for study.

Menno's earlier concerns about David Joris and his spiritualistic piety and lower regard for the authority of the Scriptures now proved to be valid. Menno frequently encountered people under the influence of Joris who tended to minimize the authority of Scripture and emphasize their own private spirituality.

There were also other voices that Menno saw as perverting the gospel, being what he called "corrupt sects." His responsibility as a leader in the church made him conscious of the fact that he needed to take a strong stand against such persons. As to Joris, Menno became direct in his words. He wrote a sharp letter in 1542, denouncing Joris as a "dunghill of a man" who was teaching trash. Joris's spiritualistic emphasis, which lacked a call to faithful discipleship, seemed in Menno's thinking to lack moral integrity; it was not truly spiritual.

He wrote a lengthy treatise on what he called "heretical article." Near the end, he asked his readers pointedly,

> Do you mean to say that the doctrine of Christ and his apostles was incomplete and that your teachers bring forth the perfect instruction? I answer that to teach and believe this is the most horrible blasphemy. . . . Deceived children, where is there a letter in the whole doctrine of Christ and the apostles . . . by which you can prove and establish a single one of your erring articles?

He showed it to Gertrude. After reading it, she looked at him silently for a moment and then said, "It is quite sharp, Menno. I would urge you to show more of the gentle side of your spirit. I know you well, and the sharp arguments come naturally and may even be necessary so that some people will hear you, but it never hurts to be more gracious. And you have that side as well."

Menno sat in silent thought, digesting her comments. At first he wanted to react angrily, but then he nodded, and replied, "It is not that I mean to be defensive or introduce argument for my own sake, but when the integrity of the gospel is at issue, my spirit waxes bold."

"I know," she said. "I've even heard you using some words

that I'm sure come from your background on the farm. You have referred to some people as 'clods' or 'dullards,' and you even called Joris a 'dunghill of a man'! Be careful, my dear."

Menno's face flushed with embarrassment, but he nodded in recognition. "I'll try to edit this, my dear, and I'll remove any words that are vitriolic."

~

When news came to Menno of the growth of the church in Amsterdam, a conviction grew in him that he and his family could go there and help the churches. He knew something of the problems the congregations were facing, and as he prayed for the brothers and sisters in the city, his sense of calling increased.

One morning, after their prayer at breakfast, Menno looked across the table at Gertrude. "My dear, I am almost obsessed with a conviction that we should go to Amsterdam. From reports that I have been receiving I am sure that we should spend some time there to help the church in view of the difficulties they face in the city. A number of our friends with whom we have worked earlier have now moved into Amsterdam, and several have passed word along that they need my support."

Her response amazed him: "This is no surprise to me. I have been thinking about some of our friends there as well. The church would benefit from your teaching and your leadership influence. God can use you to strengthen the suffering church in Amsterdam."

They made preparations, and within a few days they set off. It was a long trip to the south and then they turned west, crossed the Rhine, and headed through very difficult terrain, with polders and dikes. When south of the sea, they headed for the village of Amersfoort. There they found friends who opened their homes to them, and Menno and Gertrude felt it wise to stay for a few days, giving the family an opportunity to rest. Menno met with a small group of believers in the evenings and enjoyed the interchange with them in the Scriptures. When it was time to move on, they bid their new friends *adieu*.

As they drew near to Amsterdam Menno recognized the more familiar landscape. He had traveled through the area as a young man a number of times in his trips to Utrecht. He had always enjoyed the sights of the windmills against the sky along the Zaan River. Now as they came near, he explained to the children their important service to the farms and businesses of the area.

Bettjie begged for a ride in one of the boats on the canal. Menno assured her they would have opportunity for that, especially in Amsterdam. She was satisfied with his promise, even though she continued to watch and talk about the different boats on the Zaan.

The family made their way carefully into the city, mingling with the farmers who were tending market. They found lodging for the first night on the second floor above a pub, then found a home where they could stay. Menno was soon busy preaching in numerous evening gatherings.

One of those who responded to Menno's preaching was a bookseller, who was of great assistance in spreading Menno's writings among believers in the city. This sharing of his writings added much to Menno's influence there. Once people knew that the author of the pamphlets they were reading was among them, attendance at his services increased.

Menno kept his promise to Bettjie about taking a boat ride on the canals. He took the family along on several trips, but in a different way than any of them had expected. One of the brothers in the church was a ferry master and owned a boat on which he transported people. Menno arranged for a small group to travel in the boat while he sat in the prow and taught them from the Scriptures. Bettjie and Jan sat by his side, trailed their hands in the water and enjoyed the ride. At times Bettjie listened intently to her father. Menno observed her and thought that she must have some understanding of his teaching. He decided to discuss it with her later, to see how much she was grasping.

The adults on the boat could listen without fear of being apprehended. They entered into a discussion of Menno's message. It was a good and somewhat secure way of conducting a Bible study, so Menno arranged several of these trips. The pilot of the small boat knew the canals well and made a circular tour. This meant that the people disembarked not far from their homes and disappeared down different streets, giving no impression of being an organized group.

~

The Simons family stayed nearly a year in Amsterdam. Menno taught and preached, and Gertrude enjoyed the city life, its culture and opportunities to associate with other women. She also led a Bible study for women of the free church. Menno kept very busy baptizing new converts and giving guidance to the elders of the congregations. Small groups of disciples held gatherings in many parts of the city.

By the end of their first year in the city, the Catholic Church had won the political battle; now intense opposition to all other movements immersed the city in violence. Representatives of the Catholic Church took a poll across the city, and anyone who did not attend Catholic services was viewed with suspicion.

It was clear to Menno that the officials would eventually find him and his family and that it was necessary for them to leave the city. Their associates and friends were reluctant to see them go but agreed that it was a wise choice. Those who owned property and had a family history in Amsterdam had a bit of security; the Simons lacked this.

Before leaving Amsterdam, Menno met with several of the communities of Anabaptist disciples, and he offered words of encouragement in his farewell comments to them. This had long been home for most of them, and they meant to stay in the city if possible. Menno urged them to be true to Christ as Lord in spite of opposition. He counseled them to be faithful to the call of Christ and not to be led astray by the followers of David Joris or Jan van Batenburg. Batenburg was a former Münsterite who had gathered a following and continued teaching Joris's apocalyptic message. Batenburg believed that the Lord was calling him to help set up the future kingdom and that the use of the sword would be expected of them when that revolution came. But now both of these men were teaching that one could avoid persecution by outwardly identifying as Catholic while the inner mind was set on God.

Menno and family set off quietly early one morning among the group of market people who routinely left the city at that hour to purchase produce from other farmers. Dressed in similar work clothes, they appeared to be part of the group. The children were placed in the bottom of a cart, covered over as they slept. Once again God helped them find their way safely.

～

A few days later, Menno wrote to the community of believers in Amsterdam and reiterated some of the warnings he had expressed upon his departure.

> Concerning the shepherds who pose as shepherds of Christ, who pasture the sheep for what they get out of it, as Ezek. 34:8 has it, pasturing themselves—you see how little they bother themselves about the sheep, whether they have pasture or not. Just so they get the wool and the milk, then they are satisfied. They pose as shepherds but they are deceivers. They are very different from the shepherds of which we read in Jeremiah, shepherds after His heart whom the Holy spirit has sent. These other shepherds have not the love of Chris which Peter had and therefore Christ's commandment to pasture His lambs does not apply to them. . . . They are not the shepherds who lead them to the sparkling waters, but to the

stagnant pools which they have prepared with their feet,
that is, by their glosses and human notions.

Therefore it is necessary to separate from them and to
depart, as we read in Matt. 7:15, Beware of false prophets.
As Paul says, beware lest any man spoil you through philosophy and vain deceit, after the tradition of men, after
the rudiments of the world, and not after Christ. Col. 2:8.

The church of Christ is the bride of Christ, and Christ
does not want His bride to conceive except of the incor-
ruptible seed. I Pet. 1:23. As Paul says, I have espoused
you to one husband, that I may present you as a chaste
virgin to Christ. II Cor. 11:2. . . . How then can some
say this is a matter of liberty? Of this liberty any sensible
Christian may judge."

After leaving Amsterdam, they found lodging with friends in
the small villages to the east. But they were in need of a more permanent lodging place to limit the stress of travel. For the next several weeks, the family moved quietly from one community to
another, being passed from friend to friend. But they continued
to make their way east and then north, knowing they would be
safer to the north in Germany. Being so cautious made travel slow.

At times Menno made some journeys alone, traveling to various locations with communities of believers and there finding the
family's next lodging place. As she stayed with the children in the
home of some new friend, Gertrude was continually concerned for
his safety. She would remind him often that what had happened
to others could happen to him, and she would occasionally review
with him the number of friends who had been executed.

"Menno, I don't want to be a fussbudget. I mean to support
you, but I am not indifferent to the risks you run."

"Yes, my dear, I understand, and if you were not concerned,
it would bother me even more."

Menno kept his own fears to himself lest he upset the children as they set out on the long trek toward Lower Saxony.

Gertrude continued to be haunted by memories of friends, such as Anna of Rotterdam, who had been burned at the stake in January 1539. As Gertrude reflected on Anna's death, she often thought about what it would mean if she herself were apprehended and had to leave their children without a mother. A few months later, word had come that several other friends of their circle, Arent Jacobs of Rijp with his wife and oldest son, had been drowned at Monickendam in north Holland. They had been executed because they spoke of having been born again by the Spirit of God, a charge that they would not repudiate. And now, as the months passed, the number of martyrs included scores who were converts to the Anabaptist fellowship.

Though she was emotionally disturbed by these alarming reports, another matter added to her concern. She needed to tell Menno that she was expecting their third child. A larger family meant more joy, but also increased difficulties.

Late one evening after Menno returned from a mission trip and the children were tucked in bed, the two sat quietly together. Gertrude knew it was a good time to tell him. "Menno, I have news again that I must share."

He looked at her with the lift of one eyebrow, and quipped, "And it involves me?"

"It sure does!" She chuckled. "Yes, Menno. If not for you this news wouldn't be fact."

Suddenly his face changed as it began to dawn on him. "You mean—we are to have another child?"

Gertrude smiled, and nodded her head modestly. "Yes, Menno, that is what I've been wanting to tell you. I've known for a few weeks now."

He reached out and took her hand. "This is a blessing from the Lord."

Yet he too had mixed feelings. Late into the evening, over tea, they talked about what this could mean for them. They agreed that this ought to be their last child. It would be best for the two children they already had, but in Menno's mind it was even more important because Gertrude had been having health problems they regarded as serious. The difficulty of getting medical attention increased as they traveled.

⁓

For several years they had scarcely been able to stay for more than a few months in one place, except when they had lodged at the Von Dornum estate. Most of the time they needed to keep moving from barn to house to barn, being helped by many friends. Menno was satisfied that now they would make their way far north to the region of Wismar by the Baltic Sea.

This was a lengthy trip for the family, but enjoyable. They moved slowly through the countryside and into the rolling terrain near the Baltic. The landscape was beautiful, and the smell of the sea was exhilarating. There at Wismar, on the edge of Germany, they found lodging with a family they knew who were members of the local congregation. It was a relief to Gertrude in her condition to be able to settle down for a bit longer.

Menno had worked across Friesland for seven fruitful years, but the intense search for him by the Anabaptist hunters made this relocation satisfying. He was sure that he could work from north Germany and perhaps make a few trips into Friesland. This would be a radical change for him but much safer for the family. In northwest Germany, the severe edicts of the emperor and the regent were not in force; many of the rulers and lesser nobility were much more tolerant than those in the Netherlands.

Gertrude had told Menno numerous times that she would enjoy being a Bible teacher, like Elizabeth Dirks. Now she asked Menno, "Do you think I could find a way to fulfill my dream of being a teacher in this more tolerant area? Or do you think that I should think of God's calling for present as primarily to teach our children?"

Menno nodded and said, "I think you have the answer. I'm

sure the latter. It seems wise for the present for you to share with the children. But I also know that if you were a teacher it would not be easy to keep hidden. We cannot run this extra risk in addition to the threats I face."

A few days later came a report from an area of their earlier work at Wormer, in the Waterland region. Authorities had executed Dirk Krood, Pieter Trijnes, Claes Roders, and Pieter Claes Jans, all of whom had helped develop the church in that area. Menno and Gertrude were so deeply grieved that for several days they were virtually immobilized. They constantly thought of their esteemed colleagues, with whom they had enjoyed a brief but meaningful fellowship.

Menno and Gertrude prayed together, claiming the promise of the Lord, "Lo, I am with you always, even unto the end of the world." They thanked the Lord for the confidence that he had been with their friends to the very end, and they prayed that the Spirit would use the testimony of these wonderful saints as a witness to many in that community.

The determination of Emperor Charles V to crush the movement became even more evident when ten believers were executed before a large crowd on the Krommenersdyke. This was done, according to the report, as a warning from the *stadtholder* that Anabaptists would not be tolerated.

Menno and Gertrude also learned that their friends Jacob and Seli, a delightful couple with whom they had traveled after leaving Amsterdam, had been arrested, taken into Amsterdam, and perfunctorily burned at the stake. The deaths of friends so close to them hit them like a thunderbolt. It seemed as though they had lost members of their own family.

"And now," Gertrude said, "the word is again spreading that the authorities are offering rewards to anyone who helps find you. They mean to put a stop to your leadership."

"Yes," Menno responded, "but Dirk and I have been appointing many others to serve as elders, and this should relieve the need for me to be on the move so much. I meant to tell you this earlier. At our last leader's meeting we ordained Adam Pastor and Hendrik van Vreden as elders for Westphalia. This will also be a great help in reaching into areas of Germany. And, as you know, Dirk often joins me in the work, and being on the move is actually important for his own safety."

Menno also gave Gertrude a report of the good number of people who had converted to Christ over the past several weeks. Now many were becoming quite involved with the free church, including Hendrik.

"This is a gift of God," Menno said, "for he has now become a co-worker with us for the region. Should something happen to Dirk or to myself, we have a competent brother to serve as a leader."

This was especially important for Menno and Gertrude. Now rather than traveling so much, Menno had someone who could stay in the region and provide leadership.

"He will be a good worker," Menno said. "And actually further to the south we have appointed other leaders, Anthonius van Keulen for the Rhineland and to the north of Amsterdam Gillis van Aken in the region of Antwerp to work with the Flemish believers. We have also ordained a brother named Frans Reines Kuiper to serve in Friesland. Since there is such an attempt across that region to find and arrest me, this will let me avoid travel in that territory and to trust more of the work to Kuiper.

"Gertrude, even though I keep hearing of more attempts for my arrest, I've said little about it lest it bother you and the children. The pressure seems to have increased ever since Regent Maria sent out that mandate from her office in Brussels. The strength of her mandate is that it authorizes the courts of Friesland to pardon a penitent Anabaptist if they would betray me. We need to be especially secretive. I promise you that I will try to be very careful in my travels and be very secretive about where we are living, lest someone report our location."

He reached over and picked up his Bible and, opening it to Psalm 46, began to read:

> God is our refuge and strength, a very present help in trouble. Therefore will not we fear, though the earth be removed, and though the mountains be carried into the midst of the sea; though the waters thereof roar and be troubled, though the mountains shake with the swelling thereof. Selah. There is a river, the streams whereof shall make glad the city of God, the holy place of the tabernacles of the most High. God is in the midst of her; she shall not be moved: God shall help her, and that right early. The heathen raged, the kingdoms were moved: he uttered his voice, the earth melted. The Lord of hosts is with us; the God of Jacob is our refuge. Selah. Come, behold the works of the Lord, what desolations he hath made in the earth. He makes wars to cease unto the end of the earth; he breaks the bow, and cuts the spear in sunder; he burns the chariot in the fire. Be still, and know that I am God; I will be exalted among the heathen, I will be exalted in the earth. The Lord of hosts is with us, the God of Jacob is our refuge. Selah.

But they soon learned that the danger for Menno had just gotten worse. A decree Charles V made in late 1543 offered to commute the sentences of any fugitive who enabled Menno's arrest. This offer was in addition to the reward of one hundred guilders to anyone helping bring Menno in.

The magistrates well knew that this increased the possibility of disclosure. Someone not so involved in the movement but close enough to have some information about Menno just might turn him in for the reward. Or someone with a family member in prison might negotiate a release by betraying Menno. The announcement of the amnesty offer confirmed Menno's conviction that it was better for them to live in Germany.

Menno and Gertrude agreed that it would be wise for him to limit the trips into West Friesland for the present, even though his leadership was needed by the congregations, and they loved and respected him. Many in the movement supported Menno and Gertrude financially, but they were all concerned for his safety.

13
Increased Opposition and Persecution for His Writings

1546–1547

During this time, Menno made a complete break from the Melchiorites, a break clearly spurred on by his writings against the teachings of David Joris, who now lived in Antwerp. Menno had diligently sought to lead Joris to a correct understanding of Scripture, and their break over the issue of biblical authority was now evident to others. Menno's approach was not conciliatory; he was quite direct in his comments.

The more he heard Joris speak, especially on his eschatological views from the book of Revelation, the more Menno actually considered Joris and his followers to be "corrupt sects"—viewing them as a sect, not a church—and placed them alongside the heretical Münsterites. He saw little difference between Joris's followers and the Melchiorites, even though the Melchiorites repudiated violence.

Word had come from Gillis van Aken of Antwerp that Joris actually claimed to be the "Messianic David." Menno now produced a pamphlet, rejected that claim outright. In response to Menno, Joris claimed that through dreams and visions he had been given a divine mission to assemble Christ's flock for the last days.

Menno learned that this claim had begun to influence the church in Amsterdam, and he wrote a strong letter to refute it. He emphasized that believers were called to be disciples of Christ, not of men. True believers will confirm this commitment to Christ by their covenant in baptism and will be identified with the church as the visible body of Christ. For discernment, he sent the letter to brothers with whom he had worked in the city.

Menno and Joris continued to exchange some very sharp writings for some time. While Menno emphasized the authority of the written Word, Joris emphasized the inner word, even rejecting externals including adult baptism. To Menno's consternation, Joris minimized the significance of the incarnation, failing to emphasize the truth of God as being seen most fully in the person of Christ. In one of his writings, Joris stated emphatically, "Faith is revealed in the power of the Spirit and in the power of truth, not in the telling of the biblical story, nor in the story of the miracles of the apostles and prophets, nor in the corporeal proof of the outer cross of Christ, nor in his incarnation, his death or his resurrection, nor in his second coming."

Menno felt that it was important for leaders of the Anabaptists to meet with Joris and his group for a debate. Menno's associates agreed. The meeting, they felt, should involve Nikolaas van Blesdijk, the emerging leader of the Davidians, as Joris's followers were now being called. They believed that God had awakened in Joris a work of the divine Spirit and that he was beyond comparison among his peers. Menno was sure this claim needed refuting.

The city of Lübeck, a beautiful seaport on the Baltic in Holstein, Germany, was chosen for the meeting. It was one of the "Wendic cities," so named from their setting along the northern sea. As early as 1543, theologians in this region had taken steps to exclude Anabaptists coming from the Netherlands. But for some years things had been relatively quiet, so by 1546 it seemed a safe meeting place. Though the city was quite a distance north of him,

Menno would be there as the Anabaptists' leader. Other brethren would include Dirk and the young associates Leenaert Bouwens, Gillis van Aken, and Adam Pastor.

The participants each made their way to Lübeck, where they conferred for several days, arguing extensively, especially about infant baptism. Rather than coming to agreement, their disagreement increased. The beauty of the surroundings made little contribution to any congeniality.

Menno debated with Van Blesdijk, the leading proponent of the Davidians. But soon Bouwens, Pastor, and Van Aken became involved in a very free and forthright conversation. In fact, Menno listened respectfully while Van Blesdijk and Van Aken engaged in a heated debate that lasted nearly four hours.

People left the meeting convinced that their position was the correct one. Menno left with heaviness in his heart. He and Dirk walked together until parting to their own homes. Both were concerned for the future of the movement.

A few days after returning from Lübeck, Menno wrote a letter to "some persons who formerly agreed with me, but now think otherwise," namely Van Blesdijk. Within a few weeks Van Blesdijk wrote a reply in which he called those associated with Menno "Mennists," a name commonly used in the region—to Menno's embarrassment—to distinguish the peaceful Anabaptists from other groups. Van Blesdijk made a special point to defend the baptizing of infants in the Reformed Church so they could thereby be as inconspicuous as possible.

Menno wrote a response in which he attempted to balance the emphasis on the inner word and the outer Word. He wrote a brief statement on the role of the sacraments and especially emphasized the bonding nature of covenant and the external expression of religious ordinances as a witness to an experience of grace. He made a distinction between a *witness* of grace and rites that *mediate* grace. He sought to be clear with his readers about the limitations of spiritualistic movements that internalized everything.

Faithful reader, do not imagine that we insist upon elements and rites. I tell you the truth in Christ and lie not. If anyone were to come to me, even the emperor or the king, desiring to be baptized, but walking still in the unclean ungodly lusts of the flesh, and the un-blamable, penitent and regenerated life were not in evidence, by the grace of God, I would rather die than baptize such an impenitent, carnal person. For where there is no renewing, regenerating faith leading to obedience, there is no baptism.

Menno's caution about Joris was confirmed when he and his family left Antwerp and traveled to Basel, Switzerland. The move was not unusual, except that Joris was apparently now living under an assumed name, Johann van Brugge. With this new identity he had become known in Basel as a wealthy and respected Reformed refugee. He lived with his family in a small castle in the inner city, and his daughters married into the city's elite without the social group knowing the family's true identity. (Joris's true identity was learned several years after he died; the city's religious leaders had his body exhumed and burned along with his books.)

⁓

Menno and Gertrude prayed daily for God's grace in keeping them and their children safe from persecution. Together in their commitment, they asked God to be a cover for them as they sought to serve him, to help them point many to discipleship in Christ, and to enable others in ministry.

Menno and Gertrude were determined not to surrender to fear. But they were also determined not to be careless. Their lives were in God's hands, and they wanted to be careful not to move from his grasp. This conviction gave them strength. Menno frequently quoted from Isaiah, "They that wait upon the Lord shall renew their strength. They shall mount up with wings as eagles, they shall run and not be weary, they shall walk and not faint."

"I've preached from this text," he said to the children, "making clear that this is strength to hold high ideals, strength to meet the crises of life and strength to walk in the routine of day-by-day living."

In his writing, Menno declared his daily goal as faithfulness to Christ. He was careful to emphasize his place as a simple servant. It was in the recognition of what God had given him that he was committed to integrity in life and service. This stood in contrast to some people whom he saw as pretenders:

> Brethren, I tell you the truth and lie not. I am no Enoch, I am no Elias. I am not one who sees visions. I am no prophet who can teach and prophesy otherwise than what is written in the Word of God and understood in the Spirit. Whosoever tries to teach something else will soon leave the track and be deceived. I do not doubt that the merciful Father will keep me in His Word so that I shall write or speak nothing but that which I can prove by Moses, the prophets, the evangelists and other apostolic scriptures and doctrines, explained in the true sense, spirit, and intent of Christ.
>
> Oh dearest reader, I repeat that I have formerly acted shamefully against God and my neighbors; and I still do sometimes think, speak, and act recklessly, which however, I sincerely hate. What am I that I should boast, seek, and teach anything else than the ever blessed Christ Jesus alone, His Word, sacraments, obedience, and His God-pleasing, virtuous, and unblamable life. He is the only one of whom it is written that He was begotten of the Holy Ghost; that He knew no sin; that guile was not found in His mouth; and that His doctrine, Word, will, and commandments are life eternal. . . .

My writing and preaching is nothing else than Jesus Christ. I seek and desire nothing (this the Omniscient One knows) but the most glorious name, the divine will, and the glory of our beloved Lord Jesus Christ may be acknowledged throughout the world. I desire and seek sincere teachers, true doctrines, true faith, true sacraments, true worship, and an unblamable life. For this I must pay dearly with so much oppression, discomfort, trouble, labor, sleeplessness, fear, anxiety, care, envy, shame, heat and cold, and perhaps at last with torture, yes, with my blood and death. . . . I say with John the Baptist, Christ Jesus must increase but I must decrease. John 3:30.

All Scripture both of the Old and New Testament rightly explained according to the intent of Christ Jesus and His holy apostles is profitable for doctrine, for reproof, for correction, for instruction in righteousness. II Tim. 3:16. But whatever is taught contrary to the Spirit and doctrine of Jesus is accursed of God. Gal.1. There is but one cornerstone laid of God the Almighty Father in the foundation of Zion, which is Christ Jesus. Isa. 28:16, Rom. 9:33, I Pet. 2:6. Upon Him alone we should build according to His Word, and upon no other.

All Scripture, Menno wanted his readers to understand, should be read "according to the intent of Christ Jesus." This was his central hermeneutic. The reader should discern the intent and meaning of a passage, not just quote the words. This was, he believed, the only way to read the Old Testament and to be consistent with the way of discipleship presented in the New Testament. He was concerned that the church be built on the one sure foundation, which is Jesus Christ.

Menno gave more attention to his wife and family, especially to Gertrude. Bettjie was a help to her, but the demands of their life were taking a toll on Gertrude's well-being. She didn't complain, but Menno could see her pain and struggles.

Menno bowed in prayer at their bedside and asked the Lord for a special gift of his healing grace for Gertrude and grace for more sensitivity and thoughtfulness on his part. He meant to be a good husband, but he was so passionate about the call to ministry that he was often absent when needed by the family. Being away from them so much was the one regret he carried. Yet he thanked God for the wonderful privilege of family and the joy they brought to one another.

～

The Mennists, as they were now commonly called in West Friesland, had evangelized all across north Holland, and in many areas nearly two thirds of the populace had come to the faith taught by the Anabaptists. The believers church movement now permeated the country. But the spread of the Reformed movement brought new dynamics to the region. This branch of the Protestant Reformation held a very different position on the matter of relations to the state. As a consequence, they were gaining political power and were becoming the persecutors of the free church.

In contrast to the Anabaptists, the Reformed were ready to take up arms against the Spanish, who were occupying the Netherlands as agents of the Roman Catholic Church and the Holy Roman Emperor Charles V, himself a Spaniard. In contrast with the Reformed Church, the Mennists were committed to live by nonresistance, peace, and nonviolence. Somehow the two groups would need to resolve this difference or, in the minds of many, the threat from Spain could not be overcome.

The persecution intensified; the magistrates, both Catholic and Protestant, wanted to rid the country of Anabaptists. Menno felt this opposition to be a real contradiction in interpretation of faith because the Reformed leaders were inclined to use the old covenant to defend the use of violence, and they believed that the church needed to be in control of territory. Because of their opposition to Menno, he had to be especially secretive with travel plans and the family's lodging. The Simons family was indebted to the many brothers and sisters who offered hospitality and who would send word to friends in the next community to have lodging arranged by the time they arrived.

Though moving from place to place was difficult for the children, they would carry a supply of bread and bologna from one place to the next. Although the bread got a bit hard, Menno was able to cut pieces for each of the children while he and Gertrude usually chewed on the crust. Meager though this diet was for growing children, Menno could occasionally find beets or turnips to supplement a meal. Although this helped, the children talked of how much better the beets were when their mother cooked them. Occasionally he also secured eggs from farmers, which they sometimes boiled over a campfire.

Menno was unwilling to be silent in the face of persecution over religious differences. He wrote to the state authorities, addressing them in his letter as "servants of God" and challenging them to conduct themselves accordingly:

> If you regarded your role as given you by God, you should then conduct yourselves in a way pleasing to God. This should mean respect for differences of thought, and granting freedom for conversation rather than exercising capital punishment of persons who differed on matters of faith.
>
> Henceforth, beloved rulers, see to it, you who call yourselves Christian, that you may be that also in deed and word. Water, bread, wine, and the name do not make a Christian, but those are Christian who are born of God, are of a divine spirit and nature, are of the same mind as Christ Jesus . . . love their neighbors as themselves; lead an unblamable, regenerate, pious life, and willingly walk in the footsteps of Christ. . . . These the Word of God calls Christians.

Menno emphasized the need for the state to respect the place of the church in its own right, granting the church freedom to interpret its faith from Scripture itself. To clarify this he referred to Luther's statement regarding the church: "The marks of the church are two, where the Word of God is rightly preached and the sacraments rightly administered." These exercises, Menno wrote, were unique to the church and were functions that the state authorities could not fulfill. But they should let the church be the church and in turn the church would respect the state.

"Luther has a good but limited focus," Menno thought. "It is necessary to add something to Luther's statement. His statement says nothing about the nature of the new community of believers and of the Christian's accountability to our one Lord and Sovereign or of what it means to hold one another accountable to live as disciples of Christ."

To clarify this concern, Menno wrote more on his understanding of the true church: it is a community of the reborn, a fellowship of disciples who hold each other accountable to live by the teachings and spirit of Jesus, and a community that lives and walks in the Spirit. In the Anabaptist understanding of Scripture, he said, there are marks that might be described as internal, that is, within the congregation of believers. They are marks by which we know one another as a people of God; we each confess Jesus as our Lord, and we hold one another accountable to live consistently with our covenant.

The external marks of the church, meanwhile, are those by which society can recognize the true church. One of these marks is witness and evangelism—sharing the mission to which Christ has called his disciples. A second mark is the freedom of the church in relation to the political powers. The church should be free from control by the state, which should support the well-being of the whole society. The church, then, will be a positive influence for good when it is guided by the priorities of the heavenly kingdom.

Menno's intent was to make clear that the true church is not interested in power and control of society but in freedom to be itself in faithfulness to Christ. This freedom, he said, should be no threat to society, for all that was being asked for was the freedom of people to determine their religion without being coerced.

∼

Menno and Gertrude received an inspiring letter from Elizabeth Dirks, their colleague from Leeuwarden. Her letter offered personal reports of her work teaching the Bible and ministering as a deacon. But it also contained sad information of the suffering of several of her friends from Leer, and this gave Menno and Gertrude prayerful concern.

Many of her close friends from Leer had walked with her in the early development of her faith. Because of the threat on their lives, they had fled, traveling to Ghent in Flanders. But soon after arriving there, they had been betrayed to the authorities and were arrested and imprisoned. After some weeks, they were bound to the stake and, without death by strangling, were horribly burned to death.

These wonderful friends and fellow believers, Elizabeth wrote, had given a clear testimony of their faith. One of them, Wouter Denijs, had boldly called out to the observers, "Citizens of Ghent, we suffer not as heretics, or those who hold in one hand a beer mug and a Testament in the other, thus dishonoring the Word of God and dealing in drunkenness; but we die for the genuine truth."

Then as the fire was being kindled, the martyrs had called to one another, "Let us fight valiantly, for this is our last pain. Hereafter we shall rejoice with God in endless joy."

As Elizabeth told him these words, Menno exclaimed, "What faith, what assurance! This is nothing other than the work of the Spirit of Christ in them. But what a trial." His voice faded, and he became silent, thinking of the terrible anguish a death like that entailed.

Gertrude looked at him, knowing well the thoughts that must

have been in his mind as he reflected on the threats on his own life. She watched him in silence, not interrupting his thoughts. Then she commented, "Menno, this is not in God's plan for you. We shall continue to pray for his covering hand for your role as a leader among his people."

He looked at her with a smile, knowing that she had read his thoughts, and simply nodded in affirmation.

To justify persecution of so-called heretics, the state church authorities appealed to the parable of the tares in Matthew 13, declaring that the church contained both true believers and non-believers. The Anabaptists, they claimed, had separated themselves from the state churches and were declaring themselves the true church. The authorities of the state church, now guided by Reformed doctrine, claimed that a true or pure church was not possible in this world, and they interpreted Jesus' parable to mean that the wheat and tares should grow together in the church until the judgment.

Menno responded that the parable of the wheat and tares supported the very principle of toleration he preached. He pointed out that Jesus did not say that the wheat and tares were growing together in the church; rather they were described as living together in the world. The field in which wheat and tares grew together is the world, not the church. The church, as wheat, was called to be "in the world but not of the world." Being disciples of Christ, we live in the world as "salt and light," at peace with all men, rather than in a context of violence. Our focus is to "seek first the kingdom of God and his righteousness."

What Menno found contradictory was that, despite this teaching, the state church did not let the two grow together, in the church *or* in the world. They still persecuted the Anabaptists, calling them tares, and continued to issue imperial decrees against the heretics.

~

The Reformed Church had become established in the Netherlands quite recently and had spread rapidly. With the freedom granted by Protestant rulers since the Diet of Speyer in 1529, they were able to almost force their movement on the people. The tensions between them and the Anabaptists was not unnoticed by various governmental authorities, who desired a more unified social order. In a quest for national unity, opposition to the Anabaptists intensified, and the persecutions increased. Rather than seeking peace among diverse points of view, the authorities sought to remove those differing with the state.

From his new, safer home in northwest Germany, where there was greater tolerance from the government, Menno could travel into Friesland when necessary. He had some emotional pain about the move, but is was best for the family, he was sure, and he could continue with some secret trips.

At first the family lived in East Friesland, where the Countess Anna of Oldenburg reigned from the palace in Emden. The climate was cooler there, but the community more peaceful. Since the country was in transition from Catholicism to Protestantism, the countess was working to promote greater unity and peace. She appointed John a'Lasco, a Zwinglian reformer from Poland, to reorganize the new Protestant state church. At the time, there was at least a bit more tolerance for the Anabaptists. In his new role, Lasco soon became aware of the difference between the fanatical sects and the relatively orthodox Mennonites.

When he learned of Menno's presence in the area, Lasco discussed with the countess the possibility of a public debate with Menno and his associates. As a member of the Reformed Church, the countess was committed to seek a way for greater harmony in her district. Her husband, Count Enno, had been quite active in arresting Anabaptists. But after his death, she had taken a more tolerant position. She called the conference to be a theological discussion between John a'Lasco, now superintendent of the East Friesland Reformed churches, and Menno Simons, spokesperson for the Anabaptists. Menno was assured that he would be granted safe passage.

Menno and Gertrude discussed this together and decided that he would go. A few days later, he left to make his way to Emden on the sea, a region of lower Saxony in west Germany, on the border of East Friesland. Saxony had witnessed the martyrdom of numerous Anabaptists, and Luther's writings against them had kept the opposition strong across the region. Now, with the Reformed influence of Countess Anna, there were gestures toward understanding.

Though Menno was assured safe passage, there were still dangers. He and Gertrude had lived there earlier, and Menno knew the community well. He'd had considerable freedom when they lived in the nearby village of Oldersum, from which base Menno had carried on his itinerant ministry.

As he came again into the city of Emden, a bustling seaport, Menno relished the smell of the sea and the wonderful view of the blue waters of the Baltic stretching to the north. How peaceful the gift of God in nature, he thought, and how he wished society would be as peaceful. It was here that Melchior Hoffman had in 1530 baptized three hundred people in the vestibule of the *Grosse Kirche*. And it was here that Sicke Snyder had been baptized by Hoffman's successor, Jan Trypmaker. Menno thought of the impact that Snyder's martyrdom at Leeuwarden had made on his own thinking while still in the monastery.

~

The arrangements were for the debaters to meet in the Franciscan monastery, and sessions were scheduled from January 28 to 31, 1544, four days of discussion. Upon his arrival in the city, Menno ran into Gellius Faber of Leeuwarden, a former Catholic priest who was now a Lutheran minister.

Faber had come to the meeting out of personal interest. He wanted to be present because several years earlier he had read an

Anabaptist letter explaining why the Anabaptists could not unite with the Lutheran Church, and it had deeply irritated him. He wrote a seventy-eight-page book in response, and now he wanted to see that some of the issues came up at the meeting.

The meeting opened with intense debate that drew crowds of observers. People took sides between Lasco and Menno. Those who sided with Menno were called Mennists, though Menno repeatedly rejected this name, affirming instead that the community of faith be known simply as a free church.

The debate soon became personal as charges were leveled against Menno. One charge was that he minimized the meaning of baptism for infants in the covenant community; a second claimed his understanding of Christ was not an adequate grasp of the incarnation and the humanness of Jesus; a third criticism concerned the itinerant nature of ministry among the Anabaptists. When Faber spoke on this point he charged them with being "hedge preachers" who ministered in fields and barns rather than in proper worship settings. Menno didn't answer back, though he wanted to point out that this was not by their choice.

Lasco was the primary speaker for the Reformed group, so he and Menno had the primary interchange. When it was his turn to speak, Menno emphasized the visible nature of the church as the expression of the body of Christ in the world. To talk of only the invisible church as the true people of faith and the visible church as the sociopolitical institution was nothing more than an old Constantinianism. Menno reviewed his interpretation of the true "marks of the church," saying that beyond Word and sacrament there needed to be the life of faithfulness as disciples, of what Paul called "the obedience of faith" in opening his letter to the Romans.

Menno focused other parts of the discussion on discipleship and moral accountability to the Lord as the gracious Redeemer and the Reconciler of all who come in faith.

The meeting closed with each side thinking it had bested the other. Menno's colleagues were very affirming of his presentations, stating that he had answered the accusations clearly and with a biblical approach. But those who had called the meeting believed that the Protestant position carried the day. At the conclusion of the assembly, the countess announced that all adherents of any sect, including the Anabaptists, must leave the city in accordance with Charles V's mandate.

Menno found the countess's action regrettable, but unavoidable. Clearly, she had called the meeting to justify expelling the Anabaptists. Menno was eager to leave and to make his rather short journey back to his family.

Arriving home, he told Gertrude, "I think we've done our part as well as we could. Now we must leave it to the Spirit of God to use this witness. It appears that our fellowship may need to suffer a lot more before we come to a new level of social freedom."

Gertrude nodded and said, "I'm sure you presented the Scriptures well, and we can leave this to God."

During the following weeks, while the memory of the discussion was still clear in his mind, Menno fulfilled a promise he had made to Lasco during the debate and wrote a consistent statement of biblical doctrine in a lengthy treatise he called "A Brief and Clear Confession." As usual, he opened the treatise with 1 Corinthians 3:11.

In the document, Menno sought first to answer the accusations that he was heretical on the doctrine of the incarnation. He was eager to establish the integrity with which he worked at interpreting the written Word. He admitted that when he began his study of the sacraments while still a priest, he had been influenced by Melchior Hoffman's teaching on the idea of the "celestial flesh" of Christ. But he wrestled with this issue in prayer over the Scriptures and discerned that it was not a term that he could use. He had come to peace with the mystery of the incarnation:

Jesus was Son of God and son of Mary in the mystery of conception by the Holy Spirit.

> This eternal Word of God has become flesh. It was in the beginning with God and was God (John 1:2). Conceived and come forth of the Holy Ghost (Matt. 1:18), nourished and fed in Mary, as a natural child is by its mother; a true Son of God and a true son of man, born of her, truly flesh and blood. He was afflicted, hungry, thirsty, subject to suffering and death, according to the flesh; immortal according to the Spirit, like us in all things, sin excepted (Heb. 2:9). Truly God and man, man and God, not divided or separated. . . .
>
> The heavenly Seed, namely, the Word of God, was sown in Mary, and by her faith, being conceived in her by the Holy Ghost, became flesh, and was nurtured in her body; and thus it is called the fruit of her womb, the same as a natural fruit or offspring is called the fruit of its natural mother. For Christ Jesus, as to his origin, is no earthly man, that is, a fruit of the flesh and blood of Adam. He is a heavenly fruit or man. For his beginning or origin is of the Father, like unto the first Adam, sin excepted.

Menno thought of his brothers and sisters in the faith who would also read the document, and he wanted to strengthen their faith by giving clear testimony to those opposed to them. He presented careful arguments that, although primarily in reply to Lasco, could also be helpful to others. A central emphasis was on the divine disclosure in Christ and the need to hear the words of Jesus as well as worship him as the crucified and risen Lord. As he interpreted the new covenant and its expectation of discipleship, Menno consistently clarified the Christian ethic as a doctrine of absolute love and nonresistance.

> As disciples of Christ, we are to seek such an infilling of divine love that we can love even our persecutors. . . . We

are taught and warned not to take up the literal sword
nor ever to give our consent thereto, except the ordinary
sword of the magistrate when it must be used, but to
take up the two-edged, powerful, sharp sword of the
Spirit which goes forth from the mouth of God, namely
the Word of God.

At last, after much fasting, weeping, praying, tribula-
tion, and anxiety, I became by the grace of God comforted and refreshed at heart, firmly acknowledging and
believing by the infallibly sure testimony of the scriptures, understood in the Spirit, that Christ Jesus forever
blessed is the Lord from heaven, the promised spiritual
seed of the new and spiritual Eve.

Writing at length on the deity of Christ, Menno addressed
Lasco's specific questions.

In the sixth place, you say, God could not suffer. If
Christ's flesh were not on earth or of Adam, but from
heaven, then he could not have suffered, and consequently could not have died.

Be impartial and judge rightly. Your conception is
that Christ Jesus as to the Spirit is of the Father, in
which Spirit He was, as you say, not subject to suffering
and death, but you hold that He was not of the Father
according to the flesh. According to the flesh, in which
He suffered and died, you teach that He is of the earth
in order that thus the law enjoined upon man with
threat of condemnation might by the earthly man,
namely, Christ, be fulfilled; that He (we being in Him,
by the oneness of His human nature and blood with
ours, whereby He has fulfilled in our flesh the righteousness of the Father) might save us. This foundation is
implied in your Latin syllogisms. We will not controvert
this by subtle syllogisms nor by acute human cavilings,

for we do not have them. But we controvert it by the plain testimony of the Word, which cannot be turned by glosses, nor broken by human reason.

Menno wrote more on his understanding of redemption, drawing from Scripture his affirmation that, in Christ, God was suffering for our reconciliation, quoting from Paul's second letter to the Corinthians (5:18-21). He argued that it was the entire Christ, divine and human, who was sent from the Father and who suffered and died on the cross, referring to the amazing and clear expressions of Paul in the epistle of the Philippians (2:5-12).

Dealing with the matter of Adam's sin and fall, Menno affirmed that those who receive the promised seed are born from above by this same Seed, the Word, Christ Jesus. He made a special point that being born of the Spirit does not mean that this is something other than identification with the incarnate Lord. Finally, Menno stated that this section should be adequate to conclude his defense of the incarnation.

But a second section of the treatise was even longer than the first. As Menno wrote about the calling and character of pastors and ministers, he focused on his understanding of Christ Jesus as the Bishop of bishops, the Shepherd of shepherds, who said, "As my Father hath sent me, even so sent I you" (John 20:21).

> As they had received the knowledge of the kingdom of God, the truth, love, and Spirit of God, without price, so they are again prepared to dispense it diligently and teach it without price to their needy brethren.
>
> And as for the temporal necessities of life, the begotten church was sufficiently driven by love, through the Spirit and Word of God, to give unto such faithful servants of Christ and watchers of their souls all the necessities of life, to assist them and provide for them all such things which they could not obtain by themselves. O brethren, flee from avarice!

Menno paused and noted that his teaching was consistent with article 5 of the Schleitheim Confession, written in 1527, which states clearly that pastors are to be supported by the congregation that called them. Menno thanked God for the way in which the faithful people of God met the needs of his little family.

After writing extensively and positively on the nature of the calling to ministry, he concluded the treatise.

> That is enough for the time being. Differentiate properly between Christ and yourselves; between His love and yours; His spirit and yours; His purpose and yours; His doctrine and yours; His sacrament and yours; His life and yours. And you will no doubt find wherein you err and fail. May God the merciful Father, grant unto you and to us all, true wisdom, understanding, faith, knowledge, and true judgment; a fervent heart, true fear, love, doctrine, life, sacraments and ordinances, through Christ Jesus our Savior and eternal Deliverer of the world. Amen. Enter ye in at the straight gate. Matt. 7:13.

A few weeks after the treatise was published, Menno learned that Lasco had published his own "Defensio," which attacked Menno's work and attacked him as a writer. Now they would wait patiently to see what reactions would come from the church. Menno was confident that his position would stand scrutiny, yet he was certain that a time would come when he would have to answer Lasco.

⁓

Persecution against the Anabaptists continued broadly across the Netherlands, Flanders, and even north Germany. Menno was not unaware of the threats on his life, but he was pleased that the family was in western Germany, where there was at least less intensity in the search for him.

Menno wrote to fellow church leaders and shared the difficulties that constant hiding caused him and his family. He lamented, saying that he was not able "to find in all the countries a cabin or hut in which my poor wife and our little children could be put up in safety for a year or even a half a year."

In late 1544, he received repeated reports of cruel executions. He was disappointed that there was still little tolerance for new ways of thinking and practicing religion, and many people were still being put to death. His heart cried out, "When will freedom come?"

Menno learned that Jan Claeszen had been hanged at Amsterdam. Claeszen had arranged for six hundred copies of Menno's writings to be printed at Antwerp; he had distributed two hundred in Holland and the rest in Friesland. There was also another shocking report about a group of men arrested and immediately beheaded at Rotterdam. This was followed by the arrest of a group of women, including a girl of fourteen, who were executed by being bound in a skiff and drowned under the ice. He shuddered as he considered the cold chill of crossing over the river of death.

This cruelty disturbed Menno deeply; the acts of persecution that were once primarily at the hands of Roman Catholics were now being carried out by Protestant state-church authorities. They, of all people, having themselves dissented from Rome, should respect the freedom of others to do so.

Menno was concerned for the integrity of the church, so he felt it imperative that he also respond to Faber, who had also written extensive charges against Menno since the Emden meeting. If the two of them could come to some understanding, it might enhance the spirit of tolerance by others. Menno was careful to provide scriptural answers to charges Faber made against him and the Anabaptists. He introduced his "reply" with a general comment:

> To all pious and well-intentioned people, whether of high

or low estate, who seek diligently the firm position of God, and who may read or hear my much-needed reply, do we wish a clear, spiritual vision, a sound mind, and an honest judgment in the truth, from God our heavenly Father through His dear Son, Jesus Christ our Lord, in the grace and illumination of His eternal and Holy Spirit. Amen.

This writing was not a minor treatise. Its first section answered seven general statements by Faber. The next ten sections included an autobiographical account in section 7 and dealt with the mission and vocation of the preachers whom Faber had derided as itinerant. Menno followed with twenty-two sections about baptism, responding to Faber's attacks in his seventy-eight-page book. Menno then wrote four sections on the Lord's Supper, then eleven on discipline, including the need for excommunication of persons choosing to live in sin, to thereby keep the church pure. This led Menno into a reply to fourteen statements by Faber about the nature of the church, and the remaining three sections refuted six of Faber's accusations.

Knowing of Faber's move from Catholicism to Lutheranism, Menno shared some personal and somewhat private aspects of his conversion to Christ. He paid respect to the writings of Martin Luther, which had helped him in his search for the life of faith, and he related some details of his own stance in refuting the Münsterites, of his seeking what it meant for him to know and live in the Spirit.

"After about nine months or so," he wrote, "the gracious Lord granted me His fatherly Spirit, help, and hand. Then I, without constraint, of a sudden, renounced all my worldly reputation, name and fame, my unchristian abominations, my masses, infant baptism, and my easy life, and I willingly submitted to distress and poverty under the heavy cross of Christ."

In evident humility he wrote of how the Lord called him and "produced in me a new mind, humbled me in His fear and taught me to know myself in part turned me from the way of death and graciously called me into the narrow pathway of life and the communion of His saints. To Him be praise forevermore. Amen."

Because Menno felt the document was very important, he stayed at his desk for hours. Writing the lengthy treatise took nearly two weeks. Gertrude was very patient, granting Menno this freedom. Even the children understood and were supportive. At least their father was at home with them! And the children could always tell when their father was deeply involved in a project. He would write, stop and read to check references, spend time in prayer, and then write again.

Actually Menno was somewhat amazed with himself at all the arguments he developed in an imagined conversation with Faber. He prayed that God would use the treatise to increase the freedom of the Anabaptists in relations to the Reformed believers.

While Menno was in the house writing, Gertrude took the opportunity to leave the children in their rooms and visit with friends. One day, while visiting a very a special acquaintance with whom she had become friends, she heard of the execution of another friend, the remarkable Maria van Beckum, whom she had met on a ministry trip. The report deeply affected her spirit, and when she returned home, Menno noted her sorrow.

He interrupted his work, and they sat together as Gertrude shared the news. Through her tears, she expressed respect for Maria and joy in her faithfulness and that of a woman who had died with her. Maria had come to the faith against her mother's wishes and was a radiant witness of the assurance of salvation. She was an especially influential witness of faith to many in the community. Maria had gone to visit her brother, John van Beckum, and was arrested. As she was being led away, John's wife, Ursula, made the unusual offer to go with her. Maria responded, "Only if you ask your husband's approval." He had reluctantly given it, and the two were led away together.

The report was that that their trial was by open court at

Belden, where they gave a clear testimony before many sympathetic persons. They were sentenced to be executed without delay; Maria was burned at the stake while Ursula watched. Then the authorities turned to Ursula and asked her to recant the "preposterous" claims Maria had made, but she would not. They took her to the stake and there, firm in her faith, she was burned also. This was a very great sorrow to her husband, who had let her accompany Maria for support but had not expected her to be executed.

∽

Gertrude was carrying their third child now, and she needed Menno's help with the family. He readily gave his time to help her, and they agreed that he would spend more time at home. An injury to his leg and the use of a crutch now made his trips increasingly difficult and actually increased the chances of being apprehended, because he was more vulnerable. When around people not known to him he would find a way to withdraw and carry his crutch rather than use it. Now, as often as possible, he went by carriage or by boat on the canals.

Though his trips did not end completely, on his most recent preaching mission, he hurried home to be with the family. He had no communication from Gertrude while away, so he was anxious to get home. He was concerned that their third child would be born while he was away. He hurried as quickly as possible, the last steps giving him pain with his lameness.

Gertrude greeted him warmly at the door with her usual gracious expressions of love. "You are in time, Menno, as you can see," she said, smiling, her hands on her large stomach.

And he was just in time, for in the afternoon only two days later, as Menno worked at his desk, she called for him. "You should go and bring the midwife, dear; it is time."

Menno quickly grabbed his coat and hurried on his way. He was soon back with the midwife, who was very efficient. Again Menno waited with concern and empathy for Gertrude, prayerfully pacing the floor in the next room. He soon heard the cry of a new baby. Their third child had arrived, another beautiful little girl, born without any problem.

"I'd have liked to have given you another son, Menno," Gertrude said, "but I am pleased to have a second daughter. Are you too disappointed?"

"Not at all, my dear. This is in God's planning," answered Menno. "We have a son, and when he grows up we can work together. We have a wonderful family and so much to be grateful for. We will trust God for our future, but thank him for each day together."

Gertrude smiled at him with no comment, continuing to quietly rock the baby. She truly loved their other two—and she practically adored Jan, their "little Menno."

Now the cries of a little one and the care of attending her changed the routine of the home. The two older children joined Menno in caring for their mother and the new baby. Each, in turn, handled the little infant as though she might break. Menno and Gertrude hovered over them and smiled in the joy of family togetherness.

As Menno gazed into the little face of their new daughter, Mariken, he thought of the Creator's greatness in this gift of life, of the wonder of bringing a child into the world. But he also thought of the threat of man's tyranny, and he pondered what the future would offer this little one. Whatever her lot, Menno could wish her nothing better than to walk with Jesus. For this he prayed, and also that each of the children could share in a church that was "without spot or wrinkle" in faithfulness to the Lord Christ.

⁓

As the persecutions continued, Menno and Gertrude discussed whether to move again. Such a move would be difficult for them, now with three children. The one security was that the magistrates were looking for Menno, the Anabaptist leader, not for a family, and the five frequently traveled with a small group to further disguise themselves.

After lengthy discussion with the elders, they agreed to commission Menno to work for a while in the city of Cologne. Within a few days they set out, traveling together as a family. They slowly made their way south, stopping for lodging at homes of believers. Dirk and his family would follow, but the two families would not spend much time together to remain inconspicuous.

After a few days, they turned west and came again to the Rhine, where they found passage on a small boat heading south. The boat stayed near the bank while the large barges plied the deeper waters. Menno promised that someday he'd take them on a boat ride on the Rhine at Cologne. After an hour they disembarked and began walking toward the city.

As they traveled with several other families, they moved very secretly from one farm house to another. Many of the houses where they stopped were too small to accommodate many guests, so quite often Menno and the family would sleep on the straw in the barn or a stable. A member of a congregation would often travel ahead and arrange lodging for them. In the community of faith, they never lacked an invitation to a believer's home, in spite of the danger to anyone found hosting Menno.

The constant moving was taxing for Gertrude, yet she didn't complain as she sought to support Menno in his ministry. As they traveled the last distance into the city, Menno carried Mariken while Bettjie and Jan walked alongside them. The two older children were often running and playing with other children in the small group of itinerants. The spirit of the children was innocent and joyful. Menno was sure that they did not fully understand the reason for their many moves.

Menno looked at Gertrude with a smile and said, "How carefree and trusting. I pray that they live in a time of great freedom and get to enjoy what we are prevented from having."

She reached out and took his hand, and they walked on with tears in their eyes but with the comfort of their love.

It had been thought wise by the leaders from East Friesland and the district of Holstein in Germany for Menno to move into the Rhineland, and when they learned of Dirk's feeling, they also commissioned his family to join the Simons family. It was best for Menno to leave an area where he was increasingly well known, lest he be found and arrested. Dirk and his family met the Simons family days later after they were out of the region and felt it safe to travel together for the remainder of the journey. The children of the two families had fun together despite the age differences.

Menno understood what it was like to be constantly sought by the authorities, and he knew well the tensions Dirk carried in seeking security for his own family and helping to find cover for Menno and his family. Members of the congregation were often questioned about them, and it put the members on the spot as how to answer. The congregation found it increasingly difficult to hide Menno in their community, so a move was fair to everyone involved. There were emotional farewells, and the Simons family set off south. Now that they were accompanied by Dirk and his family, the details of travel were more readily arranged. Dirk was sometimes able to secure carriage passage for them.

As they made their way carefully toward the city, Menno pointed out the changes from rural life to the more congested urban life that marked a large city. Suddenly, at a turn in the road, the whole city came into view. The spires of the great cathedral stood against the sky. Menno stopped and called the children's attention to the sights.

"The cathedral," he said, "is one of the largest in all of Europe. Someday I will take you all to see it, even show you inside."

"Will you explain it to us?" Bettjie asked, "and tell us the meanings of the differences in their religion?"

Menno looked at her with surprise. "If you are interested,

yes, I will tell you all about it and why we do not go to cathedral for our worship. This you should understand."

He looked over at Gertrude, and she nodded her head with a bit of a smile.

Although the elders had urged Menno to move for the safety of the family, Cologne would also provide him a new area for ministry. Once in the Rhineland, they were to meet Brother Antonius, an elder in the local church. Menno would serve with him as a bishop of the region. Menno hoped that they could stay in Cologne for some time, because there was greater tolerance in this city, and he could work with colleagues and spread the word of grace. Dirk thought that he would find a smaller community and work from that setting, perhaps in nearby Cleve in the edge of Germany.

~

Cologne was the capital of the Prussian Rhine province. It boasted a large and significant university and one of the largest and most famous cathedrals in the country. In many ways, it was a fortress of Catholicism, but in the shadow of the university many non-Catholic movements had found expression.

Earlier, there had been a dissenting movement led by a Cologne native, Gerhard Westerburg, who had gone to Münster in 1534 and was baptized. After his baptism, he and his brother Arnold baptized many in Cologne. Opposed by the archbishop, their work was violently suppressed. But word was passed that there was more tolerance in Cologne, where there was even a group of peaceful Anabaptists.

Menno's mission would be to work with this group. They had received a letter from Brother Antonius, and as they arrived at the outskirts of the city, he met them, welcomed them warmly, and then guided them to the home of a believing couple with whom he had arranged lodging for them. Antonius said he was sure this was a city large enough to hide the family while Menno ministered to the various small groups in the believers church.

Menno and the family were well received in Cologne. He was surprised at the new sense of freedom as he moved among friends in the city. After several days, Dirk took his family down the Rhine, to the nearby German duchy of Cleve, which would enable him to work with Adam Pastor, a tireless traveling evangelist in the region, while also relating with Menno, a short distance away.

The ruler of Cologne, Herman von Wied, had been trying to reform the evangelicals. When Anabaptists were apprehended, he sent clergy to convert them in prison. He was not against reform, but he wanted it along the lines of Erasmus, that is, discussion of differences with efforts at unity and respect. At least this approach allowed small Anabaptist circles to exist, and Menno was able to share the Word meaningfully among them.

The months passed peacefully for the family, and they enjoyed their life in Cologne. The children had a freedom they had not known elsewhere. They also joined others of their age in classrooms provided by the community. It was a good experience at study, building on what their mother had taught them in their home. Gertrude liked meeting with other women to shop, something she had not been permitted to do for a long time.

One day after lunch, Menno called the family together. "Today we visit the cathedral. There is no service this afternoon, and I should be able to show you the building and its beautiful symbols."

The two older children were enthusiastic, and the family set off. Soon they were in the heart of the city, and then in the courtyard around the cathedral.

They stood, looking up at the tall towers, impressed by its gigantic size. Jan said, "It makes me feel so small. I cannot see the top. And look at the size of the doors! Can we go inside?"

Carefully Menno opened a door and led them in. They paused to let their eyes adjust to the darkness. Then Menno began to explain, pointing out that the building was laid out in the form of the cross as a reminder of the death of Christ. They looked up at the tall arches, which, he explained, were supposed to keep the worshipper's focus lifted toward heaven. As they came nearer to the front, he pointed to the altar, the large crucifix, and the other symbols used by the priests to interpret their worship.

Bettjie said, "Why don't we worship in a large building like this? Its beauty is very attractive and must have special meaning for the people."

Menno knelt on one knee so that they could hear him better. "The church is not a building; the church is a fellowship of people who are followers of Jesus. It would be wonderful if there was the freedom in our country for people of different faiths to all have big buildings to worship in."

He paused, then continued. "Why we don't worship in this kind of building? Well, your mother and I once did just that. We understand the ritual and the claims made by the priests in baptizing infants and in performing a mass as though the sacrifice of Jesus happens over and over again. But once we met the risen Jesus, came to know him as our Savior and Lord, all of this was so empty. Salvation is in being forgiven by the Lord; it is in being a friend of God and living in obedient faith. We are the church."

He stopped and looked into their faces. "To know the new life in Jesus, to know that we are his children, this is the most important thing that we know and the one thing that your mother and I want each of you to know."

His eyes were wet as he looked into their faces. Almost embarrassed, Bettjie nodded her head, looked over at Jan, and said simply, "I think we are beginning to understand."

A priest moved through the area in front of the altar, and an attendant came to assist him in arranging for the next service. Menno discerned that it was time for them to leave, and he took the family quietly to the door where they had entered and stepped out into the pavilion. They paused for their eyes to adjust to the bright light, then they started down the street to make their way home. Menno and Gertrude walked quietly for some time, reflecting on the children's reactions to the cathedral.

~

During the following weeks, Menno was able to minister widely in and around the city. His travels frequently took him into Bonn, to the south. He enjoyed these trips, first making a brief walk from their home across the city of Cologne to the Rhine River. He was usually able to get passage on a barge up the river, even offering his help in a turn at one of the oars. He enjoyed the scenery, the slow pace of the time on the river, and watching the other boats they passed. He found himself dreaming of the day he could take Gertrude on a long ride up the river, perhaps even to Switzerland.

His ministry in Bonn was fruitful, as it was in Wesel, in the territory downriver near Cleve, where he sometimes worked with Dirk. On one occasion he took Bettjie and Jan along on a riverboat, as he had promised, and they met the Philips family.

Sitting quietly through the whole evening meeting in one of the homes was a challenge for the children. Bettjie found herself studying the faces as they sat in rapt attention, listening to her father interpret a passage from the book of Romans. They spent the night with Dirk and his family, and in the early morning made their way back to Cologne.

~

Membership in the free church continually increased. People responded to Menno's teaching by being baptized. His work had an increasing influence, and he was respected and welcomed by many new acquaintances. Menno reveled in the freedom to minister in the Word and interpret Scripture to his listeners.

He also ministered in various towns, such as Fischerswert and Illekhoven. He was grieved that a boatman who gave him passage down the Meuse River to Roermond was apprehended and then executed for this kindness. Menno made a very meaningful acquaintance with a deacon, Lemke Bruerren, at Illekhoven, and gratefully shared his hospitality. The two men developed a meaningful friendship.

After nearly eighteen months in the city, the active Protestant reformer in the area, an influential pastor named Albert Hardenberg, challenged Menno to a public disputation. This was not a new test for Menno, but the debate did not remove the difference between them, and tension continued to increase.

It seemed wise to Menno to again move his family. After serving in Cologne for more than a year and a half, they were on the road as fugitives from their oppressors.

"How I long for the day," Menno said to Gertrude, "when there will be freedom in society for people to believe as they choose, to stand before the Lord without the authorities trying to determine their faith."

"That would be wonderful," she said. "We must pray that the day will come when that will be a reality." She paused, and then added, "If not for us, then for our children."

They traveled first down the Rhine, the children once again enjoying the sights along the shoreline, but they also enjoyed watching the water carry them along. Larger ships in midstream frequently passed them. Menno chose to disembark by early evening, and they made their way toward the Maas River region to the north. They were able to find lodging there, negotiating with the landlord a reasonable price for a lengthy stay. Menno and Gertrude enjoyed the community and were content to live there for a few months, developing a small fellowship of believers.

But they soon felt that they needed to move again, this time to Schleswig-Holstein to the north. It was now late fall in 1546, and the weather was cool. The leaves were turning yellow. As the family traveled, they made their way east toward the Baltic Sea. There were many Mennists there who had fled the Netherlands and the persecution that had become so intense. Menno found lodging for the family in Wismar with brothers and sisters in the fellowship. While he knew this might only be temporary, it was an important stop for them. Gertrude had become ill and needed some time of seclusion and rest.

Menno found numerous Davidians in the area. Joris had preached in this region much earlier, and many continued to teach what they had learned from him. Menno could not remain silent in the face of this challenge and found himself engaged in discussions. He learned that the free church movement had lost some members of their Anabaptist fellowship in East Friesland to the Davidians.

In response, he wrote a letter that expressed his convictions regarding the kingdom of Christ, which is known by its impact as a leaven in society, as a salt to the earth and light to the world. "The kingdom is not present as an organization or as a visible structure but as the power of spirit and of faith in the one Lord, Jesus Christ," he wrote. He emphasized that the church is founded only on Jesus Christ, his redemption, and resurrection.

> That Jesus is Lord is the expression of his followers who are willing to be disciples even in suffering. As disciples we do not seek power or a dominant role in society. The disciples of Christ are "citizens of heaven" while living here in the world. We will do society the greater good by maintaining our integrity.

While the most intense opposition and difficulty for the Anabaptist movement was the persecution by the state in their attempt to crush the free church, Menno saw the Davidian doctrine as a threat as well. Confusion in the fellowship would rob it of stability. He had long been burdened by Joris's heresy; he considered it a serious challenge to the church's doctrinal integrity.

The debates between the two groups, however, increased the public awareness of both. In deep anguish Menno was confronted by the continued arrests of many of his elders, arrests often encouraged by the state-supported clergy. The result was the martyrdom of some of Menno's associates, a very serious loss for the church. Both Protestant and Catholic leaders were now in common cause against the Anabaptists.

~

Menno returned from a very fruitful preaching tour and hurried back to the family. He actually carried his crutch the last short distance, exhausted but eager to be with Gertrude and the children. They heard his knock, and as Gertrude opened the door, the two embraced while the children jumped around in excitement. Menno hugged each of them as he sat down in his favorite chair. In her usual helpful style, Bettjie brought tea for them each.

As Menno and Gertrude drank and the children gathered around, he reported to them the good response to the gospel. He told of the many people who had gathered to hear his sermons and of dozens who had responded to the gospel of Christ in repentance and faith. "Upon their testimony of a new birth in the Spirit and their commitment to live as disciples of Jesus, it was my privilege to baptize each in turn. There were several dozen persons baptized in various places."

The children listened intently to his report, and Gertrude said simply, "Praise the Lord. He is faithful as always."

Menno smiled at her, and said, "Yes, he is faithful, my dear, and that even with my limitations."

The children looked at his crutch and then watched as he bent over to kiss their mother with a lingering embrace. "You are not well, Gert," he said. "I had hoped you would be fully recovered. I'm sorry that I have not been here with you."

"But you were where you needed to be, Menno, in his ministry. The Lord takes care of me, and that with the children's help." She smiled at Bettjie and leaned back in the chair.

In the following weeks, Menno spent a more relaxed time with the family. He did try to give some special attention to his lame leg, but said sorrowfully, "I will need to live with it. The break didn't heal properly."

14
Church Tensions in
Lübeck and Emden

1547–1550

Like it or not, Menno had to recognize that his followers were being called Mennists. It was 1547, and he was called by the elders to come north again to Emden and debate with Adam Pastor. In a previous debate about baptism and other questions with Nikolaas van Blesdijk, Menno had been supported by Adam. At that time, along with the brethren Dirk Philips, Leenaert Bouwens, and Gillis van Aken, their brother Adam had been an amiable colleague. But in the months that followed, he had become more individualistic and independent.

The debate was called because Adam had come to hold a view that Jesus Christ did not exist as the Son of God previous to his coming into the world. Adam believed that Jesus had become divine by an indwelling, an incarnation in which God dwelled in Christ. This was a humanistic universalism contrary to the orthodox faith of the Christian church as expressed in the Apostles' and Nicene creeds. The Anabaptists held with both creeds, along with most Christian communities. Therefore, the elders were asking Menno to assist in holding Adam accountable to relate his views to orthodox Christian thought and if necessary to discipline him through the community of faith.

Menno once again secretly traveled north to Emden. Knowing the city well, he soon found his way to the lodging place of which he had been informed. The wind felt cool on his face, and the smell of salt in the air from the Baltic brought back good memories for him. He always enjoyed this city with its beautiful seaport, actually the largest city in East Friesland.

Located on the border area with west Germany in Lower Saxony, it showed a measure of tolerance, though Menno could not presume on this. After all, he recalled, Melchior Hoffman had come here in 1530 and had united the Sacramentarians who had fled here from areas of the Netherlands. The Reformed clergy had accepted him to some extent, especially because of his work among the Sacramentarians. They had allowed him to perform some three hundred baptisms in the vestibule of the *Grosse Kirche*. But the accommodation had been temporary, for it received enough attention from the civic and clerical authorities that they aggressively resisted his work. Hoffman had fled to Strasbourg, but before leaving he had installed the very effective Jan Trypmaker as his successor in the city.

Menno had learned of this man some years earlier through his deep interest in the faith of the martyr Sicke Snyder. Trypmaker had baptized Snyder two weeks before Christmas 1530. As for Adam, Menno and the other bishops agreed with the Reformed pastors that his views of Christ were heretical. This matter couldn't be ignored, both for the sake of the Anabaptist communities and for the sake of their reputation among the other church associations. Menno and his colleagues sought to include Reformed clergy at the Emden meeting. The authorities, under encouragement of the Reformed clergy, guaranteed safe passage. Though Menno was assured that he would not be arrested while in Emden, he kept his travel schedule and his time in the city very secret. But he moved among the group with freedom.

The Reformed pastors challenged Menno and his associates to bring clarity to issues concerning Christology, and this led to an intense but wholesome discussion. Both the Protestant leaders and the Anabaptist leaders rejected Adam's arguments, which clearly rejected the full deity of Christ.

Menno made a strong defense of the Anabaptists views on the basis of Scripture and the historic creeds. His conviction rang clear and strong that Jesus Christ is the only begotten Son of God, the one foundation on which we can rest our faith and life, distinctions similar to those of the Protestant leaders. It was especially important for Menno to speak to this because he had been accused of having a Melchiorite view of the incarnation. Now, as clearly as he could, he rejected this view of the "celestial flesh," even renouncing some of his earlier and somewhat vague presentation.

As he spoke, Menno affirmed the mystery of the incarnation, but declared that even with the mystery he was led by the Scriptures to affirm the divine and the human aspects of Jesus the Christ; quoting specifically from Philippians 2. While he did not know how the two natures were imparted to Jesus, he accepted this mystery with Paul. He quoted Paul's statement to Timothy, "Great is the mystery of godliness; God was manifest in the flesh, justified in the Spirit . . . received up into glory." Further, he quoted one of his favorite verses, from the beginning of the epistle to the Romans: Jesus was "declared to be the Son of God with power by the resurrection from the dead."

The day after the conference, Menno and his associates met to discuss the need for action with regard to Adam. As leaders, they had met to hold him accountable to the faith of the church, as they themselves were accountable. They were agreed together, and they acted together, in excommunicating him, which they did even while they assured him that they hoped for continuing conversation. The elders were in agreement that they couldn't just walk away from a man they had known as a brother. Menno sought to make clear to Adam that they were still praying for a change in his views and that they hoped that in the future they would see him walking with them again.

~

As Menno made his way home, he found himself resenting the inconsistency of the antagonism toward Anabaptists, as the persecution was now coming from the professing Christians of the Protestant state church. They themselves were dissenters from the Roman Church, and it was gross hypocrisy that they would not recognize the freedom of Anabaptists to be dissenters as well.

When Menno arrived home, he was still troubled by his thoughts of resentment. He sat down at his desk to write a cutting blast at the Protestant pastors. Menno's intent was to expose the shallowness of their claims. They had broken from the Catholic Church, true, but they had not fully broken from its formalities or from the habit of absolutizing religious rites. Nor were they tolerant of those who were dissenting from them. His language was earthy, but clear in his ridicule of their hypocrisy. He was appealing for them to recognize the free-church movement to be just as legitimate as their own movement.

Menno reflected on one of his earlier discussions with John a'Lasco. Menno had asked him whether a new Reformed theologian, John Calvin, was supportive of the hostility his church was expressing toward the Anabaptists. Lasco had quipped back, "I'm sure that he supports us, for he has read something of your writings and has written about you in specific words. For example, Calvin has said, 'You cannot imagine anything more conceited than this ass, anything more insolent than this dog.'"

Menno had made no comment to Lasco, for he himself had made cutting remarks about others with whom he disagreed. He simply smiled as he remembered how Gertrude had reminded him to be more understanding and mild in spirit. Later he learned that while in Strasbourg, John Calvin had married Idaletta Storder, the widow of the Anabaptist, Jean Storder, who died of the plague in 1536. Perhaps, he thought, this new relationship in Calvin's life would influence his thinking and his attitude toward the Anabaptists.

As Menno wrote, he became more and more intense about the issues and heatedly expressed his views. He wrote pointedly about what he saw as a perversion in the Protestant church's teaching on the way of salvation. Having broken free from Rome, the Protestants were actually little better in their lifestyle and showed little restraint in behavior. He wished that in their emphasis on salvation by grace through faith, they could understand grace as God's acceptance of us into covenant relationship and that discipleship was "the obedience of faith" expressed in this covenant. This walk in faith was their assurance, their security, and their joy in being reconciled to God in and through Christ. He hoped that they would take covenant accountability more seriously.

For Menno, the new life in Christ meant a reconciled relationship with God, expressed in daily discipleship with dependence on the power of the Spirit for holiness of life. This new life in Christ was something far more rewarding, more satisfying, than anything he had known as a priest in the Catholic Church. His disagreement was with them as well, but he focused especially on his difference from the Reformed clergy.

> All they desire is that men say what they ask of them, especially the priests of the papacy. Bah, what dishonorable knaves and scamps these confounded priests and monks are! The devil take them. The rascal pope with his shorn crew have deceived us long enough with their purgatory, confession, and fasting. We now eat whenever we get hungry, fish or flesh as we please, for every creature of God is good, says Paul, and nothing to be rejected. But what follows in Paul's statement they do not understand; namely, them which believe and know the truth and partake with thanksgiving. How miserably the priests have had us poor people by the nose, robbing us of the blood of the Lord, and directing us to their peddling and superstitious transactions. God be praised, we caught on that

all our works avail nothing, but that the blood and death of Christ alone must cancel and pay for our sins.

They strike up a *Psalm, Der Strick ist entzwei* and *wir sind frei*, etc. [Snapped is the cord, now we are free, praise the Lord] while beer and wine verily run from their drunken mouths and noses. Anyone who can but recite this on his thumb, no matter how carnally he lives, is a good evangelical man and a precious brother! If someone steps up in true and sincere love to admonish or reprove them for this, and point them to Christ Jesus rightly, to His doctrine, sacraments, and un-blamable example, and to show that it is not right for a Christian so to boast and drink, revile and curse, then he must hear from that hour that he is one who believes in salvation by good works, is a heaven stormer, a sectarian agitator, a rabble rouser, a make-believe Christian, a disclaimer of the sacraments, or an Anabaptist!

This burst of emotion was a release for Menno. He hoped to expose the inconsistency of the state churches. But that exposure had to be done with integrity, and it had to show his faith in the community of believers he led.

Menno pursued his writing with even more diligence than in the past, now that his ability to travel had become limited, especially with his crippled leg, the difficulties with his crutch and the need to avoid being easily detected. It was one way he could help the church to be a disciplined community and to express the new life in the Spirit.

∼

About this time Dirk Philips brought news to Menno and Gertrude learned that their close friend and colleague in ministry at Leeuwarden, Elizabeth Dirks, had been executed on May 27, 1549. The news hit them hard, and they were distraught. For some time they wept in each other's arms. Later Dirk provided great detail about her arrest and trial.

Elizabeth had been imprisoned and then executed in Leeuwarden, her adopted hometown, where she had been working and was so well known. On returning from one of her Bible-teaching treks, she had been arrested along with an associate, Hedgie Fritz.

The magistrates who arrested Elizabeth, knowing that she worked closely with Menno, claimed at first that she was Menno's wife. Elizabeth was forthright in saying, "In no way, I belong only to the Lord; I have never known any man."

They cruelly tortured her on the rack and with thumbscrews crushed her nails until the blood ran, seeking information that could lead them to Menno. Under excruciating torture she prayed for God to relieve the pain, who answered by giving her freedom from pain and a boldness that amazed her captors. She had been brought before the council in repeated sessions and grilled with questions, which she answered with brief yet pointed statements.

The lords asked, "What are your views with regard to the most adorable, holy sacrament?"

She answered, "I have never in my life read in the holy Scriptures of a holy sacrament, but of the Lord's Supper."

They responded, "Be silent, for the devil speaks through your mouth."

Elizabeth said, "Yea, my lords, this charge is a small matter, for the servant is not better than his lord."

"You speak from a spirit of pride," they replied.

To this she said, "No, my lords, I speak with frankness."

Again they asked, "What did the Lord say, when he gave his disciples the supper?"

She asked in turn, "What did he give them, flesh or bread?"

One of the lords said simply, "He gave them bread."

Elizabeth said insightfully, "Did not the Lord remain sitting there as they ate? Who then would eat the flesh of the Lord?"

The procurator general had been very rough in the trial, seeking to get Elizabeth to recant, or at least to expose her partners in the faith. But at no time did she implicate others; she was steadfast and forthright in expressing her own faith in Christ.

Dirk said, "We are so grateful for her witness, her clear expression of faith, and her care in not exposing any of us. If my role were as well known by the authorities as yours, I would be sought in the same searching manner that you are."

Elizabeth and Hedgie were in adjoining cells, Dirk reported. The turnkey had a special attraction to Hedgie, a middle-aged widow, and in sympathy for her, he left her cell door unlocked, which he dared not do for Elizabeth. Hedgie made her escape and disappear into the countryside. There seemed to have been no pursuit because the magistrates were primarily focused on Elizabeth, probably because of her popularity and her effectiveness as a teacher.

After a very lengthy trial, the procurator sentenced Elizabeth to death. They led her from prison to the river, where she was placed in a bag and drowned for her faith in Christ. A priest had offered Elizabeth the crucifix and urging her to kiss it in penitence. She had said simply, "This is not my God; my God and Savior is in heaven."

Menno and Gertrude sat in silence as Dirk continued his report. They were gripped with deep sorrow, contemplating the loss of another effective ministry partner. Menno could still smile as he thought of her ingenuity in escaping from the convent at Leer in the clothing of a milkmaid. When he was in Leeuwarden, they had studied the Scriptures together, and along with Hedgie, they had witnessed and taught Bible. Menno had shared the privilege of commissioning Elizabeth to serve, like Priscilla in the early church, as a deacon among the Anabaptist congregations of the region. It was a great loss to the church; she was loved by the people in and around Leeuwarden as a Bible teacher, as a deacon and as a leader. To Menno and Gertrude, Elizabeth's martyrdom felt as though one of their own family had been executed.

Menno rejoiced that the answers Elizabeth had given were true to the faith. He was quite impressed with one of the insights that she had shared. "Her comment that Jesus was sitting there in his body when he broke the bread and gave it to the disciples, saying, 'This is my body given for you'—that's a very insightful remark. And how true. Jesus was pledging himself to the death for them in that symbol, and this is an expression of the new covenant. And our sister, in her answer, was pledging herself to the death for Christ and his truth."

More women in the free church were literate than in the larger society, and Menno knew that, through Bible teachers like Elizabeth, the congregations had grown so rapidly. As women, they were able to conduct Bible studies in their homes without being readily detected. Menno was sure that with Elizabeth's death, God would raise up others in her place, but it was not easy to say goodbye.

"Elizabeth was free to do what I would have liked to do if not for my family duties," Gertrude said softly. "But I wouldn't trade having the children." Menno nodded, knowing how deeply she felt about her desire to teach.

As something of a tribute to Elizabeth, Menno resumed writing *The True Christian Faith* with renewed vigor. The title page carried the familiar words, "For other foundation can no man lay than that is laid, which is Jesus Christ." The document was a beautiful evangelical statement of the centrality and uniqueness of Christ. Menno sought to clarify the nature of what it means to walk with the risen Lord, of the joy of a life of holiness, and of freedom through the Holy Spirit. He found pleasure in taking pen and putting his thoughts to script.

> Behold, my reader, such a faith . . . is the true Christian faith which praises, honors, magnifies, and extols God the Father and His Son Jesus Christ through loving fear and fearing love, for it recognizes the good will of the

Father toward us through Christ. It recognizes, I say, that all the promises to the fathers, the expectation of the patriarchs, the whole figurative law, and all the prophecies of the prophets are fulfilled in Christ, with Christ, and through Christ.

It acknowledges that Christ is our King, Prince, Lord, Messiah, the promised David, the Lion of the tribe of Judah, the strong One, the Prince of Peace, and the Father of the age to be; God's almighty, incomprehensible, eternal Word and Wisdom, the firstborn of every creature, the Light of the world, the Sun of Righteousness, the True Vine, the Fountain of Life, the true Door and Shepherd of the sheep, the true Foundation and the precious Cornerstone in Zion, the right Way, the Truth, and Life, the promised Prophet, our Master and Teacher, our Redeemer, Savior, Friend, and Bridegroom. In short, our only and eternal Mediator, Advocate, High Priest, Propitiator, and Intercessor; our Head and Brother.

~

Thinking of the martyrdom of so many in their circle, Menno and Gertrude regarded each day together as a gift from God. They cherished the children the Lord had granted them. It was a joy for Menno to see how the two older, Bettjie and Jan, did much of the housework for Gertrude, whose health continued to deteriorate. Whenever the family needed to move, they were especially grateful for Bettjie's assistance, young as she was.

As the children grew, Menno felt it was time to share more fully with them the reason they were constantly moving. Again and again the children had begged to stay at a place they liked, and it was painful to tear them away and move once more. But now they began to understand the pressures under which their parents lived.

"Father, I'd much rather be on the move than to lose you," Bettjie said.

Menno smiled as he hugged her. "Thank you, my sweet, and I don't want to miss out on being with you."

Menno held her by the shoulders. Looking into her eyes, he asked, "And what makes you think that you might lose me? Aren't we in God's care?"

"Well, some of our friends have told us stories of the death of people because of their faith. They have told us that they are concerned that this doesn't happen to our parents."

"In God's providence he will protect us if we are careful, for he has given to me and to your mother the privilege of being parents for you, my Bettjie, and for Jan and Mariken, and we will share as fully as we can."

That evening he sat with the three of them, Mariken on his lap, and Bettjie and Jan on the floor at his feet. He told them stories from the Bible.

"You know, children, how much your mother and I love you, and we wish only the best for you," he assured them. "We've wanted you to go to school with other children, but this hasn't been possible. We wish that we could live at one place, and you would not need to leave your friends so often."

They nodded, and Bettjie said, "And so do we!"

Menno smiled at her outburst; Bettjie had become quite insightful. "But we are called to serve our Lord and his church. You have heard me preach, and you know that Christ Jesus and his gospel are the most important things in our lives and the most important things for others. We are called by God to share this good Word."

Menno knew that the children could understand only a little. But he also knew that they would grow day by day in knowledge and come to their own personal faith commitment. Menno was sure they were covered by the grace of God in Christ. Over the next few years, they would come to the age of moral discernment and accountability. He wanted them to each understand the gospel so that they could respond on their own to the call of the Spirit.

What a privilege it would be when that time came to share in their baptism! Menno and Gertrude were confident that at the appropriate time, the children's' moral accountability would bring them to a public commitment to the Lord.

After their meal that night, Menno gathered the children around and asked them to join in the evening prayer:

> We pray Thee humbly, as our dearly beloved Father, to look upon us, Thy children, persecuted for the sake of Thy holy Gospel, and earnestly desirous, in our weakness, to live devoutly in this world. Be pleased to keep us in Thy Word in fatherly fashion, in order that to the end of our days we may remain constant in Thy Word and Gospel, revealed by Thee to the plain and simple, and hidden to the wise ones of this world. Look upon us with thine eye of pity, as Thou didst upon the prodigal son, upon Mary Magdalene, upon the woman of Canaan, the centurion, the thief on the cross, Zacchaeus, and upon all those who have with tears desired Thy grace.
>
> And feed our souls in like fashion with that heavenly bread, Thy holy Word, by which our poor souls may live, and give us to drink of that living water, the Holy Spirit, who can lead us into all truth, whom the world cannot receive because it knows Him not, nor sees Him, even as Thou Thyself, O Lord, hast said. For the world lieth in wickedness, said John, and we will perish with all that is therein; but he that doeth the will of God abided forever. Amen.

In the following weeks Menno made numerous brief trips

without involving the family, the most extensive one being into Prussia. A number of Anabaptists had earlier fled there from the Netherlands, and there were people from Flanders among them, so Menno asked Dirk to make the trip with him to minister to these believers and ordain leadership for the flock.

It was a long journey to Danzig, across farmlands, past brick kilns and bakeries filling the air with their aroma. Once they arrived, they met with a group of believers and enjoyed their fellowship for the next days, helping them to form a congregation. It was a joy to see their emerging sense of community, something much needed by those who'd settled there. He and Dirk had appointed leaders, and Menno was pleased with the strengths of the people chosen.

After a week with them, Menno was ready to return home. Because he had a deep sense of the Spirit's work and guidance there and was assured of the group's faithfulness, he encouraged Dirk to stay longer among them as an elder and a theologian. Menno told the group, "Dirk is without doubt the leading theologian in our group. He is much better at theology than I am." Dirk smiled at this compliment, his eyes twinkling above his full beard, even as he bowed his head in modesty. Menno continued. "I can leave now with confidence in the strength of this fellowship, knowing that Dirk's work with your appointed elders will bring unity and stability."

Menno set off in the early dawn to make his way home. One of the farmers in the group gave him a ride on his cart for some kilometers. From there he traveled by foot with the use of his faithful crutch. The trip was strenuous, but he was able a number of times to find a ride, which made the trip briefer than many previous ones.

Menno was scarcely home when news came of another martyrdom. The inquisition had increased its activity, and more of their friends had been arrested. Niel Kyper, a close friend and brother in the Groningen area, had been executed. Kyper's wife,

Gerrit, and the family were left without support. Gertrude and Menno had enjoyed Gerrit's hospitality in the past, and they were now concerned for her and children.

"Menno, you must write to her," Gertrude urged. "She needs our comfort."

He wrote a tender and encouraging letter, expressing their faith in her steadfastness to Christ and admonishing her to live in victory of spirit with her children.

> Much grace and peace, and a kind greeting! Fervently beloved sister in the Lord, whom my soul cherishes and loves! Since the Lord has now called you to widowhood, my fatherly faithful admonition to you is, as my dear children, to walk as becomes holy women, and I hope that you may, even as the pious Anna, serve the Lord in the holy temple, that is, in His church with a new and upright conscience, with prayer and fasting, night and day serving the needy saints which the virtuous widow of Sarepta in Sidon did for faithful Elijah in the time of drought and scarcity when she received him in her hospitality and fed him with her tiny bit of meal and oil. So shall the meal of the holy divine Word be not lacking in the vessel of your conscience, and the joyous oil of the Holy Spirit from your soul. . . .
>
> This brief greeting written to you in true paternal faithfulness receive in love and ponder it earnestly. All the saints that are with me salute you. Greet all pious friends. Pray for me. The eternal saving power and fruit of the crimson blood of Christ be with my elect and much beloved sister forever. Amen! M. S., your brother who loves you fondly.

Gertrude affirmed the letter's approach. "I am trying to hear it as she will in reading it," she said. "I'm sure she will be encouraged by that letter and will know of our love and prayers."

"Gert, before we send this we should have a special prayer for God's blessing on it." They bowed their heads and he led in prayer, "We pray thy Fatherly mercy, with sorrowful hearts, and out of the depth of our souls, for all men, for kings, and for all magistrates, in order that we may live a quiet and peaceful life in all godliness and gravity. For, said Paul, this is good and acceptable in the sight of God our Savior, who would have all men to be saved and come to the knowledge of the truth. Amen.

"O Lord, be pleased to enlighten them with thy grace, those that are still in darkness and who walk in the ways of death and err unwittingly and receive all those who with a firm trust come to thee seeking thy grace and mercy, confessing that they know not, and that henceforth they would live after the will of God, to reform their lives, do penance, be converted, be born again, believe the gospel and obey it, confess it before the world and live it. This we pray, O holy Father, for thy great name's sake."

∿

Menno now preached frequently at evening gatherings in the region. Because of some of the issues brought to him about discipline in the life of the congregation, he emphasized the meaning of a covenant with Christ and a new birth in grace. "This covenant," he said, "emphasizes a call to discipleship and a life of faithfulness in the church. As a congregation, we need to support one another in prayer, to counsel each other on principles of Christian living, and to discipline one another when needed to keep the church true and authentic as a community of the regenerate. This church, purchased by his own blood, is truly a *gemeinde*, a fellowship of the regenerate."

When Menno consulted with the elders of the region, they expressed a need for integrity in the life of the church but also for special care in exercising discipline and accountability. They were concerned that discipline should not be discouraging, especially to new believers. Menno agreed to consider writing on this subject in the future. He too wanted to safeguard discipline from becoming a legalistic function that would eclipse grace, so in 1550 he wrote a booklet entitled "On Excommunication." After his typical introduction citing Jesus as the foundation, he offered an extensive treatment on faithfulness to Christ.

> I dare not go higher nor lower, be more stringent or lenient, than the Scriptures and the Holy Spirit teach me; and that out of great fear and anxiety of my conscience lest I once more burden the God-fearing hearts who now have renounced the commandments of men with more such commandments.
>
> It is evident that the congregation or church cannot continue in the saving doctrine, in an unblamable and pious life, without the proper use of excommunication. For as a city without walls and gates or a field without trenches and fences, and a house without walls and doors, so is also a church which has not the true apostolic exclusion or ban. For it stands wide open to every seductive spirit, to all abominations and for proud despisers, to all idolatrous and willfully wicked sinners. Yes, to all lewd, unchaste wretches, sodomites, harlots, and knaves, as may be seen in all the large sects of the world which however pose improperly as the church of Christ. Why talk at length? In my opinion, it is the distinguished usage, honor, and prosperity of a sincere church if it with Christian discretion teaches the true apostolic separation, and observes it carefully in solicitous love, according to the ordinance of the holy, sacred Scriptures.
>
> It is more than evident that if we had not been zealous in this matter these days, we would be considered and called by every man the companions of the sect of Münster and all perverted sects. Now, however, thank God for his grace, by the proper use of this means of the

sacred ban, it is well known among many thousands of honorable, reasonable persons, in different principalities, cities, and countries, that we are innocent of and free from all godless abominations and all perverted sects, as we also make known and announce very deliberately to the whole world, not only by our doctrines and walk, but with our possessions and blood in evident deed.

As Menno continued the treatise, his concern was that the peaceful Anabaptists should be understood not as legalists but as believers committed to being faithful. He didn't want the Anabaptist church to have members who were careless about sin, something he saw in the Protestant churches. The attempt of the Protestants to cover such persons by simple doctrinal declarations was little better in his mind than the way the Roman Catholic Church justified some people through their interpretation and use of the sacraments.

Menno learned that leaders of the Reformed church frequently accused him of being heretical in his interpretation of the incarnation and on other matters of doctrine. This was a carryover from his earlier identification with the thought of Hoffman, and he had sought to clarify this at the Emden conference. On the occasion of that meeting, he had written that all believers should recognize the incarnation as a great mystery, affirmed by Jesus' words, "I and the Father are one." Menno prepared a short tract on this theme to clearly express his faith in the divinity of Christ as the Son of God. In the tract, he sought to make clear that he continued to reject the views of Adam Pastor. While Adam did believe that Christ is the only mediator between God and man, he did not believe in the eternality of Christ or that Jesus was the eternal Son of God.

In the fall of 1550, after some conversation with Gertrude, Menno took special pains to write a clear and gracious tract on this matter. He entitled it "Confession of the Triune God." Following his customary title page, he began his composition:

Menno Simons wishes all his beloved brethren and sisters in the Lord, grace and peace, an unbroken, sound, and pure faith, genuine brotherly love, a sure and living hope, and a God-pleasing, irreproachable conduct, confession and life, from God our heavenly Father, through His beloved Son, Christ Jesus, in the power of the Holy Ghost. Amen.

We believe and confess with the holy scriptures that there is an only, eternal and true God, who is a Spirit; the God who created heaven and earth, the sea and all that is therein; the God whom heaven and earth and the heaven of heavens cannot contain, whose throne is heaven and whose footstool is the earth, dwelling in light which no man can approach unto; whom no man hath seen, nor can see; who is an Almighty, powerful, and an ever-ruling King, in the heavens above and on the earth beneath; whose strength and power none can stay; a God above all gods, and a Lord above all lords; there is none like unto Him, mighty, holy, terrible, majestic, wonderful and a consuming fire; whose kingdom, power, dominion, majesty, and glory is eternal and shall endure forever. Besides this only, eternal, living, Almighty sovereign God and Lord we know no other; and since He is a Spirit so great, terrible and invisible, He is also ineffable, incomprehensible, and indescribable, as may be deduced and understood from the scriptures.

This one and only eternal, omnipotent, incomprehensible, invisible, ineffable and indescribable God, we believe and confess with the scriptures to be the eternal, incomprehensible Father with His eternal incomprehensible Son, and with His eternal, incomprehensible Holy Spirit. The Father we believe and confess to be a true Father, the Son a true Son, and the Holy Spirit a true Holy Spirit, not physical and comprehensible but spiritual and incomprehensible. For Christ says, God is a Spirit. Inasmuch as God is such a Spirit, as it is written, therefore we also believe and confess the eternal, begetting heavenly Father and the eternally begotten Son, Christ Jesus. Brethren, understand my writing well, that they are spiritual and incomprehensible, as is also the Father who begat; for like begets like. This is incontrovertible.

Menno went on to quote from the Gospel of John, chapter 1, that "the Word was made flesh and dwelt among us." Again he quoted from Colossians 1, that the Christ "is the image of the invisible God." And he quoted at length from Philippians 2, as he often did, of the incarnation of the Christ, "who being in very nature God humbled himself to become in very nature human," calling this the greater christological passage.

Dearly beloved brethren, understand me correctly when I say He is the eternal Wisdom, the eternal Power. For as we believe and confess that the Father was from eternity and will be unto all eternity; that He is the First and the Last, so we may also freely believe and confess that His wisdom, His power, His light, His truth, His life, His Word, Christ Jesus, has been eternally with Him, in Him and by Him; yea that He is the Alpha and the Omega.

Menno wrote at greater length on this matter than was often true of his polemics, for he saw this as a major theological issue. He finally concluded,

Dear brethren and sisters in Christ Jesus, receive this with the same mind in which I have written it. Read it plainly among the brethren, and understand it in a Christian manner, and beware, beware, yes beware, of all disputations, discord, and division. This I desire from my inmost soul for the Lord's sake. The sincere, evangelical peace be with all my beloved brethren and sisters in Christ Jesus. Amen. September 9, 1550.

15
Mediator for Harmony from Westphalia to Groningen

1550–1552

It was April, and the beauty of spring was everywhere across the land. The new life was an inspiration to Menno's spirit even though he felt the chill of the early spring weather. As he walked, he was anxious for the warmth of a house. The churches of the area had recently celebrated Easter, and Menno had enjoyed teaching on the resurrection of the Lord Jesus. Now he was traveling again, and the weary miles took their toll. He was making his way carefully into West Friesland, once again to visit brothers and sisters in Groningen and in Leeuwarden. This was familiar territory, and at times he sought roads that were off the main thoroughfares so he would not be sighted.

As Menno traveled, he paused frequently for rest, and as he viewed the polders he reminisced about working with his father. It was always a challenge to arrange the ditches to drain the land and then arrange the pumping of water from one level to another so that it would flow to the sea. In their small operation, much of this movement of water had to be done without the help of a windmill.

Menno had left Gertrude and the children in Holstein while he made this extensive and difficult trip. Although his leg was much better after extended rest, his limp and the burden of his increased weight made travel a test of his fortitude. He often set out in the early morning before many others were on the roadways. When he could, he arranged to be carried by farm carts between villages, the farmers often covering him with hay. Occasionally he was able to get passage on the water, selecting carefully among the numerous boats on the canals.

Secretly and somewhat fearfully, Menno made his way to the edge of Leeuwarden. It didn't take him long to find the home of Klaas Jans, where he was greeted warmly. Frau Jans wanted to hear all about Gertrude and the children and was especially concerned about Gertrude's health. Menno reviewed in detail the story of the last days of their associate Elizabeth Dirks, recounting her clear witness before the council and her victorious death in the river. The community of faith was deeply saddened yet, rather than being disheartened by the persecution, was strengthened by her witness.

During the next few days in the community, Menno learned that the magistrates possessed an updated description of him. In 1550, a man captured at the Maas near Roermond, Jan Neulen from Visschersweert, had confessed under torture that he had heard Menno preach in a pasture at night. He described Menno as a stout, heavy man, with a brown beard, who had a serious limp that made it difficult for him to walk. Now, as Menno was frequently traveling about in the community, small groups of Anabaptists walked with him and several of the men used walking sticks so that Menno's use of the crutch would not be so conspicuous. Sometimes the pain in his hip was so severe he would need to stop and rest, and those walking with him would stay nearby.

But moving around at night, under the cover of darkness, Menno was able to preach to gatherings of many interested people. These meetings were held in various barns in different areas around the edge of the city. In response to one of Menno's messages on justification by faith and the new life in covenant, a godly sister expressed that her spirit was deeply troubled by the depravity of her nature. Menno answered briefly that only by facing our limitations honestly can we appropriate the Spirit's power for victory. But he promised to write her a more extensive treatise.

Back at the Jans' home, he wrote a meditation that he hoped would help the woman to know the assurance of her salvation and not to be discouraged by a perfectionist view of discipleship. He emphasized that we are not a community of perfection but of dedication to be disciples of Jesus.

With a brief introductory statement on the love of God and a quotation from 1 John 3:1 concerning the marvel of his love that we should be called his children, Menno wrote a few lines to undergird her faith.

> Since it is plain from all the scriptures that we must all confess ourselves to be sinners, as we are in fact; and since no one under heaven has perfectly fulfilled the righteousness required of God but Christ Jesus alone; therefore none can approach God, obtain grace, and be saved, except by the perfect righteousness, atonement, and intercession of Jesus Christ, however godly, righteous, holy, and un-blamable he may be. We must all acknowledge, whoever we are, that we are sinners in thought, word, and deed. Yes, if we did not have before us the righteous Christ Jesus, no prophet nor apostle could be saved.

Menno slipped in and out of Leeuwarden with great care and, for those few days, avoided detection by the magistrates. He saw his time in the city as a special ministry of strengthening the believers and seeking greater unity in the community of faith. There were many differences of thought that were more cultural than theological. Some members were Flemish immigrants to the region. But Menno emphasized that unity was to be found in their commitment to Christ and in their common respect for the God's Word.

Back home, the children seemed to have grown so much, though he had been gone only two weeks. It was no longer easy to hold Bettjie and Jan, now ten and eight, on his lap at the same time. Bettjie had matured considerably and now, as a somewhat precocious hostess, she brought her parents each a cup of tea, pulled up a chair, and settled herself to listen to her father. But Mariken, the most precocious of the three, was in Menno's lap as always, hugging him and asking for another story. Menno felt wonderful as he held them and basked in the intimacy of his family.

After some days of rest and regaining his strength, Menno felt he must continue writing. In the first weeks that he was home, he just wanted a time of freedom in his own wonderful circle of love. But he had also used the time for church ministry in a few group meetings, though much of his ministry now was through his writing.

With the Prussian brothers and sisters in mind, Menno wrote to the leaders in Danzig. He sent special greetings to Dirk, assuming that he was still there, and assured them they were not forgotten. Menno reported that he had talked with the elders at Leeuwarden and Groningen, and they supported Dirk and the ministry in Danzig. They wanted Menno to encourage Dirk to spend even more time with the refugees in Prussia, developing their congregational life.

Some weeks later, after he had regained strength, Menno pushed himself to make several trips into the border areas of the Lowlands. More of his recent travels, however, had been in the region around Emden. In these meetings he was always on the lookout for people the Lord had gifted for the ministry. When he found such a person, who was confirmed by the community of disciples, Menno would commission him for ministry. At the Emden conference, Menno was impressed with the insight and effective presentations of Leenaert Bouwens. Soon after the conference, he and Dirk presented Leenaert to the congregation there and, with their vote of support, Menno then ordained him to the ministry. He was very thankful for colleagues like Dirk and now Leenaert to share the responsibilities of ministry.

Leenaert had become a very effective evangelist and was able to travel to areas too risky for Menno, particularly to the west. Menno continued to work with the congregations in the region of Emden and the lower Saxony. In view of Leenaert's influence and mobility, Menno ordained him as a bishop.

Over the next few months, Menno met frequently with Leenaert. They studied Scripture, and Menno served as his mentor. Leenaert's attitude was very positive; he found joy in the spread of the movement. He reported great success in evangelism, and within the first several years of his ministry he baptized nearly four hundred in north Holland, with many more converts across West Friesland.

Leenaert's enthusiasm bubbled over in his encouraging reports. "I've just come back from Flanders," he told Menno. "And in spite of the persecution, people are eager to know and to follow Christ! It seems that on each occasion when people are executed and give their lives for their faith, many others are impressed that there is meaning and satisfaction in being a disciple of Christ. People are hungry for an assurance of salvation by faith more than a religion of form."

"That is wonderful," Menno replied. "I am thankful to God for the ministry that he has given you. I've prayed for younger people to carry the work far beyond what I am now able to do. At present I am ministering more to believers in our congregations, but they always bring seekers along to the meetings. And I am finding similar attitudes and responses. Evangelism is happening through the witness of the members of our congregations when they share with their neighbors. People are deeply disappointed in the state churches, in the compromises of the Protestants, for people are seeking more than doctrinal answers; they want assurance of salvation in the grace of Christ."

"Yes," Leenaert said. "They have found that the sacraments administered by the priests do not in themselves give them peace with God, and neither does simply reciting creedal formulas. But they have also become concerned for the society and want a faith that offers freedom and social well-being."

"We have a message for them," Menno said. "Rather than being kept in slavery to patterns of religious works that don't bring peace, we can engage them in walking with Christ. I am finding that many thinking people respond to the gospel when the focus is on Jesus. In Him they understand the Scriptures as a call to a new life. And as we have found, there is nothing to match what it means to walk with the risen Lord."

"Yes, Menno, and the response is so great in these regions of Friesland that in some areas the majority will soon be Mennists."

"I wish we didn't use that name, Leenaert. We are followers of Christ. I wish that name had never been used to describe us."

"I know, but your leadership has united the movement, and like it or not, this is our identity in the land."

"But the church is the body of Christ. He is Lord and we are simply his servants."

Leenaert nodded. "Menno, it is so wonderful to work with one whose spirit is complementary rather than competitive, and you are that kind of person."

Menno was grateful for the compliment. "Remember that, Leenaert, for someday you will be standing where I am, the senior leader to others who will need your support."

Menno enjoyed the opportunity to meet and encourage Leenaert's wife, who asked him how Gertrude was able to accept and survive the strain of the threats. She herself was in constant fear for Leenaert's safety.

Menno said kindly, "For her understanding and support I am forever grateful. I'm sure it is because she shares the same vision that motivates me and counts this work as her calling as well as mine."

She looked at him in silence for a bit, and then said simply, "Thank you for that word. It speaks to me."

Menno and Leenaert were able to travel secretly and to preach at numerous gatherings in the region. They visited Harlingen, the seaport village where Leenaert and his wife had lived. They made a trip south to Warga, where Leenaert had been well received. Many people had been brought to the faith through the remarkable Bible teaching of his colleagues from several years earlier, the martyr Elizabeth and her associate Hedgie.

After a fruitful time in the Warga community, they felt led to travel on to Workum, where they held meetings in barns or in the fields away from the villages. This region was more familiar territory for Menno. Menno and Leenaert actually were near Menno's boyhood home of Witmarsum, but they skirted it. Menno wished they could visit Pingjum and call on his brother Theo, but it didn't seem wise.

Workum was not very far inland from the coast, and Menno enjoyed time at the shore. They were hosted by a family whose house was the meeting place for a small group. The people of the Lowlands were so very gracious to him, welcoming him back into their community with great joy. There were many immigrants from Flanders there who responded enthusiastically to the message of Christ. But their culture and lifestyle created some distinctions among the believers, for the Flemish and the Frisians each had deep pride in their own culture.

"We'll need to keep the conversation open between these various groups," Menno told Leenaert, "or we'll have a division in the church over matters that aren't important."

"True enough, Menno. However, it is never easy to discern when things are only cultural differences or when the truth itself is carried in different cultural forms."

"That's true," Menno said, "but at least we can distinguish between the principles taught by Scripture and the applications we make of those principles as practices in life."

"I think I understand. However, I do want people to take the applications we teach with all seriousness. Somehow discipleship needs to be made visible."

This comment gave Menno a twinge of concern. He didn't want to push Leenaert on it, but lately he had been discerning a more dogmatic spirit developing in his brother—something that in his thinking seemed too legalistic—and he thought Leenaert should be more discerning of the differences. He wanted to talk about this but waited for a more fitting occasion.

～

In the community of Workum, the two men heard a report about Nikolaas van Blesdijk that came as no surprise to them. He had followed David Joris to Basel and married Joris's oldest daughter, Susanna. The earlier writings between the Menno and Van Blesdijk had focused on their differences rather than their respective family life. Menno learned that Van Blesdijk was continuing to write, but there was evidence that on some things he had come to differ with the views of his father-in-law.

It was not long until Van Blesdijk renounced Joris and began to cooperate with the state church, becoming an eloquent opponent of the teaching of his father-in-law. After having written to counter some of Van Blesdijk's earlier teachings, Menno was now confronted with a man whose views were more like the Reformed Church.

At Emden, Menno had sought to encourage some of the Flemish believers. He tried to help them discern the cultural differences that influenced their discipleship. He sought to help them understand that when we read Scripture, we must recognize elements we bring to our reading that can shape our interpretation. A reader must be totally honest and open to the written Word.

Menno taught one simple rule in reading the Old Testament, and that was to discern when a passage was only descriptive and when it was intended to be prescriptive. He had found this to be helpful in his Bible teaching, and he was sure that it would help the congregations there to adjust to cultural differences.

Several months earlier, while traveling from Germany into Friesland, Menno had stayed with Claes Jansz, who was supportive of his ministry. Claes himself had a very effective ministry, which was a joy to Menno. Now, a few weeks later, Menno learned the sad news that Claes had been arrested as an Anabaptist and beheaded for having provided shelter to Menno.

As Menno made known his sorrow and deep grief over the death of this wonderful brother, one of the members of the congregation came to him with some additional reports. He handed Menno copies of several letters from other friends who were now imprisoned in Antwerp. Menno read them carefully, finding them to be refreshing testimonies of faith.

But the letters gave him only part of the story, for another report came to him on September 1, 1551. Menno's friend Jerome Segersz, along with Hendrik Beverts, had been burned at the stake in Antwerp. Jerome's wife, Lysken Dirks, had been imprisoned with Jerome, but in a different cell. The two were held in the Steen Castle, on the Scheldt River near Antwerp, which was used as a prison. Because Lysken was pregnant, the authorities postponed her death until after she delivered the baby. During their imprisonment, both Jerome and Lysken wrote numerous letters that were wonderful expressions of faith and admonitions to faithfulness.

The letters—ten by Jerome and three by Lysken—were rich with meaning, faith, and their understanding of Scripture. The congregations of the region copied them and passed them through the region. Menno received several and carried them with great gratitude to share with Gertrude.

As Menno read and reviewed the letters with Leenaert, the faith of these remarkable people gripped them. The letters were amazing expressions of trust in the Lord and commitment to the way of the cross. They also revealed much about the suffering inflicted by the authorities and the nature of the inquisition. Menno was impressed by the support of the congregation of believers, who not only prayed for prisoners but also risked their own lives to take food to the prison and provide the couple with notes of encouragement.

When Menno got home, he tenderly told Gertrude of the death of their friends, the execution of the men, and of Lysken's pregnancy and the difficulty of her imprisonment. They shared their sorrow and concern together while reading several of the letters. Together they prayed for Lysken in her suffering, asking the Lord to give her the strength of his Spirit, that she would know the presence of the Lord in her cell and freedom in her spirit even in her suffering and loneliness. Gertrude took the letters and hid them in their quarters, saying that she wanted to read each of them carefully—but later.

As Menno reflected on the death of his friends, he was well aware that this could just as easily have been him. But God in his grace was sparing him for his work, and he meant to use his freedom diligently. But with the wonderful expressions of faith and victory even in death, the testimony of the martyrs was something to celebrate rather than mourn. Menno began to write a few verses for the congregation to use in group singing.

> We are people of God's peace as a new creation.
> Love unites and strengthens us at this celebration.
> Sons and daughters of the Lord, serving one another,
> A new covenant of peace binds us all together.
>
> We are children of God's peace in this new creation,
> spreading joy and happiness, through God's great
>   salvation.
> Hope we bring in spirit meek, in our daily living.
> Peace with ev'ryone we seek, good for evil giving.

We are servants of God's peace, of the new creation.
Choosing peace, we faithfully serve with heart's devotion.
Jesus Christ, the Prince of peace, confidence will give us.
Christ the Lord is our defense; Christ will never leave us.

Several weeks later, a small delegation came to Menno and
asked if he would be willing to meet again with Adam Pastor. They
believed that Adam had taken Menno's writings seriously, and they
hoped that he might be persuaded to return to the fellowship.
They wanted to arrange this meeting at Lübeck in Schleswig-
Holstein, not too distant for Menno. This would mean a trip for
Menno back to the beautiful Baltic seaport where they had met
earlier with Van Blesdijk.

He agreed to the meeting, and the elders made arrangements
for it to take place in the late summer of 1552. Menno wanted
to take Gertrude along, but they decided it would not be wise.
He decided he must take the hymn he had just written, as it
would speak to the issues discussed there.

As Menno and the elders met with Adam, the discussions
focused on the understanding of the incarnation and of the sovereignty of the Lord. But congenial as Adam was, he was quite inflex-
ible. After the first conversation, he and Menno shared in a few sub-
sequent meetings that were rather fruitless. Adam made some
adjustments, but even so, instead of being reinstated into the fellowship, he chose to continue following his more independent stance.

"Well, at least we tried in a brotherly spirit," Menno said to
the elders. "Our attempt at reconciliation was the best we could
do." On that note, they bid each other God's speed and went each
his own way home.

A few weeks after the meeting, Menno learned that Adam had
moved into the Rhineland for freedom to carry out his own mission. He ministered there briefly, and a few months later Menno
heard that he had died in Münster with a few followers.

~

When Menno was back home, he began to edit his brief but moving document on the grace of God, "The True Confession of Faith." He was sure he must prepare it for publication; he thought it might be his best work yet. It sought to relate his doctrinal insights with more practical questions of faith and life. As he wrote, he emphasized that our reconciliation with God is solely on the grace we know in Christ.

> For all the truly regenerated and spiritually minded conform in all things to the Word and ordinances of the Lord. Not because they think to merit the atonement of their sins and eternal life. By no means. In this matter they depend upon nothing except the true promise of the merciful Father, given in grace to all believers through the blood and merits of Christ, which blood is and ever will be the only and eternal medium of our reconciliation; and not works, baptism, or the Lord's Supper. For if our reconciliation depended on works and ceremonies, then grace would be a thing of the past, and the merits and fruits of the blood of Christ would end.
>
> Oh no, it is grace, and will be grace to all eternity; all that the merciful Father does for us miserable sinners through His beloved Son and Holy Spirit is grace. But reconciliation takes place because men hear the voice of the Lord, believe His Word, and therefore obediently observe and perform, although in weakness, the things represented by both signs under water and bread and wine.

Soon after his return from Lübeck, Menno suffered a mild stroke. The doctor ordered him an extensive period of rest, to Gertrude's relief. She was certain that his condition had been brought on by extreme exhaustion, and now she became his caregiver, keeping him from exerting himself. This was difficult for Menno to accept, as he was not given to idleness.

After a week, the most difficult stage of his illness passed, and he concentrated on doing things with the family. For the next several weeks Menno simply enjoyed being with them and sought the Spirit's gift of patience.

The family was now living somewhat secretly and relatively safely in the region of the Overijssel. Menno became impatient over the confinement and his inability to function freely. He wanted to continue writing about issues in the church. But, for the present at least, he found it difficult to mentally engage in his usual arguments with the clarity he wanted. Perhaps due to his stroke, the threat of persecution now weighed more heavily too. His fear that he and his family might be found increased, so together they began to pray about where it was best for them to make their home.

In this time of illness and fear, Menno began composing some lines in verse that might be sung by the church. He entitled the composition "Prayer in the Hour of Affliction" and saw it as an expression of his inner joy and sadness, structuring the verse in lines that would fit a well-known tune.

> A sad and doleful care,
> This news, dear brother, share,
> Which God hath now for me prepared.
> > A chastening He applies,
> > My inmost heart He tries,
> > My flesh in sore affliction lies.
>
> His godly wisdom sure
> That ever shall endure,
> > Knows perfectly
> > That now I lie
> > In anguish sore.
>
> Help, Lord, I Thee implore
> That I by grace once more,

After this grievous blow
May comfort know!
In His grace.

Ah, faithful Father, Lord,
My flesh has strength no more,
This earthly house Thou breakest sore.
The vile world hates me quite,
For this Thy witness bright;
Thy cross I bear, with grief not light.

And yet—adversity!
Thy hand Thou lay'st on me,
And presses so
My flesh lays low!
Yet rest I me

Upon Thy promise free
Which ever sure shall be;
And praise Thy majesty
In all eternity!
My Father, God and Lord.

Incline Thy face once more
In this disease and sickness sore;
Give patience, strength, in grace
The brightness of Thy face,
Mid sorrows that come on apace!

That I may constant be,
Whate'er Thy way with me;
And not the last,
My soul hold fast!
Yes, Father, so kind.

Preserve in pious mind
Thy sons, who sadness find,
 In faith and doctrine whole,
 So prays my soul!
 I rest in Thee.

~

After two months, Menno was quite well again—"his old self," as Gertrude said. The family was fond of the community in which they were staying, but the extra attention the doctor had given Menno became known, and he feared it might increase the threat. They decided to move again, for the safety of the family, to be sure, but also for those who had shielded them.

They did not want to say where they might journey to, but together they agreed they would travel in north Germany and even toward Prussia.

"Perhaps," Menno said to Gertrude, "with my more weakened condition, we needn't travel very far this time. Hopefully we can find a place to live in Holstein and find some measure of peace. If that is possible, we can share more time with our growing children, and I will write and extend my ministry by the printed page."

With raised eyebrow she said, "That would be good, even though I think you are up to the rigors of travel. Let's pray for guidance to find a place where we can be at peace and you can do just that. You may even be able to share the faith more broadly if we can find a printer near our next home."

"That may be true, but with my crippled leg, it becomes more difficult for me to travel. In my recent trips, one thing has become obvious—the church is growing far beyond any work I am able to do. God has raised up so many voices, men and women, who are witnessing and teaching the Scriptures. Dirk is a wonderful colleague, a theologian, and Leenaert is an effective evangelist and also a very exacting pastor."

"They are effective leaders," Gertrude said. "But I'm also glad that we have been led to include women in ministries of teaching the Word. They touch many lives, especially other women, who might be difficult for men to reach."

"Yes, I'm sure that is one reason the movement of our peaceful Anabaptists is spreading so widely. There are now many small gatherings in homes to study the Scriptures. But Gertrude, the women are paying a price along with the men."

Gertrude looked down and said, "Even so, I'm glad for the freedom for women to serve."

"I think such a leadership role for women is unique to our movement, Gert. I don't find this happening among the Lutheran or the Reformed churches. And in the Roman Church, such a role for women is so very limited, as you know from your time in the Beguinage."

Once settled in Holstein, and with the encouragement of Gertrude, Menno began rewriting some of *The Foundations of Christian Doctrine* and seeking wider distribution for it. He also was concerned that he be heard with clarity on the kingdom of God as the divine rule and as a kingdom of peace. He wanted it understood that the peaceful Anabaptists were not seeking to overthrow the government but were asking only for a new level of freedom. They would still be a minority in society but a community of faith committed to follow Christ according to their understanding from the New Testament.

Charles V continued to use violence to keep the Holy Roman Empire intact. He had earlier waged struggles with the Protestants, but after making some adjustments for them, he continued the intense persecution of the Anabaptists. He had defeated the Protestant princes in the Schmalkaldian War in 1547, but then he signed the Treaty of Passau, in which he gave the Protestants free exercise of their religion. But that freedom only led to another Diet that attempted to find agreement on religious liberty and political equality between Protestants and Catholics. In none of it was there any indication of greater tolerance for the Anabaptists.

This intolerance and the continued executions haunted Menno. In some way, he believed, the authorities must be made aware that they would answer to God on this matter, that tolerance and social freedom was the only way for the future.

There continued to be many reports of the death of leaders who were friends of Menno and Gertrude. Their esteemed brother Hendrik Anthonisz, an associate from Amsterdam, was arrested with five associates in June, then they were severely tortured on the rack and with thumbscrews all summer. All six were burned at the stake on August 6, 1552.

Menno knew most of these men. He bowed his head in tears, praying for their families and for an end to the atrocities. Anthonisz had been a gracious host to them when they had first gone to Amsterdam to minister. Menno contemplated writing a letter to the authorities in an appeal for tolerance, urging that matters of faith should be discussed and religious differences should not be met with capital punishment. With a price on his head, he felt it could not get much worse for him as a result of the letter.

Late in 1552 he wrote this focused treatise and called it "Confession of the Distressed Christians." He sought to encourage his brothers and sisters in their suffering.

> The brightness of the sun has not shone for many years; heaven and earth have been as copper and iron; the brooks and springs have not run, nor the dew descended from heaven; the beautiful trees and verdant fields have been dry and wilted, spiritually, I mean. However, in these latter days the gracious, great God by the rich treasures of His love has again opened the windows of heaven and let drop the dew of His divine Word, so that the earth

once more as of yore produces its green branches and plants of righteousness which bear fruit unto the Lord and glorify His great and adorable name.

The holy Word and sacraments of the Lord rise up again from the ashes by means of which the blasphemous deceit and abominations of the learned ones are made manifest. Therefore all the infernal gates rouse themselves, they rave and rant and with such subtle deceit, if God did not show forth His gracious power, no man could be saved. But they will never wrest from Him those that are His own.

On a visit from Danzig, Dirk was commissioned by the elders to consult Menno about an unfortunate situation concerning their esteemed brother, Gillis van Aken, one of their most effective evangelists. Van Aken traveled extensively across Friesland and north Germany, baptizing many. But his popularity had gotten him into trouble; there were reports that he was guilty of adultery with several women in different locations. The elders of the region had asked Dirk to find Menno and meet with a group at Mecklenburg, Germany, where they'd deal with the matter.

Menno lived not far from the city of Mecklenburg, yet with the rigors of travel he suffered from the strain on his hip. It was helpful not to travel alone, and Dirk was able to secure a wagon on several occasions for them to ride. When they arrived at Mecklenburg, the group welcomed them enthusiastically; it was something of a reunion, with Menno as their leading elder.

They asked Menno to guide their deliberations. He called them to prayer, then gave a brief message on why this discipline was necessary for the integrity of the movement. After careful reporting and review of the charges, it was agreed that they must excommunicate Van Aken, banning him from ministry and fellowship with the church until he should give evidence of repentance.

~

In his next treatise, Menno wrote extensively on a variety of topics, seeking to stimulate conversation. He began with justification by faith, discussing the character of genuine faith as covenant offered in the grace of God in Christ by which we are enabled to believe. This he followed with a section explaining the errors of the state church preachers and why the Anabaptists do not hear and follow them but rather read and follow the Scriptures for themselves.

The next sections clarified the Anabaptist interpretation of the Scriptures where it differed from that of the Protestant preachers. Menno sought to show the importance of discerning the meaning of a passage rather than simply quoting single texts. He did this on various topics including believers baptism, infant baptism, and the Lord's Supper. Expounding on the text of Micah 6:8—"He has showed you, oh man, what is good, and what the Lord requires of you, to do justly, to love mercy and to walk humbly with thy God"—he wrote that faith brings us to a quality of righteousness that is relational and consequently leads us to a pious and unblamable life in Christ Jesus.

Menno interpreted the Lord's Supper as a sign of covenant, as opposed to other preachers' claim that it remits sin. He wrote against swearing the oath and giving ultimate loyalty to the king as contrary to Scripture that calls us to serve the King of kings. Finally, he wrote a conclusion calling people to reject the teachings of apostate and worldly religious leaders and to follow the Word of the Lord, which "Christ Jesus Himself has taught us from the mouth of His Father and sealed it with His own blood. Rev. 1:5, 1 Pet. 1:19, Acts 20:28."

Menno concluded this treatise with a brief statement about Jesus' teaching on love for God that issues forth in love for others. It is this love that enables us to treat all people with justice and respect, to extend peace in a quest for mutuality for all peoples. He quoted Jesus' words in answer to the attorney who had questioned him about the great commandment, stating that the first commandment is to love God with all of one's heart, soul, mind, and strength, then adding that the second commandment is of like character, to love one's neighbor as oneself.

"On these two commandments, says Christ, hang all the law and the prophets," Menno wrote. "Love is the total content of Scripture. Everyone that loves, says John, is born of God and knows God. He that loves not knows not God; for God is love. And he that dwells in love dwells in God and God in him. Without this love, life is all vain, whatever we may know, judge, speak, do, or write."

Menno laid down his pen and leaned back in his chair with a sigh. He would much rather preach the gospel to hungry listeners than to deal with problems in the church. But the church has always had problems because of our humanness, he concluded. God's transforming grace keeps changing us, but we are never perfect. He thought of Romans 8:29, "We are predestined to be conformed to the image of his Son," bowed his head and began to pray.

"Father, it is you that I seek in longing, and I long for only you in my seeking. It is you that I find by living in love, and I love you in my finding. Help me to worship you in joy, and above all to enjoy you in worship. This I pray in the grace of Jesus Christ my Redeemer. Amen."

16
Publishing and Dialogue from Wismar and Lübeck

1553–1557

Menno and his family now lived in Wismar, in the Mecklenburg region of Germany, and it turned out to be one of their longest stays in one place. They kept the location secret, but there was less of a threat in this region and consequently they had a measure of peace. They really felt like a family, and it was evident that Menno's health was better.

Gertrude frequently asked Menno not to risk himself by being so open in his ministry and not to travel so much. "Your writings are in print, and they are being spread across Germany as well as across north Holland," she said. "This is a unique ministry, and it provides in a concrete way a base for stabilizing the thought and discipline of the renewed church."

"Yes," Menno responded, "but my writings also identify me as one whose stance is neither Catholic nor Protestant, and from those writings pronouncements are made against me. I am so indebted to the grace of God that I continue to be free, that he enables us to share life together. Even so, I must continue the work to which God has called me."

⁓

News came of another group of martyrs executed in Amsterdam. Herman Jansz, a maker of long, hooded cloaks, was arrested while carrying out his business on the corner of the city's Popelstreech. Four other Anabaptist men with him were also arrested. All were executed by burning at the stake. The sentence read that Jansz was a disciple of Gillis van Aken.

Menno was so very grateful that he and the family were, at least for the present, able to have escaped persecution. With some respite, but with the continued persecution constantly on his mind, he picked up his pen to write an appeal to the authorities, called "A Pathetic Supplication to All Magistrates." In it, he called for understanding, tolerance, and conversation. Menno affirmed his belief that the better course for all was a free society in which divergent views could be aired, but those holding such views would still be considered loyal to the state.

He introduced the treatise with a lengthy section on the teachings of Christ, the apostles, Cyprian the martyr, the African bishops, the Nicene Council, and the apostle Paul. He then distinguished the peaceful Anabaptists, now generally called Mennists, from various heretical sects, including the Münsterites who, "contrary to God's Word and every evangelical scripture, also contrary to proper policies, set up a new kingdom, incited turmoil, introduced polygamy, etc., matters which we oppose vehemently with God's Word, condemn and censure as is evident and patent from all our acts and public activity."

Menno addressed the authorities respectfully as "Honorable and Wise Sirs," as "Your Highnesses," and as "Dear and Noble Sirs."

> Be pleased, in godly fear, to ponder what it is that God requires of your Highnesses. It is that without any respect of persons you judge between a man and his neighbor, protect the wronged from him who does him wrong, even as the Lord declares, execute judgment and justice, assist against the violent, him that is robbed, abuse not the stranger, the widow, the orphan. Do vio-

lence to no man, and shed no innocent blood, so that your despised servants and unhappy subjects, having escaped the mouth of the lion, may in your domain and under your paternal care and gracious protection, serve the Lord in quietness and peace, and piously earn their bread, as the scripture requires.

Under the continued emotional weight that she carried and with the intensity of the opposition and persecution around them, Leenaert's wife, Maria, wrote a very pointed and concerned letter asking Menno for his help. She specifically made a strong plea for him to release her husband from the ministry because of the persecution the Mennists were suffering. Maria related how she lived in fear for her husband's life, and she entreated Menno and the elders to grant Leenaert a release. She needed here husband with the family, and she feared for his safety.

Menno recalled his many good times of fellowship in their home, and he understood something of Maria's tender spirit and her fear. He wrote her in deep empathy, but reminded her that they all lived under the sovereignty of God. Menno was confident that God would fulfill the purpose of their lives and their mission. He then stated that actually it was not himself but the church that had called Leenaert to the ministry, and it was not in Menno's power to release him. He sought to encourage her to walk in faith and submission to the Lord.

Dear sister, strengthen your husband and do not weaken him, for it is required of us that if we love God, we shall also love our brethren. In short, prove yourself to do to your neighbor what Christ has proved to be to you, for by this only sure and immutable rule must all Christian action be measured and judged. Behold, worthy and true sister, as the church calls our beloved brother to the office and service, I cannot conscientiously interfere unless I should love flesh, your flesh, more than Christ Jesus my

Lord and Savior and my sincerely beloved brethren. May
the Almighty merciful Father act in this matter according to His divine good pleasure and guide the heart of
my beloved sister so as to be resigned to His holy will. I
sincerely thank my beloved sister for the gift of love that
you have sent me. The Lord repay you in heavenly riches of eternal glory. My wife greets you with the peace of
the Lord. The Lord Jesus Christ be forever with my most
beloved friend and sister. Amen. Your brother in the
Lord, Menno Simons.

Knowing that he was considered the leading elder in the
Anabaptist brotherhood, Menno took his responsibility with
great seriousness. In recent years his work with Leenaert had been
an encouragement and a blessing to him. He rejoiced over this
brother's success in evangelism. There were hundreds of new converts, Leenaert reported to Menno, and there were many baptisms. This growth kept Menno busy ministering to many groups
and seeking to unify the rapidly growing church. New converts
also added new ways of thinking in a congregation, and it was a
challenge to help members hear one another in respect and love.

In another written defense of the faith, Menno crafted a
lengthy polemic to express his convictions on the nature of salvation. He emphasized that we are being saved by grace as a special gift of God, then followed it with an explanation of the
nature of the believer's new life in Christ. The booklet, like all
his writings, opened with his favorite quotation from Paul, "For
other foundation can no man lay than that is laid, which is Jesus
Christ." He wrote with pastors in mind, even though he hoped
laity would read it as well, so he entitled it "A Brief Defense to
All Theologians."

For the Protestant pastors, he addressed ten topics, stating that he wished to engage in a theological disputation with the state church. Menno hoped the treatise would open dialogue with the Protestants. They too had left Rome, and they should have an understanding spirit toward their free church neighbors in the Anabaptist movement.

The list of themes on which he wrote was extensive: the qualifications of evangelical preachers; the unchangeable character of the doctrine of Christ; Christ's perfect teaching and perfect sacrifice; the source, nature, and fruit of regeneration; Christian faith and love; obedience to God's commandments; Christian baptism; the Lord's Supper; ecclesiastical excommunication; and the Christian life. These were all topics on which he had been criticized, and he attempted to give biblical perspectives on each. He wrote at considerable length, seeking to provide clarity and an exercise in biblical interpretation.

Menno was disappointed that, as the writing was circulated, he received no reply from the Protestant clergy and no request for discussions. In fact, he received only one response—from the clergy of Wesel on the lower Rhine, who said that instead of discussion, they preferred that the executioner deal with Menno! This attitude, also reflected in the neighboring town of Cleve, was the very attitude Menno was addressing.

With this sharp retaliation, he wrote another address, entitled pointedly "A Reply to False Accusations," in which he sought to further answer the criticisms.

"These accusations," Menno wrote, "include the charge that we are Münsterites; second, that we are disrespectful and disobedient to the magistrates; third, that we are seditionists; fourth, that we hold all property in common; fifth, some have invented the charge that we practice polygamy; sixth, that we deny penance and grace to persons who after baptism should fall into sin; seventh, they say that we are vagabonds not realizing that this fugitive pattern is not our choice but forced upon us by intolerance and persecution."

He wrote at length to interpret the Anabaptist separation from the state church, delineating many points of difference.

"This writing," Menno commented in summary, "in spite of my limited education should show such that I do have a knowledge of the Scriptures. At least it is my attempt to speak to the issues which they should want to discuss and on which I desire to share with 'learned theologians.'"

He waited, but again they gave him no audience.

⁓

As Menno and the family enjoyed living in lower Saxony, a request came for him to make another trip into Friesland. The elders in the region wanted him to assist a congregation in calling a leader to replace one who had been arrested. Menno and Gertrude wrestled with this decision in prayerful contemplation

"Menno, do you think you are up to this?" Gertrude asked him.

"Well, I've been traveling around here in ministry. I believe I can make this trip if the Lord gives us his confirmation of peace as we consider it."

"What about the threats for your arrest? Do you not have fear of that?"

"Yes, Gert, I have some fear, and that makes me be very cautious."

"You are courageous."

"Ah, but courage is not the absence of fear. It is a refusal to surrender. Once we surrender to our fear, we then stop living."

She nodded, "Yes, true, but let's take a few days to pray and think about it."

Two days later, they decided Menno would make the trip. Gertrude urged him to spend the money to take passage in a carriage as often as possible. It was increasingly difficult for him to walk except slowly, having hurt his leg again with a twist that he was sure had affected the socket in his left hip.

After a few short rides with farmers on their carts, he took passage on a carriage. Concerned that he not be trapped inside the carriage, he asked the driver if he could ride on top, seated next to him. He said he could better stretch his game leg by letting it hang down, and riding there would also enable them to visit. The driver agreed, and Menno climbed up beside him.

They had traveled some distance when they came to a roadblock where soldiers were checking all who passed by for identification. With no way to leave the carriage, Menno sat there contemplating what he might do.

Several soldiers walked over to the carriage and asked, "Is Menno Simons in there?" Quickly Menno swung down, hiding his pain, opened the door of the carriage and called loudly to the passengers inside, "Is Menno Simons in there?" They called back a resounding "No. He isn't in here." Menno turned to the soldiers very respectfully and said, "They say he isn't in there." Acting indifferent, he climbed back up to the carriage seat, again concealing the pain.

The soldiers conferred for a moment, and then said to the driver, "You may go on." As they drove off along the road, he looked over at the driver, who seemed unaware that Menno had just escaped with his life.

⁓

Though the trip was difficult for him, Menno was able to complete his mission. He stayed for several days and shared in a number of congregational gatherings. The spirit of their expressions of faith and the quality of the candidates they had chosen pleased him. He assisted in the ordination of leaders for several of the congregations. He also was encouraged to receive blessings for his ministry, which was leading the congregations to unity in Christ.

He knew that Gertrude would be concerned about his wellbeing, so he hastened to get back home. He found passage in a cart hauling produce to the next city, yet the driver took him beyond that, to another farmer who would take him further.

There seemed to be changes each time he returned home. Bettjie was becoming a fine young woman. She was an avid reader, and it taxed her parents to find books that she could borrow. Menno was amazing how Gertrude's teaching had helped each child in their development. How he thanked God for his Gert and the children. He prayed for God to give them a more relaxed family life together and asked for a wonderful future for each one.

In the late evening, Menno gathered the children around and told them a story from the Bible. Then he asked them to join him as he prayed,

> Blessed Savior, Thou hast in the Gospel taught Thy children that fear Thee saying, "Take no thought for thy life, what ye shall eat and what ye shall drink, nor for the body what ye shall put on. Is not the life more than food and the body than raiment? Consider the birds of the heaven. They sow not, neither do they reap, nor do they gather into barns, and your heavenly Father feeds them nevertheless. Are you not much more than they? Which of you can add one cubit to his stature by being careful for it? And why do you take thought for raiment? Consider the lilies of the field how they grow. They toil not, neither do they spin—I say unto you that even Solomon in all his glory was not arrayed like one of these.
>
> "If God so clothe the grass of the field, which today is and tomorrow is cast into the oven, would He not much more do such for you, O ye of little faith! Therefore, do not be filled with care saying, What shall we eat, or, What shall we drink? Or, Wherewithal shall we be clothed? After these things do the Gentiles seek, but your Father knows that ye have need of all these things. Seek ye first the Kingdom of God and His righteousness and all these

things shall be added unto you. For this reason we pray, Our Father which art in heaven, hallowed be Thy name. Thy kingdom come . . ."

And the children joined in quoting the remainder of the Lord's Prayer.

Menno kissed them each and sent them off to bed. Turning to Gertrude he said, "What a wonderful blessing God has given us that we were graced with these three lives. His grace to us is awesome." She smiled, pleased that he recognized this.

Menno told her about the soldiers stopping the carriage and his quick action. She chuckled as she shook her head and said, "God is so good, once more he has kept you safe."

～

While they were enjoying a measure of peace, persecution continued unabated, especially in West Friesland. In most of the areas Menno knew well, numerous people were put to death for their faith. But at the same time, hundreds of people were being converted and joining the Anabaptist movement. It was evident that the testimony of the martyrs encouraged others to examine the faith and respond to the gospel.

While living in Wismar, the brothers called on Menno to meet a special emergency. In the winter of 1553 a group of Zwinglian Reformed Protestants in London had come under persecution by the authorities there and had found it necessary to flee England. Having been refused entrance to Denmark by the Lutherans there, they had arrived at the seaport at Wismar. It was the dead of winter, and the boat was marooned in the ice just off shore in the Baltic Sea. The refugees were desperate, but the Protestants of Wismar would not help them.

Menno called the elders together, and they agreed their congregations should meet this difficult challenge. Although most of the Protestant people of the area were afraid of the consequences if they offered aid, the Anabaptist community gathered food and clothing. While the boat was marooned, the people were able to walk on the ice and pull light sleds with supplies. A small contingent of Anabaptists from the congregation carefully braved the ice and met the group, offering them food they had brought along. The Anabaptists then offered the refugees the shelter and warmth of their homes.

Once they were all ashore, Menno talked with the leaders of the English group, among them John a'Lasco, formerly of Poland and an earlier acquaintance, and Hermes Backereel. The language barrier made conversation difficult for most of the group, so they sent to Norden in East Friesland for Martin Micron to interpret. The Reformed believers wanted Micron's help to engage in further conversation with Menno. Many of them were interested in understanding the faith of their gracious Anabaptist friends.

The discussion was a very intense interchange, perhaps due to Micron's service as interpreter. He focused on their differences rather than on what they had in common. But they discussed the paths they had walked. Both had rejected the position of the Roman Catholic Church and its sacramentalism, but this meant they needed to be clear on the way of salvation by faith.

For Menno, salvation was experienced in a personal faith response to Christ, a conversion through participation in his grace, evidenced by identification with him as his disciples. But for Micron, it involved a more philosophical discussion of the role of grace in God's electing a people to be his own. He placed less emphasis on conversion and a lifestyle of discipleship.

Menno's position on the nature of the church was also different from Micron's. Menno emphasized that God's primary calling was for us to respond as believers, which meant a personal conversion to Christ in which we become responsible members of his covenant community. This conversion resulted in a community of believers who were disciples of Christ in their lifestyle; they were separate in society, a fellowship of the powerless rather than a movement seeking to be among the powerful.

Micron expressed the Reformed Church's commitment to serving Christ as a calling to which God predestined them. In response, Menno affirmed that the Anabaptists were also seeking to serve Christ and that he recognized that no one group had control of the kingdom of Christ. But they needed to be true to their convictions from the Word of Christ; they needed to ask how they could best impact society, seeking the freedom to live for Christ and his kingdom.

Menno also engaged in discussion with Backereel. The talk between these two men was more practical; they met on more common ground as lay theologians, yet Backereel was very Zwinglian in his interpretation, seeing a much more immediate relation between the church and state.

Menno and the family had at this time moved again to Emden, which made it possible for Menno to arrange for further meetings with Backereel. In one session, Backereel asked Menno where he lived, but Menno did not reply. However, Backereel learned from a neighborhood child where Menno's home was. Menno's only recourse was to agree to another interview only on the condition that the location of his dwelling be kept secret. Backereel gave his hand on this, promising that it would not be divulged.

To Menno's sorrow, just a few days after their discussion, the people of Emden knew where he lived. Within two days, Menno quietly took the family and left Emden. They moved some distance to the south in secrecy, living like fugitives for a few days before making their way to Holstein, where they found lodging on the estate of Baron von Ahlefeldt, who had welcomed the Anabaptists to settle in his territory. During his military service in the Netherlands, Ahlefeldt had gotten to know the peaceable Mennists and had great respect for them. He was very hospitable to many refugees, and he strongly defended his practice to the government authorities.

~

Menno had not been at Holstein long when the elders of Mecklenburg asked him to make the short trip to meet with Gillis van Aken. They had been working with him for some months, and they had been assured of his regrets, repentance, and recommitment to faithfulness to the Lord. But the elders wanted Menno present if they were to release him from their ban and give him freedom to minister among them.

Menno met with the group, sitting with Gillis and listening to his testimony. Gillis's renewed level of integrity impressed Menno, and he agreed that he should be reinstated to ministry in the church. Yet, as he journeyed back to the Ahlefeldt estate, Menno wondered whether Gillis could succeed as notably as he had earlier.

The episode reinforced to Menno the need for leaders in the church to provide encouragement and accountability to one another. As this conviction grew, he began sending word to his friends in leadership, inviting them to a conference of elders. This meeting, he affirmed, was important for building the strength needed by elders for the work, for promoting integrity within the church, and also for encouraging each other. Persecution was taking a serious toll; so many leaders had been put to death that the young congregations often needed to call inexperienced people into leadership.

Within a few weeks he welcomed his friends to the gathering. They met at a place he arranged in the city of Wismar, which was readily accessible for them. Among those who came to the meeting were Dirk Philips, the younger leader Leenaert Bouwens, Gillis, who was just a few years older than Leenaert, Herman van Tielt, Hans Busschaert, Hoyte Rienk, and a few other brothers and sisters.

Menno was very pleased with the group that gathered for this conversation. With a great spirit of camaraderie, all shared in commonality but not in competition. And in relation to the members of their congregations, they carried a very affirming role.

Menno wanted the elders to recognize the importance of discipline. While it was needed to safeguard the witness of the church, its focus should be on helping and reclaiming those in error. He was concerned for the integrity of the holy life, but knew that love for the erring person must be the central aspect of any discipline.

The few days together were refreshing, even though there were times of intense debate. They discussed what they had learned about the earlier Schleitheim Synod, held two decades earlier in 1527 by their associates from south Germany and Switzerland. Menno related how the group, in prayer and conversation, had come to a clear sense of the Holy Spirit's presence and leading. He saw it as a model for them, and as the group prayed and discussed issues together, they also came to a clear sense of unity in the Spirit.

They then drafted what was to be known as the Wismar Resolutions, which contained nine articles. The first five called for clear and severe discipline of one another. The sixth article dealt with marriage requirements, the seventh with the use of litigation before a worldly court, the eighth concerning restrictions on the bearing of arms and any exceptions for such, and the ninth on limiting the teaching and preaching functions of the church to those properly called and ordained by a congregation. The meeting concluded with the hope that these articles would help unify rather than divide the community of faith.

The group was conscious that divisions between communities had emerged as groups migrated due to the persecutions. As Menno listened to the discussions, he recognized the cultural differences among them, and some of the proposals struck him as too legalistic. Hearing views that were oriented to the Old Testament law, Menno felt the need to clarify the relation of law and gospel. He did this not as Luther or the Reformed theologians did, but simply by clarifying how Jesus gave a new relational meaning to righteousness, how discipleship and salvation by grace interrelate.

Like the Protestants, Menno saw that the law shows us our

need of a savior, for no one could perfectly fulfill the law. But beyond this he wanted to emphasize that when one is reconciled to God in Christ, one then lives with integrity in this new relationship. "When one understands the covenant of grace and its transforming power," Menno said, "it follows that the expression of the new creature will be in conformity with Christ. When we are born of the Spirit, this regeneration recreates us as new persons, as persons who will express in life the true humanness which God intended in creation and which he now enables in the new creation."

The group urged Menno to elaborate further. He didn't hesitate, but opened the discussion to the group. Menno was confident that together they recognized Scripture to be authoritative for the individual believer and for the community of faith, even pointing to the way of righteousness for society. He emphasized that law and the gospel relate as justice and forgiving mercy.

Menno noted that the Word of God, especially in the Sermon on the Mount, outlines the life for the disciple of Christ. It condemns sinful disregard of this standard, but it also serves as a guide for the regenerate who now live and walk in the Spirit. Menno reminded them of an earlier work in which he had written of spiritual resurrection as an inner transformation.

"Under the work of the Spirit," Menno said, "the law is like a deadly hammer that shatters the pride of the heart, but the gospel consists of rays of fire lighting up the inner man.

"The true church is the body of Christ, a body which makes Jesus visible to society," he said. "It is a fellowship of people made new by the work of the Spirit. When people are transformed from within and become new creatures in Christ, the outer expression of life will correspond to an inner quality of peace and assurance as children of God. Church is more than a lot of people attending a service for a sacramental exercise; rather the church is a communion of persons who gather in the presence of Christ, a community of the Spirit who are committed to live in fidelity to our Lord. It is to this assurance of salvation in Christ and to the integrity of faith to which we are called and to which we are calling others."

The assembly closed with a strong affirmation that the church's primary work should be, with the help of the Spirit, creating a new people, recognizing the function of the law not as saving but as a means of calling people to true penitence. Together they agreed that over and beyond the law is the Spirit's work on the basis of true faith in Christ. In this work the Spirit changes people internally and externally.

As a corrective to both Protestant and Catholic emphases on the law, the group agreed that, while the moral principles of God's earlier laws were carried over in the New Testament, the law of love that Jesus brought was more complete. The way of dealing with offenses was changed as well, with the exercise of forgiveness and reconciliation. In Christ the approach for the church is one of transforming grace rather than punishment. They reviewed again the account in the Gospel of John of the legalistic religious leaders asking Jesus about stoning the woman taken in adultery. Jesus exposed their own sins and then said to the woman, "Neither do I condemn you, go and sin no more!"

Menno affirmed to the gathering that he would do more writing in an attempt to help the Anabaptist communities find a clearer understanding of the gospel of grace. Grace, he said, does not exclude action but enables discipleship of Christ. He quoted from the epistle of James, "Show me your faith without action and I will show you my faith by my actions." Menno returned home satisfied with the meeting and its conclusions.

～

Just a few days after his return, it became evident that Jan had contracted an illness. While Gertrude gave their son special care, he suffered with something they didn't understand.

After being out briefly one day for a short trip to visit a neighboring family, Menno came home and found his wife holding their son, very anxious over his condition. She was bathing his brow in a vain effort to lower a fever. Menno summoned the village doctor, but he could not help. A few hours later, as they held him in their love and helplessness, Jan died.

Menno and Gertrude stood by the bed, embracing and weeping together. Bettjie and Mariken were sobbing at their feet.

Finally, Menno gathered their girls in his arms, with tears covering his face, and spoke words of assurance to them. Their brother was with the Lord, and they could trust Jesus for Jan's safekeeping. It was difficult for him to pray just then, but he did so, for the sake of the girls as much as for himself and his beloved. "Father, you understand and share our pain. It hurts. Yet we submit our Jan to you. We believe that he is accepted in your grace, and we trust him to the arms of Jesus." His voice broke, and they stood arm in arm, weeping.

Baron von Ahlefeldt made the arrangements for Jan's burial. Servants on the estate prepared the small coffin. A private memorial service was held in a meeting room on the estate, the baron's family and staff joining with them in their sorrow. To help keep the Simons family safe, the baron registered Jan's death as that of a child of one of his tenants.

Menno loved each of the children, but he had long imagined Jan becoming a partner in ministry when he was older. Now the death left a great void in his heart. For several days Menno retreated into solitude, then told Gertrude, "God's grace is sufficient for this as well. We need to surrender our disappointment to him."

Gertrude's eyes were wet with tears, but she looked at him with compassion, knowing how deeply this had cut into his soul. She said, "Yes, Menno, and I'm praying that we can discover that for each of us."

The days passed slowly as the family grieved and prayed for the Spirit's healing.

Out of the pain in his soul, but also in compassion for others in the suffering flock of whom he was pastor, Menno wrote a strong treatise called "The Cross of the Saints: An Admonition on the Suffering, Cross, and Persecution of the Saints." Addressing the community of saints, he focused on the relationship between discipleship and grace to bear the cross of suffering. One excerpt in particular expressed his inner turmoil over the suffering and limitations imposed on them as a family:

> For how many pious children of God have we not seen during the space of a few years deprived of their homes and possessions for the testimony of God and their conscience; their poverty and sustenance written off to the emperor's insatiable coffers. How many have they betrayed, driven out of city and country, put to the stocks and torture? How many poor orphans and children have they turned out without a farthing?
>
> Some they have hanged, some have they punished with inhuman tyranny and afterward garroted them with cords, tied to a post. Some they have roasted and burned alive. Some, holding their own entrails in their hands, have powerfully confessed the Word of God still. Some they beheaded and gave as food to the fowls of the air. Some have they consigned to the fish. They have torn down the houses of some. Some have they thrust into muddy bogs. They have cut off the feet of some, one of whom I have seen and spoken to.
>
> Others wander aimlessly hither and yon in want, misery, and discomfort, in the mountains, in deserts, holes, and clefts of the earth, as Paul says. They must take to their heels and flee away with their wives and little children, from one country to another, from one city to another—hated by all men, abused, slandered, mocked, defamed, trampled upon, styled "heretics." Their names are read from pulpits and town halls; they are kept from

their livelihood, driven out into the cold winter, bereft of bread, (and) pointed at with fingers. . . .

Yes, any man who is not ready for this hated and scorned life . . . cannot be the Lord's disciple. For it can never be otherwise. They must take upon themselves the heavy cross of al poverty, distress, disdain, sorrow, sadness, and must so follow the rejected, the outcast, the bleeding, and crucified Christ. . . .

My most beloved brethren in Christ, be of good cheer and be comforted in the Lord, you who have freely and voluntarily used your shoulders and your back under the cross of Jesus Christ. Yes, this is and remains the only strait and narrow way and door through which we must enter and pass. Whosoever will follow after me must deny himself and take up his cross and follow me. If you would be the people and disciples of the Lord, then you must bear the cross of Christ. This is undoubted and true.

But as he wrote, Menno was conscious that anyone who would endure suffering must have the resources of the Spirit of Christ. With this in mind, he added words of encouragement, endeavoring to cultivate a spirituality that had the power to support one in suffering.

Pray fervently and prepare yourselves, for through much oppression we must enter into the kingdom of heaven. Here is the patience and the faith of the saints. Oh, my brethren watch. . . .

Therefore, O ye people of God, gird yourselves and make ready for battle; not with external weapons and armor as the bloody, made world is wont to do, but only with firm confidence, a quiet patience and a fervent prayer. . . . The Lord is your strength, your comfort and refuge; He sits with you imprisons and dungeons; He

flies with you to foreign lands; He accompanies you
through fire and water. He will never leave you nor for-
sake you.

Menno sat thinking about the place of so much suffering at
this stage in the history of the world. It was believed by most
everyone that the end of history was near, that God was com-
pleting his work. Menno pondered this matter at length. Yes, he
believed that the Lord would return and bring his work to its
culmination, but Menno questioned whether this would be
soon. He said to Gertrude, "Somehow I believe that in the providence of God there may yet be a new order of freedom that will
come to society and the suffering we endure might by like the
birth pangs of a new age. I dream of freedom for the people of
God in society, a freedom for which I pray repeatedly."

"This would be so wonderful," she answered. "Whether it
comes in our lifetime or not, it will make it possible for many
more people to come into the fold of God. That would be so
wonderful for our children and . . ." She sat in silence.

Menno looked at her tenderly, quite sure that she thought
of their daughters and of Jan's passing.

～

Menno continued to give himself to writing. He wanted to
answer some of the questions that had been raised by his audiences.
He had earlier written a strong reply to Gellius Faber in Emden,
with the hope that a treatise of the true church, the "*Gemeinde* of
faith," as he liked to refer to the believers church, might lead to
greater tolerance and respect.

Menno now wrote that the Protestant leaders had only
moved partway toward reforming the church; they needed to
understand the New Testament picture that the church was to be
free in the state. He placed special emphasis on the church as the
visible body of Christ in the world and that the state needed to be

more tolerant of differences of belief among its citizens. Rather than capital punishment for differences of belief there should be freedom for different perspectives. This very diversity could be an enriching challenge for conversation. Once again he shared the content of his writing with Gertrude.

"This is good, Menno," she said. "You need to let them know how you think but also how you feel about the atrocities against our people and the threats against us."

"Yes," Menno said, "I owe it to our brethren who have given their lives for the cause of Christ to offer some defense or interpretation of the cause for which they have died."

He sat in silence for some time, thinking of some of those who had been recently executed. Then, thinking about the constant threat under which he lived, he picked up his pen and resumed writing. This would be something of a personal note in conclusion.

> "He who purchased me with the blood of His love and called me who am unworthy to His service, knows me, and He knows that I seek not wealth, or possessions, nor luxury, nor ease, but only the praise of the Lord, my salvation, and the salvation of many souls. Because of this, I with my poor weak wife and children have for eighteen years endured excessive anxiety, oppression, affliction, misery, and persecution. At the peril of my life I have been compelled everywhere to drag out an existence in fear.
>
> Yes, when the preachers repose on easy beds and soft pillows, we generally have to hide ourselves in out-of-the-way corners. When they at weddings and baptismal banquets revel with pipe, trumpet and lute, we have to be on our guard when a dog barks for fear the arresting officer has arrived. When they are greeted as doctors, lords, and teachers by everyone, we have to hear that we

are Anabaptists, bootleg preachers, deceivers, and heretics, and be saluted in the devil's name. In short, while they are gloriously rewarded for their services with large incomes and good times, our recompense and portion must be fire, sword, and death."

Menno said simply to Gertrude, "With this I rest my case. Since we are building on the one foundation, Jesus Christ, we will trust the work to him."

~

Major political news came in October 1555. Emperor Charles V had led a brilliant assembly in Brussels. Evidently, he was making steps toward retiring and had ceded his lands in Italy and Burgundy to his son Philip. His explanation was that this act reduced the amount of burden he carried. It also suggested coming changes within the empire. This gave Menno hope for the end of the heavy-handed oppression under which they suffered.

More immediate for Menno were the tensions that continued in the church itself, not because of persecution, but because of differences in opinion among the leaders. One issue confirmed his concern that Leenaert had a tendency to legalism.

In 1555 Leenaert had banned a man from the church in Emden. He then asked the man's wife to join in shunning her husband. She refused to do so, and Leenaert banned her as well. This created great tension in the congregation, and its leaders needed help. They called on Menno.

This meant another trip to Emden, which Menno made with a heavy heart. When they met, Menno urged Leenaert to take a more moderate position, to negotiate with the church leadership toward a more satisfactory position. But Leenaert maintained his rigid stance and was far too controlling of his colleagues. To Menno's disappointment, he gained no concessions from Leenaert, and the tension in the group continued.

Leenaert's influence was wide because of his extensive travels as an evangelist. The elders had actually banned him from this ministry while he considered his position. The ban had lasted about six months, and he was then reinstated. But the issue went unresolved and tensions remained.

Menno later received word from a struggling congregation at Franeker that faced a serious dispute over the ban. Menno felt that their local elder, Hendrik Naldeman, should try to mediate. He planned to write a letter with instructions on discipline.

The dispute over the ban was spreading through the believers church. On one side, many believed that their elders had been too quick to discipline, and an offending person should be admonished three times regardless of the seriousness of his or her sin. A further question was whether a person who fell into sin should always be excommunicated. Could a believer who fell into sin through weakness be brought to repentance without the ban? Menno wrote a short treatise to try to help.

> Out of great distress and sorrow of heart I write to you in the year of 1555, because a letter was handed to me signed by five brethren of good report, from which I learn, may God better it, that a violent dispute has arisen among some of you concerning the ban. One party insists, if I understand correctly, that no sin or work of the flesh should be punished with excommunication without three admonitions going before, a position with which I cannot agree; for there are some sins, like murder, witchcraft, incendiarism, theft, and other like criminal deeds, which eventually require and imply punishment at the hands of the magistracy.
>
> Now if we were to admonish such transgressors before they were expelled, the unleavened lump of the church would be changed into an ugly leaven before the whole world. Therefore act with discretion, and do not judge

such matters involving capital punishment, especially if they are public, as you would other works of the flesh which do not constitute an offense and cause for reproach in the eyes of the world.

The other party urges, if I understand correctly, that all works of the flesh are to be punished with excommunication without any previous admonition at all, and that all penitence must take place outside the Church. That doctrine and position is, according to my humble understanding, altogether contrary to the word of Christ, of Paul, and of James. For avarice, pride, hatred, discord, defamation, and contention with one's neighbor, are patent works of the flesh, and work death if not mortified and repented of. Yet they are not punished without three foregoing admonitions according to the Scriptural requirement. I wish that men would consider that even as sin when completed yields death, so also does repentance and a contrite heart together with the ceasing from sin bring forth life once more, as may be seen in the case of David, Peter, the thief on the cross, Zacchaeus, and others.

I also understand that these same brethren are of the opinion that if some brother should secretly have transgressed in some deed or other and then in pain and sorrow of heart should lament to one of his brethren, that he has sinned against his God in this way, then this same brother would be obliged to bring it to the attention of the church and if he should fail to do so he would then be punished with the transgressor.

This is not only unheard of, but also wholly frightful in my way of thinking. For it is clearly against all Scripture and love. Matt. 18; Jas. 5; Col. 2; Eph.5. If the ban was instituted for the purpose of repentance, how then if repentance is already shown (namely in the contrite sorrowing heart), can excommunication be pronounced against such? O my brethren, cease from such plans, for it tends to destroy and not to reform.

May the Spirit of Christ, rich in peace, protect you all, sound in doctrine moreover, ardent in love and without offense in life, to the edification of His church and to the praise of His holy name. Signed by me, the one who is lame, your brother and servant, November 13, A.D. 1555. Menno Simons.

Menno had scarcely sent this writing by way of a friend when another facet of the problem came to his attention. The churches in south Germany had reacted to the stringent discipline now being pursued in the Low Countries. A delegation from the south German communities, which were a part of the Anabaptists known as Mennists, made the long trip in late April to visit Menno at Wüstenfeld, in north Germany. They had come this considerable distance prepared to stay for at least a week, but told Menno that they were willing to extend their visit into early May if necessary.

This group included Lemke Bruerren, a deacon in whose home Menno had once stayed, and Zelis Jacobs, an Anabaptist elder of Monschasu in Eiffel, Germany, whom Menno had known in Cologne. There were also other elders, including Herman van Tielt and Hans Sikken. If there was to be a continued relationship between this group and the churches in the Lowlands, a better policy on discipline would be needed.

The group from Germany appealed for a more open relationship with people under discipline. They believed that, as Anabaptists, they needed to be more accepting of differences, just as they wished from others. They wanted to know whether Menno was siding with Leenaert and Dirk or if he had a mediating solution.

"My brothers," Menno said, "the church is the body of Christ and being one body calls for harmony and integrity so that each part can function properly."

"That is very true," Lemke said. "But there is diversity of parts."

"But we can have unity with diversity," Menno replied. "Unity doesn't mean uniformity. You may wear lederhosen in the south, but we needn't do that here in the Lowlands. Our styles and our languages need not be the same. Those are cultural matters. But there are issues in moral behavior where we must hold each other accountable."

"Give us an example, Menno," Zelis said, "something other than sexual morality."

Menno thought for a moment. "As a church, we are committed to rejection of the sword. We leave it in the hands of the state. What would you do if a member insisted on carrying a sword?"

Zelis simply nodded his head in agreement; he and Menno understood one another. Yet as the meeting continued, Menno felt that Zelis was somewhat aloof and hesitant in expressing his own convictions.

Menno had also worked with Van Tielt; he had been an intermediary between Menno and John a'Lasco in 1533. His presence encouraged Menno to be open with the brothers, and Menno affirmed his deep convictions that elders had a responsibility to maintain integrity among the membership in their congregations.

"The church is to be true to the covenant with Christ, a covenant to walk in truth and love," Menno said.

The group had agreed before coming that they would argue for a more moderate position on church discipline, and they now expressed their agreement to Menno. As he listened to their comments, he basically agreed. But he was caught between moderation in relationship with them and the need for fidelity to the colleagues he had long worked with there in the Lowlands.

Menno admitted to those at the meeting that he was in a bind. He could promise only that he would try diligently to converse with Leenaert and Dirk, trying to help them to a more balanced position on discipline. But it was now clear that the rigorous position of the Dutch communities was creating a wide gulf between them and the German Anabaptists.

Menno's personal conviction was that discipline should happen in the community in which people meet in the presence of the risen Christ and act in faithfulness to him. Discipline was not to be a method used by an elder to control a congregation. Rather the community of believers was responsible to hold one another accountable. This conviction was central in Menno's message on nurture as well as on discipline. He had often reminded his followers of the words of Jesus, "Where two or three are gathered in my name I am there in the midst of them."

The true church was a community of the Spirit, and it was the Spirit who created unity as well as correcting elements that spoiled unity. Menno believed that people were to be held accountable for their covenant and that an elder should call the congregation to exercise a role of discernment and nurture. A violation of a covenant commitment called for the offender to be disciplined. This discipline included excommunication for carnal behavior. But it was the manner of this practice of discipline that was now creating stress in the church.

∽

Most of the group left Menno's home without being fully satisfied. Zelis stayed behind and visited with Menno. He affirmed that he was in basic agreement, but wanted to safeguard his influence with his brethren. He joined them in taking a firm stand against any abolition of marriage by the ban, as had happened under Leenaert's leadership. He and Lemke were in full agreement on this matter. Menno heard the concern, and though he agreed, he could again promise only that he would talk with his associates.

Gertrude was more sympathetic to the concerns of the

group from the south. Menno pondered this at length, knowing well that he must talk soon with his fellow elders.

A few weeks later, a meeting was arranged in the eastern region of Friesland, which made it easier for Menno. He made his way to the meeting with a heavy heart, knowing he would have to confront Dirk and Leenaert.

Menno met with the elders and engaged discussion with his younger colleagues. He was impressed by their idealism for a "church without spot or wrinkle," but he cautioned them against being too perfectionist: "We are not a community of perfectionists but of compassion, and our ministry must serve the weak as well as the stronger."

Verbally they agreed, but as they talked further, the two men pushed Menno to take a more strict position, one that his sense of compassion would not let him endorse. He was caught in an intense inner struggle about being involved in a practical question that was becoming such a divisive issue. These brothers insisted that the spouse of an excommunicated member be required to shun that member along with the rest of the church. This had resulted in grave tension for those congregations. Already various factions had begun to separate from each other.

Menno protested this factionalism, pointing to the consequences of broken fellowship. But Leenaert and Dirk became more and more defensive. "Menno," Leenaert said, "for the sake of integrity in leadership, you need to support us, or . . . or you too may be put under the ban."

Menno drew back in amazement. "You would do that? When I have trusted you, called you, and ordained you. Where is your respect?"

Leenaert looked over at Dirk, and nodded. Dirk said softly, "My brother Menno, you are highly regarded, and it is only as we as elders stand together that the church can be united on this matter."

"But the church is already divided on this," Menno said. "If we are not more considerate of different views, if we don't negotiate a base of agreement, your approach will tear the church apart. Dirk, you've spent time in many communities, especially with the brethren in Prussia, and you know there must be room for some variation in practice."

Dirk smiled. "Yes, I understand what you mean. I have a commitment to our Prussian congregations, and I hope to take my family back to Danzig and share in the work there. It is a community in which we feel at home. But Menno, we are working here to keep the church as one body, and we need your support for a unified approach to discipline."

As the meeting came to a close, the elders prayed together, and the group disbanded, slipping out one or two at a time. Menno could hear Dirk and Leenaert chatting, sharing comments on the need to seek purity in the community of faith.

Turning to Menno, Dirk said simply, "Menno, we trust you to weigh this carefully. We have already made up our minds on this procedure."

Menno bid them farewell, slipped out of the meeting room, and made his way back to the quarters where he was staying. He walked with a heavy heart. This was not what he wanted to see in the church he loved. He felt some resentment over needing to add this to other matters in his already heavy load. For instance, he had recently begun carrying on a literary battle with the Protestant Martin Micron, and it had not lessened. He didn't need this new problem.

∼

After a long trip, he was home with his Gert, and her advice was helpful, as always. "Be patient, Menno. Give the Spirit time to work. You shared your perspective and God has given you influence. We will see what becomes of this as we wait on the Lord. You need now to free yourself from this and continue your other work."

Menno was grateful for her counsel, and he soon returned to writing a response to Micron. This interchange took a lot of his time. He needed to proceed carefully, to study the issues, and then to seek to refute the various charges against him. Menno wrote long treatises in which he tried to provide as much clarity as possible.

He wrote that his position on basic doctrines had remained consistent from his earliest years in Holland as an Anabaptist leader. "You can check from those who have been under my ministry in the years from 1536 until the present time in 1556," Menno wrote. He smiled to himself as he thought of having had a twenty-year tenure of service.

He also wanted to be clear that he was independent from the earlier influence of Hoffman and the Melchiorites. He hoped that Micron would read him without bias and hear him purely out of his own understanding of the Holy Scriptures.

Menno began the "Epistle to Martin Micron" with an affirmation that "love is the total content of scripture. Everyone that loves, says John, is born of God and knows God. He that loves not, knows not God; for God is love. And he that dwells in love, dwells in God and God in him. Without this love, it is all vain, whatever we may know, judge, speak, do, or write. The property and fruit of love is meekness and kindness. Love is not envious, not crafty, not deceitful, not puffed up, nor selfish. In short, where love is, there is a Christian."

He was emphatic in stating that he intended to stand firmly on Scripture as his one sure foundation for faith and life. It was the authority of the Word rightly interpreted that tied his movement to the apostles and to the church of the New Testament.

After a lengthy treatment against a religion of mere ritual, of a verbal profession of doctrine but no corresponding life, he made some quite sharp comments.

So I have written, my worthy brethren, against the doctrines, sacraments, and life just considered, imperial decrees, papal bulls, councils of the learned, long standing practices, human philosophy, Origen, Augustine, Luther, Bucer, imprisonment, banishment, or murder meaning nothing; for it is the eternal, imperishable Word of God; I repeat, it is the eternal Word of God, and shall so remain forever.

In January 1556 came a momentous political change, one of great importance for Menno and for society in general. Charles V had ceded more of his domains from his responsibility and was retiring to a monastic order for the rest of his life. There, by meditation and prayer he would seek the cleansing of his soul and seek peace with God. He ceded his Spanish domains and those in the New World to his brother Ferdinand. And he abdicated his imperial crown and moved to the Jeromite monastery of St. Justus in Estremadura, Spain.

In Menno's mind there was no question that Charles V's conscience must have called him to repentance. The move to a monastery for the remaining years of his life might well be his inner quest for peace. Menno recalled well a similar quest in his own soul and the wonderful peace and assurance he now enjoyed in the fellowship of Christ. He could only pray for Charles V and wish the same experience of grace for this man who had been his enemy.

Menno was traveling less now, but he was sure that he would need to travel again to meet with Dirk and Leenaert.

After he finished the "Epistle to Martin Micron" he spoke frequently with various people who called on him. In 1557, representatives from Alsace and Switzerland asked to meet with him. This group of believers came seeking greater unity in the church. They wanted to help their Dutch brothers and sisters come to a more moderate position on discipline.

Menno wanted the brothers in the Lowlands to take these Swiss brothers seriously. He admired their biblical understanding and perspective. After their brief visit he promised to do what he could in negotiation with elders of the Lowlands, especially with Dirk and Leenaert. In turn he knew that this group would share his comments with their mutual friends, Lemke and Zelis Jacobs.

Since the previous meeting in Friesland, Leenaert and Dirk had continued what they saw as a call to maintain the integrity of the disciplined church. But the resultant tension was leading to more division within the church. Menno heard these reports and felt that he needed to make another trip into West Friesland, much to his regret. As usual, the journey was not without risk and needed to be undertaken in great secrecy.

He talked this over at length with Gertrude, and they agreed that he had to set out. This time he would travel to Harlingen, where Leenaert had long been at work and where, he learned, Dirk had joined with Leenaert.

Many Anabaptists around Franeker were more tolerant than the two leading elders, but the elders had a sizable group of conservatives who stood with them. The more liberal Flemish, now under the leadership of Jan Scheedemaker, were in the process of forming their own fellowship. The Frisians regarded the Flemish, who had immigrated north to flee persecution in Flanders, as too liberal in rejecting the Frisian style of plain living. In turn, the Flemish regarded the Frisians as too materialistic because they lived in ornate houses.

After a long and difficult journey, Menno arrived at Harlingen. When the meeting convened, he spoke frankly to the group about the need for more compassion and consideration toward each other. He reviewed their earlier meeting at Wismar and assured them that he had continued to give the matter much prayer and thought. But as he sought to bring the group to a basic agreement on a position, Dirk and Leenaert overruled him. They were insistent on discipline for the specific case before them and wanted the ban to be applied to the woman living with her excommunicated husband. She would need to either shun her husband and separate herself from him in the marriage, or she herself should be banned.

A small group of conservative elders then met with the larger church council. Menno withheld comments on the specific case they were discussing, though he found it difficult to refrain from challenging his friends. Finally one of the elders asked for his thoughts. He replied that he was hesitant to speak to the case because he was too far removed from their community. Consequently, with little restraint by fellow elders, Dirk and Leenaert summarily banned the woman in question and upheld the ban on her husband.

To Menno's consternation, they even extended the ban to any persons who supported the woman in disagreeing with the elders' decision. Now Menno needed to speak: "What makes you so sure that you have discovered the mind of Christ? Can you not hear his words of forgiveness, 'Neither do I accuse you. Go and sin no more'?"

To his amazement, the conservative wing once again threatened to break fellowship with Menno. Leenaert said bluntly, "Menno, if you fail to support the church in enforcing this ban, we will need to announce that you are a dissenter in the discipline of excommunication."

Menno said, "I can't believe that you two would be so carried away with your own opinions that you would exclude me."

Leenaert reacted by suggesting that Menno was identifying with the Scheedemakers, a group named after their leader, Jacob Jansz Scheedemaker, who had been less demanding on the matter of shunning in the use of the ban. He had been excommunicated by Leenaert Bouwens in 1555. Leenaert condescendingly called this group the *Scheedemakers*. Having been reinstated to his office, Leenaert exerted his leadership even more decisively.

Menno was shocked. He had worked with these men closely

through the years, and their rigid stance did not fit what he had long shared with them in the grace of Christ. He sat in silence as the meeting was brought to its close, and with sadness he took his leave.

Menno immediately began the long trip home to Wüstenfeld. As he traveled, he reflected with great thankfulness on the privilege he enjoyed in life. God had blessed him with a wonderful marriage and family life. He was deeply grateful for the security his family enjoyed on the estate of Von Ahlefeldt, whose gracious hospitality was unusual. Menno was eager to be home to enjoy a respite from the extensive travel.

∽

Menno had been able to develop a relationship with a printer who was producing and shipping his books and pamphlets for him. He was delighted with the arrangement. Several weeks earlier the printer had shipped fourteen barrels of his most recent book, which made their way by canal boat to Amsterdam.

It was painful to tell Gertrude what was taking place around Franeker. It involved people they knew well and respected. Because of Leenaert and Dirk's rigid position, several groups were withdrawing from the churches. Leenaert spoke condescendingly of those that withdrew, saying that the dissenters included people he was sure needed to be disciplined. He had even derisively called the dissenting church group *de drekwagen* (garbage wagon).

Menno recognized that this legalistic attitude was threatening the unity of the church in the Lowlands, where there were now thousands of Anabaptists, but it was also creating friction with the Anabaptist churches in south Germany and Switzerland. Menno felt that the only thing he could do was write and publish his own views on the nature of discipline and help the church through this difficulty. He sought a mediating position in his writing, but he was unable to shake free of the contentious discussions at Harlingen.

As he wrote, Menno addressed the disputes over the ban, but he failed to conciliate on the issue. He soon heard that the Anabaptists to the north, known as the Waterlanders, had adopted the stricter position and now distinguished themselves from the Flemish believers. With this division they no longer used the name Mennists. This was no problem for Menno, except that it symbolized the estrangement of the parties. But he knew that this was the risk of the free church, of being the body of Christ with no visible head as a pope or any authoritarian overseer. The tie as Christians to the apostolic tradition was the authority of Scripture.

To Menno, interpreters of the Word needed to be honest and humble in recognizing what they brought to their interpretation. It was not what the Scriptures *said* that divided a community, but rather what people *understood* it to say. The cultural differences of the various groups tended to be as divisive as their theological differences. To be a church required a dedicated community that would exercise a mutual dependence on the Holy Spirit as it sought to properly interpret the Word.

Menno recalled reading of a conversation between Martin Luther and Master Eck, a Catholic, about the danger of giving the Bible to the relatively untrained laity. Master Eck asked Luther, "Do you know what you are going to have if you do this?" Of course he had in mind that it meant chaos.

Luther quickly answered, "Yes, more Christians."

"Yes," Menno thought, "in many ways both were right."

He and Gertrude prayed for their many friends and for the brothers with whom Menno had met, asking God for a moving of the Spirit to safeguard the unity of the church they loved.

17
Home at Oldesloe and Gertrude's Passing

1558–1559

Menno was now torn by a more personal heartache. Gertrude's health continued to decline, and it became increasingly evident that she was not going to get well. He was quite anxious about this, and he had their host arrange for a doctor to look at her condition while not telling the doctor who she was. This was a difficult experience for Menno; he had to keep himself hidden while the doctor examined Gertrude and gave his report to their host. The medication of herbs helped little.

Menno knelt by her bedside frequently, placing his hand on her head and praying for God's healing grace. He was so grateful for their love and the more than two decades they had been together. It was so short a time. He prayed their time could be extended so that together they could enjoy more peace from the oppression that had been so tenacious.

Their little home in Wüstenfeld, a little village in Holstein near Oldesloe, did provide a quiet setting for them for a rather extended time. The earlier move from their location in Wismar had not been an easy one, especially for Gertrude. But her health had improved somewhat. They had, for some weeks following, some happy times being with their daughters in Wüstenfeld. But for what seemed a more secure setting, Menno soon moved the family to the town of Oldesloe.

Menno and Gertrude would sit together in the evening and reflect on their dreams, the loss of their son, and the limitations they faced with the threat of arrest. They dreamed of a day when the social and political order would bring a new birth of freedom.

"It is in God's hands," Menno would say, as he laid his hand on Gertrude's shoulder, "just as is the church. It is his work, not ours, and we are only his servants."

She would smile and look into his eyes, and in that gaze they would both see the pain in the eyes of the other. "He knows his way for us," she added. "I am at peace with that."

Bettjie and Mariken were gracious with their mother and provided loving care and support. Mariken spent the most time with her, and her deep affection for her mother was evident in her tenderness and in her prayers. Bettjie carried most of the responsibility around the house, shopping for food and doing the cooking. Menno was proud of her, and he thanked her again and again for doing so much while he needed to remain hidden. At times he told her of his dreams for her future. She would smile and thank him, almost embarrassed when he mentioned marriage.

Gertrude's health continued to deteriorate, and the three of them sought to encourage her and support one another. With deep inner pain Menno watched his beloved become weaker and weaker. In their second year at Oldesloe, Menno sat by her side as she grew more and more weak. They shared words of love, for as he said to his daughters, "I want your mother to know how much she has enriched my life and how meaningful her support and her sharing has been through these nearly two dozen years."

Menno was almost constantly at her bedside, sharing tenderly in her care and offering words of love and encouragement. He watched helplessly as Gertrude succumbed to her illness. Menno was quoting from her favorite psalm, 46, when she closed her eyes and began to breathe in a more labored manner. Menno held her hand, his eyes wet with tears, as her breathing slowed and then finally stopped.

His beloved Gertrude was gone, at rest with the Lord, he was sure. Even so, the parting left him with a deep void. When their son had died, they were together in sorrow. But now he was alone. His daughters, quite mature young women now, did their part to comfort him, but the pain and emptiness could only be processed by his own faith and the comfort of the Spirit.

Menno suffered daily from the loss, feeling as though a part of him was missing. He traveled less in the days that followed, deeply affected by his grief and his physical handicap. He spent time with his daughters, knowing they too shared his deep grief.

Late summer turned to fall, and nature all around them was beautiful. The September colors of the aspen enriched the landscape alongside the windmills that marked the skyline.

Menno found the grieving process to be a continuing experience and not something on which he could close the door. He had been strengthened by Gertrude's great courage, her insight, and above all by her very faithful support. News had come of posters with the price on his head, but she would always say, "Menno, we are in the hand of God, and it is his work in which we share. He knows when we will have finished our journey. He will give life as long as he expects us to work."

As a result of his writing and also of several debates, public attention now refocused on him. The number of adherents to the faith had grown remarkably, and his colleagues warned him that various magistrates continued searching for him. But he was hopeful that he would not need to take his two daughters and move once again.

When Menno had found their lodging at Oldesloe, he and Gertrude had hoped it would be their home as long as possible. She had planned to continue teaching their daughters, but Bettjie was so accomplished that it was primarily a matter of encouraging her and finding materials for her to study. She was especially helpful with Mariken.

After Gertrude died and Menno chose to engage less in travel, the little family had considerably more time together. Bettjie and Mariken were a wonderful encouragement to him. Each participated enthusiastically with him in the life of the church.

It had been a great joy to Menno and Gertrude when their daughters each made their commitment to Christ and to a life of discipleship. Menno had asked one of his associates to instruct them for baptism, because he wanted them to hear their faith confirmed by someone in addition their parents. But Menno led their baptism service. His eyes were wet as they knelt before him, and with his associate, he baptized them, one and then the other, "in the name of the Father, the Son, and the Holy Spirit." Taking each by the hand, he asked them to arise and quoted from Paul, "Like as Christ was raised from the dead, even so you also shall walk in newness of life."

As Menno recalled this wonderful occasion, he was thankful this had taken place while Gertrude was with them. She had been privileged to witness their baptism and to support them in this step of faith.

But now that his wife was gone, it was like one of his arms was cut off, leaving him handicapped. But Menno considered the safety they were enjoying as a special blessing of the Lord. So many of his friends had died for their faith, and he was continuing to elude his pursuers. He saw this as evidence of God's hand upon him as a leader in the growing church.

Word came that on July 10, 1557, Gillis van Aken was beheaded in Antwerp. Menno recalled how he had needed to discipline and expel him from the ministry several years earlier, but in repentance and restitution Gillis had been reclaimed and became an effective minister. While Menno felt a deep sorrow over the loss of Gillis, he also felt a deep satisfaction that the man had been faithful to his death.

Menno's time now was given primarily to writing and publishing. With the services of his printer, it had become a very satisfying ministry for him. He traveled less, both to be with his daughters and because he need a crutch much of the time.

~

After the loss of Jan, Menno and Gertrude had reflected at length on the role and responsibility of parents. Now, as something of a memorial to her, he wrote a reflection on family life, "The Nurture of Children." In it, he urged parents to help their children with the best education possible and to discipline with care. Any punishment should be given with discretion and moderation, without anger, and children should be kept away from corrupting, worldly influences. Above all, they were to be instructed in the Christian faith. He urged parents to rule their household as well as themselves with honor and virtue, in keeping with the Word of God.

He continued the family theme with a brief and beautiful tract, "Meditations and Prayers for Mealtime," in which he drew on select psalms, along with other Bible passages. He promoted the practice of grace and thanksgiving before meals as part of the parental responsibility to help children come to know and worship God. He wrote that parents should teach not only by their words but also by their example. His writing was stimulated by the wonderful memories he carried of his life with Gertrude.

In his writing, Menno once again expressed his concern for people across the land who were caught in poverty. He urged the Christian community to be compassionate, to give them aid not only in material ways but also by extending privileges in education and social development. He affirmed again and again that "true evangelical faith is never indifferent. It clothes the naked, it feeds the hungry, it gives aid to the poor and promotes the way of peace. And this peace seeks mutuality for all humanity."

Menno reflected on the unfairness of life's experiences. The princes and others in authority, Catholic and Protestant, knew little of the suffering that he and his many associates in faith had to endure. Of the Protestant reformers he wrote, "[They] live in luxury and splendor, yet they suffer many of their own poor, afflicted members to ask alms; and poor, hungry, suffering, old, lame, blind, and sick people to beg their bread at their doors." It was a matter of deep discomfort to Menno that the peasant people were forced to live with such meager means when those in authority wasted so much.

Menno reflected on his experiences in ministry with deep gratitude to God. Each execution of a person for the faith stimulated in him a renewed sense of dedication and determination to serve his Lord more effectively. Driven from one home to another, never able to provide all he would have liked for his family, he thought of the many people who had given them aid. He carried a debt to so many and also to the congregations whose support had enabled him to have lodging and food, all at risk to their own lives. Thinking on this he wrote some further admonitions:

> If we wish to save our neighbor's soul by the help of the Spirit and Word of our Lord, or if we see our neighbors in need or in danger, driven forth for the Word of the Lord, then we should not close our doors to them. We should receive them in our houses and share our food, aid them, and comfort and assist them in their troubles. We should risk our lives for our brethren, even if we know beforehand that it will be at the cost of our own lives. This example we have in Christ who for our sakes did not spare himself, but willingly gave up his life, in order that we might live through him.

The year passed slowly for Menno in his deep sorrow over the passing of Gertrude. But he soon endured another very different but very real sorrow—the increasing tension between the Dutch and the south German churches. Menno had met with the delegations from both sides but with little success.

In Menno's opinion, Dirk and Leenaert continued making grave mistakes in acting so legalistically. The overly authoritative Dutch elders now acted to ban the south German churches from their fellowship. As far as Menno could see, the estrangement would last far into the future.

In addition to this, the group in the north who called themselves the Waterlanders, and whom Menno had long known as the Frisian believers, continued defending their division from the Flemish to the south. Leenaert had considerable influence with the Frisian community, while the Flemish tended to look to Dirk for their counsel. This division would not be healed any time soon.

Menno was convinced that the things dividing the churches were primarily human applications of truth and often not the essential truth itself. It was a real challenge for him to help people make that distinction. In his messages he emphasized the danger that follows when people regard their applications to be absolute. Unless the distinction between basic principles and human applications was respected, there was no way, in his thinking, to prevent division. In the face of this, he would continue writing and teaching to encourage the unity of the church in its discipleship.

Menno was well aware of the cultural differences, having frequently encountered them in his many travels over the years. Cultural preferences, he was certain, contributed much in creating the current divisions. The Flemish were a carefree and worldly people, while the Frisians were staid and thrifty. These characteristics were a part of their lives, and in various ways they incorporated them into church life. Menno tried to emphasize what he saw as a central truth—being separated from the world had to be balanced by first being separated unto God—and he tried to assure his brothers and sisters that the Spirit who creates the church will work for its refinement and unity.

He found encouragement in continuous reports of faithful witnesses from each wing of the movement spreading the message of the gospel; many gave their lives for their faith in Christ. One report came by way of two men from Franeker in West Friesland who had come the long way to share with Menno the account of the death of Lenaert Plovier. This faithful brother was a well-to-do cloth merchant in Meenen who had served Menno on various occasions. When appointed to a political role as an assayer of cloth, he refused to swear an oath and as a consequence lost the appointment. He then fled to Antwerp, where he had developed a silk business. There he was arrested, along with two others, Janneken Eghels and Maeyken de Hont. The three were put in sacks and drowned in the wine cask at Steen Castle.

The two men who visited Menno had gone to Antwerp as friends of Plovier the night before the execution of this faithful servant of Christ. They had listened outside the castle wall where Plovier's cell was located and had heard him pray, expressing his confidence in the Lord's grace. They also told Menno of the arrest of Hendrik Leerkooper and his wife. He had been executed, on October 8, but, as far as they knew, his wife was still in prison.

After some time of sharing hospitality with the two men, Menno thanked them earnestly for making the long journey to visit with him. He was encouraged, he said, by the Spirit's work in bringing to birth such a vibrant church. When he asked them how they had been able to find him, they told him that this information came from one in the church, but only after a lengthy time of giving evidence that they were believers and not betrayers.

The two men bowed their heads together with Menno and shared in prayer. They each asked God to give his faithful people a special sense of his presence and grace, protecting them but also enabling them to be open in witness to the new life in Christ. In concluding the prayer, Menno said, "We walk through the valley of the shadow, but you, oh God, are with us. It is your presence that comforts us and sustains us."

"I needed this word," Menno told the two as they prepared to leave. "You were sent by God. While I am concerned for the integrity of the church in its discipline, in holding each other accountable to be faithful, it is the public witness of faithful people that is most important. Through expression of faith such as this, many more will come to believe. The state church continues to be a fallen church, as has been the case since Constantine, but in God's providence I believe that things will change.

"Brethren, I live with the vision that a new day of freedom will come. I continually pray that the authorities will soon come to see that it is only just to grant freedom for each person to choose their own path of faith. One's religious beliefs should not be determined or enforced by the authorities of the state. Under God's calling, the state has its role of keeping order and securing the well-being of its citizens, but the church is called to live as an expression of the rule of Christ, an expression of his kingdom."

18
Return from Harlingen Under Threat of Being Banned

1559–1560

Menno kissed his daughters goodbye and left them with their good friends, the Ewing family. He was embarking on another difficult trip, feeling it to be in God's will. It was very different for him to travel now that Gertrude was gone; she looked after things at home. But his daughters were two wonderful partners in his work and would be safe. Bettjie was now nearly twenty, and Mariken was sixteen.

"Remember how much I love you," he said in parting. "Nothing could take me away except the work of Christ and the present need."

"We know that, Father, and we are with you in our prayers and thoughts," Bettjie said.

With those encouraging words, he placed his helpful crutch under his arm and started down the road. His thoughts were on his daughters as he traveled. Lately, there was a fine young man calling on Bettjie, and Menno anticipated that it would not be long until she would be married. He was prepared to accept this, for she should have her own life and home, and Mariken could take care of things at the house for the two of them. Both of his daughters were so much like their mother that it was a pleasure to be around them. He chuckled to himself, remembering his earlier thought that a child begotten by its father received its nature from him. It is obvious, he thought, that children do not receive everything from their father. He had "begotten" two daughters, but they carried the marks of their mother.

He paused to rest, sitting on the bank of one of the drain channels around a large polder. He had watched the sun rise, spreading its light across the land. He watched the cattle eating peacefully in the polder. While thinking about his daughters, he pondered the mystery of the incarnation and the problems in his earlier notion that Jesus received everything from his Father and nothing from his mother. "I was mistaken," he said to himself, "for just as my daughters reflect their mother, so Jesus shared the humanity of Mary. He is the only begotten of the Father, but he was born of the virgin Mary and was her child. The incarnation will always be a mystery for us, but as the Apostles' Creed says, 'He is true God of true God and true man of true man,' and John writes, 'The Word became flesh and dwelt among us.'"

Menno reflected back on the time he and Gertrude had enjoyed at Groningen and Leeuwarden and the many friends they had there. But the congregations there had suffered so much in the last several years. The authorities continued to execute those they saw as traitors to their authority. Recently, on March 14, 1559, three leaders were drowned in a tub at Leeuwarden: Claesken Gaeldochter, her husband Hendrik Euwes, and a very effective elder, Jaques d'Auchy. Claesken had been baptized in an open field at Workum about 1549 and had become a very effective Bible teacher in the church. She left three sons, saying to them that she "didn't want to leave for all of the world." She had a remarkable knowledge of Scripture and was very skilled in answering the questions of the inquisitors in testifying of her faith. The others left a similar testimony, especially the elder d'Auchy.

One of the elders Menno visited on his journey told him of

the recent execution of two brothers in Haarlem, whom Menno had known well—Joriaen Simonz and Clement Dirks. The night before the execution, the pastor of the Haarlem church, Bouwen Lubberts, boldly preached a sermon to the public in the Schoutenstraat. He declared the integrity of the two men who were sentenced to die, witnessed to the sincerity of their faith, and asked the people what kind of government would take the lives of such upstanding citizens over matters of faith when the officials themselves had differed with the Roman Church. He affirmed how much these men were needed in their community and what a loss their death would mean for everyone. How Menno wished that he could have been there to hear it. What a daring and bold, yet encouraging, thing for the pastor to do!

Menno traveled to Harlingen and made his way very cautiously to the lodging place, where he had been told he'd find Dirk. Dirk opened the door, and when they were inside the two men embraced and greeted each other in the joy of being together again. Dirk expressed his sympathy in the passing of Gertrude and shared his faith and assurance that she was with the Lord, which meant a lot to Menno. The two men spent the next few hours talking; even with their recent differences they fell into former and familiar patterns of conversation.

As they visited together, Dirk shared an account with Menno of a very striking martyrdom in Ghent of Hans van Overdam and Hans Keeskooper. While a sad happening, it was filled with expressions of unusual courage and even humor. These two had agreed while in prison that when they were led to the stakes, Keeskooper would ask permission to take off his stockings as a gift to some needy person. This type of request was usually granted. While he was doing this, Overdam had time to speak to the crowd and share their testimony of faith. The report was that Keeskooper took his time in a protracted removal of his long stockings while Overdam made good use of the opportunity. Because of his strong voice, many in the crowd heard his clear message. Then it was Keeskooper's turn. As Overdam removed his stockings, slowly and carefully, Keeskooper preached.

Menno sat thinking of the strategic and remarkable farewell of these men, and he chuckled a bit. Prior to their execution Overdam had sought to explain his position and that of his fellow Christians to the magistrates who had tried him. Since he had written out this defense, it had been preserved and was now being passed to others. Dirk had been able to secure a copy.

> Be it known to you, noble lords, councilors, burgomasters, and judges, that we recognize your offices as right and good. Yes, as ordained and instituted of God, that is, the secular sword for the punishment of evildoers and the protection of the good, and we desire to obey you in all taxes, tributes and ordinances, as far as it is not contrary to God. And if you find us disobedient in these things, we will willingly receive our punishment as malefactors. God, who is acquainted with every heart, knows that this is our intention.
>
> But understand, ye noble lords, that the abuse of your stations, or offices we do not recognize to be from God but from the devil, and that antichrist through the subtlety of the devil has bewitched and blinded your eyes. Be sober, therefore, and awake, and open the eyes of your understanding and see against whom you fight, that it is, against God.
>
> Therefore we will not obey you; for it is the will of God that we shall be tried thereby. Hence we would rather, through the grace of God, suffer our temporal bodies to be burned, drowned, beheaded, racked, or tortured, as it may seem good to you, or be scourged, banished, or driven away, and robbed of our goods, than show you any obedience contrary to the Word of God and we will be patient herein, committing vengeance to God.

As Menno read it carefully he was impressed with Overdam's statement. He had himself written in his *The Foundation of Christian Doctrine* that rulers did not have the right to determine the faith of their subjects. In his writings, Menno had continually appealed for tolerance and for the freedom to preach the gospel as they understood it. Menno recalled that he had concluded his statements with some sharp words of judgment against the persecutors both Catholic and Protestant.

> But the reviling, betraying, and agitation of the priests and your unmerciful mandates and edicts must be our scriptures, and your rackers, hangmen, wrath, torture chambers, water and stake, fire and sword (O God) must be our instructors and teachers, to whom we sorrowful children must listen in many places, and finally make good with our possessions and lifeblood. . . . This I know for certain, that all bloodthirsty preachers and all rulers who propose and practice these things are not Christ's disciples. The hour of accounting when you depart this life will teach you the truth.

During his long trip north and west into Holland, Menno endured severe pain in both his hip and his heart. But he was at peace about having made the journey. He had seen the developments of the division between the Flemish and Frisian believers. Beyond their cultural differences there were other problems resulting from people who, in seeking ways to avoid suffering at the hands of the state, had made accommodations to their Protestant neighbors. To Menno, these accommodations were a compromise.

What had been a small division over excommunication when it was discussed at Emden had grown into a major schism. The Waterlanders of north Holland (whose name comes from their being bounded by the Zaan River to the south and the Zuiderzee on the east) along with some groups from Franeker and even Emden, had withdrawn from the main Anabaptist body. These groups had come to be known as the more liberal wing of the free church. Leenaert and Dirk were leading the more conservative of the Frisians and Flemish who, even with their differences, regarded their community as the true Anabaptists. Now the two factions had actually excommunicated each other! The Waterlanders had moved to associate more with the leaders from south Germany, with their less rigorous discipline.

It was disconcerting for Menno to find that differences were emerging even in the group of Frisians and Flemish, no doubt a reflection of the differences that had now developed between Leenaert and Dirk. He had tried to avoid becoming involved, but entered into the discussion with various leaders. The more conservative group pressed him strongly to identify fully with them. They sought to hold him accountable to details that he saw as relative, and they did it by a method he saw as a mistake—using single texts as proof, then arguing for their interpretation on the basis of the infallible truth of Scripture. Menno attempted to mediate, stressing the difference between principle and application and arguing that their problems were basically the latter. But their reaction was defensive; they even insinuated that they might need to excommunicate him from their fellowship. His response was that any discernment for healing of this division would be difficult unless they were willing to look at the larger issues.

To the south, the less strict German Anabaptists held a conference in 1557 at Strasbourg. Fifty bishops from numerous countries attended. They wanted to continue relationship with the Mennist churches to the north, but they rejected the practice of strict shunning, especially of shunning marriage partners. Menno was caught between the two sides—the Swiss-German groups on one side and those from the Lowlands on the other.

The meeting he was now attending in the Harlingen region

had been scheduled with a careful measure of secrecy. Upon dispersing for the night, the participants scattered to various homes. Now in the early morning of the second day, Menno walked carefully beside his host with whom he had shared lodging. As they found their way to the gathering of church leaders, Menno was prayerfully reflecting on the matters. "How is it possible to achieve unity unless there was a special work of the Holy Spirit among them?" he pondered.

The need for mediation was great, and Menno felt he must help the church he loved, despite his distaste for conflict. Leenaert and Dirk were now at odds with each other. Menno was sure it was the result of the legalistic spirit they had shown in earlier disputes over the ban.

Dirk was accusing Leenaert of subscribing too legalistically to the position of the Frisians and then extending his influence into the community of the Flemish. As a bishop and leader in the church, working more with the Flemish, Dirk was now attempting to exercise discipline to suspend Leenaert as an elder. "Once you minimize grace and live too much by law," Menno thought, "there seems to be no end to legalism."

As a consequence of Dirk's action, Leenaert had moved again to Harlingen. He was well received by the Frisians, evidently because he had a long association with them, having ministered among them so effectively. He was well known as a traveling evangelist who had preached in nearly two hundred communities and had baptized over ten thousand people. Now things had changed, and his work was also influencing the Flemish, where Dirk had become recognized as a significant spokesperson and leader. Even so, both of them had their differences with the Waterlanders who had withdrawn from them. The Waterlanders, Menno heard, were now working on a confession of faith that would serve to unify their people. Menno thought that was a good move.

Dirk and Leenaert had agreed to meet with Menno and a group of elders to seek reconciliation. At the meetings, Menno was troubled yet exhilarated by fellowship with old friends. It was unbelievable to him that believers who had shared so deeply in the suffering church would be having this problem.

As the talks began, it appeared that his presence made it easier for Dirk and Leenaert to converse. It seemed like earlier times of good fellowship. But now, on the second day, the unresolved matters came to the fore. With patience and words of love, Menno sought to mediate between the two brothers. To his dismay he was unable to lead them to a resolution. They brought this meeting to a close but planned to meet once again the next morning. Menno spent much of the second night in prayer, not able to sleep as he wrestled with the problem.

The discussion on the third day was long and detailed, and at its conclusion the group drafted a list of things about which they were in agreement regarding discipline and conduct. Then they drew up a short statement of things left unresolved. Clearly there was much more on which they agreed than on which they were divided. Menno asked both Dirk and Leenaert to commit themselves to honest prayer over these matters.

⌒

Menno had long recognized Dirk as a special gift to the church. He strongly emphasized the visible church, which Menno also held to be very important. This concept of the visible believers church greatly differed from the Protestant idea of the true church being invisible, being known only to God in his electing grace, and including both the wheat and the tares.

In their discussions Menno and Dirk agreed that the church is to be the visible expression of the body of Christ. As his body, it should make Christ visible to the world and be a fellowship of believers "without spot or wrinkle." Dirk emphasized that the bride of Christ dare not be untrue to the bridegroom. Any people openly living in sinful acts could not be permitted to continue their identification with the church unless they repented.

Menno was in basic agreement with him on this principle, but differing somewhat on actual practice.

Menno had seldom found opportunity to read Dirk's writing. Perhaps in the future he could do this, and they could have conversation over what each was writing. At this point his task was clear: he must work on the relationship between Dirk and Leenaert. The crucial issue was their increased differences on applications of the understanding of the pure church.

The meeting ended, and they would need to trust the Spirit to help them work for understanding and reconciliation. Before leaving for home, Menno and Dirk had a brief, private conversation, primarily about the community of disciples in west Prussia, where Menno and Dirk had ordained leaders for the group. Dirk told Menno of his deep interest in the Prussian community and his plan to return. "I'm tired of this continued interaction with Leenaert," he said. "I think it may be best for the both of us if I should work elsewhere. And as you know, we have many friends in Danzig, so we are considering moving there."

Menno said simply, "I understand, Dirk, and if you feel God leading you to a ministry with our friends in the Prussian community, you have my support in this. Danzig could well be a good place for you and your family, just as I have found the Mecklenburg region to be for us."

~

Menno tramped along with the help of his crutch, occasionally taking difficult paths through the fields to avoid encounter with the authorities seeking him. As he walked along slowly, he pondered the tension between his brothers and wondered how to help them find unity. He recognized that it is unity we seek, not uniformity; we can have unity of spirit with some diversity of practices. Coping with the suffering brought on by persecution was problematic enough without these other problems.

Over and over in his mind, Menno heard the words, "For

other foundation can no man lay than that is laid, which is Jesus Christ." What things are really essential? We are new creatures in Christ, people who are given the Spirit of God. But we are also creatures of thought and culture, and these can affect how we express our walk with Christ. He is the center of our faith, the One in whom and by whom we come to God. We are not accepted because of our goodness but because of our covenant with him in his grace. This is the heart of the matter. The church must exalt Christ above all else. From this meeting he had his mandate—lift Jesus higher.

This thought encouraged Menno, despite the limited success he felt he had achieved. As he thought of his brothers, he prayed that they would do the same, lift high the message of Jesus and his resurrection power.

For the first stretch of Menno's journey, several elders had made arrangements with a farmer to give him an extra-long ride in a farm wagon. At his stop, another farmer met them, and Menno simply transferred from one cart to the other. Later his driver left him by the side of a canal, where he could secure passage for the next phase of his journey.

The boat ride was relaxing. But it took Menno another week after leaving the boat, with his slow and careful pace, before he arrived back at Oldesloe, where his daughters warmly welcomed him.

Menno noticed that Mariken was suffering from an illness. It gave him concern, but he did not comment; he made it a matter of prayer. He longed to see both of them free to marry and enjoy a family as he had.

Quietly Menno reflected on the trip. His mind went to a favorite Scripture in the second chapter of Ephesians. "For He is our peace, who has made both one and has broken down the middle wall of division between us . . . to make in himself of two one new humanity, so making peace; and that he might reconcile both unto God in one body by the cross."

He prayed, "My Father, this is your church, built on your own foundation. As sincerely as I know how, I have sought to build on the one foundation, which is Jesus Christ. I trust this fully to you as the work of your Spirit. Amen."

19
Menno's Final Days and Passing at Oldesloe

1560–1561

Menno was bone tired for days after his return. The long trip had left him exhausted, but he was refreshed by the tender care of his gracious daughters. How he missed his Gert, her love, her companionship, and her counsel. He leaned back in a chair and mused. How good God had been to bring them together. How much they had enjoyed each other! He smiled as he recalled their conversations. He had teased her that perhaps his frequent absences had enhanced this enjoyment, for they had not exhausted one another's patience.

Menno took up his pen to begin to rewrite a summary of the meetings with Leenaert and Dirk in a pamphlet called "Instruction on Excommunication." It would dwell on the need for the church to be authentic in its covenant with Christ and its walk of discipleship.

> We see all this and observe that now the bright light of the holy gospel of Christ shines again in undimmed splendor in these latest awful times of anti-Christian abominations. God's only begotten and firstborn Son, Jesus Christ, is gloriously revealed. His gracious will and holy Word concerning faith, regeneration, repentance, baptism, the Lord's Supper, and the whole saving doc-

trine, life and ordinance have again come to light through much seeking and prayer; through action, reading, teaching, and writing according to the true apostolic rule and criterion in the church, by which the kingdom of Christ comes to honor and the kingdom of anti-Christ is going down in shame.

Menno hoped to bring balance into the thinking of his fellow leaders, but he had seen that the schism was deep. Perhaps there were other factors that the men did not even recognize that made them competitive, so he wrote this treatise with them in mind. He tried to show his own balance in interpreting Scripture, showing the importance of discipline and, where one has become apostate, excommunication. He supported this by affirming that he had known about three hundred cases where a believing man or wife under the pressures of persecution failed to shun the unbelieving spouse, and ultimately they were lost to Christ and the church. But he pointed out that while excommunication was to be done with firmness, it was to be with evident love and the clear intent to reclaim the person. When excommunicated persons came to repentance, the pastor needed to carefully consider evidence of renewed life in Christ before restoring the person.

Menno also affirmed that it was important to distinguish between unrestrained acts of living in sin, as was the case of the incestuous man at Corinth, and sin that was not premeditated, as in the case of Peter denying the Lord.

Menno's inner turmoil over the difficulty of his position showed in the length of the treatise. He cared deeply about the thoughts, feelings, and responses of each side of the issue.

How he wished he could have a good chat with Gertrude. She had always been able to help him achieve balance in his emotions and expressions. She would tell him when his statements appeared harsh or when he needed to be more empathetic to those who thought differently than he did. But now he was alone, and he turned to prayer, asking the Spirit of God to grant him the gift of discernment as well as of wisdom. His longing was that his work and life would reflect his commitment to build on the one foundation of Christ as Lord.

In reflecting on how Gert would have helped him with the treatise, he thought of his daughters and their future, especially Mariken, who did not seem well. He thought of the freedom the Lord had given so many women in their movement to study the Scriptures and teach the Bible to others. But many had paid a high price, like Elizabeth Dirks, who had worked so diligently and died so valiantly for her faith. Another brave hero of faith was their friend Soetken van den Houte of Ghent. Just a few months earlier she had been martyred after a life of remarkable ministry.

～

It soon became evident that Mariken was very ill. He felt so very helpless; he could do nothing but encourage her and pray with her. He regretted that he had needed to be away and did not recognize her need earlier.

Menno had been home little more than a week when Mariken became confined to bed. A disease had invaded her body and medication was not correcting the illness. During the next several weeks he spent much time by her bedside, reading to her from favorite psalms, such as 23, 32, and especially 34.

> I will bless the Lord at all times; his praise shall continually be in my mouth. My soul shall make her boast in the Lord: the humble shall hear thereof and be glad. O magnify the Lord with me and let us exalt his name together. I sought the Lord and he heard me, and delivered me from all my fears. They looked unto him, and were enlightened; and their faces were not ashamed. This poor man cried and the Lord heard him and saved him out of all his troubles. The angel of the Lord encamps round

about them that fear him, and delivers them. O taste and see that the Lord is good: blessed is the man who trusts in him.

And he read from Isaiah 43.

Thus saith the Lord who created thee, O Jacob and he that formed thee, O Israel, Fear not; for I have redeemed thee, I have called thee by thy name, thou art mine. When you pass through the waters, I will be with thee, and through the rivers, they shall not overflow thee; when you walk through the fire, you shall not be burned, neither shall the flame kindle thee. For I am the Lord thy God, the Holy One of Israel, thy Savior.

Menno paused, and then said softly to Mariken, "Above all, we have the words of Jesus, 'I go to prepare a place for you, and if I go and prepare a place for you I will come again and receive you unto myself that where I am there you may be also.' This is our assurance, Mariken. Jesus said, 'The one who comes to me I will in no wise cast out,' and you have come, and he is as good as his word."

He spoke tenderly of salvation in God's wonderful grace, assuring her that she was God's child through her faith in Christ and that now her Lord awaited her in glory. As he prayed with her repeatedly, Mariken responded warmly and with assurance, "Thank you, Father. You have given me a wonderful privilege in knowing the truth of Christ, and I am at rest in him."

Menno's eyes filled with tears. "Mariken, there is nothing so important as to know the new life that Christ gives to us. We will miss you so very much, and there is nothing I would love more than to see you live a long and meaningful life, but we are together in our surrender to the Lord, and I am at peace, as you are, knowing that you will be with the Lord in all his glory."

Deep, wrenching pain consumed Menno as he and Bettjie stood beside Mariken's bed in the final hours of her life. They watched her breathing as it slowed. Then it stopped, and she was gone. They fell into each other's arms as they wept. And then Menno quoted the verse, "Precious in the sight of the Lord is the death of his saints." Bettjie whispered a soft amen.

Menno was grateful to their landlord for once again taking charge of funeral arrangements and the certification of Mariken's death for the authorities. Friends came to extend their sympathy to Menno and Bettjie. The loss of her sister was very difficult for Bettjie; they had been very close. At first Menno felt that, in some way, he had been responsible for the family's difficulties; perhaps the constant travel and hiding had taken its toll. But then he knew that he could not have avoided this, and that Gertrude, Bettjie, Mariken, and even Jan were also committed to be true to the calling of Christ. As he placed this before the Lord, the comfort of the Spirit brought healing.

Mariken was buried in the garden next to her mother's grave. Menno wished that little Jan's body could also be next to them. Turning to Bettjie, he said, "And when I go, you will place my body next to Gertrude. That is my wish."

Bettjie said, "I will see to that, Father; you need have no concern on the matter."

They walked back to the cottage, Menno's arm over her shoulder for balance, but also as an expression of his love for his daughter.

~

But life needed to move on, and Menno found himself in extended dialogue over issues facing the church. He was disturbed over the difficulties of being clear and compassionate while creating a disciplined church. Two brothers from the Rhineland with whom he had enjoyed past association had become particularly critical of his position on marital avoidance. The German brothers were defending a much more lenient and individualistic approach. They told him that he had become more stringent, more legalistic, in his older years. In their opinion he needed to rethink his position and not be influenced by the other leaders in Holland.

Menno received another considerate but pointed letter from his friends in Germany, Sylis and Lemke, the elders of the German church who had challenged him to do something about Leenaert and Dirk.

Recognizing the presumption of the men, Menno wrote a brief response entitled "Reply to Sylis and Lemke." He acknowledged the problem Dirk and Leenaert had in their support of marital avoidance. He also said he had met with them but had achieved little. He expressed his conviction that the Spirit would help the church to work through this, and he counseled them to have patience and an understanding spirit. He also wrote his challenge for these men to be faithful to the Lord of the church and to the Scriptures. He cautioned that they should not let their stance become a compromise or a permission for worldliness and sin in the church.

He wrote at length, for he needed to answer their central charge that, in supporting Dirk and Leenaert, he himself was guilty of causing people to blaspheme. As they saw it, a discipline that was too harsh was creating resentment against Christ. Menno wrote that he was being misunderstood, as he had no greater goal than to build on the one foundation that is laid, which is Jesus Christ. Calling them "dear friends," he appealed for them to pursue faithful discipleship of Christ as they called people to the obedience of faith and to accountability to the Lord, who is head of the church. This, he wrote, was his own commitment, and in this they were brothers. In answer to Lemke's charge that he believed people tended to build on him and his faith, Menno responded with very personal notes.

> First, if I should now or any time say to Lemke or to anyone else—the people build upon and look to me so

much, then my own mouth would convince me that I would be like unto a fool who is quick to praise himself. I trust that not only the Word of the Lord, but also common sense will teach me better. And as I have experienced it more than once in my life, the spirit of Diotrephes is not yet altogether dead, a spirit which generally clothes itself in a sheepskin sighing and complaining, oh, oh, the people build upon and look too much to Menno! By this the hearts are turned from love.

Therefore I have not said once but perhaps ten times, If the common people should build upon me and look to me so much, then I could wish that the Lord would cause me to stumble sometime (not taking His grace from me altogether) so they might learn to know not to build their foundation, hope, and consolation upon me, but solely upon the living cornerstone, Christ Jesus, who according to the will of His Father and to His honor has called us in His eternal love and married us by faith into His death and blood—but not Menno or Lemke. Oh, that they would not garble my words, nor repeat anything but the truth which can stand before God.

Secondly, I answer, If you thus turn to shame the words of my piety whereby I seek only the praise and honor of my Redeemer, which I had not thus expected, then I desire that in love you point out my error according to the truth. For although I am a poor sinner who at times am overcome by my flesh, I yet thank God for His grace that He has to this day saved His poor, weak servant without any grave offense both in doctrine and in life.

But if your vision is so poor and dim that you call it stumbling, namely, that I teach according to the Holy Scriptures that we should shun the offensive transgressors until they repent, or that the ban should be used without respect of persons, or that I am ever prepared to accept a better instruction of God or admonition and doctrine of His Holy Spirit, as I have done and given an example in regard to the matter of carnal sins, then I may well console myself that the holy apostles are in this matter no less stumblers than I am. For before God, I do not know but that I teach the essence of their Word unadulterated, and walk in the footsteps of their spirit, so far as I have received grace and strength from my God.

Within two weeks, a brother brought Menno a letter of response. It was clear in their writing that the German communities of Anabaptists could not accept the more rigid interpretation of the Dutch church on discipline. They, with the Swiss Brethren south of them, were more interested in seeking the good of the offending person and working toward restoration. They wrote that it seemed that Menno was torn by his relationship with Leenaert and Dirk and that through their association he was not free to follow his own inclinations. To Menno's chagrin, Lemke even referred to him as a weathervane changing its direction with that of the wind.

The letter was quite sharp in expressing their difference. Lemke even said that in addition to differing with Menno on the matter of church discipline, he had several other matters on which he disagreed. This was a bit much for Menno, as he felt the churches to the south were being too independent, and he was caught between negotiating with them and continuing to maintain the respect he enjoyed from the churches in the Netherlands. Menno pondered this, knowing he needed to work for what was best to maintain integrity in the Anabaptist churches of the Netherlands and unity for the larger cause as much as possible. But as they represented others in the strong German communities to the south, he needed to represent the communities of the Lowlands in which he was a leader. In response he wrote a letter exposing the problems he saw in their position.

How perilously you are sailing like a ship that goes trip-
ping along between two rocks. If it avoids the one it will
run into the other. Therefore, take heed, take heed, I say,
that you may escape the eternal shipwreck of your poor
souls and arrive in the haven of eternal peace with the
most High. Amen. Amen.

With words of deep regret, Menno stated that this letter
could officially place them under the ban as far as the Dutch community was concerned. He concluded his letter: "I write with
deep regret. Due to your attitude of rejection of my leadership
role, and failure to understand my desire for harmony in my association with the elders in the Netherlands, I must now relinquish
open brotherhood with you."

This final note was so painful for Menno, he held the letter for a few days and reflected on it further. He prayed for the
Lord's guidance on sending it, and finally did so. For the next
few days he prayed for a work of the Spirit to safeguard the letter's impact and to renew and sanctify the church in which he
had invested so much.

Menno prayed regularly for Leenaert and Dirk, and for the
south German and Swiss brothers. He especially prayed for the
church across Friesland, with all of the persecution from the magistrates and the need for unity and strength within the church.

As he closed his prayer time in the early morning, he opened
his Bible to a favorite passage in Ephesians 2: "For he is our
peace, who has made the two to be one, having broken down the
wall of partition between us, for to make in himself of two one
new humanity, through the cross, so making peace."

He continued to browse through the familiar phrases and
thought of the wonder of this marvelous expression of grace.
"This," he said to himself, "is our security, our hope, our assurance that the work of Christ will bring this church through to
maturity and unity as the body of Christ, the body that will
make Christ visible in society."

⌒

Crutch under his arm, Menno slowly made his way through the garden. It was fall now, and most of the plants were dead. The cabbage was green and full, and the celery tops stuck up from soil that had been hoed around the plants to protect them and increase their tenderness. Menno stood looking at the trees, now nearly bare of leaves. "This is the cycle of life," he thought. "Soon it will be my turn."

He made his way back into the cottage. In his favorite chair, he reached for the Bible and placed it on his knees. He opened to Paul's first letter to the Corinthians, placed his finger on verse 11 of chapter 3 and read, "For no one can lay any foundation other than the one already laid, which is Jesus Christ." He smiled as he leaned back and closed his eyes. This was his basic text, the key to his life's work.

Bettjie watched him sitting in his chair and was sure that he had fallen asleep. She left him in quiet and went about preparing their meal. Menno admired his daughter as he observed her manner as a gracious hostess and the spirit in which she adjusted to Mariken's absence. She was much like his Gert. He tried to encourage her through her grief over the loss of her sister, but it was difficult because he felt it so deeply himself.

⌒

Even though he was often tired and increasingly weakened by his work, Menno found it a pleasant ministry to counsel the many people who came to his door. Frequently it was traveling evangelists or missioners who wanted to see him. They gave long reports of carrying the gospel message to many communities across Europe.

One day a guest brought him a letter from Thomas von Imbroich, a friend he had greatly admired and respected. He had written it some time before, in 1558, as he faced his death in

prison in Cologne. Menno was deeply moved by what he read—
a farewell from a friend who knew his time was short.

> Let us be valiant; for the apostle says, "My strength is
> made perfect in weakness." . . . Hence I deem it good to
> be in weakness, if it be followed by being in reproach,
> distress, persecution, and fear for Christ's sake.
>
> Yea, if the Lord should count me worthy to testify
> with my blood to His name, how greatly would I thank
> Him. For I hope not only to bear these bonds with
> patience, but also to die for Christ's sake that I may fin-
> ish my course with joy; for I would rather be with the
> Lord than live again in this abominable wicked world.
> However, His divine will be done. Amen.
>
> And if anything should be defective yet in my life, that
> I may not have been diligent enough (which I confess),
> may the Lord blot it out and purge it through the fire of
> His love and mercy in the blood of Jesus Christ. . . . Dear
> brethren, I desire that you will all pray to God for me
> that He will keep us through Jesus Christ our Lord and
> Savior. Amen.

As Menno read the letter, he began to cry. Turning to his
guest, he said, "I am blessed by this letter. What a wonderful expression of steadfast faith! I needed this word, for it refreshes my own
faith. I've known Thomas as a brother and have rejoiced in his ministry. He had a very biblical message, especially emphasizing the
need for us to know the inner presence of the Holy Spirit. He has
preached very clearly that there are two baptisms: the outer with
water that is only a sign and doesn't save or change anyone, and the
inner with the Spirit, and this inner baptism changes, transforms,
and saves the recipient. It is the presence of the Spirit of Christ that
creates a new people and a new community."

His guest nodded, listening intently, expecting Menno to
continue his comments. Then he said, "And now our brother

Thomas has experienced the third baptism, having emphasized the baptisms with water and with the Spirit, yet now is added to this a baptism of suffering for our Lord."

"Yes," Menno responded. "Here he writes positively that he is ready to die for his Lord." Menno paused, then said reflectively, "I have had to face this in a different way, and as a fugitive I have avoided such a death. But even so, in the threats and danger of arrest I too have often faced this issue of death. I have committed myself first to serve Christ and then to die for Christ if that be in his plan. But for me the blessing of God is in answer to my prayers for grace to live for Christ, to minister his gospel. He has granted me that privilege for two dozen years. I can't ask more."

"And we are so grateful to the Lord for his protection," his guest said. "The church has so benefited from your ministry and leadership. From the impact of your service and writing, we are now being called Mennonite, a designation that marks us as a peaceful group of Anabaptists. But some of us ask, what will we do when you are gone?"

Menno chuckled, "The church belongs to our Lord, and he calls people to lead and to meet the needs of his flock. I'm sure the Spirit will call gifted people to go way beyond what I have been privileged to see and do. I am praying that there will be a new day of freedom, a day of tolerance, a day in which people of different perspectives can live side by side and share in conversation with each other. In such conversation the Spirit can certify the truth as it is in Jesus. True, we have problems in the church, because we are so human, but the Holy Spirit is building the kingdom of Christ among us and he will continue to build the church. I must confess that I enjoyed the pastoral ministry in the church more than a protective ministry."

~

A few days later, Menno said, "Bettjie, would you bring me *The Foundation of Christian Doctrine*? I would like you to read a few sections for me, just to review a few things I have found so important. Just hearing them rather than sitting here trying to rethink them may bring me a renewal of peace."

Bettjie went to his shelf and picked out the little book. As she turned the pages she found passages that he had underscored. She read as she paged along.

> In Christ nothing matters but faith working by love, the new creature and the keeping of the commandments of God. . . . Christ and his apostles teach that regeneration as well as faith comes from God and His word, which Word is not to be taught to those who are unable to hear or understand but to those who have the ability both to hear and to understand. This is uncontestable.
>
> The holy apostle Peter also declares the same and says that even baptism doth also now save us, not the putting away of the filth of the flesh, but the covenant of a good conscience with God by the resurrection of Jesus Christ. Here Peter teaches us how the inward baptism saves us, by which the inner man is washed, and not the outward baptism by which the flesh is washed. Oh, no, outward baptism avails nothing so long as we are not inwardly renewed, regenerated and baptized with the heavenly fire and the Holy Ghost of God.
>
> But it is when we are the recipients of this baptism from above, then we are constrained through the Spirit and Word of God by a good conscience which we obtain thereby, because we believe sincerely in the merits of the death of the Lord and in the power and fruits of His resurrection and because we are inwardly cleansed by faith. In the spiritual strength which we have received, we henceforth bind ourselves by the outward sign of the covenant in water which is enjoined on all believers by Christ even as the Lord has bound Himself with us in

His grace through His Word, namely, that we will no longer live according to the evil, unclean lusts of the flesh, but walk according to the witness of a good conscience before Him.

To be regenerate, to put on Christ and to receive the Holy Ghost, is one and the same thing, and according to their power not different. Do you have the one? Then you have the other also. But that does not at all concern infants, for regeneration as well as faith takes place through the Word of God and is a change of heart, or of the inward man, as was said. To put on Christ is to be transplanted into Christ and to be like-minded with Him. To receive the Holy Ghost is to be a partaker of His gifts and power, to be taught, assured, and influenced by Him as the Scriptures teach.

Menno sat in his chair with his eyes closed. As she paused, he said, "This I believe, and this is basic in our experience of faith. But read on a bit further. Share something of the nature of this new community of the regenerate." Bettjie went on silently scanning and then selected another passage.

I tell you the truth in Christ, the rightly baptized disciples of Christ, note well, they who are baptized inwardly with Spirit and fire, and externally with water, according to the Word of the Lord, have no weapons except patience, hope, silence, and God's Word. The weapons of our warfare, says Paul, are not carnal, but mighty through God to the pulling down of strongholds, casting down imaginations and every high thing that exalts itself against the knowledge of God, and bringing into captivity every thought to the obedience of Christ. I Cor. 10:4, 5.

Our weapons are not weapons with which cities and countries may be destroyed, walls and gates broken down, and human blood shed in torrents like water. But they are weapons with which the spiritual kingdom of the devil is destroyed and the wicked principle in man's soul is broken down, flinty hearts broken, hearts that have never been sprinkled with the heavenly dew of the Holy Word. We have and know no other weapons besides this, the Lord knows, even if we should be torn into a thousand pieces and if as many false witnesses rose up against us as there are spears of grass in the fields and grains of sand upon the seashore.

"Yes!" Menno burst out in a guttural response. "That I believe!" Bettjie continued to read further the words her father had written.

I confess my Savior openly, I confess Him and dissemble not. To be born of God is to become one with Christ in Spirit, faith, life, and worship. He is the Lord of the Church. We are his new community, that in which we are one by our common faith in Christ. And as Christians, we must walk as Christ walked. As Paul wrote, "If any man have not the Spirit of Christ, he is none of his." "Whosoever transgresses and abides not in the doctrine of Christ is none of His." II John 1:9.

These and other Scriptures stand immovable and judge all those who live outside the Spirit and Word of Christ, and who mind earthly and carnal things. We are called to integrity in our walk with Christ, to have contrite hearts, true knowledge of Christ, true love, an earnest desire after the Kingdom of God, dying to earthly things, true humility, righteousness, friendliness, mercy, chastity, obedience, wisdom, truth and peace. I in this matter, with my small talents, with similar intent and cause, testify openly to the truth.

Menno smiled at Bettjie. "I have been quite free with words, too free at times, but I simply want to call those about us to hear the Word of God and to come to him. Many people under false teachers are missing out on the freedom that is in Christ." He paused, straining a bit for his breath.

"Father, I understand, and I pray with you that many will come to know our Lord. We are like seed sown in the field, and in God's time there will be a harvest of plenty."

Menno nodded. "In God's time. Yes, and we are just at the dayspring. He is visiting our land. The day will come when there will be freedom and tolerance for differences of faith. You must prepare to live in the changes that will come."

It was a struggle for him now to make even a short speech. He closed his eyes, and Bettjie watched him until he had fallen asleep, tired from the exertions of the day.

~

During the next few days, Menno continued to converse with the several people who came and went from his home, but it became evident to Bettjie that he was increasingly weak. After several months, he became severely ill, finding it difficult to breathe. At times he suffered pain in his chest and would spend hours sitting in his rocking chair. He was often grumpy over his inability to be active, troubled and even tormented by the suffering that was besetting the church.

Menno was soon unable to walk without help, and his daughter kept him mostly to his bed. Many days he was in emotional turmoil, pondering memories of what he had suffered and the difficulties it had caused for Gertrude and the family. As he reflected on the divisions in the church, he told Bettjie that he was tired of fighting and that he needed to leave it to others.

He asked Bettjie to read to him once again from the second chapter of Ephesians, the last part of the chapter. She got the Bible and began to read at verse 14.

For he is our peace who had made both one, and hath

broken down the middle wall of partition between us; having abolished in his flesh the enmity, even the law of commandments contained in ordinances; for to make in himself of twain one new man, so making peace; and that he might reconcile both unto God in one body by the cross, having slain the enmity thereby: and came and preached peace to you which were afar off and to them that were near. For through him we both have access by one Spirit unto the Father.

"How wonderful," Menno said. "That is the heart of the gospel, the word which I have sought to share across the country. But read on. I want to hear the conclusion."

Bettjie continued with exuberance.

Now therefore ye are no more strangers and foreigners, but fellow-citizens with the saints, and of the household of God; and are built upon the foundation of the apostles and prophets, Jesus Christ himself being the chief corner stone; in whom all the building fitly framed together grows unto a holy temple in the Lord: in whom you also are built together for an habitation of God through the Spirit.

"Thank you," Menno said. "With that passage I rest my case. To build on the foundation of Christ as expressed by the apostles and the prophets is our highest calling and our security."

It was January of 1561, and Menno was confined to his bed. During those days, numerous visitors still called on him. He enjoyed their words of encouragement, and he continued to express concern that a faithful and true church celebrate the life in the Spirit, that as regenerate people they willingly embrace a life of discipleship and pledge themselves to one another in a covenant of love and mutuality.

Bettjie was usually busy about the house as people visited with her father, but she heard him say repeatedly to those who called, "There is nothing on earth as precious to me as the church." Of this they were all quite certain, for they had lived with him and known his ministry, and they had seen the evidence of his sincerity.

~

One day Menno called Bettjie to his bedside and took her hands, each in one of his own. "My time here will not be long," he said. "I am so thankful to you for your special care and your support. When I am gone, don't weep for me, as I will be with the Lord and with Gertrude. But look to yourself, to the daily enrichment of your faith in Christ and to your own discipleship. I am sure that God will give you a wonderful marriage and there will be children, my grandchildren whom I will not get to see. But bring them up in the nurture of Christ. May God enrich you by His Spirit to do just that."

He closed his eyes. Bettjie looked at him as her own eyes filled with tears, knowing that he was near death. Releasing his hands, she watched him silently as he slept. She shared the satisfaction of faith in Christ that he witnessed, and she knew that the Lord was with him in this hour. She was so thankful for a father who had taught her in the way of the Lord, so thankful for his example and his ministry.

Bettjie turned to a neighbor who had come to be with her and who stood by the door, saying simply, "He was a wonderful father and he lived a good life. In spite of having a price on his head, he was able by God's care to avoid arrest and martyrdom. His twenty-five years in ministry were a special blessing from God, and for him to die in bed is so much better than to die at the stake! We have so much for which to be thankful."

The neighbor listened, then stepped over and put her arm around Bettjie's shoulder. "And he has been fortunate to have such a wonderful daughter. You have been his colleague in the work of Christ." They stood together in an embrace, the neighbor shedding tears of empathy with Bettjie as she watched her father straining for breath.

~

Menno suffered quietly for several days in the last part of January, but on the last day of the month, he came to the close of his life. It was the twenty-fifth anniversary of his ordination, which came after his renunciation of the Roman Catholic Church and his joining the free church movement, as he called it. He had lived to see the development of a major association of disciples of Christ, now known as Mennonites, the peaceful Anabaptists.

Just before his passing, Menno asked those around the bed to help him sit up so that he could get his breath. He sat propped up by pillows long enough to give a short exhortation. As he emphasized faithfulness to Christ, once again he said, "There is no other foundation, only the one which is laid by Jesus Christ." Then he laid his head back, closed his eyes, and quietly passed from this life to the next.

Menno was no longer a fugitive but at peace—a son welcomed home by the Father.

Epilogue

The movement Menno Simons served is today made up of many small denominations of Mennonites. Much of the distinction between the denominations is cultural or ethnic in origin. Perhaps the diversity is conditioned primarily by the freedom in which the laity has pursued the study of Scriptures. Various interpretations have led to varied applications in lifestyle, but all the groups would claim to be biblical in interpretation of Christian faith and discipleship.

The Mennonite church actually began about twelve years before Menno's conversion, in Zurich in 1525. The movement had a very significant early formation and was known as the Swiss Brethren. It spread across Switzerland, Austria, south Germany, and into France, following down the Rhine to the Low Countries. It was there, under Menno's leadership in the Netherlands, that the church was given his name, Mennonite.

This name, initially expressed as Mennist, soon moved south until the Anabaptists in Germany and Switzerland were also called by the same name. The spread of the name was accepted in large part due to the desire of the peaceful Anabaptists to distinguish themselves from violent revolutionaries who were also called Anabaptists by the authorities.

The movement was the more evangelistic group of the Reformation. It spread rapidly across Europe. In the era of American colonization, Mennonites moved west, coming first to Pennsylvania in 1683 under William Penn, who brought Quakers two years earlier, and with many migrations following. These migrations to North America continued into the early twentieth century. Often, especially in the nineteenth century, the reason for the movement was to settle someplace where Mennonites would be free from participation in war and could live out their nonresistant commitment.

This denomination has now existed for more than 480 years and has spread to many countries of the world. It numbers 1.25 million members in as many as seventy different countries around the world. With the growth of the Mennonite churches in Africa, the majority of the denomination's members today are from other than European backgrounds. The Mennonite World Conference offices in Strasbourg, France, coordinate effective global activities, highlighted by an international conference every six years. The most recent gathering was in Zimbabwe in 2004, with a unique mix of global members.

Other global activities are conducted by various denominational mission boards and by the service agency Mennonite Central Committee. This is one inter-Mennonite organ in which Amish groups participate. The Amish are doubtless the second-largest Anabaptist group in North America and have increasingly become recognized by secular society as a people of integrity. The Amish have their background in the Mennonite Church in Switzerland, where a division took place in 1693 over the issue of discipline in congregations. The schism has kept the groups separate through the years.

The third-largest group would be the Mennonite Brethren, who are especially strong from Kansas to California in the United States and from Manitoba west to British Columbia in Canada. In addition to these groups, many smaller conferences of Mennonites seek to live by the Anabaptist vision. Numerous Baptist groups also recognize their roots in the Anabaptist movement.

The church spread across Europe in the sixteenth century through early leaders who were very evangelistic. There are accounts of several who each converted and baptized thousands, including Leenaert Bouwens, Menno's associate of the

Netherlands, and Leonard Dorfbrunner of Bavaria. It is obvious that these believers were won to Christ by the evangelistic ministries of the Anabaptists or there would not have been such numbers to be martyrs. Even today, on the cutting edges of the church in various countries, both the work of evangelism and the experience of martyrdom have continued.

After a spiritual renewal among German Lutherans in seventeenth-century Europe, which influenced Mennonites as well, the Anabaptist movement spread beyond Europe, especially to North America. Until near the end of the twentieth century, North America held the largest number of Mennonites. The Mennonite church in Africa has now become the largest in the world, enriching the denomination along the way. In some cases, especially in Africa, whole groups of Christians have joined the Mennonite church to identify with its emphasis on discipleship in Christ and the way of peace and nonviolence.

The lessening of persecution gave the Mennonites a new freedom early in the seventeenth century. This was true especially in the earliest expressions of tolerance in the Netherlands. The authorities from there appealed to those in Switzerland to become more tolerant of the Anabaptists, benefiting those churches. This soon followed in other countries of Europe. With the new freedom in the Netherlands, the Mennonites became quite involved in society, in business, in the professions, in education, and in the arts.

In the sixteenth century, the Anabaptists produced the *Ausbund*, a collection of songs written primarily by martyrs when in prison. The major writing of historical accounts of the martyrs, *Martyrs Mirror*, has bridged the centuries. Among various artists, the poet Joost von Vondel of the Mennonites of the Netherlands has been described as "the Dutch Shakespeare."

It is of special interest to my wife and me that there were numerous Mennonite artists of lasting repute. This includes Jacob and Solomon Ruisdale; Anton Mauve, whose wife was cousin of Vincent van Gogh and who introduced him to the use of color;

Govert Flink who studied under Rembrandt; and Jan Lyken, who illustrated *Martyrs Mirror* and numerous other books. Although he was not a church member, Rembrandt's association with the Mennonites has been said to have shaped much of the humanism of his paintings.

As a movement of "a third way" between Catholic and Protestant, the Anabaptist/Mennonite position has had its own uniqueness, especially in its christological interpretations, its emphasis on discipleship in loving nonviolence, and its emphasis on separation of church and state. In 1922, in lectures at Princeton University on church history, Henry Dosker spoke of the Anabaptists and their emphasis on separation of church and state as having been two hundred years ahead of its time. He said that it was not until the founding of the United States that this sociopolitical pattern could be realized. It did not happen easily, however, because the early colonies in New England were still fully identified with the Church of England. When Roger Williams sought to carry out his Baptist convictions in a way that challenged political policies, he was expelled and sent back to England. Upon his return to England, he was again expelled with his followers, and they began a new venture in what came to be known as Rhode Island. Later this position of separation between church and state became a part of the United States Constitution.

A very significant story is that of Stephan Funk, a Mennonite preacher near Thorn, West Prussia, who taught peace in a way consistent with the teachings of Menno Simons. When King Charles XII of Sweden invaded Prussia and was executing a siege of Thorn in 1703, he heard of Funk and his preaching. Learning that the Mennonites rejected warfare, he sent for Funk and ordered him to preach a sermon in the camp in his presence and prove his principle of nonresistance from the Bible. Funk complied. After the sermon, the king inquired whether all wars were unconditionally condemned in the Scriptures. Funk answered, "If anything could be allowed in the Holy Scriptures, it must be that a king who is attacked in his own realm might defend himself; but that a king march into another realm to conquer and devastate it, for that there is no freedom in the Scriptures; on the contrary, it is absolutely opposed to Christ's teachings."

In the eighteenth century, John Wesley was used of God for a movement of spiritual renewal that ultimately affected the world. His associate, George Whitefield, made seven trips across the Atlantic to bring the gospel to the colonies in America in their need for a spiritual awakening. A note of interest that too few people know about is the friendship between John Wesley and the leading Mennonite pastor of Amsterdam, Jeremy Deknatal. Wesley quoted Deknatal in his journals, and Deknatal wrote that he and his wife came to a deep spiritual experience through their friendship with Wesley. In turn Wesley shared with the Mennonites a measure of their concerns for peace, as he preached against war and violence.

The Mennonites who came to America under William Penn were from Switzerland and Germany, then from Prussia, and later from the Netherlands. Many Dutch Mennonites became wealthy as owners of shipping lines and were involved in the development of the New World, at work early in New Amsterdam, later called New York. But most of the Mennonites who came to North America came in a quest for freedom from military service in the countries from which they emigrated. As they spread to the west, they carried the Bible and the book of martyrdom, *Martyrs Mirror* by Thieleman J. van Braght, translated from the Dutch to German to English. Their industrious lifestyle carried them into new farming areas and land acquisition. There are stories of death at the hand of Indians in Virginia and central Pennsylvania, but also remarkable stories of their peaceful lifestyle enabling them to develop respect and friendship with the Native Americans.

While the Mennonites were separatists in society, they were loyal to the authorities. During the Revolutionary War, they were loyal to England until the break, and then they took their place as U.S. citizens. During the Civil War, they were committed to the way of peace and avoided participation in the military. There are moving stories of the high price that many paid for this, especially in Virginia. Significantly, the revivalist D. L. Moody, who served as a chaplain during the Civil War, stated, "On the question of war I am a Quaker."

As to the several Great Awakenings, which claimed hundreds of thousands of indifferent Americans for the church and the cause of Christ, the Mennonites were influenced by the revival but were so separatist that they did not freely participate. But God raised up Mennonite revivalists, one being John Funk, who had gone to Chicago and was converted under D. L. Moody. Funk worked with Moody but returned to work in the Mennonite church. Another was John S. Coffman, the first Mennonite itinerant evangelist in the North American Mennonite church.

To various Protestant denominations the term Anabaptist was a heresy to be avoided. This limited Mennonite acceptance by the larger church, while on the other hand Mennonite separatism extended their pattern of exclusiveness. In the nineteenth century the Mennonite church began once again to extend its mission of sharing the gospel. The Dutch Mennonites were the first, sending missionaries to Indonesia, at that time called the Dutch East Indies. The Dutch Mennonites also gave financial assistance to the Baptists for William Carey to go to India. Later, missionaries were sent by American Mennonites to India to work in famine and orphanage relief, as well as in evangelistic missions and church building.

Many Mennonites left Russia under Alexander the Great, with his good wishes, and moved to North America at the turn of the twentieth century. Responding to war and famine in Russia, Mennonite Central Committee engaged in extensive relief work. Those early immigrants from Russia selected the best grains and brought Turkey Red Wheat to America, starting the very successful wheat farming in Kansas and other states. Much later, at the conclusion of World War II, many Mennonites were displaced; fleeing Russia they found themselves in the Russian Quarter in Berlin. It was only by God's providence and the good work of Peter and Elfrieda Dyck that they were able to leave Europe and make their way to South America, where large communities still live in Paraguay and Uruguay. Mennonites have often needed to flee a place to maintain their position on peace and to escape conscription into military service.

Early in the twentieth century, the development of Mennonite colleges enriched and strengthened the life of the church. In the first quarter of the century, seven colleges were founded and developed by various North American Mennonite denominations. Later, three seminaries also were founded. Five of these colleges are associated with the denomination known as Mennonite Church USA (MC USA): Goshen College, Bethel College, Bluffton University, Eastern Mennonite University, and Hesston College. MC USA also sponsors two seminaries: Eastern Mennonite Seminary and Associated Mennonite Biblical Seminary.

Other denominational organizations have colleges and seminaries. Mennonite Brethren have Hillsboro College, Tabor College, and Fresno Pacific University, and Mennonite Brethren Biblical Seminary. They also have Bible colleges in various provinces of western Canada and an inter-Mennonite university in Manitoba. The Conservative Mennonite Conference owns Rosedale Bible College, near Columbus, Ohio.

Mennonite Church Canada (MC Canada) and the Mennonite Brethren (MB) sponsor a number of higher education institutions, including Canadian Mennonite University in Winnipeg, Manitoba; Conrad Grebel College in Waterloo, Ontario; Columbia Bible College in Abbotsford, British Columbia; and Toronto Mennonite Theological Centre. Both groups also relate to Associated Mennonite Biblical Seminary and Mennonite Brethren Biblical Seminary.

By the later part of the twentieth century, these schools enabled faculty to dialogue with Mennonite professors at universities in other countries, especially in Holland, Germany, France, and Switzerland, and to serve on faculties of universities in other countries, particularly in South America and Africa. Mennonites are becoming once again expressive of an ecumenical spirit. As Mennonite theologian John Howard Yoder pointed out, Mennonites were one of the more ecumenical denominations for "they would share with anyone anytime on the basis of the Scriptures."

Harold S. Bender of Goshen College was elected president of the American Society of Church History and on December 29, 1943, presented his inaugural address, which he entitled "The Anabaptist Vision." This remarkable presentation resulted in new interest in Anabaptist thought. After a significant historical introduction, he expressed three primary points: the rediscovery of salvation in Christian experience as discipleship, the emphasis on the church as a voluntary fellowship of the regenerate, and the emphasis on love and nonviolence as a lifestyle. George Williams of Harvard and, later, Franklin Littell followed in scholarly research along with numerous others. Highlighting the uniqueness of the Anabaptist faith, Walter Klaassen wrote *Anabaptism: Neither Catholic nor Protestant*. In his 1999 book *Theology of the Reformers*, Timothy George excelled over many Protestant scholars with the inclusion of the Anabaptists, giving a chapter of his book to Menno Simons. He also writes on Martin Luther, Ulrich Zwingli, and John Calvin.

A whole new generation of Anabaptist scholars came to the fore by the mid-twentieth century, in both America and the Netherlands. Along with Harold S. Bender were his associates J. C. Wenger, Chester K. Lehman, and Guy Hershberger. The young scholar John Howard Yoder studied in Basel under Karl Barth and became without doubt the leading Mennonite theologian of the twentieth century. His theological insights and sharp mind enabled him to touch minds for the cause of Anabaptist thought, as did Stanley Hauerwas of Duke University and James McClendon of Fuller Theological Seminary, along with many others. Within the

Mennonite church, John Howard Yoder stimulated theologians such as Hauerwas; McClendon; Perry Yoder of Elkhart, Indiana; John Roth of Goshen, Indiana; George Brunk III of Eastern Mennonite Seminary; Norman Kraus; Calvin Redekop; and many others.

One of the best scholars of Yoder's writings is Mark Thiessen Nation, professor at Eastern Mennonite Seminary. Katie Funk Wiebe, an inspirational writer, is one of many women who should be named, along with bishops, pastors, and lay leaders. These women include Elizabeth Bender, who did much of the research and writing for her busy husband, Harold S. Bender. I, of course, include my wife, Esther K. Augsburger, artist and sculptor, whose partnership has so enriched my life. Without detailed comment, mention should be made of Nancy Heisey, Mary Oyer, Beryl Brubaker, Lee Snyder, Nancy Lee, Melodie Davis, Phyllis Pellman Good, Dorothy Nickel Friesen, Mary Shertz, Gayle Gerber Koontz, Elaine Sommers Rich, Delores Friesen, and internationally of Rachel Bagh of India, Esther Kalambo of Zambia, Hellen Bradburn of Tanzania, Kadi Hayalume of Congo, Sibusisiwel Ndlova of Zimbabwe, Rebecce Osiro of Kenya, Kelemua Tefera of Ethiopia, Sidonie Swana of Congo, Nelly Mlotshwa of Zimbabwe, and many, many other women whose contribution in the spirit of Christ helps to shape the church and interpret its faith and mission.

During the 1950s into the 1970s my friend George R. Brunk II brought evangelism and revival to various Mennonite groups across North America. Others of us were privileged to share in many citywide interdenominational meetings in which we extended the Mennonite perspective in an evangelistic manner. On of the unique meetings I was privilege to conduct was the one citywide meeting held in Salt Lake City on the capitol steps for eight nights, in cooperation with the various Protestant churches of the city. Such meetings were used by God to share the call to discipleship far beyond the Mennonite church.

There have been a significant number of scholars, missionaries, and pastors who have emerged as contemporary voices for the Anabaptist faith in many parts of the world. This includes scholars from the Doopsgezinde (Mennonite) Community in Amsterdam; scholars in Basel, Switzerland; and at the Bienenberg Bible Institute, Liestal, Switzerland, such as Samuel Gerber. The growth of the church in Indonesia has been one of the more significant areas of church dynamics. East Africa has been a strong center for Mennonite mission, especially the noteworthy ministry of Donald Jacobs and his work with numerous church leaders on the continent. Other movements include the work with Africa Inland Mission by the Evangelical Mennonite Church, and the remarkable church growth in the Congo and especially in Ethiopia with the Meserete Kristos Church. One can only mention the church in South America, in the many countries in Central America, in India, and in other Asian countries.

There are many significant contemporary American Mennonite scholars whose contributions reach far beyond the Mennonite church. In ethics and theology, of note is Lawrence Burkholder of Goshen College, formerly a professor at Harvard. Another contemporary scholar of Anabaptist history and thought is Arnold Snyder of Conrad Grebel College at Waterloo University in Canada. His writings have been shared in the global community through the Mennonite World Conference. Other significant scholars and writers include Norman Kraus in theology, Wilbert Shenk in world missions, John A. Lapp in church and mission history, Elmer Martens in biblical studies, Calvin Redekop in sociology, John Toews in biblical theology, John D. Roth in history, and Katie Funk Wiebe, an inspirational writer. Some of these, and many other noteworthy scholars, are members of various Mennonite denominations, including the Mennonite Brethren, Brethren in Christ, Church of the Brethren, Brethren Church, Grace Brethren Church, and the Missionary Church.

As Mennonites, we have sought to take our place in the larger

Christian community, witnessing to an evangelical faith and its essential character as a call to discipleship of Christ. This is being promoted by colleges and seminaries of the various Mennonite denominations and by the agencies that support workers in mission in many countries. Several examples of this conviction for evangelism are seen in meetings by multidenominational Mennonite groups that gathered to discuss evangelism, first in 1972 in Minneapolis for a conference on evangelism known as Probe 72, and again in a similar conference in 1985, meeting in Denver, called Alive 85.

A good number of Mennonite leaders have attended the Billy Graham congresses on evangelism, beginning with Berlin in 1966 and numerous others, including Amsterdam and later Lausanne in 1974. We participated as well in the Graham Congress on Evangelism in Minneapolis in 1970. The Mennonite Brethren, the Evangelical Mennonites, the United Missionary Church, and the Brethren in Christ denominations have long been members of the National Association of Evangelicals, even though other Mennonite denominations are not.

At the beginning of the twenty-first century, Mennonites have engaged in numerous ecumenical discussions with other churches and denominations. These meetings have been held with members of the Roman Catholic community, with Reformed Church leaders in Zurich, and with Baptist representatives. A significant conversation was held between representatives of the Baptist World Alliance and the Mennonite World Conference in early 2002 at Eastern Baptist Seminary in Philadelphia, thanks to Larry Miller, executive secretary of the Mennonite World Conference and L. A. "Tony" Cupit, Denton Lotz, both executives for the Baptist World Alliance.

Another note of interest is reported in the work of Baptist scholar Glen Stassen, of Oxford University. His study of the earliest Confession of Faith of the General Baptists (c. 1620) found that Article 39 of the First London Confession, has extensive, almost verbatim quotes from Menno Simons's "Confession of Faith as an Anabaptist." Stassen's article, "Opening the Menno Simons Foundation Book and Finding the Father of Baptist Origins," appeared in *Baptist History and Heritage* in Spring 1998.

While the Anabaptists were the evangelists of the Reformation period, reaching the populace by itinerant missions, our evangelism as Mennonites in North America and Europe has been less direct and has been primarily related to "presence," that is, to being a witness for Christ as a community of faith. This may reflect the separateness of the denomination in the stream of Christian churches, but it may also reflect the fact that the Mennonite position on nonresistance has tended to cause rejection by other Christians who have participated in the military. Increasingly our evangelism is being thought of as the missional character of the church, as being "salt and light," seeking creative ways of sharing the gospel of Christ in society.

As Mennonites, we believe that we do society the most good by maintaining our integrity as a church. We do the larger Christian churches the most good by emphasizing a Christology that takes Jesus seriously in life and teaching as well as death and resurrection; a witness of discipleship and the life of peace; separation of church and state; and a lifestyle of love and nonviolence. Our focus on mission stresses conversational evangelism but also relates service and proclamation, balancing the evangelical and the social dimensions of the gospel. We seek to hold a christological center that sees Christian experience as relationship with the risen Christ, a relationship that holds salvation and ethics together rather than seeing ethics as something added to one's faith. In this perspective we are saved in relation with Jesus and we live in relation with Jesus.

While Mennonites have often been known more for culture than for theology, this has changed in recent years. The Mennonite church has taken seriously the call to share faith with others and has become quite active in church planting in cities like Indianapolis, New York, Chicago, Dallas, Raleigh, Seattle, Washington, D.C.,

Calgary, Toronto, Vancouver, and many more. Sometimes this has grown out of young professionals moving to the city, but frequently it has been a deliberate move in church planting.

With an increased contribution in publishing, in theological interchange, in educational and professional vocations, the church is better understood. Today, the Mennonite church is a leading voice among Protestants for a lifestyle of peace, and it has long been counted with the Quakers and Church of the Brethren as one of the historic peace churches.

The Mennonite denominations have for the past century been quite missionary in service and proclamation in many countries of the world, especially in Asia, Africa, and Latin America. We are committed to holding the great commission and the great commandment together. The relief agency Mennonite Central Committee ministers in many parts of the world. Mennonite Mission Network includes missions in some fifty countries. Mennonite Disaster Service is known for its assistance to people suffering from nature's catastrophes. Volunteer programs of various types enable young people to make short-term service ventures in bridge-building for peace and cross-cultural relationships. I once compared the percentage of our church membership who are volunteer workers with that of the Southern Baptists for a speech at one of their conventions. I found that in comparison with this much larger denominations, Mennonites were in the forefront in global mission engagements.

The Mennonite church seeks above all to hold its commitment to Jesus Christ as Lord, to live as disciples of Christ in love and peace, and to find through the Holy Spirit the ability to live the way of Christ as taught in the gospels, especially in the Sermon on the Mount, and in the epistles. In the transitions of thought from premodern to modern to postmodern, the church is committed to a theology of relationship with Christ and the community of his disciples. This commitment takes his Word as its guide for life and seeks as a community of faith to understand and interpret that Word consistently and with relevance to our context. This is the heritage of faith to which we have been called by our Lord, by Menno Simons, and by a host of others, and which we believe will extend until our Lord returns.

Bibliography

Bender, Harold, ed. *The Mennonite Encyclopedia*. Vols. 1-4. Scottdale, PA: Herald Press, 1957.

Berends, Ernst. *Der Ketzerbishof, lebena nd ringen des Reformators Menno Simons, d. 1561*. Basel, Switzerland: Agape-Verelag, 1966.

Braght, Theilemann J van. *Martyrs Mirror*. Scottdale, PA: Herald Press, 1951. Originally published in Dutch, 1660.

Brunk, Gerald, ed. *Menno Simons, A Reappraisal*. Harrisonburg, VA: Eastern Mennonite College, 1992.

Dyck, C. J. *An Introduction to Mennonite History*. Scottdale, PA: Herald Press, 1993.

Estep, William R. *The Anabaptist Story*. Grand Rapids, MI: Eerdmans, 1963.

Friedmann, Robert. *The Theology of Anabaptism*. Scottdale, PA: Herald Press, 1973.

Friesen, Abraham. *Erasmus, the Anabaptists, and the Great Commission*. Grand Rapids, MI: Eerdmans, 1998.

George, Timothy. *Theology of the Reformers*. Nashville: Broadman Press, 1988.

Hoekema, Alle, and Roelf Kuitse, eds. "Discipleship in Context," papers read at the Menno Simons 500 International Symposium, Elspeet, Netherlands, 1996.

Horst, Irvin B. *The Dutch Dissenters, A Critical Companion to Their History and Ideas*. Leiden: E. J. Brill, 1986.

Isaak, Helmut. *Menno Simons and the New Jerusalem*. Kitchener, ON: Pandora Press, 2006.

Jeschke, Marlin. *Discipling the Brother, Congregational Discipline*

According to the Gospel. Scottdale, PA: Herald Press, 1972.

Keeney, William E. *The Development of Dutch Anabaptist Thought and Practice from 1539–1564*. Nieuwkoop: B. de Graaf, 1968.

Klaassen, Walter. *Anabaptism: Neither Catholic nor Protestant*. Scottdale, PA: Conrad Press, 1973.

Koolman, Jacobus ten Doornkaat. *Dirk Philips, Friend and Colleague of Menno Simons, 1504–1568*. Translated by William Keeney. Edited by C. Arnold Snyder. Kitchener, ON: Pandora Press, 1998.

Krahn, Cornelius. *Dutch Anabaptism: Origin, Spread, Life and Thought, 1450-1600*. The Hague: Martinus Nijhoff, 1968.

Philips, Dietrich. *Dietrich Philip Hand Book*. Translated by A. B. Kolb. Alymer, ON: Pathway Publishing, 1910.

Poettcker, Henry. "Menno Simons' View of the Bible as Authority." In *A Legacy of Faith: The Heritage of Menno Simons*, C. J. Dyck, ed. Newton, KS: Faith and Life Press, 1962, pp. 31-54.

Snyder, C. Arnold. *Anabaptist History and Theology, an Introduction*. Kitchener, ON: Pandora Press, 1995.

Stassen, Glen, "Opening Menno Simons Foundation Book and Finding the Father of Baptist Origins." *Baptist History and Heritage*, Spring 1998.

Verheyden, A. L. E., *Anabaptism in Flanders, 1530–1650*. Scottdale, PA: Herald Press, 1961.

Vernon, Louise A. *Night Preacher*. Scottdale, PA: Herald Press, 1963.

Visser, Piet, and Mary Sprunger. *Menno Simons: Places, Portraits and Progeny*. Harrisonburg, VA: Eastern Mennonite University, 1996.

Voolstra, Sjouke. *Menno Simons: His Image and Message*. North Newton, KS: Bethel College, 1997.

Wenger, J. C., ed. *The Complete Writings of Menno Simons*. Scottdale, PA: Herald Press, 1956.

———. *Even unto Death*. Richmond, VA: John Knox Press, 1961.

Williams, George H. *The Radical Reformation*. Philadelphia: Westminster Press, 1962.

Yoder, John Howard. *The Politics of Jesus*. Grand Rapids, MI: Eerdmans, 1972.

The Author

Myron S. Augsburger is widely known for his leadership as president of Eastern Mennonite University and Seminary, and the Council of Christian Colleges and Universities. He has led many evangelistic, preaching, and teaching missions across North America and around the world. As a pastor, he planted and served a vibrant young church in Washington, D. C. He is the author of more than twenty books, includ-ing *Soli Deo Gloria* and *The Robe of God*. He and his wife, Esther, live in Harrisonburg, Virginia.